$\mathcal{T}$IMEPOOL

Susan Plunkett

JOVE BOOKS, NEW YORK

TIME PASSAGES is a registered trademark of Penguin Putnam Inc.

TIMEPOOL

A Jove Book / published by arrangement with
the author

PRINTING HISTORY
Jove edition / August 1999

The Penguin Putnam Inc. World Wide Web site address is
http://www.penguinputnam.com

ISBN: 0-515-12553-9

A JOVE BOOK®
Jove Books are published by The Berkley Publishing Group,
a division of Penguin Putnam Inc.,
375 Hudson Street, New York, New York 10014.
JOVE and the "J" design
are trademarks belonging to Penguin Putnam Inc.

PRINTED IN THE UNITED STATES OF AMERICA

10 9 8 7 6 5 4 3 2 1

For the Tuesday afternoon Ladies,
Cherry, Jennifer, Pamela, and Sister Rose

Chapter 1

IN THE LAST hour before dawn, Caladonia Hornsby followed the thief down to the ocean. She did not consider herself a brave individual, but she was determined to learn who had broken into her home and why.

She kept apace with the halo of light cast by the torch the thief carried across the beach. The shifting sand beneath her feet muffled her footfalls. The low clouds hiding the stars were the only witnesses to her dangerous game of cat and mouse. Even the tide recoiled from the danger passing through the night.

Anxiety rippled through Cally. The bitter bite of anger lingered in her dry mouth.

What had the thief taken from the desk in the study? It wasn't money. She kept none there. Whatever it was, he had recognized it immediately.

Finding a thief violating the sanctity of her home and thumbing through the sacred relics of her father's desk had some benefit. He might lead her to her father's killer. If not for her chronic insomnia, she might have missed the opportunity to follow him.

Ahead, the thief raised his torch to examine a spine of rocks running from the sand out to sea. The black upthrust drank in the light. At all but the lowest tides of the month, only the sharp spires of rock loomed above the water. Tonight, the extremely low tide exposed the base of the rocks. Waves, weather, and countless generations of sea life had smoothed the lower portions. The torchlight gave the harsher crags a sinister aura. The sandy beach reflected the glow of his torch in a widening arc.

Cally froze in the shadows, afraid the torchlight would expose her. Her gaze probed the darkness for a place to hide, finally settling on the rocks to her left. It was the only safe place.

The man settled on a weather-smoothed talon of rock clawed into the sand, leaned to the side, and pushed the carrying end of the torch into the sand. He peered into the night, his head tilted. Listening? Waiting?

The pendulum of her heart-pounding anxiety swung toward fear, then back toward excitement. *Hide.*

The thief drew a knee up to brace himself, then cupped his hand behind his ear. Cally's racing heart battered her ribs in a frantic attempt to flee. It took every ounce of willpower she possessed to remain where she was. For if he was involved in her father's death, she would meet the same dismal fate if he caught her.

The thief turned away.

Cally drew a quiet breath. Prudence dictated she abandon her pursuit. But being prudent would cost any chance of discovering the identity of the thief.

Even if you run away, you're not safe. You could be next.

The voice of logic pounded the panic in her temples into submission. She stood her ground. Although it was a chilly night, perspiration gathered between her breasts and melted into her corset.

Straightening her shoulders, she took a deep breath, then angled toward the rocks thrust up from the sandy beach, away from the torchlight. She knew every boulder and outcrop on the shore. Right now, the jagged spires she had played hide-n-seek in as a child offered the greatest promise. Like a miniature mountain range with sharp peaks and hidden valleys, it offered a sense of safety the damp, dark night lacked.

Careful not to cut herself on the barnacles and broken rock, she sidled into a recess that stretched over her head.

Moments later, the sound of approaching horses sent her scurrying deeper into her pungent-smelling sanctuary. Groping in the darkness with her free hand and refusing to think about the slippery things crunching beneath her feet, she found the alcove she'd been seeking and wiggled inside. The acrid odor of seaweed and salty creatures lodged in the back of her throat and left a bitter taste on her tongue.

"You two got good timin'. I ain't had to wait on ya very long."

Cally's chest tightened with the realization of how close she was to the men. *Breathe quietly,* she admonished herself. *They can't see you; don't let them hear you.*

"Did you get it?" asked a soft-spoken tenor voice.

"Yeah. Gettin' inta the house was easy as takin' candy from a baby. The winder latch inta the li-berry was broken. The winder slid up real quiet-like."

Cally kicked herself silently. Of course the window posed no barrier. The latch had broken last week when Brendan was cleaning the windows. Apparently he hadn't fixed the lock like she had asked.

Cally stretched, trying to see the men meeting the thief. She leaned too far to the side and bumped her head on a jutting rock, then had to tug her hair free.

"Let's have it," demanded a baritone with an almost-familiar inflection. Saddle leather creaked amid the jangle of slack reins as the riders dismounted. One of the horses snorted.

"Not so fast. Where's me money?"

"You'll be paid. After I know you have the packet," the tenor assured the thief.

"I'll be paid, alright. I done got what ya asked for. It weren't easy sortin' through them drawers without mussin' anything up, but I did. No one'll know I ever been there."

"Good work, Freddy. Very good," crooned the soft-spoken tenor.

On tiptoes, Cally strained for a glimpse around the rocks. No luck. Teeth gritted in determination, she wedged the toe of her shoe into a crevice. Her fingers stumbled for a higher hold. Still, it wasn't enough to see over the top. Balanced on one foot, she searched for the next rung on the slippery rock face. When she found it, she levered herself upwards.

"Dammit! This isn't anything but an old manifest. What're you trying to pull, Freddy?" demanded the baritone.

"Wait a minute here. I got what ya asked for. Ya told me not ta look inside, jest get the packet with his initials on it. That's the only blue leather one in the desk. Are ya tryin' ta welsh on our deal?"

Even craning her neck, all she saw was the tops of their heads. Both horsemen wore hats, but she had an excellent view of the balding crown of Freddy the Thief's pate.

Something with a lot of legs crawled onto her hand. Instinct begged her to shake it off. She tightened her grip. This was no time to get queasy. Reflexively, she swallowed, but her mouth was as dry as the sand on the beach and just as gritty.

"There is no deal. You didn't get what we wanted." She could barely hear the soft-spoken tenor's claim. The small hairs at the nape of her neck fluttered. Quiet men were dangerous men.

"I got what ya told me to get. It were just where ya said it'd be, too. In the desk. I tell ya, I checked every drawer ta make sure there weren't another. That there's the only blue leather pouch there were, I tell ya."

Using her toe, Cally felt for another jut. A few more inches, and she ought to be able to see their faces. *Careful. If you can see them, they can see you.*

"Is that so?" came the more patient baritone.

"Yeah. That's so. Now, I want me money."

"Could she know?" asked the tenor.

"Not likely, but not impossible. She's a smart one."

Finally, Cally found a handhold. Just as she started to pull up, her fingers slipped. Biting her lips, she grappled in the dark to keep from falling.

"Maybe too damn smart for her own good. We need those papers back," said the tenor.

"She may have inadvertently switched things around after Peter's death," said the baritone in a pensive tone. "My sources are sure she has no idea how important those papers are."

Try as she might, Cally couldn't remember what papers her father had kept in the blue leather pouch. She inched upward, her heart beating in her throat, fear flowing from her pores as perspiration. She had to see who they were, who had killed her father.

"Sun's comin' up. Give me over me money. Iffen you want me ta go back there again, it's gonna cost ya. Freddy Hansen don't work for nothin'."

"Pay the man," ordered the baritone.

Cally peered over the top just in time to see Freddy the Thief scramble toward her. His terrified eyes glittered in the shadows.

He shouted when he saw her.

A single shot rang out.

A flinch cost Cally her tenuous hold on the rock. Reaching, grasping at air, she tumbled into the bottom of the crevice.

"What was that?" demanded the tenor.

"The tide coming in. Let's get him to the water."

"I heard something and it wasn't the tide or critters. It came from the other side of those crags."

Cally held her breath, her body trembling. Dear God in heaven, they shot him. Killed him. If they found her, the next bullet would be for her. Every cell in her body screamed for her to run. Her stunned limbs remained still, refusing to move. A crab scurried over her hand. Something slimy oozed beneath her calf.

"Freddy isn't going anywhere. Let's be sure."

They were coming. Panic charged her limbs into motion. Ignoring the scrapes and aches, Cally wiggled to her feet. Groping with one hand, holding her skirts with the other, she half-ran, half-fell out of the crevice.

Frantic, she searched the inky darkness. The safety of the dunes lay out of reach. Even if she fled down the beach, they would easily spot her against the pale sand. Staying in the shelter of the rocks was her only hope.

Panting in terror, determined to escape, she followed the upthrust, crawling along and letting her hands guide her in the darkness. Her unblinking eyes remained wide. The break in the rocks was here. Somewhere. Soon, too soon, the sun would light the eastern sky and melt the protective cloak of darkness. Then she'd be exposed and at the mercy of men who had just proven the only mercy they had was in a well-placed bullet.

She shimmied between a gap in the rocks just as the two men rounded the back of the rock formation. The feeble fingers of torchlight illuminated the garish specter of a large crab dining on the remains of a small creature. If she wasn't careful—and lucky—she would meet the same fate as the crab's unidentifiable dinner guest.

"Come on. It was Freddy's scrambling and falling that knocked a few rocks loose," insisted the tenor.

"Like hell. Look at this."

Cally didn't wait to hear what they found. She scrambled along the fetid passage. Crustaceans clinging to the crags tore at her palms. Sharp edges, invisible in the darkness, sliced at her groping fingers. Her pulse hammered in her temples and shortened her breath. Any second a hand would grab her. The portent of long fingers reaching, scratching at the air behind her made her skin crawl.

The gentle lapping of ocean waves beckoned ahead. At least she was going in the right direction—away from the killers. Dimly, she realized she couldn't stay in the rocks longer than the tide remained low. When it changed, anything caught in the crags would be dashed and broken by the powerful waves.

"Get Freddy's torch and go around the far side. We'll trap whoever's in there between us," called the baritone. "Can you drag Freddy to the water?"

"Yes. The sooner we get rid of him, the better. Damn, we're too close to . . ." The soft tenor voice faded, which was just as well for Cally.

The first glimmers of morning brightened the gray clouds overhead. Ahead, the sea melted into the gloaming fog. The descent of the outcropping into the sea signaled the end of her flight. And probably her life.

The cry of gulls waking with empty bellies announced the new day. The birds circled, calling out like spectators at a public execution. A couple of seals resting on the rocks in the surf barked approval for the dawn.

With her arms extended for balance, Cally picked a path along thick tufts of slick sea plants and barnacles that crunched beneath her feet. Each step carried her further into the cold water. At the final thrust of black rock splattered white by countless generations of gulls, she gathered her skirts around her hips. At least whatever inhabited the dark water pulsing in the basin wouldn't shoot her. She stepped down into the tide pool.

Her feet slipped out from under her. She plunged into the chilled sea. Only by catching the edge of the rock, did she manage to keep from being completely submerged in the water. Still, her skirts tried to drag her down. She scrambled to get her feet righted beneath her.

Trembling, Cally drew a shaky breath, then caught the billows of her skirts between her legs. The caprock of the formation hiding her loomed overhead. Weather had hollowed the underside. She took advantage of the scant protection by wedging herself as far under it as possible. Barnacles and mussels poked at her back. Something pulsed on her left shoulder blade, but didn't move when she tried to reposition. Inches from the crown of her head, the underside of the rocks was alive with tiny creatures gurgling, burping, dripping, and scurrying. Fear had her in its icy grip and she didn't dare even shiver in the cold water numbing her fingers and toes.

Legs braced, Cally shrunk into the deepest shadowy recess. She watched the sky brighten over the ocean. Still, the petulant fog hugged the breakers visible beyond the gentle wave swells surging across the submerged rock basins. She willed it to roll in and hide her.

"Where the hell did he go?" The soft-spoken tenor sounded impatient, worried, and out of breath. "Help me with Freddy."

Cally hunched against the rock as though she could blend into the crevices and pores.

"If somebody is out here, we'll find him. There's nowhere to go that we can't see him."

Cally's breath came in small, shallow pants. She didn't want to die. Especially not at the hands of those responsible for her father's death.

The men were close enough for the sound of their splashes to reach her.

"Do you have a good hold on him?" asked the baritone.

"Yes. He's damn heavy with all these rocks in his pockets."

"They'll keep him from floating away until the tide takes him out later."

A series of grunts preceded an enormous splash directly in front of Cally.

She gasped. The rapid blinking of her eyes was the only defense against the stinging salt water running down her face. The scream in her throat rattled inside her head. She stared at Freddy the Thief's lifeless face undulating with the incoming tide.

If they found her, she would end up bobbing in the water beside Freddy.

Breathing through her mouth, she recoiled, pressing her body into the rock. Razor edges of crustaceans and broken shells scraped her exposed skin. The weight of her sodden clothing pulled and pushed with the tide, trying to draw her closer to Freddy the Thief. She dug in her heels and pushed against the rock, trying to get even further away from the corpse.

The rock seemed to give, allowing her to retreat. She continued staring at Freddy's dilated eyes lit by the now-gray dawn.

A wave lifted the corpse higher, broke over him, then slapped her in the face. She bit off a cough and gave her head a quick shake. She'd choke to death before she gave herself away.

When the next wave came, she was ready. Clutching the rock, she cowered into the craggy niche poking her back.

"The tide's coming in," said the tenor.

"Freddy will stay put. Let's check the rocks again. Somebody was out here. If he's in the rocks, the tide will flush him out." A sudden splash preceded a curse from the baritone.

"Watch it. And watch the beach. Don't let him get away." Confidence oozed from the tenor's soft voice.

"We have all morning to wait him out, don't we?"

The sounds of fading splashes as they retreated sent Cally's heart plunging. She had to move. Soon. Or drown. But if she moved, they'd kill her.

Another wave crested, gently lifting and turning Freddy's surprised face toward the shore.

Cally cringed against the rock. This time, it gave way. The surging water from a large wave hurled her backwards. The craggy surface disintegrated. She lost her grip and began falling.

And falling.

Through the water.

Into spinning darkness.

MONTEREY, CALIFORNIA, PRESENT DAY

As the first rays of dawn lit the eastern sky, Narcotics Agent Requiem Maguire parked his Harley beside the beach. With deft fingers, he unfastened his black half-helmet, then hung it on the high end of the ape-hanger handlebars. As he swung off the bike, he reached inside his leather jacket for his cigarettes.

The nicotine habit and the Harley were trappings acquired out of necessity. Like his long hair and the tattoos on his back and arm, they were part of his assumed persona. Eventually he'd quit smoking. Lasers could remove the ink coloring his pores. But the Harley was here to stay.

Over two years of walking with one foot in the shadows and the other on the edge of his grave had formed calluses over his emotions. Circumstance had forged Requiem Maguire into a hard case.

Right now, he stood at a crossroad in his life and craved guidance as to the best way to go. It didn't have to be a blinding flash from the Almighty. A fifteen-watt bulb would do.

The decisions he faced should be easy. No-brainers.

But these days nothing was simple, especially not decisions with consequences. He didn't want any more responsibility. He was tired of intrigue, subterfuge, and the ever-present anxiety of discovery. One false step, one slip . . .

Ten years in Narcotics, the last twenty-nine months undercover, had turned him into an old man, used up before his time.

He lit a cigarette and leaned against his bike, his long legs straight, his black motorcycle boots crossed at the ankles.

Dawn was his favorite time of day. Despite the ugliness and misery he'd witnessed during this period of his life he'd forever consider his dark time, the new day still promised hope. At this hour, he had the beach to himself. The illusion of possessing so much space imparted a dizzying sense of freedom.

The first glimmers of a late October dawn worried patches through the leaden cloud blanket. He watched the sand brighten against the gray-black sea. A dark rock formation created a rift in the expansive beach. A wall of fog shielded the breakers beyond the slash of craggy rocks.

For the past couple of years, he had identified with the rocks straddling the edges of two very different realms. The jagged structure reminded him of a fallen giant reaching desperately for the sea. But time and circumstances had ensnared the imaginary giant and locked him to the shore before he made his escape. Now the formation posed an obstacle the patient waves punished without remorse.

Req knew about obstacles. And retribution. And darkness.

"It's over," he whispered in a long exhale of smoke. "Almost."

He heard the lie rise with the smoke curling into the dawn as he exhaled, and wanted to believe it.

Putting away the bad guys was his objective when he had taken the assignment. The trouble was, they didn't stay put away. And they had friends and hired assassins who extracted retribution. Even after he testified, it wouldn't be over—not until he was dead.

Of course, he could choose not to testify. But then he'd have to quit his job, and he wasn't sure he wanted to do that either. For the past three weeks, he hadn't been sure of anything. And that was part of the problem.

Something moved in the surf.

He tossed his cigarette away and straightened.

Squinting, he made out an arm reaching for the beach.

"Shit." He started running. The expanse of sand seemed to grow as his heavy boots carved valleys into the soft surface.

"Damn druggies." He stripped away his leather jacket and struggled out of his boots. As soon as each boot was free, he tossed it in the direction of his jacket.

Cold salt water spattered his face when he challenged the incoming tide at a dead run.

Someone was in the surf. Someone battling hard, flailing at the surging waves instead of using their momentum to get to the beach.

A wave slammed into Req's thighs, slowing him.

The brightening gray sky added definition to the form in the water.

A woman, he realized, diving into the waves. Not far. Another thirty feet.

A strong swimmer, Req stroked toward the faltering woman. Going against the tide was natural. He'd done it most of his life.

When he reached the woman, she surprised him by pushing away. Well, hell, maybe she wanted to die after all.

"Don't fight me or you'll drown us."

". . . not die alone . . ." She spit out a mouthful of water, her dark eyes wide with terror.

Req treaded water. "Lady, I don't intend to let you pull me down." The ocean chill seeped into his bones. "And I'm not going to let you drown." A wave lifted him and washed over her. Didn't she realize she was minutes away from taking her last breath? He answered his own question. Druggies didn't realize anything except that they needed another fix.

The woman popped above the surface coughing, her gaze locked on him. "Stay away," she said, then coughed again.

"Right. If you can't help, don't fight me."

Her arms worked frantically to keep her afloat.

When the next wave dunked her, Req caught her long, blond hair and pulled her around. She broke the surface screaming. He ignored her and slung his arm over her shoulder, between her breasts, and grabbed her at the opposite armpit.

"Hold still, dammit. If I wanted you to drown, I'd have watched from the beach." His legs pumped hard to keep their heads above water.

She stopped fighting.

She seemed of average size, but it took all his considerable strength to keep her afloat and swim toward shore. The slim shoulders he dragged through the waves must be attached to hips the size of China. How else could a woman with such slender arms and shoulders weigh so much? He adjusted his grip and found his answer. Hell, her torso was encased in full-body armor.

When he was finally close enough to safety to put his feet down, he was grateful they didn't have to swim another ten feet. He held onto her as she struggled to stand. Waves pummeled their backs, propelling them forward.

Req swore when her knees buckled. His grip on her arm tightened, bracing them both against the onslaught of the next wave, until she righted herself.

"Who . . ." She coughed and doubled over, but kept staggering forward.

Req looked down at her. Her blond hair coiled around her face and shoulders. Her determination to reach the beach didn't fit with someone bent on dying.

Jeez. She was dressed for a bad trip. How the hell she made it two feet off shore wearing that long dress and yards of petticoats amazed him. She had to have been in the water for at least five minutes, long enough for him to park the Harley and smoke a cigarette. Her drug of choice must have given her the tremendous strength necessary to stay afloat with the tonnage buttoned to her body.

Adrenaline did strange things to a user's high. He watched her closely, prepared for her to turn violent.

She glanced up at him through streamers of long, wet hair. Gooseflesh rippled over his arms when she met his gaze. Fear. Resignation. Exhaustion. He noted the spectrum of her emotions in a flash. Beneath them all, anger burned.

At the water's edge, she faltered again.

"A little farther," he coaxed. "The tide's coming in." He pointed at his jacket and thought only of the warmth it promised now that the cold, morning air bit into his every pore.

Her arm trembled, but she shuffled toward the dark spot on the sand. A few feet short of his jacket, she dropped to her knees then collapsed face first onto the beach and began shivering.

"Helluva hard comedown from a bad trip, huh?" He plopped down beside her, his wrists dangling over his spiked knees. "You dressed for it, lady."

Her back rose and fell with the sheer exertion of breathing. Her labored breath reminded him of a runner at the end of a marathon. He wondered how long it would be before she took another bad trip and went swimming for the last time. Damn, she was trembling so hard, she might go have a seizure any minute.

"Before you shoot me . . . tell me why . . . why you killed my father."

Chapter 2

"THAT'S REAL GRATITUDE. I pull you out of the ocean, and you accuse me of killing your father," he murmured. "The connection is crystal-clear."

Cally cursed her depleted body. She had done everything possible to avoid becoming easy prey like Freddy the Thief, but she had failed. Whatever the killers had in mind, they didn't want her dead. Yet. Through the ringing in her ears a small voice begged her to get up and run far away as fast as possible—before the man next to her realized she didn't know anything. There may be a gun among his things. He might be aiming it at her back right now. Fear kept her heart pounding louder than the surf. All she could do was lie on the sand.

For what seemed an eternity, she tried to catch a full, clear breath in her burning lungs and listened for the sound of the hammer drawn back and the click of the cylinder rotating for firing. The strength required to lift her head was more than she could muster. She wanted to turn and see the gun she suspected he had, then look him in the eye when he pulled the trigger.

Despite her valiant efforts, she was defeated. He had caught her, hauled her to shore, and—

"Why?" she breathed.

"Why what?"

"Why didn't you let me drown?" she panted. He would rue his efforts when he realized she had no idea what her father had kept in the blue leather pouch.

"Beats the hell out of me. Maybe my perverse nature and a moment of weakness because I couldn't stand seeing anyone get what they wanted."

With great effort, she lifted her hand high enough to scrape the hair from her face. "Is that why you killed my father?"

"Lady, I didn't kill your father."

"Had him killed."

"You need to detox. If you can't stay away from the drugs, get a better mix for your next trip."

The deep rumble of his voice penetrated the ringing in her ears. The silken edge of his gruffness possessed a unique, unfamiliar tone. She closed her stinging eyes. "I have no idea what detox is or why you think I'd need it. I'm not ill. Why would I need medicine?"

The derisive bass laugh rising from behind her added to the shivers already wracking her body.

"Yeah, why? How the hell do I know why you're on drugs? The best I can hope for is that you've scared yourself enough to leave 'em alone. Next time, you might succeed in becoming shark bait."

Cally drew a long, quavering breath. The voice was all wrong. He was neither a baritone nor a tenor. His voice was a lower, bass tone that reached inside of her when he spoke. He wasn't one of the men she'd heard on the beach. A flash of relief gave way to outright panic. If he truly was a Good Samaritan who had risked everything to rescue her, they were both in grave danger. Judging by the brightness of the sky, not more than a few minutes had passed since the sea had sucked her under and then dumped her in the surf. "They're looking for me."

"I'm sure *they* are."

The sound of his movements sent her shrinking against the sand. Maybe he wasn't one of the men who killed Freddy the Thief, but he was involved. He had just admitted he knew they were looking for her. "You're one of them, aren't you?"

"One of who?"

"The men who work for them. They killed Freddy after he did a service for them. The same fate may await you when you finish their bidding."

He stopped moving around. "Freddy who?"

"The thief they hired to break into my house and go through my father's desk. I heard him." She flattened her hand in front of her mouth to hold back the sand flies hopping on and off her face. Lord, she was tired and dismayed that she hadn't escaped. But she had to convince him that he was on the wrong side. If she kept talking, maybe he would realize there was no advantage in killing her.

"I saw Freddy as he was leaving the house. I followed him out here, then hid in the rocks. Two men met him. I tried to see them, but just as I got my footing, they shot him, and I fell. Then they started looking for me. There was no place to hide, except the pools. But they threw him into the water in front of me." She shuddered at the vision of Freddy's death mask. "The tide came in. The next thing I knew, I was trying to swim for shore."

"Back up. You saw someone get shot?"

Hadn't she just explained that?

"Freddy."

"Freddy who?" Req asked for the second time.

She thought for a moment. Her brain felt like a beehive, thoughts humming, swarming, and flitting in erratic directions. The sense of lying vulnerable on the open beach increased her agitation. The man beside her had rescued her, but that didn't make him an ally. "Whatever they're paying you, I'll double it if you get us off the beach before they find us."

"Nobody's paying me." He resumed his movements.

Cally scraped every bit of energy she could garner and pushed herself up to a sitting position. The fog crept toward her from the breakers. The gulls screeched over the rock formation on Cally's right. She looked down the beach and cried out. "They're coming." Fumbling, scrambling, she tried to stand. The volumes of saturated petticoats and skirt fought against her. Her trembling legs buckled.

"Look closer, lady. Those are a couple of joggers. The worst they'll do is run over you."

Frantic, she crawled, trying to get her feet under her, determined to get away. The next thing she knew, strong fingers closed around her upper arms and hauled her upright. Dark green eyes framed by short, thick lashes glared down at her.

"What kind of drugs did you take?"

Her mouth opened, but the words stayed locked in her throat. She shook her head, stunned by the intensity of his eyes. They seemed to see so much, but apparently not the danger. "Run," she finally whispered, more afraid for him now than of the two killers.

"Did you see a man murdered here?"

A quick nod was all she managed. This man was dangerous. She saw it in his hard, cold eyes, but she couldn't look away.

The strength of his grip on her upper arms promised he could snap her in two.

"When?"

"When . . . what?"

"When did you see the murder?"

"Th-this morning. Just before dawn."

"Lady, I was here then. I didn't see or hear anything."

"They shot him." Did he think her stupid? Only a blind man could have missed the torches the killers carried on the beach.

"I have a fine ear for the sounds of gunfire. There wasn't any."

Cally tried to pull away from his tight grasp. The two figures moving down the beach were larger now and while she couldn't make them out, she couldn't wait until they were close enough to shoot her. "Please. Let me go," she pleaded, frantically trying to wiggle free.

"Sure." He spread his hands and stepped back.

Suddenly off balance, she struggled to maintain her footing. Wary of his easy compliance, she shuffled away, not quite turning her back on him. She fled for the safety of home.

"For a minute there, I almost believed you saw someone get killed."

She didn't care what he believed, as long as he didn't try to stop her. She stumbled beneath the oppressive weight of her sodden dress. Before she hit the ground, he caught her arm.

"Come on, lady. The mystery masquerade ball is over. It's time for detox."

The way he referred to "detox" set her instincts on edge. She wanted no part of whatever it was. "I'm going home."

"Sure. You can go home. After the drugs wear off. The law is on your side. They can't keep you." He steered her toward the crest of the dune.

Cally looked over her shoulder and her heart nearly leaped through her chest. The two people running on the beach darted through wisps of incoming fog. Her heart skipped a beat, and her mouth became a desert. They were almost within shooting distance. All they had to do was look her way.

Fear lent strength to her rubbery legs. For an instant, she was grateful the man followed her up the dune willingly. She lacked the energy to drag him. The terrain, made more difficult by her heavy yardage collecting thirsty sand and leaving a damp trail, demanded her attention.

Her thighs burned. Her desperately taxed lungs, confined by

the bones and laces of her corset, screamed for a full, clean breath. She put one foot in front of the other, anxious to reach the dense foliage at top and get out of sight of the two people on the beach.

She finally reached the crest of the dune and to her surprise, she almost ran straight into a split-rail fence.

"This way." The man tugged at her.

Staring at the fence, she accompanied him without protest. Her pulse thudded in her ears as she wondered who had put up a fence. And when. Even after he led her through a break in the weathered structure, she continued staring at it. Amazingly, it looked old. But it couldn't be. It hadn't been there an hour ago.

When she started to question the man, her voice locked in her throat. Noise suddenly assaulted her from every direction.

And light. Little fires burned on poles everywhere.

They hadn't existed an hour ago.

Lights blazed beside the road and inside strange houses that had sprung out of the sandy ground and sprouted people within the last few minutes.

They glowed on noisy, funny-looking conveyances traveling at incredible speeds without horses.

The pungent scent of something raw bit deep into her brain with each shallow breath she took.

The shock collapsed Cally's legs. Dizziness further disoriented her as she crumpled to the ground. Reflexively, she reached for her temples. Disbelief hammered through her veins. The sensory overload was too much to fit into her head.

"Dammit, lady. Don't have a seizure on me. I'm too damn tired for it."

Cally slid her hands over her ears, but her eyes refused to close and blot out the impossible things before her. Genuine panic, the breadth of which she never suspected possible, clutched her. Abruptly the sights disappeared and she was staring into the man's green eyes. They were now the only familiar sight to behold.

He slid her hands from her ears. "Breathe deeply. Come on. Deep breath. Clear your head."

The patient hypnotic voice penetrated the abrasive cacophony of sights and sounds that seemed to vibrate from the earth. Some part of her grabbed at the lifeline of sanity he offered. Dimly, she realized this wasn't a dream she would wake up from and then dismiss as part of her grieving process for her father.

The reality of her situation bludgeoned her senses. Even the air tasted different.

"That's it. Another deep breath."

Staring into the green eyes looking back at her, she obeyed. Gradually the dizziness cleared.

"What happened?" she breathed, not daring to look away from him. Flashes of light whizzed back and forth fifty feet away on a road that shouldn't exist. As long as she didn't confront the stark, overwhelming reality assaulting her, she wouldn't start screaming.

"You're crashing."

Crashing. It made as much sense to her as the gaslights suspended on poles. "I think I've lost my perspective."

"Perspective hell. You lost more than that when you decided to escape into drugs."

Now she wanted to scream, but had neither the breath nor the energy. "I'm not on medication."

"Right."

She shook her head. "Wh-where am I?"

He snorted, glanced away, then looked back. Through the miasma of peripheral sights and sounds, she detected sorrow in the furrows above his arched eyebrows.

"Coming down from a bad trip. Ride it out. It might get worse before it gets better. Come on, let's get you on your feet."

Because he seemed to have an answer for everything, she let him help her stand. Her legs trembled. Not once did she allow her gaze to stray from his eyes. She groped behind her for the fence, found it, then rested against the top rail.

"Deep breath," he encouraged.

She obeyed, letting her eyelids droop into a long blink. A flash of something snagged her attention. Her eyes opened wide.

It wasn't possible.

She blinked again, but the wings on his black shirt remained. Without thinking, she reached out and touched the orange, silver, and black picture an artist had painted on the thin fabric stretched across his chest. The image felt smooth where the paint wasn't cracked. Her fingers brushed over the words "Harley-Davidson Toy Run, 1996." The two-wheeled fixture in the center of the wings reminded her of a cumbersome bicycle. It was "1996" that captivated her fragile senses.

A woman who spent her life grounded in pragmatism, she dared a slow perusal of her nightmarish surroundings. Lights blinked on and off in the grand houses beyond the dark strip of road frequented by an increasing number of horseless carriages. One by one the glow on the tall poles beside the road winked out. The globes weren't gas; they were electric. Everywhere she looked the marvel of electricity was flaunted in an impossible abundance.

She shook her head and closed her eyes for a moment. When she opened them, nothing had changed.

This wasn't the same place she left a few hours ago.

Washington Irving's absurd story of Rip van Winkle waking up after a twenty-year nap flashed through her mind. Fiction. Fantasy. Besides, she hadn't fallen asleep. But suddenly the classic story didn't seem quite so outlandish. Something had happened to her. She was the same. Monterey Bay was still in the same place. The rocks, hills, and mountains hadn't moved. But everything else was different. From the looks of things, Rip van Winkle had it easy. It would have taken far more than twenty years to build what she saw around her.

"Tell me it's not true," she whispered, her gaze drawn back to the numbers on his shirt. Surely that couldn't be the year. Time was not a tide changing at the whim of the sea.

"It's not true," he assured her.

"Thank God." Her eyes closed as she exhaled a heavy sigh of relief. There was a logical explanation. "For a moment . . ." Ridiculous. Ludicrous, really. "I feared you had dragged me from the sea and into the year 1996." Embarrassment for the absurd conjecture spilling from her lips crept through her shock.

"What?"

"Your shirt. For a moment I had the absurd thought that 1996 was the year."

"It isn't."

Relief escaped as a sigh.

"I made this toy run a couple of years ago. The shirt's old."

"No. It isn't possible. . . ." If his painted shirt from 1996 was old . . . The realization delivered a stunning blow that nearly jolted her off the fence.

Req lunged for the woman and barely kept her from slipping off the top rail. She was dead weight one minute, rigid the next. He wedged himself between her legs and braced her.

"Lady. Come on. You're young. You'll get over a lost year or two." Why people who emerged from a prolonged drug hiatus were surprised they'd lost time amazed him. Maybe this one had scared herself enough to change her future. If not, one morning some jogger would find her washed up on the beach.

For an inexplicable reason, the prospect further depressed him. One minute she seemed to have so much spirit and spark. The next . . .

She moved against him.

Hesitant to relinquish his hold, he looked down. The gray morning heightened her ashen pallor. Dark, coffee-colored eyes gazed up at him with soul-crushing desolation that reached the marrow of his bones.

He followed the fixed direction of her wide-eyed stare to his shirt. "What did you expect? Snoopy?"

She swallowed twice before responding, "What happened to me? How did I get here?"

"I don't know. Where'd you come from?"

"Eighteen ninety," she whispered.

Req stiffened. "Eighteen ninety. What's the rest of the address?"

Her head lifted sharply. The depth of her anguish sent a wave of gooseflesh up his arms. She swallowed hard before answering. "Eighteen ninety is not a residence, sir." Her voice lowered to a whisper. "It is the year."

"Right." And he was king of Atlantis. "I suppose that's when you started doing drugs?" He didn't even try to temper the sarcasm dripping from his tone.

A defiant push at his waist registered her objection. "What is the preoccupation you have with medications? I've never even taken laudanum." She turned her face away. "But . . . considering . . . perhaps I—"

"Considering what?"

The panic pinching her even features melted. As he watched, she transformed. From someplace within, she garnered an amazing composure. The trembling he felt in her arms and shoulders eased. Slowly, rigidity returned to her spine. A hint of warm color touched her cheeks when she became aware of his stance between her legs. "I think I had best stop talking or you will deem me a lunatic."

Impressed by the change she managed, he tried to reassure her. "I'd rather deal with a lunatic than a drug addict." On the street, sometimes it was hard to tell the difference.

"I see." She attempted to draw her left leg away from his, but he remained firmly planted between her thighs.

"You probably don't, so I'll explain. In my book, a mental breakdown isn't always something people can avoid." He should know, he was feeling pretty close to having one himself. All his instincts told him to turn her over to the local police or social services and walk away. But the desolation he had seen in her eyes matched his own, and he couldn't turn his back. The recognition of a kindred lost soul wouldn't allow it.

"And if you decide I'm a lunatic? What will happen to me?"

"Nothing."

She nodded, seemingly arriving at a decision. With a prim thrust of her chin, she regarded him. "How did you do it?"

Req exhaled loudly. "Do what? I already told you I didn't kill your father. Or have him killed."

"How did you bring me here?"

"As I recall, we sort of stumbled and walked up the beach."

"No. How did you bring me to . . . to this . . . *here*?" She pointed a finger at the sandy ground lapping up the water dripping from her skirts.

Req thought quickly, then stepped back to better see her face. She balanced on the split rail, quickly closing her legs when he released her thighs, and laced her fingers on her lap so tightly her knuckles turned white. The earnestness of her question burned in her eyes. "I reached out and grabbed you." Req stopped short. Lunatic or druggy, he couldn't play her demented game.

"Can you reach back? I must go home."

He shook his head and met her gaze pleading for his understanding. "You've been hallucinating."

"I wish I were." Her head bowed, but not before he saw the forlornness creep back into her soulful brown eyes. "It seems I find myself in dire need of advice, Mr. Davidson."

Confused, Req studied her through narrowed eyelids. "Davidson? I'm not Davidson." She didn't belong in a detox center. She belonged on stage. Or in a psychiatric ward.

She stared at his shirt for a moment before looking up at him. "I beg your pardon. I assumed Harley Davidson was your name."

"You assumed wrong. What's your name?"

"Caladonia Hornsby," she answered softly.

"Look, Caladonia—is that what people call you?"

"You may call me Miss Hornsby," she said with a straight-faced sincerity that rocked him. A fine tremble in her hand thwarted the smooth gesture of straightening the snarls of hair clumped around her shoulders.

Req turned away. Memories of another dark-eyed girl haunted him. Three years ago, he had pulled a few strings and gotten Malika Escobar into the Betty Ford Center in lieu of prison. It hadn't done any good. Malika had left Betty Ford, caught a bus back to San Jose, and met her old dealer at the station with an open wallet. One injection of bad heroine was all it took to kill her and any chance of salvation.

Miss Caladonia Hornsby was either hooked hard on something or mad as a hatter. The question was, which?

He struggled with the decision of what to do with her. If he turned her over to the authorities there was no telling how she would cope. The vulnerability he sensed in her smacked of innocence. Yet innocence was virtually impossible among users and the dichotomy bothered him.

She looked afraid, confused, but too healthy for a hard-core addict. Although pale, her face colored too easily for her emotions to have desensitized from everything except her next fix. "Something's not right," he murmured.

"I beg your pardon?"

He turned around. She sat prim and proper, like an actress in a movie. Water still dripped from her sand-encrusted skirt. Pale blond strands of dry hair fluttered over the wet clumps plastered to the side of her face and along her clothing. Hell, her party costume did look like something right out of 1890. Had someone spiked her drink with a designer drug? Maybe left her on the beach and suggested she continue celebrating in Hawaii—on the economy plan?

Then he met her worried brown gaze. Beneath the sand clinging to her cheek, she was an attractive woman with wide-set eyes framed by thick, dark lashes. Her even features and straight nose reminded him of the wholesome cover models on the *Ladies Home Journal* magazines stuffed in the supermarket checkout racks. But it was more than her looks and the curves of her body he'd felt in the water that drew him to her. Damn, he would give anything if he didn't identify with the sense of being lost that was so clearly reflected in her eyes.

"You said you needed my advice, Miss Hornsby."

"Yes. If I am truly no longer in 1890—"

"You aren't."

"I, ah, have no idea where I should go." Fear pinched her features when she glanced at the road where a car in need of a new muffler roared by. "I cannot imagine not having my home."

"Well, I suppose a lot of people who spend their days panhandling on the streets feel the same way. When you make the wrong choices, you shouldn't be surprised when you wind up homeless. Friendless." He looked down the beach at the waves. *Lucky to have your life.*

"This place you mentioned, this detox—what is it?"

"A place you can get counseling while you purge the drugs out of your system. You'll have a bed, food, and they'll give you some clean, dry clothes."

A shiver of revulsion stiffened her spine and curled the corners of her mouth in disdain. "The detox place doesn't sound like anywhere I want to visit."

He studied her, wondering if she had been through the system before, if she had a record of drug use or dealing. The naiveté he sensed heaped doubt on the probability. That doubt gnawed at him. Circumstance and her irrational assertions said one thing; the instincts he had relied on to stay alive said she was a victim: harmless, vulnerable. Hell, the system would chew her up and spit her out.

He glanced at the beach where they had recuperated after their swim. If he didn't have a weakness for watching the sun light up the ocean in the morning, she would have already found *escape*.

"You'll go with me." The solution emerged without thought. His willingness to take responsibility for her startled him. Gradually, he understood the reason for the protectiveness she engendered. If misery loved company, desolation craved companionship. She exuded both in spades.

"Is there nowhere else I can go except . . . detox?"

"I'm not taking you to detox."

"Then . . . where will you take me, Mr. . . . ?"

"Requiem Maguire. But you can call me Req." A lopsided smile forced its way across the left side of his mouth. "No 'Mister.' Please."

"Whatever you prefer. Is there a place for people who have become . . ." she searched for a word before concluding, "displaced?"

For the first time in over a month, a genuine smile spread across his face. It felt good. So did his impetuous decision. She was a screw-up, but harmless. His brother-in-law, Dr. Robert Starkey, would know how best to help Caladonia Hornsby. Quietly. Without putting her into the system. Robert's work with troubled kids had taught him how to use the social services system without tagging a kid for life. "If you mean a people lost and found, no."

"Then where will you take me?"

"Someplace safe. Someplace where you can get your bearings."

"Where?"

"Home with me." This was probably the dumbest thing he'd done in twenty years. But then, making good decisions wasn't his strong suit since the emotional crash-and-burn he'd experienced after emerging from undercover. Now he was fresh out of logic and growing thin in the sanity department.

He retrieved his helmet from the high grip of the ape-hanger handlebars. "Hold this."

He finger-combed his long hair back and fished a rubber band from his pocket. Once he had his ponytail in place, he checked his pockets for another rubber band and came up empty.

Miss Hornsby cocked her head and stared at him while clutching the helmet as though it was a Waterford crystal vase.

"Push your hair back and pull the helmet on. I'll help you fasten it."

Dubious, she obeyed, but slowly, as though weighing her choices and finding none better than what he offered. "You will not have a hat if I wear yours."

"Yeah, well, we're not going far. Besides, pretty soon rush hour will keep the boys and girls in blue too busy to notice a helmet-law infraction."

Once he fastened the helmet on her, he took off his jacket and helped her put it on. "It gets cold riding on the motorcycle."

"Then will you not need it? You have such small sleeves on your shirt, and it looks so thin."

Anxious to get on the road, he stooped to play her game. "Would a man offer his coat to a lady in 1890?" he coaxed.

"Why, of course. It is only proper etiquette."

"Well, consider this proper motorcycle etiquette." He zipped up the front of the jacket. "Let's get out of here."

She made it halfway to the Harley before freezing in her tracks.

"Come on. The sooner we get going, the sooner we'll be warm and dry."

"H-how does one ride upon such a bicycle contraption?"

Req winced. "Please, Miss Hornsby. This is hardly a bicycle. It is a Harley-Davidson motorcycle. Made in America and the finest machine on two wheels anywhere." He climbed onto the motorcycle. "Get on behind me and be sure to bunch those skirts."

She stood unmoving, her fingertips peeking through the sleeves of his jacket, her hair hanging in sandy clumps around her face, her skirts still dripping onto the gritty asphalt parking area. The expression she wore was one of terror mingled with fascination. He felt like a cobra enticing an innocent victim. All he lacked was Zamfir on the flute.

"Come here," he called softly.

She hesitated. Then the strain in her features eased. The macabre fascination in her expressive eyes lingered. Although clearly afraid, she responded to his summons.

When she stood beside him, he bent low and reached between her ankles. He pulled the back hem of her dress between her legs and gathered up the excess yardage. "The tailpipes get very hot. I'd hate for your skirt to catch fire. Now, climb on behind me."

She shook her head, horrified. "Sitting astride such a thing is most improper. My limbs will be exposed."

He leaned to the side. "Yeah. That's the general idea. You have nice legs, but nobody will see them under those stockings. The shoes aren't bad for bike-riding either."

"I don't think I can do this, Mr. . . . . Req."

"I don't think you have a choice, Miss Hornsby. I'm not leaving you here."

"But perhaps that might be best."

He shrugged. "Chances are, if I leave you, and you're real lucky, you'll end up riding to the police station. After a few hours, they'll send you on to detox, or the psych ward. So lift your leg over the seat, tuck your skirts around you, put your feet on these," he said, tapping the foot pegs. "Then hold onto me like a second skin. Lean when I lean, not the opposite way. Got it?"

She was so pale, he thought she might faint. Instead, she looked over her shoulder at the ocean where morning joggers were already wearing out the beach.

"Will you call a priest if I die?"

The temptation to laugh withered in his throat when he realized she was serious. "Yes, Miss Hornsby, but I don't think you'll die on the back of my Harley." He plucked his sunglasses from their perch beside the speedometer and put them on.

She climbed onto the back, trying to keep herself covered and secure her skirts. When she was satisfied, Req straightened the bike, then started it. The distinctive Harley-Davidson rumble pulsed through his veins.

It pulsed through Caladonia Hornsby's, too. They hadn't even reached the street and she was holding onto him so tight, he'd probably have internal injuries before they got home. The pressure of her helmet against his back promised bruises.

It wasn't until he stopped at an intersection that he heard her praying.

What the hell had he gotten himself into?

Chapter 3

C ALLY'S PRAYERS RAN the gamut from giving thanks for her narrow escape on the beach, to penitence for all real and unintentional sins, to an entreaty for an explanation for her awful fate.

Though she kept her eyes closed and her helmeted head bowed against Requiem Maguire's back, the spectrum of smells and sounds that assaulted her reinforced the notion that she was no longer in 1890. The acrid stench of the new world intensified whenever they slowed or stopped.

Blaring noises and the sporadic wail of something being tortured ebbed and flowed through the wind slamming into her ears. Unable to process more change, Cally dared not open her eyes and see that they traveled at an impossible speed.

The thrumming vibrations of the motorcycle and Req Maguire wedged between her thighs added to the chaos besieging her senses. And the scope of her prayers expanded with the intrusion of what she considered inappropriate sensations that began between her thighs and warmed her belly.

"We're here," he said over his shoulder.

Cally forced her eyes open. *Here* was a mansion behind iron gates swinging open by an invisible hand. Lush trees, a myriad of sculptured, groomed plants and gardens, and an expansive lawn surrounded a sprawling house with a red-tiled roof and the creamy white stucco reminiscent of a hacienda.

The motorcycle eased through the gates, which immediately closed behind them.

Cally openly gawked at the fine, cobblestone road winding up to the house. Ferns, fuchsias, camellias, late-seasoned roses, and countless small plants hugged the ground in precision that defied a single leaf to fall. The sense of enormity sent her retreating behind closed eyelids.

When he pried her hands off his abdomen, it took a moment for her to realize they had reached the end of their journey. The contraption beneath them no longer rumbled, although the ghostly vibrations continued in her legs and body. The tingling was most acute along her inner thighs and the juncture of her legs.

"You can get off now," Req said.

Cally opened her eyes. At first she wasn't sure if they were in a part of a house or a barn. Morning sun mingled with light from overhead. Aware of the ache in her arms from holding him so tight, she shifted her trembling hands onto her damp skirts.

"Where are we?" Beside them sat a gold-colored vehicle similar to those she had seen on the road by the beach.

"In my garage. Let's go inside. You can get out of your party dress and into a warm bath. You must be freezing. I sure as hell am." He climbed off the motorcycle, then unfastened the helmet he'd made her wear and hung it on the handlebar.

She wanted to ask questions, but wasn't ready to give the situation more reality by voicing them, let alone hearing the answers. Sifting what she already knew required more fortitude than she could muster. She clung to the safe, numb state that insulated her from the stark terror of unconditionally accepting that she was part of this loud, smelly, mind-boggling place.

"Is there someone I can call for you?" he asked. "Someone who might be worried or looking for you?"

"Who would I pay a call on? I know no one here." Cally accepted his offered hand and extricated herself from the Harley as gracefully as possible. Her sand-encrusted skirts and petticoats imposed a heavy burden as they tumbled into place.

Her knees buckled. Instinctively she grappled for stability. Her fingers caught in Req's shirt as he steadied her.

"Easy," he whispered, hauling her against him.

Staring into his shadowy green eyes, Cally found sorrow and salvation. The uncertainty he reflected pierced her fragile defenses. She nearly cried out in anguish at the blatant emotion she saw there. The raw intensity singed her paltry defenses. She wanted to look away, but could not. The emotion evident in his eyes changed again. He regarded her with a coldness that seemed to emanate from his soul.

The sudden shiver riding her skin had nothing to do with temperature. For reasons she could not fathom, she did not want him to think ill of her. Faced with the impossibility of her situation, it shouldn't matter what he thought of her. But it did, and she didn't know why.

He swore under his breath and turned his head. "The party's over, Miss Hornsby. Time to get clean and sober."

She wanted to object, but couldn't find the words. Instead, she gathered her feeble strength and straightened. As she had done countless times, she tried to shake the wrinkles from her crumpled skirts. The old habit imparted a sense of normalcy. Sand clung to the folds and wet patches.

As he led her into the house, he pushed a button. With less noise than the motorcycle made, a great door descended from the ceiling, lowering steadily.

Cally bit back a scream, her heart pulsing in her throat. Steeling herself to suppress what was beginning to feel like a perpetual state of astonishment, she watched as a wall descended, sealing her away from the daylight. All the while, she continued the ritual of brushing sand from her skirts.

"Could you move a little faster? It's cold out here." He tugged on her upper arm, which was sure to be bruised by now.

Cally lowered her head. "My apologies."

The door she walked through led to two more in a room lined with cupboards, big steel boxes with dials rising behind them, and a deep sink. Everything was white. All of it was overwhelming, especially the lighted ceiling.

She followed him through a door and then a hallway marked by doors and lovely artwork. Slack-jawed, she moved along the gallery she would have loved to spend an hour examining. She was still gawking at the art when he opened a door and led her through a darkened room.

"You can use this bathroom."

Req touched a panel by the door and without warning, bright light flooded the shadowy darkness, forcing her to squint.

"The towels are fresh," he said without the bite in his tone.

"I . . ." Cally stood in the center of a room more bizarre than her vivid imagination could have ever conjured. "I . . . thank you."

Req turned away.

She glanced over her shoulder in time to watch the door close. She started to turn back, then paused, gasping.

Staring at her disheveled image in a mirror covering the entire wall, she could barely believe she was alive.

She continued staring. The reflection was the only familiar

thing she had seen since leaving the ocean. And the safest place to look for the moment.

A tremor crept up her spine. Riding on the motorcycle behind Requiem Maguire had been the most terrifying, exhilarating experience in her life. Even with her eyes closed the entire trip, the sounds and scents battered her beleaguered senses. Holding his hard torso had kept her grounded in the strange reality of a place in a time he took for granted.

Cally knew a miracle when she saw one. This impossibility engulfing her was just that: a miracle.

She should be dead. The men on the beach should have found and shot her. The ocean should have drowned her beside Freddy the Thief. The surf should have held onto her heavy skirts and pulled her into the depths.

Instead, she was alive because Requiem Maguire had dragged her to the shore of a different—

"Time," she breathed. Speaking the word made it real in ways she could not deny. She was alive. In the same place, but another time.

A miracle of this magnitude had to be ingested one bite at a time, much the way one might eat an elephant.

And eat this miraculous elephant she would.

Determined to make the most of the opportunity, she undressed. By the time her clothing lay in a sandy heap around her feet, she was cold. Turning on the water in the shiny red bathtub was easy. Figuring out how to keep it from running down the drain took a bit of experimentation.

Cally washed and rinsed her hair under the tub spigot. She suspected there might be an easier way, considering the numerous portals in the side walls of the bathtub and the funnylooking bibcock staring at her on the long side of the tub.

With a heavy towel wrapped around her head and another tucked firmly around her body, she washed her clothing in the tub, then cleaned the sand from the floor. These mundane tasks kept her from dwelling on what awaited beyond the gleaming white-and-red bathing room.

A sharp knock on the door startled her. She whirled around and stared at the closed door. "Wh-what?"

"You've been in there two hours. Just wanted to make sure you were still breathing."

The disturbing smoothness of his bass voice jolted her out of the blessed numb state she had cultivated. The concern thrumming through his tone vibrated inside her. The odd sensation heightened her agitation.

"I, uh, was waiting for my clothes to dry, Mr. . . . Requiem."

"They'll get that way a lot faster in the dryer."

A dryer? For clothing? Cally shook her head. How many nameless marvels awaited her on the other side of the door? She sought neutral ground in which to hide her ignorance. "I'll trust your judgment on that issue, Mr. Maguire."

He muttered something.

"I'm sorry. I didn't hear you."

"Are you decent?"

"Of course not. My clothing is too wet to don."

"Put on the robe hanging beside the shower door."

Frantic, Cally looked around, then spotted a white robe hanging on a gold hook. As she pulled on the fluffy garment, she peeked into the upright bathing enclosure. Next time, she would wash her hair in the little room with the glass door.

"Now are you dressed?"

"Ah, well, I have the robe on, but I'm hardly presentable for mixed company, Mr.—"

The door opened.

Her heart skipped a beat. She tucked the fluffy lapels of the robe together under her chin.

"Relax. I'm not going to eat you."

She blinked several times. The way his gaze devoured her, it seemed that was exactly what he had in mind. She turned away and glimpsed her reflection. The brief image lent assurance she was in no danger of attracting any man's attention. Swathed in white toweling from her head to her bare toes, she stole another peek at him.

He, too, was barefoot. There the similarities ended.

Dark blue denim trousers, faded at the knees, hugged his long legs and narrow hips. Her perusal lingered at the worn material outlining the male bulge at his crotch. Wicked curiosity warmed her body and encouraged her visual exploration.

A thin, collarless black shirt proclaiming "Shit Happens" in blazing red clung to his abdomen and flared across his chest and broad shoulders. In the gleaming light, she noticed every ripple and strategic hard plane of her rescuer's finely honed physique.

Fascinated, her gaze roamed higher. He was tall, perhaps an inch over six feet. His dark hair, now dry and combed, was tucked behind his ears. She envied him the natural waves curling the thick, lush mane. She squinted. Was that an earring hole in his left ear? To her knowledge, only sailors and pirates pierced their ears. Then perhaps one of those was his profession. He was certainly sun-darkened enough.

His olive complexion appeared freshly shaven. Life had etched care-lines around his eyes and mouth. He had sharply defined cheek bones, a strong jaw, and a generous mouth she suspected capable of both soft endearments and crass cruelty.

"You can quit taking inventory. You're not my type. I like my women straight in every sense of the word."

While she wasn't sure what he meant, she was too embarrassed at being caught studying him to ask. Avoiding his face, she stared at a dark lock of hair curling over his collarbone. "I . . . uh . . . might you have a curl I can borrow?"

"A curl?"

Mortified, Cally's gaze darted to his face. The dark arches of his eyebrows lifted a fraction of an inch. "A comb. I meant a comb," she said quickly.

Not a hint of his reaction showed in his features as he reached for a drawer between the twin sinks. His shirtsleeve rode up his biceps displaying a Celtic dado-patterned tattoo encircling his arm. "Here's an extra toothbrush you can have." He searched the back of the drawer and found a comb, which he laid on the counter beside the toothbrush and a tube of something.

"Finish up. I'm fixing breakfast. How do you like your eggs?" He scooped up her clothing from the side of the bathtub.

"Poached," she answered, picking up the tube and reading the brightly colored letters. The ingredients astounded her. But then, it seemed everything did. "Is this safe?"

"Excuse me?" Holding her clothing, he paused at the door.

"Do you use this?"

"Yeah. You looking for a commercial endorsement?"

A tight headshake was all she managed as he walked away, leaving the bathroom door open. With a shrug, she uncapped the toothpaste. It tasted minty and clean. She brushed her teeth, deciding she could grow to like the pleasant aftertaste, then worried the snarls from her hair.

"Miss Hornsby! Your *poached* eggs are getting cold," Req shouted from a distant part of the house.

Cally returned the sundries to the drawer and hurried through the door. She stopped in her tracks. The bedroom was decorated in a plethora of floral prints and ruffles. A canopy bed dominated the center. Shiny, square, white furniture lined the walls. Rows of neatly arranged books filled two bookcases. Nightstands with gold drawer pulls stood on both sides of the bed. A desk and mirrored dresser flanked opposite walls. Against the wall at the foot of the bed was a large, hollowed-out dresser with a rack of black rectangles hosting strange symbols. To the right of the stack, another rectangle that reminded her of a great eye stared blindly at the bed.

"Miss Hornsby!"

Cally collected herself and followed the direction of Req's impatient bellow. "You eat an elephant one bite at a time," she murmured, realizing she would have to chew and swallow very fast. Digestion was another matter.

The scrutiny of his house guest during breakfast made Req uncomfortable. She watched his final meal preparations as though she'd never seen a kitchen before. "Okay, what it is? You don't like your poached eggs?"

"These are scrambled eggs," she said, staring at the coffeepot as though it was a poisonous snake. "Delicious scrambled eggs. Thank you."

"You're welcome. I don't do poached eggs, just fried, boiled, and scrambled." Watching her, he silently admitted that he'd finally stumbled across someone he couldn't read. Too much about her behavior didn't add up to drug abuse. When she'd rolled up her sleeves so she could eat without dragging them through the food, the insides of her arms were clean. Not even a freckle marred the soft flesh. Maybe she didn't use needles. Yet. He would know soon enough how heavy her habit was.

There was nothing wrong with her appetite. She ate as though she hadn't had a decent meal in weeks. The genteel manners she employed as she ate the last scraps of her breakfast reminded him of meals in his mother's dining room, of life before the dark time. Whatever else Miss Hornsby faked, fine table etiquette came naturally.

"I have to go into town." Req refilled his coffee cup. "I'll pick up some clothes for you. What size do you wear?"

"My clothing . . ." She looked out the window as though searching for them.

"It's in the dryer." The woman didn't do things halfway. Her costume appeared authentic right down to the woolen stockings. The baggy drawers—he couldn't call them panties because panties implied femininity—were more like flimsy culottes that buttoned at the waist.

He had seen plenty of lingerie and bustiers in his time and not one had felt like a Kevlar vest or looked like the utilitarian torture device Miss Hornsby wore.

"May I make a personal inquiry?" Anxious brown eyes turned on him.

"Shoot."

She winced, obviously disliking the term. "As to the matter of your profession, are you a man of the sea?"

"A man of the sea? You mean a sailor?"

"Yes."

"Why do you think I might be a sailor?"

The whiteness of the terry cloth bathrobe accentuated the faint pink blush creeping up her neck. "It appears your ear is pierced. I have not seen a man with such a . . . with an earring hole, other than a sailor."

Nonplussed, he rocked back in his chair. "Where have you been living? Under a rock?" Req caught himself almost believing her. Oh, she was good. Damn good. Method actors could take a lesson from her on living a role before they stepped in front of a camera.

Req folded his arms over his chest. Maybe she wasn't a junkie, just a nutcase trying to escape into the past.

"I told you, 1890, but I know you doubt my veracity."

That wasn't all he doubted.

She collected the plates in front her at the table. "If you will tell me where I might find soap, I'll wash these."

"Just throw 'em in the dishwasher."

The way her shoulders slumped he may as well have asked her to do the windows too. "Dishwasher," she murmured, setting the plates in front of her.

"Are you going to tell me you don't know what one is?"

The hint of a sad smile caught the corners of her sensuous lips. "For as long as I can remember, Irene has been our dishwasher. And our cook. And our housekeeper. And . . ." Acute sorrow replaced the ghostly smile. "She'll wonder where I am. And worry."

"Call her." He gathered up the dishes and took them to the dishwasher. "There's a phone on the wall beside the refrigerator."

"Phone? Alexander Graham Bell's invention?" Her brown eyes widened. "You have one?"

"There are six here. Use any one of them."

"Six?" Her gasp diverted his attention from placing the dishes in the dishwasher. No one got excited over a telephone. Except Miss Hornsby. Maybe she escaped from a private mental hospital where she had never used a phone or done her own dishes. But hell, she must have gotten a clue from television. Unless the staff didn't allow her to watch it.

He placed the butter knives in the dishwasher's basket. Maybe he ought to lock up the cutlery before he left. If she did something drastic while he was gone, he would have a hell of a time explaining. Worse, he would have to give up this place and find another, less comfortable hidey-hole until the trial. He'd never trust Sal Terragno, his boss at the Narcotics Division, to arrange a safe house for him. Too often he had the feeling Terragno would enjoy throwing him to the enemy. The only thing stopping him was the need for his testimony once they got the cartel to trial.

"Call your housekeeper," he urged softly. *Maybe she'll come and get you and we can both get on with the business of surviving,* he added silently.

She shook her bowed head. "How does one telephone 1890? I doubt even sixty telephones could reach that far." She rose from the table and tucked the robe tighter around her throat. Errant strands of pale blond hair caught on the terry cloth loops. The thick tresses hung straight down her back, nearly to her narrow waist. Not even the bulky robe hid the inviting curves beneath.

Req slammed the dishwasher.

Stupid. That's what he was. Here he was avoiding the men he worked with and for, and hiding from the drug dealers who wanted him dead—preferably before the trial. And what did he do? He brought home a druggy. A loony. Why? Because he thought he recognized a kindred, dispossessed soul. Jeopardized everything because of a momentary weakness, a whim. Damn. He was the one in need of institutionalization.

"Look, Miss Hornsby. Maybe I better take you someplace where you can get proper care." *And commit myself at the same time for risking unnecessary exposure.*

She paused at the kitchen door. "What do you mean, proper care?"

He muttered a curse. What did he mean? "I don't exactly know. I'll make a few calls." Maybe his brother-in-law, Robert, would handle it. Quietly and anonymously.

"I'm sure you know what is best, and I detest being an imposition. Under the circumstances, I have no choice but to trust your judgment on the matter and place my faith in your expertise."

"I wish you wouldn't." Her sincerity cut through one of the weak spots of his conscience. Hell, she seemed harmless.

"Wouldn't what?" She turned, her fingers still entwined in the lapels of the bathrobe.

"Trust me."

"Are you untrustworthy?"

"Not normally. But I'm not . . ." What was there about her that reached inside of him, rattled his reasoning, and loosened his tongue? "I don't want the responsibility of your trust."

"Or me," she added for him. "I understand that much."

"Your mental state—"

Melodic laughter filled the kitchen and swirled around him. "I assure you, sir, the things I do not question are my mental state, and the miracle that brought me here. I have a thousand, no, a million questions. The most imperative is how I return to my own home. In 1890. I have a business to run and people who depend on me." She took a step forward, all traces of her laughter fading into a heat-forged tenacity. "And I want to find out who killed my father. And Freddy the Thief. And who tried to kill me on the beach."

Req stared at her, his skin tingling with an eerie awareness. The same instincts that kept him alive while working undercover whispered that she was telling the truth. *Her* truth, he amended, not necessarily *the* truth.

She closed the distance between them as she spoke, her eyes intent on him. "As far as I'm concerned, my being here is a detour, a temporary inconvenience. I'll unravel the mysterious events that brought me here, then be on my way." She halted in front of him. "If I have to move heaven and earth, I'm going home, Mr. Maguire. I want justice. I have to have it. For my father. For myself. Has your soul ever wailed in the dark for the harsh light of justice? Have you ever cared for something so passionately that no obstacle was too great? No price too high to achieve it?"

He knew what she spoke of, how the aching need for justice could burn away the periphery of life, could become a tunnel you walked through even though you knew death waited at the other end. He understood the gleam of unshed tears in her eyes. If she started crying, she might never stop.

He wouldn't call anyone, wouldn't place her in a system that he knew with every fiber of his being would destroy her.

Instead, he listened to his instincts.

"I'll be back in a few hours. Meanwhile, don't answer the phone or the door." He turned away before he yielded to the impulse to grab her, hold her against his heart, and seek solace for them both.

Life was simpler when he didn't allow himself to feel anything. Since emerging from deep cover three weeks ago, he'd sought to reclaim what he considered his *human* side. A helluva mistake. He'd forgotten how much chaos dwelled in the ability to feel. Like an avalanche caused by a snowball, there was no stopping it after the first roll.

If he was wrong about Miss Hornsby . . .

If she did something drastic . . .

If she did something stupid while he was gone, he'd turn her over to the county and never look back.

"Thank you," she murmured.

"For what?" He grabbed his leather jacket from the end of the counter.

"For trusting me."

"I never said I trusted you. If you want trust, be here when I get back. Alive. Breathing. Alone." He reached for the knob.

"I haven't figured out where to go or how to get back. Are you bringing company when you return? Or will you be alone?"

She was slick, alright. "I'll be alone." He left, chastising himself because he wasn't ready to turn her over to anyone, not for her own good, not even for his.

He took the car, positive she wouldn't be tempted to ride the Harley. Once in town, Req focused on the tasks before him. He needed to check in, but not with his boss, Sal Terragno. From a pay phone on Cannery Row he called Terragno's boss, Daryl Rydell and monitored the second hand on his watch. He spoke for twenty-seven seconds, then hung up. Let Terragno bitch about his jumping the chain of command. The man had never gone undercover. He didn't have a clue what coming out was like.

Rydell had worked undercover nine years ago and was still looking over his shoulder. It had cost him his wife and kids in divorce court. He knew what it was like to see and do things that went against the grain of conscience, to remain quiet and feel his gut burn, to choke back the bile when cruelty and human misery made him want to vomit. He knew the price of growing calluses over everything except the instincts that kept him alive.

Other than his own sister, Req trusted Rydell as much as it was possible for him to trust another human being.

When Req went undercover, no one told him he would lose his humanity layer by layer. At the time, it wouldn't have mattered. Back then, the last thing he wanted to do was feel. Now, he was paying for it. It was like coming out of anesthesia after surgery; the pain returned in waves until a scream filled his chest. He didn't want the anesthesia, but he didn't want the reality either. God help him while he fumbled in the middle ground, groping for a path in the dark.

He went shopping for Miss Hornsby, guessing at the sizes. She damn sure couldn't wear that dress and body armor. Finding something suitable from the skin out took longer than anticipated.

When he returned home, noise blasted him in the kitchen. He dropped the packages on the kitchen table and stripped off his jacket as he hurried through the house.

He approached the open bedroom door. Books lay open across the bed, on the floor, over the desk. The stereo played heavy rock music. A talk-show hostess prodded a woman in a tight, red shirt and big hair to explain the reasons for her sex change.

Miss Hornsby was nowhere in sight.

He turned off the stereo and television. The bathroom door was closed.

With a rapidly beating, heavy heart, he opened the door and stuck his head inside.

Sleeping soundly, Miss Caladonia Hornsby lay curled in the bathtub hugging a pillow. A loose fist coiled around the terry-cloth lapels at her throat. The front edges gaped open below her knees. Day-old scrapes, cuts, and bruises marked her calves.

"Shit," he breathed, so relieved she hadn't done something stupid that his hands trembled. He went into the bedroom and cleared the bed in one powerful sweep by pulling back the bedspread.

Carefully he lifted Miss Hornsby out of the tub. He carried her to the bed and laid her down, then covered her with a blanket before her eyelids fluttered.

"Mr. Maguire?"

"What the hell were you doing sleeping in the bathtub?"

"It was the only room I knew how to work things in." She yawned, then turned onto her side, closing her eyes. "I pressed too many buttons. I'm sorry."

He tucked the blanket over her shoulder. "Go to sleep."

She surprised him by turning back and gazing up at him with weary, worried eyes. "A man came. He didn't see me, but I saw him."

"Someone came here?" Every muscle in his body stilled. "What did he do?" He kept his voice soft, not wanting to alarm her.

"He had a little box he held up to the house. He walked around, lifting the box. When he finished, he stuck a calling card under the front door." She reached for the business card lying on the nightstand, but Req beat her to it.

"He's from the electric company," he lied. Damn Terragno! Couldn't he wait? Or did Terragno think he'd found a way to make him heel? Terragno would love to have him begging for protection. *Not in this lifetime,* Req promised.

Without thinking, he placed a kiss on Miss Hornsby's forehead. When he straightened, he wasn't sure which one of them was more surprised. He looked away. "I have to go out again. I'll try to make it back today. Same rules as before. No phone, no visitors. There's food in the kitchen. Meanwhile, get some sleep. Things will look better when you wake up."

"I highly doubt that, Mr. Maguire." She turned onto her side, her fingertips absently touching the spot on her forehead where he had kissed her.

As he left the book-strewn room, he realized he may have saved her from the waves, but she was drowning him in a sea of emotion.

Ten minutes later, he'd changed clothes and backed the car out of the garage. He needed to talk to Terragno. This time, he would do it from Reno and take his time explaining things. He could catch the afternoon flight, make a connection, then return before dark. If things went well.

Considering the day's events, he was not encouraged.

Chapter 4

SLEEP HAD HELPED clear her mind. Patient experimentation had paid off as Cally learned how to operate the largest of the magic boxes in the bedroom. It was a good thing she lay on the bed when she changed the image in the great eye.

A couple writhed in the throes of passion among tangled sheets. Except for short blond hair, different color eyes, and a lack of tattoos, the man reminded her of Requiem Maguire. Despite all the complexities surrounding her, tussling in the sheets with him was exactly what her body wanted. Astonished by her licentious thoughts, Cally pressed the button on the device in her hand. The picture changed.

Determined to restrain her wild thoughts concerning her host, she stared back at the great eye.

"Don't be a fool," she muttered at a woman inviting her to smell her toilet. "Now, why would anyone want to do that?"

She punched the button again.

This window on a different time was incredible. Scary, but amazing. How many newspapers and books might she have had to read to learn what the people inside the great eye could teach her in a short time?

The longer she watched, the more she understood Requiem Maguire. Small wonder he was so sure she indulged in medications. Total strangers hawked pills, potions, and ointments for treating the most personal, private, and embarrassing conditions.

More shocking was the candor with which people revealed their worst sins in front of audiences. She had watched part of such a program with a macabre fascination and revilement. If she had done or experienced the things the people on the stage discussed openly, she would crawl into a hole and starve to death before exposing the deed.

Cally drew her knees up and hugged them over the blankets. Resting her chin atop the peak, she became mesmerized with her window on this new world.

Slot machines dinged, jangled, and enticed passersby inside the doors of the casinos Req passed. The anonymity of a place as public as the strip in Reno was just what he needed. The pay phone he headed for was well used and safer than entering a casino with cameras recording every person. He didn't doubt Terragno would have the call traced. He couldn't prevent that. But he damn sure wasn't going to draw him a picture—or give him one.

He had made a last-minute connection to Reno, as he'd planned, and intended the same expediency, but using a different route, back to Monterey. He checked his watch. Less than two hours before his flight. Damn, he wished he had the right equipment to make his calls untraceable so that he wouldn't have to go to such elaborate lengths every time he needed to call his boss.

Soon, he promised himself. However, *soon* did nothing to alleviate his sense of urgency to return to Caladonia Hornsby. She may not be playing with a full deck, but his own actions proved he wasn't either.

Req slapped two rolls of quarters on the ledge beside the telephone. After affixing the microphone attached to a small recorder in his pocket, he punched in the memorized number, then fed the coin slot with as much zeal as a quarter-slot machine player on a streak did. He didn't worry about a tap on Terragno's line. The scrambler on the office telephone line would keep their conversation private.

"Terragno," came a tired voice over the receiver.

"You sent people to look for me. You broke the arrangement, Sal." Req scrutinized the people passing on the street. Paranoia was an asset in his line of work.

"I don't know what the hell you're talking about." Fatigue turned to feigned boredom in Terragno's voice.

Req checked his watch. He knew the ploy better than he wanted to. "Cut the bullshit and games, Sal. You think you're the only one who gets reports from me?"

"I'm the only one who should, Maguire. You keep forgetting

we have a chain of command. You report to me. You're my responsibility—"

"Then act like it. And remember, if they get me before I testify, the entire case is down the tubes."

"Then, come in, dammit, so we can ensure your safety," Terragno said quietly.

"Like Paul Sandavol?" Christ, it still hurt to say his ex-partner's name. "I stand a better chance of making it to the trial taking care of myself."

"That's a low blow, Maguire. Sandavol's death wasn't my fault."

"The hell it wasn't." Req spotted a pickpocket relieving a tourist from the burden of his wallet.

"You're paranoid and looking for someone to blame. If it makes you feel better to blame me—"

"I warned you they were onto him, and you didn't pull him."

"We couldn't pull him. He was so close—"

"So close, he ended up with a bullet in the back of his head. The difference between Paul and me is that I don't trust you. I record everything you and I say, Sal, so if something happens to me prematurely, you can kiss your career good-bye. The whole fuckin' world's going to know about you, not just Daryl Rydell."

The brief silence promised he'd hit a nerve. He kept the momentum going. "If I so much as catch a whiff of anyone watching me that I haven't personally asked for, I'll come in and drag your carcass over the coals personally. And you sure as hell won't like the fallout. Listen carefully. I'm only going to say this once. If I come in, I won't testify."

"Dammit, we'll subpoena you," Terragno hissed.

"You can put me on the stand, Sal, but you can't make me say what you want to hear. I've been walking this tightrope for over two years. I put my life on the line every damn minute. Right about now, the only thing I care about is staying alive. You're a liability to me. Stay in Dallas, Terragno, and keep your leash pets with you, and away from me, unless you want to go to another funeral." Req checked his watch.

"Don't threaten me, Maguire."

"The only threat I see is you not abiding by the agreement we hammered out in Rydell's office. The rest is fact, Terragno. You want to test me, track me down yourself." Req wouldn't kill him. Not intentionally. But since Paul Sandoval's death six

months earlier, he'd wanted to hurt Terragno. Badly. Killing
was too easy.

"You're ignoring standard protocol for protecting a witness.
I can't be responsible—"

"Don't I know it! The only thing you need to be responsible
for is seeing that I get what I need through the channels Rydell
and I set up. You compromise that, Terragno, and so help me
God, I'll come after you." Req whipped the microphone free,
then slammed the receiver into the hook. The Plexiglas shield
around the pay phone shuddered from the impact. Two
passersby glanced his way.

"Shit," he muttered, scooping the remaining quarters into his
hand.

Armed with expertise gleaned from the great eye and something called an infomercial, Cally figured out how to operate
the amazing microwave oven in the kitchen. Finding it in the
gleaming expanse of white countertops and cupboards was an
accomplishment in itself. A surface she realized was the stove
dominated the center island of the kitchen. The microwave was
located on the countertop beside the tall double doors of the refrigerator. The way it matched the cupboards, she thought it
looked more like an armoire than an icebox.

Her stomach growled as she searched the frozen food in the
icebox, which was an advancement from her era that bordered
on phenomenal.

She read the back of a square box labeled "Turkey Potpie,"
almost dropping it when she heard a noise from the cavern she
decided was the carriage house where he kept the Harley beast.
A glance at the clock on the wall behind the table showed it was
nearly two in the morning. No wonder she was tired. But she
was hungry too.

She sat at the table and picked up the pencil she had used to
write down four pages of questions that she wanted Req to answer. Like everything else, she had to push a button to make it
work. That was all right. She was adapting. If she remained in
this place very long, she would have calluses on her fingertips
from pushing buttons.

The kitchen door opened and Req entered the brightly lit
room. Wherever he had been, and whatever he had done, hadn't
improved his mood. The small lines around his scowling mouth
seemed more pronounced. The tight way he carried himself bespoke a tension she was familiar with.

"Ah, Mr. Maguire, you're home."

"Who else were you expecting at two A.M.?"

"Why, no one."

"The name is Req. Okay?"

"Alright. If that's what you prefer." He was the most disconcerting man she'd ever met. Off balance, she looked away and changed the subject. "I've learned how to work the lights." The small triumph had kept her from bashing her shins in the dark. The simplicity of flipping a switch had made her laugh as she turned on most of the lights in the house.

He stopped in his tracks and stared at her.

Suddenly nervous, conscious of her state of dress, she clutched the lapels of the soft, white robe. "I couldn't find my clothing."

"I bought you clothes." He removed his jacket and tossed it on the counter.

"You bought clothes for me? How? Why? I mean . . ." Flustered, she wondered where they were and how she might have missed them when she practiced with the light switches in various parts of the house.

"In those bags you've shoved to the far end of the table. I had to guess at the sizes." He picked up the coffeepot on the way to the sink.

The embarrassing growl of her empty stomach forced her to look away from the enticing bags that crinkled when she touched them. They seemed entirely too small to accommodate the clothing she was used to wearing. Recalling the garb people wore on the great eye, she swallowed hard and wondered what kind of fashions Wal-Mart made.

"Did you eat anything?" Req rinsed the glass carafe and started making a fresh pot of coffee.

She watched closely. Earlier, she would have loved to fix a cup. The best she had managed was tea brewed with hot tap water. "I, ah, was just about to experiment with the amazing little oven that pops corn and cooks a turkey in minutes."

The way his green eyes narrowed added to her sudden discomfort. "I found a turkey pie in your frozen icebox," she said, feeling guilty for invading his supplies. Thank heaven she hadn't opened the chocolate ice cream.

"Did you find anything else interesting in there?"

She blushed. Of course she had. He probably wanted to know if she had eaten his ice cream. "I am not in the habit of invading my host's larder. I prefer to ask permission, particularly since I have imposed on your good hospitality to a far greater extent than I suspect either of us is comfortable with."

"Lady, I'm too tired for these games. You want something to eat, fix it and eat it. Just clean up after yourself." He turned his back and reached into a cupboard for a mug. "You want coffee?"

"Yes, please, if you don't mind."

"If I minded, I wouldn't have asked."

For a moment, she silently gritted her back teeth. She was trying to be polite. Good manners seemed the least she could do under the circumstances. Then again, she had seen little evidence of what she considered common courtesy or good manners among the people inside the great eye.

"Yes, please," she said, lifting her chin. "I would like a cup of coffee." She set the pencil on top of the tablet. "And I'd like to eat something too."

"Help yourself." He set a second mug on the countertop beside the coffeepot and closed the cupboard door. "The coffee will take a few minutes."

Apprehension mingled with relief when he left the kitchen. She quickly retrieved the meat pie and reread the directions as her stomach growled again. She was hungry enough to eat it frozen. Confident she knew how to cook it, she followed the steps and put it in the microwave and pushed Start.

"It won't cook any faster if you watch." Req had reentered the room and approached the coffeepot.

"This amazing invention must save hours from a cook's day," she mused, still hunched over and watching the meat pie move in a slow circle inside the oven. "Who makes the meat pies? How do they arrange to sell them? Where do the ingredients come from? I didn't recognize some of the ones listed on the box. Are those new spices? If so, where do they come from?"

When she looked up, Req was staring at her as though she had grown a third eye. "It's a potpie. You buy it at the store. Who the hell cares how it gets there?"

"I do. I want to know everything about this time and place. The more I learn, the better chance I have of finding my way home."

He carried two cups of steaming coffee to the table and glanced at the list of questions. "How the hell does knowing the life cycle of a potpie help you?" He cleared his throat and set down the coffee, then picked up the notebook. "What's this?"

The oven buzzed, startling her. She opened it and started to reach inside. "It's steaming. How do I get it out?"

"You never heard of hot pads?" He dropped the notebook and pulled open a drawer beside the stove. "Use a plate, too. Just scoot the whole thing onto the plate with the hot pad. The plate catches the crumbs and makes clean-up easier."

She did as he suggested, feeling foolish. At the table, she set her meal where her notebook had been, then started searching for a fork.

The sound of a turning page made her self-conscious. Although she'd hoped Req would answer her questions, she hadn't meant for him to read them or her notes. Especially not the one about—

"You're good, Miss Hornsby. Damn good. You ought to consider a career in Undercover Ops." He slapped the tablet against the table edge. Suspicion hardened his expression. He didn't so much as blink. "Or do you already have that kind of career?"

The great eye had taught her a lot, but obviously not enough. "I don't know what you're referring to. I slept under the covers. Is that what you mean?" It felt wrong. The disgusted scowl darkening his sharp features gave his response. "I believe we suffer from idiomatic differences within the language," she said slowly. Some of the things people laughed at in the great eye had escaped her comprehension too. There was so much to learn and so little time to learn it.

"Idiom. Idiot. Whatever. I'm too tired for this. In the future, eat what you want, when you want. Just don't leave me a mess." He nodded at the bags at the end of the table. "Don't forget your clothes. Tomorrow or the day after, we'll get you some running shoes."

"I have shoes. Besides, who would I run from here? The only consolation I take from this bizarre situation is that no one knows me, therefore, no one wants to kill me."

She set her dishes on the countertop, then reached for the bags. Her curiosity prickled with a mixture of dread and excitement. No man, not even her father, had bought clothing for her more personal than a scarf.

The blend of colors and fabrics inside the bag begged for her touch. She obliged, drawing out the lacy black garment on top. Confused, she held it up. The curving bones beneath the breast cups defined it as a support garment. It seemed too small to replace her corset. Then, recalling the pictures on the great eye, she realized that was part of its purpose and held it up for closer

examination. The lace cups lacked the same full measure of
material on the tops as on the bottom. She reserved judgment
whether this was in fact an improvement over the corset. It certainly appeared so where comfort was concerned. Holding it
against her bathrobe revealed how flimsy, even seductive, the
foundation was. There was something deliciously wicked about
the design of the lacy pattern that exposed the flesh beneath.

She looked at Req, wondering why he had purchased such
provocative undergarments for her. These were certainly nothing like the cotton ones advertised on the great eye.

His scowl and the gruff manner in which he turned his head
told her what her body already knew. He wanted her, or at least
he had when he selected the seductive lingerie. There was
something darkly thrilling in knowing he wanted to see her in
the flimsy garb. A small sense of satisfaction mollified the but-
terflies beating invisible wings in her stomach. At least now she
knew that the attraction wasn't one-sided.

She dropped the bodice on the table, then reached into the
bag for the other black scrap of lace. "How did you know this
would fit me?" Despite the sense of power and sexual excitement, embarrassment warmed her when she thought of actually
wearing the lingerie. A fleeting glance at Req made her thick
robe seem like gauze and promised she was flirting with a new
form of danger.

"Guessed," he said in a thick voice.

The bottom counterpart to the provocative black bodice was
unbelievably intriguing. If not for the education provided on
the great eye, she would never have guessed these were panties.
Looking at them, "panties" was an exaggeration in describing
the lacy, thong garment she recognized from the Playboy chan-
nel. "Incredible."

Req cleared his throat and shifted in his chair. "What?" His
hands dwarfed the coffee mug that he clutched as though it was
an anchor.

"That women wear this kind of . . . of . . ." She held up a tri-
angle holding two loops together. Judging by the hint of color
on his tanned neck, whatever it was, he liked it. A lot.

"Underwear," he finished.

A sexual tension drawing her nerves taut made her shift from
foot to foot. She could put an end to it by stuffing the black lace
into the bag. But she couldn't help playing with the fiery desire
crackling in the air between them. She ran her fingers over the
lacy black panel, then held it across her hips. "Like this?"

Req nodded once, his discomfort readily apparent, but he didn't appear the slightest bit embarrassed.

The predatory gleam in his unblinking eyes made her feel stalked. Yet she had brought this on herself. She tried to turn the tide by focusing on the absurdity of wearing the flimsy undergarments. "I may never become accustomed to the differences between this time and my own."

Req sat back in his chair and folded his arms over his chest. "If you need help dressing, call me. I'm at your service."

The sudden shift of the heated tide cresting between them left Cally with the feeling that she was swimming around a shark. A hungry one. "Thank you for the offer of assistance, but I'm sure I can manage."

"Fine," he said. "It's late. I'm going to bed." The slight lift of his left eyebrow beckoned with a tantalizing invitation.

She clutched the noisy, crinkly bags, tempted beyond reason to accept. The realization jolted her into standing a bit straighter. Inside, she had never been more off balance.

With a faint smile more like a smirk, Req took his coffee and the notebook off the table as he stood.

Truly, he was the strangest, most enigmatic and enticing man she had ever met. But then, she hadn't met any others in this time.

Lying in bed, Req read the first page of questions before deciding he was too damn tired to make sense out of the situation. He turned off the light and tried to sleep. Oblivion eluded him.

He wanted her. Hell, his body was screaming for him to drag her under him and answer all the questions she'd written down.

"Don't think about it," he admonished through clenched teeth. He tried to shift mental gears, tried to forget the beautiful lush body hiding behind that robe.

The questions she'd written out surfaced. It was safer to wonder why anyone wanted to know about inflation rates over the past century. The same thing held for currency coefficients. Who cared what a dollar was worth in 1890 compared to today?

Miss Caladonia Hornsby, that's who.

His brain wanted to believe she had an act, one she was very, very good at performing. His gut twisted, wondering if she was a plant, maybe one of Terragno's people. Terragno didn't know anyone of that caliber. Besides, Rydell would never have approved such an assignment anyway. He had better uses for a woman that talented in the art of illusion.

Req's heart promised his brain that his gut suspicions were wrong. She was vulnerable, caught up in something neither of them understood, and making the best of it. He'd lived an illusion of his own creation and knew how damn real it could get, how hard it was to return to old realities. Maybe that's what had happened to her.

The only thing Req knew for certain was that his loins were screaming for him to do something about the agony of fullness he experienced each time he looked at her. Or thought about her. Like now.

The thought of her wearing the lacy lingerie kept surfacing. It was all he could do to stay in his own room. How satisfying removing that bulky robe from her sweet-smelling skin would be. Exploring . . .

He punched his pillow, angry with himself for being so obsessed with a woman.

He needed sleep, not fantasy. Summoning the discipline that had kept him alert and alive while undercover, he forced Caladonia Hornsby out of his mind.

Eventually, the ache in his groin eased and he drifted into a restless sleep. Shortly before dawn, he awakened drenched in sweat and out of breath.

His heart raced and fear mingled with outrage and a sorrow so profound it nearly crushed his chest. Each time he blinked, he saw the dingy warehouse on the run-down industrial side of the San Diego wharf, and heard the gunshot as Gutierrez put a bullet in the back of Paul's head.

Req stared at the dark ceiling, admitting to himself that he would testify regardless of what Terragno did. He owed it to Paul. Hell, he owed it to himself, to Victor, and to Malika. All he had to do was live long enough to tell his story to a jury.

"Got to," he seethed. How else could he extract payment for all the misery-laden debts Gutierrez owed? And if he didn't force payment, who would?

"No one."

He threw the covers back. The morning air chilled his sweaty body. He headed for the bathroom and showered. Ten minutes later, he climbed on his Harley and headed for the beach.

He needed to see the sky brighten over the mountains and the water come alive with the dawn. Each time he saw the sunrise brought him one day closer to the day of retribution. As a lost soul who belonged nowhere, it gave him purpose.

• • • •

Cally woke in a panic. For a moment, nothing was familiar. As sleep fled from her fuzzy brain, she recalled where and *when* she was. The dangerous game she had played with Req in the small hours of the morning crashed into her awareness.

She showered and collected the scanty underwear she had washed in the sink before going to bed. There was so little to the garments, they had dried quickly. For a moment, she wondered if they had shrunk. Putting them on brought back the memory of Req's expression when she had held the panties up. He had remained stoic, but she had felt the sexual hunger roaring inside him.

"No more playing with fire," she muttered, then looked in the mirror as she reached for a pair of socks on the countertop.

The intimacy of the clothing Req had purchased was even greater when she wore it. The lacy drawers were little more than a silky scrap riding high on her hips. The brief corset replacement molded her breasts until they overflowed the cups that simultaneously confined and exposed. Wearing the undergarments, she felt naked.

She quickly donned the denim trousers, soft blouse, and fleecy over–shirt he'd purchased. Fortunately, the attire covered her from head to foot. Although they fit reasonably well, she doubted she would become accustomed to wearing anything other than skirts.

"As Saint Ambrose said, 'When in Rome, do as the Romans do,'" she muttered, tucking her hair into a coil at the back of her neck. "But he didn't mention how long it took to become accustomed to Rome's ways."

In the kitchen, desperate for a cup of coffee, she experimented with the brewing pot. The aroma crawled into her nerve endings. Maybe today Req would explain how to use the stove nestled in an island surrounded by chopping blocks. The pots, pans, and lids hanging from a contraption fixed to the ceiling looked well used. Someone cooked. She had a niggling suspicion it wasn't Req.

The rumble of the Harley heralded his arrival. She hadn't realized he had left the house. At least there was coffee.

She poured two cups and settled at the table. He hadn't returned her tablet, so perhaps he would answer a few of her questions.

Req entered the kitchen and tossed his black leather jacket on the countertop beside the door. She realized that in the philoso-

phy of everything having a place, that particular spot belonged
to Req's jacket.

The same deep-rumbling thunder she had experienced on the
Harley rode his features. He walked quietly despite the heavy
black boots he wore. The way his jeans hugged his muscular
thighs and narrow hips drew her eye to the pronounced bulge
of his sex where the blue material was faded from wear. She
wondered what kind of underwear Requiem Maguire wore and
how he looked in it. And without it. Speculation heated her with
the intensity of a hot, summer sun. Dry-mouthed, she lifted her
gaze to the animated white shark scowling on the front of his
black tee shirt. Given the mood he projected, the predator
seemed a self-portrait.

"Coffee," he grunted.

"I just poured a cup for you." She gestured at the mug steaming across the table from her. Overall, it seemed wise to wait
until he started on his second cup before asking questions or
probing for answers.

They eyed one another covertly, their gazes catching, darting
away, and returning. The raw emotion bubbling inside Cally
vacillated between anxiety and the powerful signals her body
foolishly sent. Finally, she studied him, trying to figure out how
this dark, dangerous man managed to make her feel things she
had never even dreamed about.

"What are you staring at?" Req set his coffee down and
turned in the chair until he faced her squarely.

Although flustered, she refused to bow to intimidation or defeat by lowering her gaze. "You intrigue me. I've been surrounded by men all my life, but I've never met anyone like
you."

"Let me guess. You want to get to know me better?" He drew
a deep breath and released it slowly. The sorrow of disappointment furrowed his brow.

"Not particularly, as I suspect you are also a very dangerous
man. I have enough danger in my life. And enough problems to
solve." She braced an elbow on the tabletop and studied the
wariness in his eyes.

"That's a helluva line you have, Miss Hornsby. Do you always come on to men before breakfast?"

Come on. What had the people in the great eye said about
that? Something . . . "I haven't asked you to go anywhere," she
murmured, trying to divine the new meaning of the two words.

"Don't bother. I travel alone. You're here as the charity case."

The connotation struck a devastating blow. The truth of it bit deep into her self-respect. "I . . . I can work." Oh, God, she didn't want charity. "Show me. Tell me what you need done. I can learn." The sting of humiliation blurred her vision, forcing her to look away. "It's all so different, but surely there are chores in need of doing."

He sat back, his hands resting on the edge of the table. "That bothers you?" Disbelief and skepticism shone in his eyes. "Enough to work?"

Mortified, Cally bowed her head. Of course she was a charity case, she just hadn't thought of his hospitality in that light. "Greatly."

"So now what? You profess not knowing how to do anything. What's your next ploy? Offering your body as payment for your keep?"

A physical slap would have smarted less. Revilement, bitter and stinging, rose in her throat. Slowly, her head lifted. Coldness swept through her as she regarded the man she had fantasized about in his underwear—and without it—a short time ago. To her chagrin, he was as enticing as ever, and even more dangerous.

Deliberately, she pushed away from the table, then stood. "Please excuse me. I think I have overstayed my welcome."

Chapter 5

REQ CAUGHT HER wrist as she rounded the table. The fine trembling of the flesh beneath his fingers betrayed her deep anger. She had no right to be angry, not after the little panty game she had played. Hell, he was starting to get used to the hard-on he went to sleep and woke up with. "Sit down."

"I think it best that I do not, Mr. Maguire. I'm sure there is employment in town, something I can do to earn enough to repay you for my clothing and food. I had best get busy finding it."

He looked up, meeting the overly bright glaze in her eyes. "Why the hell are you crying?"

Her jaw clamped, her lips pressed together as though holding back an acrid retort. "I most certainly am not crying."

Technically, she wasn't. At least she wasn't shedding any visible tears. "Sit down," he repeated.

She remained rigid.

How much easier it would be if she was a drug addict. It had been over twenty-four hours, and she showed no withdrawal signs. Not drugs, he conceded. A harmless mental case. He couldn't let her leave. Not yet.

"Please," he growled through gritted teeth. He couldn't remember the last time he had said *please* to a woman besides his mother or sister.

"So you can insult me? Insinuate that I'm mad?" She yanked on her wrist. His fingers tightened. "Suggest I'm a woman of compromised principles and low morals?"

"Look, Miss Hornsby, you got nowhere to go and no way to get there—unless you're lying and your friends are waiting close by." He let the implication hang as hard, dark fury turned her eyes into agates. He couldn't tell if he had caught her in a lie or if she was genuinely outraged over the accusation.

"A lie would be so much easier for you to believe, but I refuse to lie to either one of us. And I do have somewhere to go—out of this house and away from you, Mr. Maguire. I'll worry about what comes later when I'm gone." The rancor of indignation returned some color to her face, though she continued regarding him with the disdain she might reserve for a large cockroach.

"Alright. I'll try not to insult you. Fair enough?"

"There is nothing *fair* about this situation. Nothing! Fair is my father being alive. Fair is me in my own home. In my own kitchen. In my own clothes." Her voice broke, then softened. "In my own time where I know how things work and who people are. Even my enemies."

She stuck to her story like she believed it. The wistfulness tormenting her features promised she did. Twenty-four hours without drugs or withdrawal symptoms lent credibility to her impossible tale. If she wasn't an addict, and she wasn't lying . . .

She was hallucinating, he decided. "Life isn't fair, Miss Hornsby. Not to you. Not to me."

Cally glared at Req, obviously not mollified by his philosophizing. "Regardless of all that, circumstances have not reduced me to the point of bartering my keep for . . . for . . ."

"Sexual favors?" Thank heaven it hadn't, although part of him wished it had. The rapid pulse in her wrist burned him alive.

"Yes," she whispered. The tension easing in her face almost cracked his facade.

"First off, I'm not asking you to go to bed with me. We've got enough trouble without complicating things." With Caladonia Hornsby, it would be a serious complication. If she got this upset over an innuendo, getting rid of her after he explored the body she kept covered like a security code to nirvana would be damn-near impossible.

Her gaze narrowed into a squint. "This trouble you mentioned—are we in it together or separately?"

"Looks like both to me." In more ways than he had imagined when he'd brought her home from the beach. "You being here complicates the hell out of things."

"For you?"

"Yeah." He released her. "And for you."

She rubbed her wrist, but remained in place. "I did not believe my life could become more bizarre. Are you going to explain, or do you think I'm too demented to comprehend?"

He gestured at the chair she'd vacated. "Sit down, and I'll tell you what I can."

She turned toward the chair, hesitant.

He couldn't miss the way her curvy bottom filled out the jeans. The motion of her hips sent the pulse below his beltline into high gear. As she walked around the table, he imagined her clad only in a pair of the scanty panties he'd selected. The black ones she'd held up earlier.

He closed his eyes to temptation, but he couldn't escape the images of her soft, pale flesh adorned in lacy, black thong panties and an equally provocative bra that offered her breasts to him with every movement.

He cleared his dry throat and tried to get rid of the erotic images of the delectable Miss Hornsby. Looking beyond the prim manner in which she sat across the safe barrier of the table, he saw curiosity. Her cowed anger waited for a wrong move before it sprang again. He turned his head, imagining those coffee eyes looking at him from over her naked shoulder, asking, wondering, waiting for him to show her how damn good sex between them could be. "What the hell have I done?" he seethed under his breath.

"I beg your pardon?" She leaned closer as though expecting him to repeat himself.

"Nothing." For the first time in his life he wondered if he possessed a death wish. Nothing else accounted for his lack of forethought or caution. He had brought her home, now he was stuck with her until he was ready to move on. In short, she knew too much: where he lived, what kind of car he drove, and there was no telling what she'd learned about the house security system during his sojourn to Reno.

Some time before he awakened yesterday morning, his brains must have dribbled out his ear. The substance that filled the void was incapable of rational thought.

Shit for brains, he concluded. The trouble with that was shit didn't think. The difficult situation he'd created smelled like he was already hip-deep and sinking fast.

It could get him killed.

That sobering thought sent his gaze back to Miss Hornsby.

It could get her killed too.

The only death he wanted to be a party to these days was Gutierrez's. That he wanted badly.

"I'm waiting for your explanation, sir."

"Save the sir crap, Miss Hornsby," he grumbled, still searching for a place to start and a way to say it.

"Are you in trouble?"

He met her probing brown eyes and found compassion. He preferred fury and ice. "Being with me could wind up being trouble for you. People want me dead. The sooner the better. They aren't too particular about taking out anyone who happens to be with me either. Understand?"

"I understand people wanting you dead, but I don't understand why anyone would want to take me anywhere," she answered softly.

"They'd kill you, too," he said flatly.

"Oh." She sat a little straighter. "Do you know why they want you dead?"

Every nerve in his body stilled when he stared into her eyes. "Yes. I'm dangerous to them."

"Can you go to the authorities?"

Req snorted. Hell, he *was* the authorities. "The law isn't after me. They can't help me. They think they can, but they can't. Understand?"

"You have reason not to trust them," she said thoughtfully.

"You got that right. It only takes one phone call to make the world a very small place."

"You don't trust anyone, do you?"

"Trust is a luxury I can't afford these days."

"Would you tell me why?"

Christ, she was a bulldog. "Last time I trusted someone to do something, he didn't do it. And a man died." The black sorrow that had become his companion since Paul Sandavol's death slid over his emotions. Like anesthesia, it melted the hard edge of his physical desire and numbed the softer side of his emotions.

"Someone you cared about was . . . murdered?" she asked.

"Yeah." He looked into his coffee mug. It was empty, like his soul.

"I'm sorry." She turned her head.

He studied her profile. She wasn't hard to look at, but she wasn't a classic beauty either. What the hell was there about her that turned him into a blathering idiot? "You have nothing to be sorry for."

"It hurts to lose someone you love or care for deeply. It hurts even more when they're murdered." She picked up both mugs and went to the coffeepot. "The authorities don't always help. I thought Detective Goodman would find out who killed my father. Maybe he tried. At first, I thought he did, but nothing ever came of it."

She carried the mugs back to the table and sat down. "That's part of what makes me believe in an afterlife. Somewhere, somehow there has to be justice."

"For your father?" he asked softly, suspecting that she had learned about compromise and corruption the hard way.

She pushed his mug across the table. "I know you don't believe me. It no longer matters. Either way, nothing changes my circumstances. What I'm trying to say is, in a limited way, I understand that by performing an act of . . . charity . . ." She swallowed as though the word caught in her throat. ". . . you complicated things for yourself."

"And you."

She laughed sadly. "You know, Req, I doubt that's possible. I may not know much about contemporary society, but I watched the great eye long enough to realize things would not be very nice for me now if you had taken me to detox yesterday morning. I didn't understand then. I may not fully understand now. Even so, I thank you from the bottom of my heart."

"The great eye? You mean TV? Television?"

"It is that. They tell all sorts of things to total strangers." Her lashes lowered as she picked up her mug. "And do things." She sipped her coffee. "When I leave here, I will never mention your name or this place. It would be most ungrateful of me to reward your generosity with betrayal."

"Silence would be appreciated. However, you don't have to be in a hurry to leave. If it looks like I've got trouble breathing down my neck, I'll warn you." She confounded him on every level. She was intelligent, quick-thinking, unassuming. And living in a fantasy world. Perhaps he might learn more about her by exploring her alternate reality. He tucked that thought into the wallet of his mind.

"What this place affords more than anything else is privacy. Comfortable privacy," Req said. "The gardeners come once a week. I know them, and I'm not worried they'll talk to the wrong people. I let the maid service go, so it will be just you and me here."

She seemed to consider his words seriously. "Until this

morning, the impropriety of my being here with you was the least of my concerns. From what you've said, I doubt I can anticipate the addition of a chaperone."

"A chaperone?" Christ, he hadn't heard that term in years. Even then, it implied *impediment.*

"Perhaps it is a cultural safeguard gone by the wayside over the years." She glanced around the kitchen, her eyebrows drawn close over the bridge of her fine nose. "Does your family own this magnificent house?"

"The place is mine." She telegraphed her doubt hard enough to tug a wry smile at the corners of his mouth. "Don't you think a guy like me would own a fancy estate on millionaire acres?"

"It is a beautiful home and more spacious than it appeared at first glance." Her gaze slid from the stove to him. "I don't really know what 'a guy like you' is. I don't know you. Let's just say the way this home is put together doesn't suit what I've seen of your personality. The only personalized room is the one you gave me."

"I inherited the place from Victor Escobar," Req heard himself say, then clamped his mouth shut. He didn't owe her an explanation. Besides, he didn't give a rat's ass how the place was decorated. It had a bed, a stove, a refrigerator, and a television. Even with the south wing closed up, maintaining the house was a real pain since he'd dismissed the cleaning service. "Tell you what. You keep the rooms we use dusted. Run the vacuum cleaner."

Her brow furrowed in consternation. "How does one clean a vacuum? I thought there was nothing in it."

Here we go again, he thought. She probably didn't do windows or ovens either. "I'll show you," he conceded. "You do the cleaning, and that'll earn your keep. Deal?"

"Food, too?"

"Sure. Can you cook?"

"I can make meat pies in the little oven," she said proudly. "And coffee."

"I'll take your word on the first. We'll work on the second." He looked into his cup at half an inch of grounds. "Meanwhile, are you interested in making breakfast?"

"Yes. Would you like a meat pie?"

"Not normally."

"Ice cream?" she asked hopefully.

He stared at her for a moment. "You really don't know how to cook, do you?"

A hint of color brightened her cheeks. "I'm afraid not. It never seemed important to learn. I was more interested in the ships and trade routes." She stood abruptly. "I must get home soon. I have duties waiting."

For a moment, he almost believed her. "Tell you what. I'll do the cooking for a while."

"You could teach me. I'm quite educatable."

The kind of cooking he wanted to teach her was best done in a bed. "I'm sure you are." He eyed the height of the kitchen countertops.

Requiem Maguire defied her understanding. One minute, he didn't want her within a hundred miles. The next, he regarded her with a nerve-shattering intensity. Then, it seemed he wanted to devour her the way the couples on the television did. If the notion didn't hold so much appeal, she could ignore it the same way she used to turn a blind eye on the ogling dockhands at the wharf.

He was right about trouble and danger. He was both.

Considering the nature of her new job, he was also right in the selection of her attire. The close-fitting dungarees made bending and moving easier than the yards of petticoats and skirts she was accustomed to wearing.

She plugged the vacuum cleaner into one of the outlets Req had indicated provided "juice," and continued her chores. She didn't understand how it worked, nor did she care, except when she went too far and pulled the plug out of the receptacle. The chores might earn her keep, but they did nothing in the way of helping her find a way home.

Regardless of how many mind-boggling innovations time had forged, this wasn't where she belonged. The score she had to settle with the murderers on the beach would remain unchallenged if she didn't return.

Self-interest and an eye for profit would keep her two partners at Golden Sun Shipping going. Twice since her father's death, Chauncy Cunningham, the man who'd started the shipping empire with her father, had offered to buy her out.

A snort of contempt fueled her vigorous efforts with the vacuum cleaner across the living room carpet.

Neither Thomas Barry, the youngest partner in Golden Sun Shipping, nor Chauncy Cunningham believed a woman had a place in the business world. It made not a whit of difference that she knew every detail and had started learning the intricacies of the business while sitting on her father's lap at age five.

At times, her father's old partner Chauncy Cunningham was blatant in his disapproval of having a female partner. Thomas Barry thought she belonged in his home and pregnant with his child.

If Thomas had incited a fraction of the tempestuous desire Requiem Maguire did with just a look, she might have considered it.

Her traitorous mind had gone full circle and brought her back to Req.

The vacuum cleaner stopped. Dismayed, she saw that she had pulled the plug from the receptacle again. The abundance of electricity had limits. Muttering, she found a wall outlet in the hall leading to a part of the house she hadn't explored and resumed her task.

Diligent, she ran the noisy machine over floors that looked clean in one room after another. She opened the door to the final room at the end of the hall, and stared.

"Turn that thing off," Req snapped without looking up from the desk.

Reflexively, Cally obeyed. "Is that a surf thing? Like on the television?" Curiosity overrode propriety as she abandoned the vacuum cleaner.

"It's a computer. Yeah, you can surf the Web." He finished tapping on the small boardlike thing before him. As she neared, she recognized the order of typewriter keys. There all similarities ended.

She rounded the desk. Lines of text moved up the screen. Before she could focus on a line long enough to read it, it was gone. Without warning, all the text disappeared.

"Merciful heavens," Cally breathed, certain she had seen a genuine miracle. A natural skepticism had kept her from believing the television claims of going anywhere you wanted to go with the aid of a little chip. "It is true."

"What's true?" He continued manipulating a small arrow over the screen. The picture changed each time a *click* broke the silence.

"You can go anywhere in the world with this." The concept was so enormous, it refused to fit into her reality, even though she was looking straight at it.

"Not anywhere," he mumbled.

"Can it send me back?" Hope as bright and shiny as a new

dime sent excitement racing through her. The heady excitement of being close enough to inhale the faint spice of his skin compounded the sensation.

"To where?" he asked, eyeing the butter-cream-colored leather couch on the far wall.

"Home. To my house, in 1890," she snapped, exasperated by his intentional denial of her situation. If she didn't learn how to control her body's response to Requiem Maguire—and soon—she would be in no physical condition to go home.

"No." Leaning back, he turned in the chair and regarded her suspiciously. "But there is plenty of information about . . ."

The sudden silence dashed her optimism and reinstated her stubbornness that fed her self-preservation. The barrier rose between them. In a moment of clarity, she realized that he thought her crazy or conniving, but hadn't made up his mind. "About what?"

"All sorts of things." He turned back to the screen and clicked the funny-looking thing beneath his palm. Within seconds, the screen went dark. He touched a button on the panel beneath the picture. The subtle hum emanating from beneath the desk silenced.

"Things you don't think me capable of understanding? Things you want to hide from me? What *things*, Requiem? Why did you turn it off?"

"I'm done using it." He rose abruptly. The chair wheels clattered over the edges of the glossy, patterned tile floor. "Don't vacuum in here. Leave things as they are." Without another word he caught her arm and started toward the doorway.

The short debate Cally had with her rising temper ended when she reached the vacuum cleaner. This was his house and everything in it belonged to him—except her. She had no right to expect anything beyond their agreement.

"That was the final room. I'm finished." The marvels of house-cleaning technology had lost their fascination now that she'd seen the computer.

Without a word, Req picked up the vacuum cleaner and closed the door.

The message was clear. He didn't want her in there. Cally gathered her bravado. "Would you mind if I look at the books in the library?"

"Knock yourself out." He carried the vacuum cleaner down the hall.

"May I interpret that as consent?"

"Interpret it as anything you want."

She waited until he was gone, then hurried down to the far end of the hall and into the library. The treasure trove she sought awaited on the bottom shelf of one of the bookcases lining the walls. The sheer numbers of books had amazed her when she entered the room the first time. The freedom to examine their contents made her almost giddy. They were the best windows she had discovered into the world she desperately wanted to rejoin.

One by one, she studied the books on California and Monterey history. The more she read, the greater her consternation at the accounts on the pages. Several of the books contradicted each other. How could people believe what they read?

"The winners of any conflict write the history," she muttered.

"Find what you're looking for?"

Cally's head snapped up surprised to find Req lounging in the doorway. She closed the book on her lap. "No. What I found were abbreviated, often distorted, accounts of what actually took place in Monterey over a hundred years ago."

She gathered the books and carried them back to the shelf.

He crossed the room and collected the remaining volumes strewn across the leather couch where she'd spent most of the day. "What were you looking for?"

"The truth. A clue. Something." She took the top two books from the stack he brought. "Anything about my father, Thomas Barry, or Chauncy Cunningham. Even a mention of Golden Sun Shipping." She stared at the books.

"How can there not be so much as a mention of Golden Sun Shipping? We were the largest shipping company in Monterey. We have . . . had offices in New York City."

"Really?" Req slid the final four books into the open space on the bottom shelf.

"Yes, really." A sudden anger born of frustration flared in Cally. "Why do you even ask? You don't believe anything I say."

"What's important is that you believe it." The softness in his tone put her on edge.

"And everything in my life would be just fine if I stopped believing I came from 1890?"

He kept his gaze trained on the bookshelf as he stood.

"You think it's all in my head, Mr. Maguire?"

He turned away without answering. "Dinner's ready. If you want to eat, come on."

"Answer me!" She wanted to shake him, but knew if she touched him, felt the heat of his skin on hers, it was she who would shake. Already she trembled in anticipation as the thought tiptoed through the minefield of her anger.

"Let's talk about it over dinner."

"That isn't an answer." She needed so many answers. Worse, she was beginning to think she needed him in all the wrong ways.

"I haven't heard your whole story. How can I make a fair judgment until I have?"

The man had an answer for everything. The trouble was, she learned nothing from his answers. She glanced at the windows, her head pounding. The entire day had slipped away while she studied the disappointing historical accounts. Brass lamps with white shades lit the room. When had Req turned them on?

"Are you capable of making a fair judgment?" Just how favorable a judgment could she expect if he knew how badly she wanted him to kiss her?

"Yeah." He stopped at the doorway and faced her. "I am."

"And you're willing to listen without bias?"

"Yeah," he breathed.

She doubted it.

Req considered Miss Hornsby's day in the library time spent to his advantage. Her intense occupation with the history books allowed him to resume his investigation of her without further interruption.

He hadn't been sure what the files would reveal about her. Lifting her fingerprints from the juice glass she'd used at breakfast had been pathetically easy. After he ran them through the system, he understood why she wasn't worried about exposure. She didn't exist in the computers, or at least her fingerprints didn't. She had never held a driver's license or an identification card in any state requiring fingerprints. She had no arrest record. And she had never applied for a credit card.

By the time he exhausted every available avenue of establishing her identity, the notion that she traveled through some sort of time warp seemed less far-fetched. According to the computer, she may as well have arrived exactly as she claimed; she damn sure didn't exist anywhere in the system. At least, not under the name of Caladonia Hornsby.

He needed more information and intended to get it. Sooner or later, she'd slip up. He couldn't help wondering if she had been studying the history books the same way a student crammed for a final exam.

Chapter 6

REQ NEEDED ANSWERS. The well-mannered Miss Hornsby damn sure wasn't going to provide them. Although he had encouraged her to speak at dinner, then again at breakfast, not once did she come close to providing the answers he sought. Instead, she had asked endless questions most twelve-year-olds could answer.

Today was not going to be a repeat of yesterday, he vowed.

When she placed the last of the breakfast dishes in the dishwasher, he pushed away from the kitchen table. "Get your jacket. We're going into town."

"Why?" She looked out the window over the sink. "It's foggy and drizzling."

Perfect weather for a trip into town with the perverse Miss Hornsby. "Do you want to go, or not?"

She neither answered nor looked away from the countertop.

"We aren't going on the Harley," he added softly, hoping to allay her fears long enough to gain her cooperation. "We'll take the car."

"The car," she repeated, then drew a deep breath and released it slowly as she lifted her gaze. "There is a first time for everything." Avoiding him, she turned away with as much enthusiasm as a condemned man on his way to the gallows. "I'll get my jacket."

He might have chalked her response up to overacting if she hadn't grown so pale. Later, he would get on the computer and research behavioral patterns of delusional people.

Req ushered her into the garage then got into the car.

She stood beside the passenger door as though she was waiting for a bus, or for hell to freeze over—whichever came first.

He muttered to himself about women wanting equality yet also expecting special consideration, got out, and went around to open the car door. As soon as she was seated, she clasped her hands on her lap. Instantly her knuckles turned white. He hoped she wasn't going to pray aloud all the way into town. Everything about her seemed fragile. Unless she relaxed, she'd shatter the first time he hit a bump in the road.

"Put your seat belt on," he ordered.

Beyond reaching for her waistband, she didn't move. "I'm not wearing a belt."

Damn, but she had a good act! Tired of the ruse, he bent over and strapped her in. As he did so, his arm brushed her breasts. Her spontaneous gasp thrust her chest forward, pressing her firm breast against his forearm. It was all he could do not to test how well her breast fit into his hand. Without a word, he closed her door firmly and resumed his place behind the wheel.

"What is this? Why did you put it on me?" She yanked at the seat belt as though the confinement it imposed made her claustrophobic.

"Not to aggravate you, Miss Hornsby," Req answered with forced patience. "If you don't wear it, some observant patrolman might spot us, pull us over, and give me a ticket. If I get a ticket, my name goes into the computer where God and his brother-in-law can see it. Your name goes with it. In less than twenty-four hours, any and all our friends and enemies will know where and when I got pulled over—if they're looking. You can be sure someone is." He backed out of the garage, then pushed the button to close the door.

"I don't understand—"

"That's an understatement," he muttered.

"—the purpose of the restraint," she finished.

"To keep you from flying through the windshield in case someone runs into us."

"I've changed my mind. I don't want to go to town with you." She began fumbling for the door latch and couldn't figure out which button or recess led to freedom. The window lowered, then raised.

Req pressed the master locks. "First it was the weather. Then the seat belt. What now?"

"I can't think of one good reason to go anywhere I might be at risk of injury." She yanked on the seat belt, trying to tear it out by the roots. "Get this thing off me and let me out! Now!"

Req stomped on the brake. The slow-moving car stopped immediately. The whiplash effect lurched them forward into the unyielding restraint of the seat belts, then back against the seats. "You're not calling the shots here, Miss Hornsby. I am. The sooner you realize that, the better. Relax and enjoy the ride."

"Are you out of your mind?"

"Alright. Then don't enjoy the ride."

"Who do you think you are?"

He turned in his seat, his left wrist dangling over the steering wheel. Having her angry was a helluva lot better than catching her watching him with a curiosity that bordered on lascivious. "Right now, I'm the best friend you've got."

"No, you're not. I have enemies who treat me with more courtesy." With a final, frustrated tug, she gave up on freeing herself from the seat belt. The upper harness settled neatly between her breasts in a gentle caress.

Req dragged his gaze from her cleavage and thanked the powers above that she was wearing a shirt, sweatshirt, and windbreaker. He kept his head up, forcing his gaze away from the tight jeans hugging her shapely legs. "Are you referring to the ones you say killed your father, or the men on the beach who threw a dead body at you?"

She grew still.

"Yeah, I suppose having courteous enemies is preferable to a hard-assed friend."

The purr of the engine changed when he put the car into gear. They drove down the long, winding cobblestone drive flanked by myriad autumn flowers and headed for the iron gates opening like an enormous mouth with silent, unseen jaws.

"Wh-where are you taking me?"

"To a place where you can pick out your own damn underwear and get yourself some shoes." He steered the car onto a winding road and waited until the gates closed before moving forward.

"What you gave me is fine. I have shoes," she insisted, glancing over her shoulder at the gate with a pinched-mouth frown that set every instinct Req had into alert.

"Like hell. You don't even have a decent change of clothes and your old boots have got to go." He watched her closely. Color faded from her cheeks and lips before they reached the intersection. "What's the matter?"

Cally drew a deep breath. Ready or not, she was about to enter the twentieth century dressed in men's trousers.

Riding inside the car, speed was not as frightening as on the back of the Harley. She retreated into her private realm and reviewed everything she had learned on the television. She suspected this excursion might be like the underwear; experiencing the real thing was far more unsettling that seeing it on a screen. Then she remembered the Harley.

"I asked you a question," Req growled. "What the hell's the matter with you? Are you going to be sick?"

He didn't want the truth, but it was all she had. "I'm preparing myself."

"For what? We're going to Wal-Mart. That takes zero preparation."

A commercial flitted through her memory. Instantly she felt better. She knew what to expect. Sort of.

This time, she kept her eyes open and concentrated on memorizing the narrow, twisting thoroughfare.

"What are you doing?"

The restrictive harness across her chest flexed as she leaned. "What you told me to do last time—leaning into the turns."

"We're in a car."

"There is a difference?" Just when she thought she knew what to do, she got it wrong.

"Uh, leaning into the turn doesn't effect the balance or the steering in a car."

"How should I know that?" she snapped, feeling foolish. "I've never been inside an automobile before."

"Right." He took a turn fast enough to make the tires squeal. Centrifugal force sent them both leaning into that turn.

Cally held the grip on the door and grappled with the handhold on her left side.

"Don't pull the brake on," Req warned.

"God, I have a brake? Where?" she demanded. Even the illusion of control would suffice.

"In your left hand. Don't—"

Elated at having a measure of control, she pulled up the lever. The car lurched and swayed. Tires screeched and a horn blasted behind them.

"Dammit to hell!" Req's hand slammed down on hers, pushed in the button, and shoved the brake down.

The car resumed its smooth downhill journey. Cally's entire body trembled with fright. She had no idea the brake would send the car into such a wild ride. The vehicle behind them was still making noises and flashing bright white lights.

No matter how hard the car turned or how fast it went, she would never touch the brake again.

"Lady, if you've got a friggin' death wish to go along with your Alice in Wonderland complex, count me out. You can go it alone."

"You want me to go away." Fright turned into anxiety. A fiercely independent woman, Cally had never questioned her ability to do what she wanted when she wanted. Suddenly, making her way in the here and now seemed a daunting prospect.

Any expectation of more help from her rescuer was unreasonable. He had already exceeded the bounds of a Good Samaritan. She would make her way alone. And she'd find the way home. She had to.

"That little stunt damn near caused an accident. Keeping a low profile with you around is like taking out an ad in the *Chronicle*."

They rode in silence while Cally sorted through her options. On the right, they passed a large shopping complex crowded with cars. So many cars. Amazing. The car continued on, and she realized they were not going shopping.

"Where are you taking me?" she managed in a shaky voice that sounded steadier than she felt.

Req swore under his breath. "Back where I found you."

Cally closed her eyes and nodded. At least she recognized the land features there. As they approached the ocean Cally took her bearings. Here, judging by the position of the land and sea, something should be recognizable. But it was all different, distorted by the advancement of civilization sprawling across the land. Everywhere she looked there were people, houses, cars, and a million things television hadn't prepared her for. The magnitude of their strangeness barely registered through the crushing sense of loss settling in her.

Req was taking her back to where he found her, then leaving. She would not see him again. The realization cut a deep, painful swath of regret through her emotions. Fighting for composure, she swallowed to ease the tightening in her throat. "Thank you for your help, Mr. Maguire. I'll repay you for the clothing as soon as possible." The dismay for the depth of her feelings for Req numbed her.

He drove straight to the beach, parked the car, and got out. Without a backward glance, he pulled a cigarette from inside his jacket and cupped his hands around the end as he lit it.

Cally had watched him closely. Working the door lever

seemed obvious now. She pulled it and tried to get out, but the seat belt held her back. Cursing under her breath, she managed to release the mechanism and got out. The swirling wind sent drizzle in all directions.

Req stood in front of the car, his right foot propped on the lowest rung of the split-rail fence defining the parking lot area. The fine drizzle in the fog beaded on his dark hair. The smoke he exhaled melted into the mist.

Cally didn't know what to say any more than she knew where to go or what to do next. She retraced the path they had taken from the beach. The foul weather deterred all but the heartiest joggers along the wet sand.

The rock formation connecting the land and the sea in a craggy grip drew her like an old friend. She ventured near the water's edge. The frothy waves of a high tide had left foam on the sand. The constants of sea, sand, and sky were all that remained unchanged. The passage of time had eroded the rock formation that she had known so well. Two of the spires were gone. Even so, standing at the edge of the ocean, everything looked as it should if she were home. So close and yet so impossibly far away.

The way home was here. Somewhere. All she had to do was find it. A sense of certainty pervaded every foggy breath she drew.

"Help me, Papa," she prayed into the thick fog rolling off the gray waves. "Help me find the right path and the way home." Her breath caught in her throat at the possibility that there was no path home. That this crowded, bizarre world had swallowed her whole and she would never again see the world she knew. Worse, that there would be no justice for her father. Or her. Or even Freddy the Thief.

That galled her more than the prospect of being trapped here.

She wanted to shout at the unfairness Fate had thrust on her. Of course, she wouldn't be standing at the edge of the ocean lamenting her plight if she hadn't slipped through the time change. She would be dead, like Freddy the Thief. The yin and yang of the situation helped her hold onto objectivity.

She drew a heavy breath and shoved her cold, damp hands into the windbreaker's pockets. Feeling sorry for herself would not find her a job, a place to sleep, or her next meal. She had best start knocking on doors. Someone would hire her. "I'm certain they would. I'm intelligent. I learn quickly. I can get a job," she murmured.

"What's your Social Security number?"

She turned sharply at the sound of Req's voice. "My what?"

He shook his head, his eyes green chips of ice. "Are you going to tell me you don't have one?"

"Why don't we change that question a little? Will you tell me where I can get one? Are they expensive?"

"The government hands 'em out free. You can't get a job without one."

The notion that someone knew the names of everyone who held a job was as mind-boggling as it was disconcerting. "Why not?"

The question, asked with unabashed naiveté, struck Req like a physical blow. The wind blew wild, damp whips of hair around her face and shoulders. Her unwavering gaze demanded an answer. In that moment, she was emotionally naked and more vulnerable than any human being ought to be.

"That's the way it is."

"Is there no democracy in this time? No republic? Government controls everything?"

She looked as pained as he felt. Whatever the source of her delusions, they were very real to her, and she clung to them with the fanatic zeal any terrorist would covet. Miss Caladonia Hornsby was the Real McCoy. She believed she'd come through time. Contrasting her actions with her intelligence, it seemed the most plausible explanation for her behavior. Ironically, he almost wished her problem was drugs. That hell he understood.

"Damn, maybe you did," he muttered, closing the distance between them. *And maybe you didn't.* Damn, he didn't know what to believe. One minute her explanation seemed reasonable, the next it didn't. But it was her own undeniable belief in herself that made him almost accept what she said. Almost.

He longed for the absolution of numbed emotions, but it was too late for the callous indifference that had carried him through the last couple of years.

"What has happened to the country?" Worry drew her eyebrows together and pinched a furrow over the bridge of her nose.

"Since 1890?" He was as sick as she was for playing along, but the way her sad eyes implored, he saw no other option. "A couple of world wars. A great depression. Foreign conflicts. Baby boomers. Nuclear armament. The sexual revolution. The technology revolution. Generation X-ers. AIDS."

She stared as though he spoke a foreign language. The midafternoon wind fluttered her windbreaker. Fine salt spray thickened the air. "I want to go home," she whispered, then turned toward the ocean.

"Whoa. Wait, Miss Hornsby. It's a little cold to go swimming." He caught her arm before she could twist away.

"I'm not going in the water. Not right now." She continued staring into the gray mist. "The answer is out there."

"Yeah?" And so were the X-Files.

"It has to be. I came through something . . . a door, out there. All I have to do is find it again."

"Miss Hornsby," he called softly. "Cally. Look at me."

Hope smoothed the hard edges of worry from her features. She gazed up at him with an unwavering certainty. "The answer is here."

"Maybe," he agreed, drawing her away from the water's edge defined by kelp benchmarks of the receding tide. The sharp tang of the seaweed surrounded them when the afternoon breeze shifted.

"Don't patronize me by agreeing when you don't believe me."

"I believe you believe it. Maybe that's enough for now." He drew her close enough to slip an arm around her shoulders. "Let's go home."

"I'd like to know how," she murmured looking out at the ocean.

"I meant back to my house."

"I thought you wanted to be rid of me."

"You scared the hell out of me and ticked me off at the same time. Bad combination these days. I took it out on you. That wasn't fair." He ought to apologize but the words wouldn't form. Instead, he gathered her in a loose embrace. He wanted to be rid of the responsibility, the uncertainty, and the complications she represented. God help him, holding her close revealed the truth—he didn't want to be rid of her. He wanted her. He needed her. Her innocence. Her dependence. Her growing trust in him. And that was the core of it. Much as he hated the notion, he needed someone to believe in him, and someone he could trust and believe in, too.

It was hell.

The fine line he walked between slipping into the self-protective mode of feeling nothing and the avalanche of emotions he'd held back for over two years seemed razor-thin today. "I'll work on not taking my frustrations out on you."

She exhaled sharply and looked him in the eye. "Until the next time you tell me to leave?"

"I don't want you to leave." Her parted lips were too damn tempting to let him dwell on the ramifications of his mission. "I want you to stay. Too much. And that could mean serious trouble for both of us."

"Then we shall have to behave responsibly. It would not be proper . . ."

What wasn't proper was waiting another second to taste her mouth. Her small cry of alarm melted with her fading restraint as she accepted the gentle kiss. The gratifying pressure of her body flowing against his sent a warm breeze across the icy desert of his soul. Famished for a taste of her, he went back for seconds. This time, she waged no protest. Instead, her hands slid beneath his jacket.

The hard kiss quickly became a warning of the kind of trouble they could expect. Hot and fiery, the kiss took on a compelling life of its own.

The glide of her probing, groping fingers along his ribs and back stoked the fire roaring in his veins. He wanted her naked flesh against his bare skin, wanted both of them so hot and greedy, they couldn't kiss or touch enough.

He followed the curve of her spine to her buttocks. His imagination went wild picturing her in the easily thwarted black lace. He deepened the kiss and held her against his erection. The only certainty he knew was that he wanted to be inside her.

Her fingertips dug into his back. The crush of her breasts against his chest shut out everything except her and what she did to him.

He dragged his mouth from hers. The forlorn whimper that escaped Cally's parted lips struck at the core of his need. Swirling fog, drizzle, and the relentless waves muted their ragged breathing. Req looked hard at the woman in his arms. Passion brightened her cheeks with color. The astonishment glittering in her eyes lingered on her lips, forming an O. The chilly, salt air in his lungs damn near froze when she pressed her lips together, then rolled them between her teeth as though tasting him again.

Had he ever *hungered* for anyone as thoroughly as he did Caladonia Hornsby? If so, he couldn't remember.

What the hell was wrong with him? How could he take advantage of an unbalanced woman who lived in a fantasy world?

"This is not a good idea," he said, each word a pain unto itself. "At least in a responsible, sensible world, it isn't."

Cally lowered her damp forehead to his chest. "You're right. Things are complicated enough."

Her easy agreement heaped disappointment on the mountain of frustrated testosterone.

The slow withdrawal of her hands—lingering, caressing, as though memorizing every inch of him—was sweet agony. When her hands abandoned him, she lifted her head. The sad smile she wore reached her eyes.

"That kiss raised as many questions as it answered." Her hips retreated, putting distance between her warmth and his need.

"Such as . . . ?" He kept the loose embrace, unwilling to relinquish her. The taste of her on his lips conjured images of a prize, one he needed as badly as he wanted it. One he had to have.

"Whether my entire sense of propriety has fled, and just how much trouble I'm facing."

"Because I want you?" *Because I'm going to have you and we both know it,* he thought.

"Partly," she whispered.

"I won't force you." The way she had responded to his touch promised he wouldn't need to do more than kiss her again to make her his.

"I know." He saw worry dart across her face. When it cleared curiosity and desire replaced it.

Req grinned in spite of the ache of denial settling into his loins. "Come on, my nomadic Miss Hornsby, let's grab a burger at a drive-through." Heaven help her, she was his. There was no point in denying it. He would not let her go although leaving might be in her best interest.

"All right," she said.

Cally enjoyed the unspoken truce. Warm air blew through vents in the car and eased the chill of damp clothing.

True to his word, Req got food without leaving the car. He drove down Church Street, passing remnants of a time Cally called home without comment until he pulled into the parking lot at the Royal Presidio Chapel.

Cally stared, hardly able to believe what she was seeing. "It's beautiful, Req. So well taken care of. So . . . so clean." She set aside her food, careful not to touch the brake although the engine was off. "Does the red lamp still burn in the chapel?"

"Last I heard, it did."

"What else has survived?" Excited, she turned in her seat. A piece of her world, even one polished to false brilliance, was a connection to home she savored.

Req listed the historic sites of Monterey and the surrounding area. Cally drank in every word, not caring that he watched her in an odd manner. Several times she corrected him on points of history, names, and dates.

He started the car and drove onto the street. "Fog's lifting. Time to go home."

Her disappointment must have shown as she gathered the debris from the food and stuffed it into a bag.

"I don't like being down here when it's clear. Makes me too easy to spot. Then I become a target." He turned onto a large thoroughfare. "That makes you a target, too. Make no mistake, Cally. Being with me is not safe."

"Then I had better find my way home quickly," she said. "Would you . . ." Her voice trailed. The notion was ludicrous.

"Would I what?" he prodded.

She swallowed her reservations, then spoke. "Like to come with me? Surely it is safer for you where no one knows you. Except me, and I wouldn't say anything." She looked away. "No one would believe me."

"You're serious?"

She nodded. "I will find a way. I have to."

"How do you propose to start?"

"What I need first is to take advantage of what is here. I need to find archives. Newspapers. Letters. Journals. Shipping schedules." Oh, yes. Why hadn't she thought of that sooner? The answers to who killed her father and why might be in such accounts.

"What do you expect to find in them?" He accelerated into a river of cars with such speed that every nerve in Cally's body tensed.

"Names. Answers, I hope."

"And if none of the names you've mentioned is in the historic records, then what, Cally?"

She recognized the tactic and it surprised her. He was bracing her for disappointment, perhaps even confrontation with her world being an illusion. He was the one slated for enlightenment. A hint of a smile escaped. "Then we'll both know I have lost my mind. But what if they prove otherwise, Req? Will you believe me then?"

He took his time before answering. "Give me three things not found in history books that took place. We'll research them."

"On the computer?"

"No. If you want me to believe, you're going to have to know, and be able to prove you know, something Joe Blow doesn't have access to."

"Who is Joe Blow?"

"Me. The guy on the street. The computer hacker—"

"I understand." She thought for a moment. "I suppose we could start with personal facts."

"Is this going to be the story of your life?"

Cally laughed. "No. I wouldn't want to risk boring you to sleep."

He nodded once. "Tell me about your father. Tell me about the people he did business with."

"How much time do we have?"

"The rest of the day and this evening. That long enough?"

Cally nodded. "Then will you answer some of my questions?"

"The ones you wrote down? Sure. Piece of cake, with the exception of the one about movies on the X-rated channels." He glanced at her. "You get off on watching?"

"Get off where?"

"Did you like watching the X-rated movies?"

She thought about it for a moment. "Once I got over the shock of seeing . . . you know, they made me sad. Besides, I felt as though I was intruding."

"Sad?" he asked in open surprise. "Why?"

"I watched their faces." She looked down at her hands, embarrassed by what she had seen. "I saw no love. No joy. No affection. My horse is more involved when a randy stallion covers her than some of those people were."

"That's an interesting viewpoint." He steered the car onto the winding road that led to the house. "No sex for the sake of sex and a hormone release."

Cally remained silent. Until he kissed her, she had thought sex and love inseparable. In the future she would have to be very careful to avoid such liberties. Too quickly they would lead to the ultimate intimacy. Heaven help her, she didn't want to feel any more than she already did for her long-haired, tattooed rescuer. *Her new friend*, she reminded herself.

Thinking about the day's events provided insight into Req. He had a gruff exterior, yet everything he had done, including pulling her from the ocean, bespoke compassion and concern. The man was a true enigma.

Chapter 7

REQ LAY ON his bed with the lights out, his ankles crossed, and his hands behind his head. He stared at the ceiling.

He'd missed the mark concerning Caladonia Hornsby.

The deprecating sound he made in the dark underscored his disdain.

She was no addict. She probably had a better grip on sanity than he did—as long as she didn't mention coming from 1890.

His normally excellent ability to judge people had failed.

She had proven quick-witted with a dry sense of humor and a proclivity for sarcasm that probably few people appreciated.

Eight hours of subtle interrogation using every soft-soap tactic he knew hadn't revealed anything new. Conversely, she became more convincing over time. He'd moved from being 100 percent sure she wasn't operating in the real world to 75 percent. During the past hour, he'd questioned his own stability. One minute he'd believe her; the next he'd tried to debunk her claim.

After she had retired for the night, he had telephoned William Potter, one of Monterey's most prestigious citizens and an old friend of Victor Escobar's. Potter could trace his family back to the early eighteen hundreds. A passionate historian, Potter's private collection of memorabilia and his knowledge were just what Req needed to break Cally's story.

Revealing his presence in Monterey to Victor Escobar's old friend was a risk Req calculated as one of low exposure. The small cadre of wealthy elderly men Victor had called friends never questioned why Victor left his wealth to Requiem Maguire. To their credit, they politely ignored Req's long hair, tattoos, and cartoon tee shirts. He suspected Victor had trusted

William Potter with the truth before he died. Only once had Potter given any inkling that he knew Req was more than the thick-skinned rebel image he cultivated.

Disguised in the heavy black garb of an old-world nun in a wheelchair, Req had attended Victor Escobar's funeral. Potter had expected him and treated him like a long-time friend. The small circle of old Monterey patrons had followed Potter's lead, each one paying respect and offering condolences for the loss of the man Req had loved like a father.

Tomorrow, he'd see how much overlap he enjoyed from Victor's friendship with William Potter.

With everything in readiness for the next morning, Req slept for a few hours. Nightmares of Paul's death woke him before dawn.

He dressed and rode his Harley to a beach north of Monterey. There, he leaned against his bike, smoked a cigarette, and waited for the sun to rise. The moments when the sky brightened with fresh hope and another chance on a new day were an oasis. In those precious minutes, a little more of his raw, ill-formed emotions spilled over the lip of the coffin he'd kept them in.

It was the only time he didn't mind feeling as lost as he knew he was. He wished he'd taken Cally with him to see the sunrise.

On the way home, he was more eager to see her than he had been for the sunrise. He admonished himself not to let her get any closer. Hell, he already liked her too much. He wanted her in bed, under him, over him, beside him, every way humanly possible.

"Not good, Maguire," he muttered, removing his helmet. "You could lose more than this decadent hideaway if you aren't careful."

The aroma of fresh coffee filled the kitchen as thickly as the fog hugged the air outside. He bent down and examined the glass carafe. Half an inch of coffee grounds churned at the bottom of the fresh brew. It was an improvement bound for greatness once Cally learned about filter papers.

"Are you always such an early riser?" Cally asked.

"Yeah. I like to see the sun come up at the ocean." For two years, dawn had marked his bedtime more often than not. Surviving another day had been enough to make him thankful and instill hope that he'd succeed in bringing down the drug ring kingpins.

"There can't be much to see in this fog." Cally reached for

the coffeepot. The stripes of her tee shirt curved around her breasts; the jersey fabric molded like a second skin. He resolved to buy a larger size for her next time. Cally's natural grace was seductive even when she stood still and breathed.

"That's the way I like it best." He set his mug beside the coffeemaker and waited for her to pour. "By the way, we're going to see a man about your past this morning."

"My past?" She flashed a wide-eyed glance at him and nearly missed his cup with the hot coffee. "There is someone else like me?"

"Not exactly." Being so damn close to her, inhaling the lingering fragrance of soap and shampoo, reminded every cell in his body how feminine she was. Hell, it had been months since he'd gotten naked for hot sex, and years since he had actually made love. Cally was definitely a woman he'd make love with. Long, slow, hot . . .

"What does this person have to do with my past?" She leaned against the countertop, held her steaming cup in both hands, and stared into it.

"Maybe nothing. Maybe something." He curled a finger under her chin, forcing her to look at him. "He's a historian of sorts. And a collector."

"Of what?"

"Local history and artifacts. It seems a hereditary trait, because his family has been accumulating things for years." He ran his thumb over her chin, then along her cheek. Her warm porcelain skin felt like it belonged against him. "Some might say William comes from a long line of pack rats, but they wouldn't say it loudly."

"Why is that?" It was an offhand remark, but the intense probing of her gaze betrayed her interest.

"William comes from old money, and he has enough social and political clout to make or break someone with a word." Req continued exploring her jawline with his callused thumb. He would have preferred exploring her intriguing textures with his mouth. "He's a collector. He keeps and catalogs everything relevant to Monterey history."

"You mean he might have papers, documents, from 1890?" Her breathless question accompanied the lifting of her chin and the lowering of her eyelids to half-mast.

The uninhibited way she savored his small examination of her face and neck was equivalent to a shout of permission to his eager body. He took her coffee and set it on the counter.

Abruptly, she stepped aside, her eyes wide with surprise. The sudden blush creeping up her neck to her cheeks told him more than he wanted to know.

She didn't want him to kiss her again, and his screaming body needed so damn much more than a kiss.

"I, uh, am looking forward to meeting your friend William," she managed, collecting her composure and coffee simultaneously.

Christ, if he hadn't kissed her at the beach, he wouldn't have known what he was missing. And that was the trouble. He did know. Remembering her sweet kiss, the press of her curvy body, and the promise of exquisite passion left him hard and aching. He didn't try to hide the effect she had on him.

"When are we going to see him?" She had retreated several steps. She clutched her coffee mug in front of her like a battle shield.

Req turned toward the refrigerator. Hell, he wasn't going to sate his greatest hunger, so he may as well slake the one in his empty belly. "At ten o'clock. You want eggs and bacon?"

When she didn't answer right away, he glanced at her. Her schooled expression underscored her determination to keep a distance. Her eyes, intent and somewhat dilated, spoke a louder message.

He wondered how long reason would hold out against the relentless, potent force drawing them together.

The finely manicured grounds and imposing Spanish hacienda architecture of the Potter home proclaimed it a mansion by any standard. Cally accompanied Req up the steps to the massive double doors. A distinguished man in a white shirt and black trousers opened the door before Req knocked.

They were ushered into a library Cally would have loved to live in for weeks. It would take at least that long to explore the stacks running from the floor to the high ceiling and the caches of a half-dozen map chests.

She had barely assessed the magnitude of the room's potential treasures when a man in his mid-seventies joined them. The first things she noticed about him were his mane of unruly white hair and the regal way he carried himself. He was a man accustomed to wielding quiet, absolute power. She smiled in warm anticipation when Req introduced her simply as Cally to William Potter. Curious but friendly brown eyes regarded her with intense interest.

Cally wished she had asked Req what he'd told William Potter about her, or for that matter why he thought it necessary to bring her here. He'd insisted she pretend to be of this era. His stance on the matter was akin to an admission of belief she was indeed from 1890. Almost.

"Requiem tells me you're a student of Monterey history, particularly the decade of 1880 to 1890," William said, gesturing to the nearest of three brown leather couches in the room.

Cally sat, absently reaching to smooth the volumes of skirts that were no longer there. Her hands trailed over her denim-clad thighs as though she could disguise her sense of nakedness. "Yes, I'm particularly interested in events from 1889 and 1890."

"Oh?" William settled in a chair across from her. "Anything in particular?"

She drew a breath, wondering if she spoke her mind whether William Potter would think her as mad as Req did. Still, honesty was the only recourse she had. "Golden Sun Shipping. And some of the events and people involved with them."

"Hmm." William regarded her for a long moment before leaning forward in his chair. "And you're interested in the fate of his company? Why? For monetary purposes?" William asked, clearly skeptical.

"I want to know who killed Peter Hornsby and why. And whether or not they were brought to justice," she said in a rush, dodging William's question. "Can you help me?"

"Possibly." William glanced behind her, letting his questions remain unanswered. She felt Req's relentless scrutiny. "Has Mr. Maguire told you that I seldom open my collection to the scrutiny of strangers unless there is some benefit to me?"

Cally shrugged, uncertain. "Do you want your house cleaned too?"

"My house cleaned?" William's amused gaze darted to Req, then to her. "Good heavens, no. I have a staff to take care of that."

She had nothing to barter or sell for the knowledge William might have locked in his head or one of the many drawers in this magnificent room. The same relentless drive to find the truth that had sent her after Freddy the Thief in the predawn hours strengthened her resolve. "What exactly do you have in mind?"

"A discussion."

Surprised, then wary because it sounded too easy, she sat a

little straighter and refolded her hands in her lap. "What sort of discussion?"

"About history," William said, settling into the comfort of the chair. "The decade you're interested in, to be specific. I've found that an exchange of studies and impressions can increase the body of knowledge about almost anything. You're interested in Peter Hornsby and Golden Sun Shipping so you're obviously well versed in Monterey's history. Why don't we start there?"

Talking about her father made him seem closer than a grave she couldn't visit. "He was a man with a rare sense of humor and infinite patience with those he loved. He was a fair, honest man who wielded a swift, sure sword of vengeance for misdeeds or injustice. During the last years of his life, he championed several unpopular causes. He became a voice for those who otherwise had none." She glanced at her hands, then back to the warm interest in William's eyes. "That is why it is so bitterly ironic, so wrong, that he was murdered and no one was brought to justice."

"And Golden Sun Shipping?"

"It was a partnership. My father, uh, told me Peter Hornsby and Chauncy Cunningham started out with one ship and the business grew over the years. In 1886, they took on a third partner. Thomas Barry. He was financially settled, and had an uncanny savvy when it came to sorting through details and making a sound business decision. Those qualities, coupled with his youth, made him a good choice."

William steepled his fingertips below his chin. "Interesting. Barry was to be the replacement when Hornsby and Cunningham retired?"

"That was the thinking. Mr. Cunningham was also working with his son-in-law, Cameron Morton. It was speculated that Chauncy would eventually help him buy into the company, perhaps even make an arrangement for Cameron to purchase his share when he retired."

"Married to Lydia?"

The question rocked Cally. Quickly, she shook her head. "No, Maudel. Lydia died of influenza in the winter of 1886, four months before she was to have wed Thomas Barry. He was devastated. We . . . everyone was. Some of the sunshine left with her." The detachment she sought refused to come, but then she had always had trouble distancing herself from people she loved.

"Fascinating. Have you any idea how Maudel died?"

"Maudel?" Maudel dead? At first, the notion was inconceivable. But in today's time, everyone she knew was dead, consigned to tidbits of history and practically forgotten.

"Who is Maudel?" Req asked softly.

Cally turned slightly. "Peter Hornsby and Chauncy Cunningham founded Golden Sun Shipping." Seeing his nod, she continued. "Chauncy married Penelope. They had two daughters, Lydia and Maudel. When the daughters grew up, Maudel married Cameron Morton, a young man who worked at Golden Sun Shipping. The family had hoped Lydia would marry Thomas Barry."

Req nodded and raised his hand. "Just wanted to know the players. Back to your story about Maudel."

Potter shot Req a look and then gave Cally his complete attention as he picked up the thread of the conversation. "The records show Maudel died in—"

"I don't want to know," Cally cried out. With every fiber of her being she was determined to find her way home. Once she got back, she did not want to look at those around her knowing the time, date, and manner of their deaths. It would drive her insane. "Please. I would prefer not to discuss anything after 1890, especially anything concerning Peter Hornsby's daughter, Mr. Potter. Can we agree on that?"

"If you like," he said softly, his gaze flickering to Req. "However, there is no mention of his daughter after that year, so it is somewhat of a moot point. Now, tell me what you know of the events at the Del Monte Hotel."

The revelation rocked her. She opened her mouth, but no sound emerged. She had to get home. There was no alternative. "No mention of her?"

"I'm afraid not, though it's possible she married. I have never been interested enough in her to trace her progress in history." Potter's eyes narrowed. "Have I upset you?"

"No. No, not at all." Of course, she'd return. The alternative was unthinkable. Besides, William Potter's archives were not complete. She settled into the safe topic of the Del Monte Hotel. "It took a year to rebuild it after the fire in 1888. But it is grander than ever." She managed a smile at a memory. "They are having a golf tournament." Her smile faded. "I mean, in 1890 they were having one. The *Wave* was filled with news of it."

"The Del Monte newspaper," William said softly to Req.

"Now, Mr. Potter, it is your turn to tell me what you know of the times in general and Peter Hornsby in particular."

"Only what is written and most of that is public record. However, the bits of gossip I gleaned from the *Wave* were fascinating. It seems Mr. Hornsby was a controversial man who often kept the social world as astir as a tide pool during a storm."

Cally listened intently to accounts of her father and the Monterey society, amazed at the accuracy. William then enticed her to elaborate on her own perception of Monterey's social life. She was so caught up in the moment that she barely noticed when Req settled on the opposite end of the couch.

Her qualms melted as the questions and answers flowed easily. William proved extremely knowledgeable about the goings-on in Monterey during the 1880s.

They discussed the politics of the times over a delicious lunch fixed the way Cally thought it ought to be—by someone other than herself. Afterwards, William led her to a large map table and pulled out one of the center drawers.

"You've been informative beyond measure, Cally. I wonder if you might be able to shed some light on a project I've been working on."

"I would be glad to try."

He turned on a lamp with a large magnifying lens in the center. Next, he spread several old photographs on the tabletop.

Cally gasped, then covered her mouth. Her heart accelerated as she stared at the closest one. "Where did you get these?" she demanded. Homesickness squeezed tears into her eyes.

"They are rare," William conceded, misunderstanding her concern. "They were among a veritable treasure trove one of my people discovered in an old house before it was demolished."

Cally stared at the photographs. She knew them well. They were hers. Looking at them was like looking at her own ghost. Her first instincts were to scoop them up and hug them to her chest.

Struggling to maintain control, she held onto the edge of the table and asked if the residence was located at the only address she had ever known. She and William stared at one another for a long moment.

"Yes, Cally. How did you know?"

"I, ah, know that house."

"How could you? It was torn down forty years ago."

She looked at Req for assistance, and got nothing. His unreadable expression hadn't changed since they'd entered William Porter's home. "What did you want help with?" she asked softly, ignoring his question.

"I've been trying to identify the people in the photographs. Most of them appear in other pictures where, with the help of additional documents, we've been able to identify them. However, there is one young woman who appears in most of these I haven't been able to identify."

Cally felt her lunch become a rock in her stomach. "Those pictures were mementos. They were never meant for anyone other than . . ."

"Than. . . What, Cally?" Potter asked when her voice trailed off.

"The, ah, young woman in them," she managed.

"Who is she?" William arranged eight photographs on the table.

"Caladonia Hornsby."

"Marvelous," William exclaimed, clearly excited. "Finally, I know who the young woman is in these photos."

Cally tamped down the outrage that had welled inside as the result of having her personal life violated. It didn't matter that eleven decades had passed. The photographs were her keepsakes.

Except they weren't.

They belonged to William Porter, a curious stranger trying to pry deeper into her life.

"Who are the men in these three photographs? They look very formal."

They were formal. And serious. Just as she had been at the time. "Miss Hornsby's ex-fiancés."

"Fiancés?" Req asked, speaking up for the first time in hours. Until now, he had been content to be a fly on the wall.

She met his unemotional stare. "Well, she was engaged three times."

"What happened to the members of the ex-fiancé fraternity?" Req leaned closer and slid one photograph after another under the harsh glare of the magnifying light.

"They remained friends with her. Two of them brought their wives to her father's funeral. The third came alone and helped her and Thomas Barry with the arrangements."

"Was he the fourth?"

"Who?" She stared at Req. He sounded like a jealous lover.

"Thomas Barry," he answered with a lethal softness.

"What?"

"Her fourth fiancé."

"He wanted to be," she admitted, realizing how it might look for a woman to be engaged so many times. In present-day society it seemed most people skipped the engagement and went straight to the marriage.

"Miss Hornsby was quite sought after, or so it seems," William said pensively. "You resemble her, Cally, particularly around the eyes. Perhaps the shape of the jaw and chin." He squinted slightly and scrutinized the image, then looked at her.

Cally pressed her lips shut, biting back a short retort. Anything she said would be wrong.

"A real man-eating heartbreaker," Req mused.

"That's not true," Cally snapped. "I—*she* didn't want to marry for any reason other than love. Sometimes love grows from friendship, and sometimes friendship remains just that: friendship. Nothing more, nothing less. You can't force the kind of feelings necessary for a heartfelt commitment to marriage. And bowing to pressure, or marrying because it might look bad if you don't, is a disservice all the way around."

William applauded, his brown eyes shining with admiration. "Well stated! A pity more young people don't feel the way you do."

Rattled, Cally turned away from the table. All her nerves grated at the censure emanating from Req. It was unreasonable. He was unreasonable. It shouldn't matter what he thought. "Would you mind if we took a little break? I'd like to go for a walk."

"Certainly," William said. "We have been at this for most of the day, haven't we? I'll show you the solarium. Actually, it's more of a greenhouse and quite relaxing."

Cally took William's offered arm and left the library. The entire situation had tested her severely.

"I would like for you to visit again, Cally. The past intrigues me. The keys to the future lie in our history. Have you ever considered how different our world might be if the countless people before us had made decisions other than the ones they did?"

She hadn't. Right now, all she could cope with were the events thrust upon her without consult or consent.

"Suppose Henry Ford had decided to stick to carriages? Or Bill Gates had decided to be a math professor? A change in those two critical decision paths would have changed the world."

Cally looked at him from the corner of her eye. It wouldn't change her world. She'd never heard of either man. She was grateful when he opened the door to the solarium.

"Thank you," she murmured.

"Enrique will bring you something to drink. Have you a preference?"

She shook her head, wanting to be alone for a few precious minutes. "Water is fine."

Once alone, she walked down the first of three aisles of exotic plants. At the far end, she settled onto the edge of an iron bench located behind a lush palm frond.

She had wanted Req to believe her. Not once had she considered how he might regard her, or what might happen if he did believe her.

"Who is she?" William demanded after he shut the library door.

"Caladonia Hornsby," Req answered evenly. Christ, she was the spitting image of the woman staring out at him from the photograph.

"Where did you find her?"

"At the beach." He slid another photograph under the harsh light. "Who are these people?"

William leaned closer. "The man on the left is Peter Hornsby. Beside him, according to your friend, is his daughter, Caladonia. I don't know who the others are. I'll have to wait for your Miss Hornsby to identify them."

"You think she can?" He studied the man Cally claimed was her father. With the help of a magnifying glass he could make out the faint traces of laugh lines around Peter Hornsby's handsome face. He'd have to give the man credit for staying fit. He looked like he could wrestle a bear and win.

"I'd bet the house that our new friend in the solarium knows who every person in those pictures is." William turned to the photographs of Caladonia Hornsby and her three fiancés for a better look. "The question is whether she'll identify them for me."

"Why wouldn't she?"

"The pictures upset her. She acted as though . . ."

Req straightened. "They were hers?" he finished.

"Yes. Most curious. She couldn't have seen them before today. They've been in this room for the last forty-plus years. Until you called, I hadn't thought about them in years."

William's sun-weathered face wrinkled with a sudden frown. "Looking at the pictures and at Miss Hornsby, I find an astounding resemblance. She has the same appearance, the same features, even the same name. Caladonia, an unusual name these days. I wonder . . ."

"What?"

William drew an audible breath, his intense demeanor coiling to receive a blow. "I've been studying reincarnation."

"I see," Req said, though he didn't see the connection. "Any conclusions?"

The understanding of a man accustomed to skepticism schooled William's aristocratic features. "Mary fought the cancer for a year before it took her from me," he said without a hint of emotion. Only the welling of tears on his lower eyelids betrayed his deep sorrow until he spoke again. "Fifty-four years of marriage wasn't enough for Mary and me. When she became terminal, we confronted our mortality and believed there had to be more."

"Reincarnation."

"Yes. Looking at Miss Hornsby, I was wondering—maybe hoping is a more accurate word—if there is some form of memory retention from one incarnation to the next."

There was probably as much chance of that as there was of someone coming through time.

"The only way she could know so much of what she's told us is if she had been Caladonia Hornsby and recalled her previous life," William mused, looking down at one of the pictures.

"You're reading too much into this, William. There are lots of ways she could have learned about the Hornsbys and what went on in the late 1880s. Or she could be making it up as she goes," Req suggested, hoping William would agree.

"It would be more comfortable for all three of us if she was." William pushed the light aside and straightened. "I watched her eyes when she spoke. She's not making anything up. What I want to know is how she knows what she does."

"She's no walking miracle or divine answer, William." It was time to get Cally and make tracks.

"Of course not, though if there is a chance she's experiencing genetic memories from her namesake, she might think about it in terms of helping her understand her own psyche. Having bleed-through memories of a past life must make this one confusing at times."

"Life is confusing," Cally said from the library door. "The only clear path belongs to the zealots."

Req caught her eye and her subtle nod. He didn't know how much she had overheard, but it was enough for her to decide to dance with the devil she knew instead of the one she didn't.

"Now, Mr. Potter, let me see the pictures again. They're very similar to the ones my great aunt had in a scrapbook. She loved to talk about the late eighteen hundreds. I heard so many stories, I began to think my ancestors were part of my immediate family."

"Was that your Great Aunt Hattie?" Req asked, catching her eye.

"Yes. The woman I told you about over breakfast." A saccharine smile served as a warning not to push her. She was lying the best she knew how. She adjusted the light and lined up the photographs. "Let's see. Who was Caladonia engaged to first? Edgar or Roger?"

"Your great aunt told you all these details?" William looked as disappointed as he sounded. "The Hornsby family tree doesn't show a female relative who might have been your great aunt."

"Then it is incomplete," Cally murmured. "My Great Aunt Hattie was only a child. She remembered the Hornsbys, the Cunninghams, and Thomas Barry. Her mother told her stories, and Aunt Hattie told me the stories. How else would I have known?"

"How else, indeed," conceded William, his dashed hopes deepening the lines of living mapped around his eyes.

Damn, she was a quick thinker and cool as a cucumber under pressure. Req liked that in a woman.

Chapter 8

"YOU OWE ME some research time," Cally said as Req turned into the traffic paralleling the ocean. The day had faded into twilight. A quick adjustment of her bearings indicated they were heading into town. "And not at William Potter's home." She had overheard enough of the conversation in the library to realize she was better off being disbelieved by Req than believed to be something she wasn't by William Potter.

"Is tomorrow soon enough?"

"Fine." Cally tried to relax in the car. She doubted she would ever become accustomed to the fantastic speeds people traveled. While the trains in 1890 had traveled faster than the thirty miles an hour they were going now, the tracks had confined the direction. Traveling beside her fellow man as they raced down lanes separated only by painted lines and at speeds she didn't want to imagine—let alone experience—required a great deal of trust.

"When you came back to the library—what did you hear?"

"I heard a sad, lonely man searching for a way to reassure himself he would be with his dead wife in the next life."

She studied Req's profile in the early dusk. Headlights flashed from oncoming cars. The shadows and light played against the angles and planes of his face. "I did not realize how he might perceive my circumstances. Once I did, I thought it would be cruel to repay his kindness by giving him false hope about his wife. Much as I hate lies, the situation seemed best served by a kind lie than a confusing truth. It also seemed wiser for me."

"He's not a bad guy," Req mused, watching the headlights reflected in the rearview mirror.

"It isn't a question of good or bad. I grew up among Monterey's wealthy and powerful, Req. Like them, Mr. Potter is accustomed to getting what he wants. This time what he wants is beyond his reach. It is beyond anyone's reach."

"If you can't help, you don't want to hurt. Is that it?"

"That's an appropriate summary," she agreed, staring back at the little girl seated behind the driver of a passing car as Req slowed.

"You're an astute judge of character, Caladonia Hornsby." He steered the car into a pullout parking area overlooking the beach. "We've got company. Let's see how badly they want to stay with us."

Cally started to turn in her seat.

"Stay still. Let them think we haven't spotted them." He lowered the windows and turned off the car. Cool twilight air rushed at Cally.

"Is this part of the trouble you mentioned following us?" The urge to look at the surrounding cars tugged at her. Determined not to do anything foolish, she stared straight ahead.

"I hope the hell not," Req said softly, watching something in the side mirror without turning his head.

Slow, rolling breakers reflected the orange, gold, and red of the sunset streaking across a purple and blue sky. The rhythm of the waves did little to soothe the raw edges of Cally's nerves. The emotional turmoil of the day had taken a toll that left her physically tired.

"He's moving on," Req said, adjusting the side mirror with the push-button controls on the dashboard. "We're not out of the woods yet. He might pull off down the road and wait. If so, that means he isn't sure it's me. Either way, he'll follow and make sure."

"How will he know which way we go?"

"He'll pick a place where he can see us but we won't see him unless we're looking hard, then slip into traffic behind us."

"What does he want?"

"I don't know, but if he wanted it badly enough, we wouldn't be watching the sunset and talking to pass the time." He shifted in his seat and adjusted the mirrors again. "We'll wait here a little while and see if he comes back."

The notion of someone watching them, waiting for them to move, increased her apprehension. She fidgeted, her discomfort growing by the minute.

"Relax and watch the sunset, Cally. We're not going to be taken by surprise. These guys aren't that good."

"Are you accustomed to being stalked?" She doubted she could ever get used to such a life any more than she'd become accustomed to the magnet draw he emanated.

"In a manner of speaking, yeah." He reached across her and opened the glove compartment. The interior remained dark, the same as he liked the inside of the car. He retrieved something that he tucked behind his back. The brush of his arm over her knees, the heat radiating from his shoulder and back, penetrated her skin and churned the river of desire sluicing through her. "This is a waiting game. So while we're killing time, why don't you tell me about the people in William's old-time picture show?"

"I'm tired of answering questions. It's my turn to do the asking and yours to answer."

"At the moment, I've given you all the answers I can. Tell me about the pictures."

"Why? After today, I think I'm better off if you don't believe me." Emotionally fatigued, she inhaled the cool tang of the night skimming the lethargic breakers. The last reds and purples were fading from the horizon. The darkness thickened the layers of intimacy settling in the confines of the front seat. "Tomorrow you can take me where I need to go for the research you promised I could do. After that, I'll explore on my own."

She heard him shift in the seat and half expected him to start the car. When he didn't, she opened her eyes and twisted so she leaned against the door. The sense of distance shrunk when he removed his seat belt. He bent low, his shoulder touching her crooked knee, and lit a cigarette. He appeared unconcerned, but she felt the tension rolling off him and another kind stirring in her. The fading light flashed in his eyes as he scanned the mirrors and assessed the beach goers returning to their cars in the sandy parking lot.

"Engaged three times, huh?" he said, then exhaled a plume of smoke the breeze carried away.

"Have you ever been engaged?" she countered. Why did his opinion of her matter so much?

"Yeah. Once."

"Did you marry?"

"No." In the final strains of light, his features took on an anguished expression.

"Why not?"

"She took a three-month vacation with the wrong crowd and came home a drug addict."

"You were engaged and she took a vacation without you?" The notion left her flummoxed.

"My job took me out of the country for a while." He cupped the cigarette and drew on it, then exhaled. "It was sort of a favor for a favor so I could tie up some loose ends. I had a transfer waiting for me when I got back. Hell, I was ready to get married, settle down, and have kids, a mortgage. The whole nine yards."

She didn't quite follow his explanation, though clearly he expected her to. "When you discovered your fiancée was on drugs, did you take her to the detox place?"

Req snorted. "Several. Her father and I tried everything. And failed. The last time, Malika checked herself out of rehab, she found her connection, and overdosed on bad heroin the same day. Her body turned up in an East San Jose crack house. A month later I found the guy who gave her that bad stuff."

It seemed an ignominious way to die. In the midst of that thought, a chill cooled the intimacy engulfing her. She had to ask, to know the depth of his dark side. "What happened to him?"

"Let's just say he's out of the drug business for good."

An awkward silence followed while he finished his cigarette. They sat in the dark listening to the ocean. Cally zipped her jacket against the night chill. She wondered what had happened to the man who had given Malika bad drugs and suspected it was violent. "I'm sorry about her. Do you still visit her father?"

"Yeah, in my own way. Victor died last year. He left me the house we're living in now.

"Malika drew up the plans for it her last semester of college. She wanted to be an architect." He cleared his throat. "She was an architect." He rested his head on the window frame.

"You loved her very much."

"Yeah. At one time, I did, in lots of ways."

"Enough to walk through fire for her?"

"I did that too damn many times. When I was a kid, she was like a little sister I had to protect. That's what I was doing when I met Victor on the Little League field." A snort that might have passed for a laugh left the impression of a good memory. "More like getting my ass beat by a couple of ten-year-olds. I was eleven at the time; Malika was five, china-doll pretty and obnoxious as hell. Victor, her father, was helping a friend organize the league. I didn't know who he was, just that I wasn't going to let a couple of bullies torment a little kid."

Req paused for a moment as though debating how much to reveal.

Cally remained motionless. The soft side of him as a child was part of the dichotomy he lived: tender one minute, callused the next.

"In short, Victor became the dad I didn't have. I became the son his wife couldn't have, only I didn't know that at the time. When I came home during college breaks, I saw as much of Victor as I did my own mother. When she remarried and moved to Palm Springs, I still came home to Monterey. As for Malika, things changed as we grew up. Getting married was the most natural thing in the world.

"Ester, Malika's mother, was dead then or she would have been as happy as Victor was when we gave him the news. Then things went to hell in a handbasket." The clipped ending of his words marked the end of the story.

"You would have married her had she finished at the detox place?" The thought of a married, untouchable Requiem Maguire cast a pall of dismay over Cally.

"Yeah. Although by the time she died, she was no longer the woman I'd asked to marry me. But I didn't give up hope. Not until she died."

"Loving her that deeply, you must understand why I did not marry any of my three fiancés." In the darkness, truth flowed easily. "I wanted a husband I could love without reservation. One who made my pulse leap when he walked into the room. A man I'd walk through fire for, if necessary. None of the men I was engaged to made me feel that way."

"I see. You believe in love and won't settle for less, right?"

"Of course. Only love would make someone willing to walk through fire for someone else. I never felt I'd do that for any of them." She laughed softly and gazed across the dark vista at the errant, foamy breakers catching the glow of headlights from the highway behind them. "Maybe a few warm embers for Roger, but that's all."

She smiled in the dark. "Given the attitude of today's society, I suppose that sounds very naïve, even foolish."

"No. Beneath the hype and glitz, that's what most people want, Cally. Walking away was the smart thing."

"The way things turned out, it certainly appears so." After

this time with Requiem Maguire, she couldn't imagine marriage to any of her former fiancés.

"Things are seldom as they appear. Let's clarify a few for ourselves."

"How?"

"By finding out if we're as alone as we'd like to be." He started the car.

"Where are we going?" She looked around wondering which car was waiting for them.

"To get some dinner."

"At the drive-through place?"

"Nope. We're going to Cannery Row. There's nothing as private as a public place, if you know the right nooks and crannies."

Cally thought of the things she had seen on television and felt her blood run cold. "Are they going to shoot us?"

"Not likely. If that was their plan, it would have happened by now."

The man had nerves of steel. She envied them. At the moment, her skin felt too tight. More than ever she wanted to look around, identify the threat, then run in the opposite direction. But she couldn't outrun a bullet. Freddy the Thief had proven that.

"Did you sleep with them?" he asked a while later.

"Who?" she asked, looking past the headlights of oncoming cars to the brightly lit streets and thriving businesses with their doors open to the people strolling the sidewalks.

"Did you sleep with your fiancés?"

She glared at Req for a moment, her quick temper threatening to get the best of her, her optimism riding high. "What an ungallant inquiry." It was none of his business. The only person entitled an explanation of her transgressions was her next fiancé, and then only if he actually wed him. "Why would you ask such a thing?"

"Just trying to put the pieces together." He accelerated through a yellow light. His gaze darted to the mirrors.

"No, you're not. You're trying to make me angry so I won't ask you questions about why we're being followed."

"If I knew, you'd know. I don't believe in keeping people I'm with in the dark." He afforded her a precious glance. "It might be something. It might be nothing. Regardless, when the shit hits the fan, you do what I tell you, when I tell you. Got it?"

"What—"

"No time for questions now. When I stop, you stay in the car," he hissed, glanced in the mirror, then jerked the steering wheel hard to the left. The tires squealed. The entire car leaned.

Cally gripped the door and almost grabbed the brake to steady herself. The sudden acceleration of her heart pounded in her ears.

He turned into a dimly lit dead end, spun the car around, slammed on the brakes, and then jammed the shift into P. He was out of the car in the next heartbeat. Dumbfounded, she watched him attack the car that pulled in behind them. Even before it stopped, Req had the driver's door open. Something shiny flashed in his hand. In the next heartbeat, he dragged a man onto the pavement.

Req seized control of the situation so quickly, Cally would have missed it if she had blinked. She'd never seen a man move that fast. She stared at the knife Req held to the man's throat with his right hand. The gun in his left hand pointed at the passenger through the open car door.

He spoke so softly she caught only fragments of conversation through the open car window. She released her seat belt and reached for the door handle. A second glance at Req changed her mind. He certainly looked like he had things under control and didn't need a distraction. Now he was listening and the man in the car was talking.

Whoever the men following them were, they were nowhere near as dangerous as the man whose hospitality she enjoyed. "Who are you, Requiem Maguire?"

He was one pissed agent-turned-witness-in-hiding. The minute he'd caught sight of them in the traffic on Cannery Row, he knew Terragno had sent the shadows. As protection, he'd no doubt insist.

Req couldn't decide if Terragno was terminally stupid or cunning enough to jeopardize the operation without appearing to do so.

He glared at the passenger over the sights of his gun in his left hand. With his right hand, he kept a steady pressure on the knife at the agent's throat as insurance. "Let's see some ID." Taking chances was foolish; taking anyone's word that they were who they said they were was suicide. He'd make damn sure his emotions weren't tangling his instincts into a Gordian knot.

"Easy. Two fingers," Req warned when the passenger lifted the placket of his jacket.

"Hey, we're just the messengers." Slowly, deliberately, he opened his jacket and withdrew his wallet. Opening the leather flap, he reached across and laid out the ID on the edge of the passenger seat where Req could see it.

"From who?" As if he didn't already know.

"District Assistant Director Sal Terragno."

Req glanced at the ID, then picked it up without relinquishing his weapon. A close study vouched for the authenticity of Agent David Hyatt's ID. Req tossed it back and lowered his gun. "What about your friend here?"

"You've got Agent Blankenship laying on his ID." Hyatt retrieved his wallet, careful to keep his hands in plain sight.

Cautious, Req took a final look around before easing the pressure on Blankenship's throat. He backed off slowly, careful not to put himself between the two men. Blankenship sat up slowly, extracting his ID from his front jacket pocket. Once satisfied with Blankenship's credentials, Req handed them back and let him stand.

"Did Terragno give you a reason to look for me, or is this just a power play to let me know he's in charge?" Req whipped the keys from the ignition, then opened the back door and got inside.

"They need you to come in," Blankenship said, massaging his throat.

"And people in hell need ice water. Try again."

"Who's the woman?" Hyatt asked, staring at Cally's outline in the car.

"Tension relief."

"Jumpy as you are, she must not be doing a very good job of it," Blankenship commented bitterly, still rubbing his neck.

"Different kind of tension. You tell Terragno, if I come in, I'm coming after him with everything in my arsenal. There won't even be ashes left when I'm done."

Hyatt turned in his seat. "Are you out of your fucking mind? Threatening a district assistant director?"

"You delivered his message. I gave you my response. Now get the hell out of here and stay away from me." He reached for the door handle. "Even Terragno wants me alive long enough to testify."

"Wait," Blankenship ordered. "There's more."

"It better be good."

"Louis Hill wants to meet with you," Blankenship said. "Terragno wants you to turn him. The prosecutor is prepared to deal for his testimony."

"Did it occur to Terragno that Hill might be a hit man and I'm the target? Hell, all things considered, he probably volunteered to do me as a charity case." Right now it seemed to Req that things really couldn't get worse. "If he does, instead of two witnesses, you boys end up with zero, and I win the pine box lottery. Did Terragno consider that?"

"Yeah. He did," Hyatt conceded. "He kicked it upstairs to Rydell."

"And?"

"Rydell wants you to cooperate. With Hill on the stand, Gutierrez won't see the light of day. Terragno says Rydell'll be heading up the operation."

"Shit." If it was just Terragno, he would blow it off. But Rydell was the man he trusted most in the department. Rydell wouldn't hang him out to dry. Req wasn't sure if he could trust these guys but he would definitely be calling Rydell tonight to make sure.

"They need you for a prelim planning Saturday night in Bakersfield," Blankenship continued. "You know the drill."

Only too well. He'd never wanted to do it again. "Yeah. Tell Rydell I'll be there. Meanwhile, you guys stay the hell away from me. All we can do is get each other killed."

What would happen to Caladonia Hornsby if he was killed?

They had picked up dinner on the way home, but Req hadn't eaten a bite. Instead, he had left her alone in the kitchen and disappeared into his office, staying there long after Cally went to bed. True to his promise, Req took Cally into town the next morning for her research excursion; although considering his surly mood after cornering the men in the alley, she hadn't expected it.

Mrs. Murphy, keeper of the sacred historic archives, literally fawned over Cally. Not until midmorning did Cally learn Req had obtained access to the priceless windows on history by making a large contribution to the library.

She had taken for granted the power of money until she'd found herself here without a penny. A *charity* case. The thought still rankled her. She could endure it. She had to until she found a way home.

"Look at this." Req slid onto the bench beside her. He spread out a brittle, yellowed newspaper, then pointed a rubber-gloved finger to an article. "I'll be damned."

Cally read the small blurb he indicated. "Thomas sold Golden Sun Shipping," she whispered, not quite able to believe it. She checked the date on the newspaper. On November 5, 1892. Almost two years after she'd left. "Are there any details elsewhere in the paper?"

"No. I almost missed this; it's such a small notice. I thought you said Golden Sun Shipping was a good-sized company."

"It is. Was."

"Seems like a prominent company would merit more than this blurb when the owner sold it."

"Yes," she agreed, worried beyond measure. If Thomas Barry was the sole owner, that meant she married him when she returned to her own time, and they bought out Chauncy Cunningham. Or she never made it home, and Cunningham died. Either way, what had happened to Cameron Morton? Her mind reeled at the possibilities, most of which she found unacceptable.

"I've checked the records for 1890 and 1891," she told Req. "There is no record of my death during those years. It doesn't appear I did anything worthy of being recorded in the vital statistics." She carefully folded the newspaper and found her notepad, then cast a sideways glance at him. Unfortunately, having him believe her didn't engender the comfort she had hoped for. "At least no one close to me died during those two years. However, Maudel had a baby boy in May of ninety-one. That means she was pregnant when I left." Had Maudel known? Or had Cally been too consumed by the aftermath of her father's death for Maudel to share her good news?

"I'm afraid what I need may exist only in an obscure journal." Cally eyed the tightly sealed glass cases.

"You look your way. I'll look mine."

"And your way is?"

"Follow the money. If Barry sold the company in November of ninety-two, what happened to the other partner and to the Hornsby holdings? That's what I intend on digging out of the paper. Then we'll see what we can do with bank records and public filings."

"Follow the money? You think my father was killed for money?"

Req shrugged. "How accurate was the newspaper account?"

"My father was a prominent man. The newspaper went out

of its way to report the details of his death accurately. He was well-loved."

"Not by everyone. Someone needed him out of the way either to make money or to protect the money they had already made. When you strip away the decorations, that's the reason for most premeditated murders. Money."

Cally thought about that for the rest of the day. The deeper they dug, the greater the possibility that Req was right. Her father's killer had acted out of greed. Those same men had killed Freddy the Thief rather than run the slightest risk of exposure.

At closing time, Mrs. Murphy volunteered to photocopy a stack of information Cally had identified as having potential. They would be able to pick it up Monday afternoon.

She and Req gathered their notes and the photocopies they'd made earlier, then left.

Cally drew a deep breath of fresh, cool air. She had a great deal of information to sift through. She glanced up at Req. He had been very quiet all day and was of far more assistance than she had dreamed. She couldn't help wonder why and suspected the answer would only ignite more questions.

Buying groceries on the way home was an amazing experience Cally would never forget. No wonder Req had no interest in how things were made. The choices available in the supermarket astounded her. She was content to push the cart and let him fill it up.

When they unloaded the bags of groceries at home it appeared he had bought enough to feed an army, providing she could microwave it fast enough.

Standing in the kitchen, she assessed the bags filling the countertops. "We have enough food for a month."

Req opened the freezer section of the refrigerator. "All I'm concerned about is the weekend. I have to go away for a couple of days. I wanted you well stocked. It's a long way to the store, as you may have noticed." He grabbed four bags of freezer goods. "Do us both a favor and stay inside the fence while I'm gone. I'll show you how to work the security locks and alarms."

A sense of dread oppressed her. "You mean, lock myself in and the world out?"

"That's it. The stakes have been raised. I'll know how far by the time I get back." He concentrated on arranging things in the freezer, then the refrigerator, with the intensity of a man with a single purpose in life.

When he finally ran out of grocery bags to unpack, he looked lost for a split second.

"What is it, Req?" She took a step, then stopped. All day they had maintained distance as though the air between them could neutralize the palpable attraction tugging in all the deliciously wrong places. It had been an illusion they both had cultivated and clung to in the dank historical archives.

They stared at one another in the glare of kitchen lights. Cally drank in the shadow of his whiskers, the diamond earring, the sheen of his dark hair, the sensuous promise of his lips capable of both cruelty and passionate tenderness. Then she met his gaze and knew the truth.

This was the man who made her pulse race when he walked into a room. The one for whom she would consider walking through fire. The one she could grow old with and find each day exciting. The one she was going to leave when she found her way home.

With a scowl that looked painful, he picked up a red and white sack and handed it to her. The bag warmed her hands and the aroma of fried chicken, potatoes, gravy, and coleslaw made her stomach growl.

Req opened the cupboard and whipped out a couple of plates. "There's a helluva lot I have to teach you and not much time to do it in, Cally."

"What do you mean?"

"You need to learn how to function in society. Where to go to get what you need. How to get there. What to do." The plates clattered on the table. He pulled on the silverware drawer so hard, Cally thought it would drop onto the floor. "Some people owe me favors. I'll work on getting you an identity." The silverware hit the hardwood table with punctuating clangs. "You're going to have to learn to drive."

Cally unpacked the red and white chicken bag, one container at a time. "I don't intend on being here that long."

"What we intend and what happens are often two different things. You didn't count on being my houseguest either. Plan for the worst, then be surprised if it doesn't happen. Chances are it will, though."

She set the table, then shoved spoons into the Styrofoam containers. "This is about last night, isn't it?"

"Leave it be."

Palms flat on the table, she leaned toward him. "How can I plan for the worst if I don't know how bad it can get?"

His green eyes became frozen emeralds. "It's bad enough for me to contemplate marrying you."

"I beg your pardon?" Stunned, she sank into the nearest chair, positive she had heard him incorrectly.

"If something happens to me, you'll be taken care of."

"Don't be absurd. I'm not getting married. I'm going home."

"You let me know when you purchase your goddamn ticket, okay? Until then, this is the only ride in town."

He was right, of course, and she hated thinking she might be stuck here. Worse, she hated the thought of anything happening to Req. Whatever he discussed with the two men who had followed them last night had changed everything. He didn't expect to survive the ordeal ahead of him. If he had, marriage would never have entered his mind.

The realization rocked her down to the soles of her feet. She could hardly envision life in this era without Req.

It was unacceptable. Surely, they could do something to keep him safe. Cally leaned back in the chair and looked hard at him. "Take me with you tomorrow."

"Not on your life. The fewer people who know about you, the better for both of us." He opened the chicken container and put a piece on each of their plates. "Don't give me more to worry about than I've already got."

"What are you worried about?"

"The last time I went to one of these setups, I ended up underground for over two years. I don't know if it's too soon or too late, but I'm not going again. I just don't have it in me anymore." He dropped a glob of mashed potatoes on her plate. "Eat. Then you're going to school in Technology 101."

Chapter 9

CALLY CHECKED HER notes against the complex panel in Req's office. The security was set to the highest level, just the way he had programmed it. As long as she accepted that things did what they did without trying to figure out how, she and technology got along fine.

She spent most of the solitary weekend studying the photocopied pages they'd brought home from the historical archives. When arranged properly, the pages told a story. The trouble was, some of the critical pieces were missing. She fervently hoped the material Mrs. Murphy was reproducing filled in some of the gaps.

Concentration was difficult. Too often her thoughts strayed to Req. When she couldn't sit still another minute and wanted to scream in frustration over his ill-defined situation, she walked the grounds. The manicured gardens and crisp air helped her put things into perspective. For a while.

Late Sunday night, she sat in the entertainment room and flipped through the seemingly endless television channels. In her listless state, nothing held her attention for long.

Near midnight, she felt Req's presence even before she heard him move through the house. She bolted up from the couch. Seeing him, reassuring herself that he was here, in one piece, was the only way she would ever be able to sleep tonight. One glimpse was all she needed.

As she rounded the corner into the living room, she ran into the center of his tee shirt-wrapped chest proclaiming him "Prime Beef" and cried out in surprise.

He caught her shoulders, stepped back, and steadied her.

She clutched the lapels of the white terry robe she had

donned after her shower. Slowly, she lifted her gaze from the red letters on his tee shirt, wanting to hug him as the tee shirt hugged his chest.

Fatigue deepened the care lines around his eyes. She touched his left temple, then gazed into his eyes.

In a flash, the fatigue evaporated. A predatory hunger lowered his eyelids to half-mast. A muscle twitched around the dimple in his left cheek.

He became a statue, neither pulling her close nor pushing her away. The only sign that he was alive was the slow working of the muscle in his left cheek. The feather touch of her fingertips stilled the spasm.

The slow journey of her thumb across his mouth parted her lips in expectation of tasting him. Being so close, touching him, built a heady excitement that pooled in her lower abdomen and hardened her nipples.

She leaned into him, bracing her hands on his shoulders, and stood on bare tiptoes. Lips parted, she wanted his mouth on hers.

Req caught her hips and held her away. "Don't start something you're not prepared to finish."

With as much certainty as the sun rising in the morning, she knew if she kissed him the intimacy wouldn't end there. He would want it all.

God help her, so did she.

"I, ah, was worried about you," she managed. Putting distance between them took all her determination. Three fiancés had taught her when to retreat, but she had never fought herself before.

"I'm back."

"I . . . good. I'll go to bed, then." She met his stare, then could not look away. He seemed to see beyond the thin veil of propriety she clung to, down to the core of unruly desire setting her aflame inside.

Req swore under his breath, then became a blur of motion. A hard yank opened the tie on her robe. An infinity of sensation swamped her senses.

Heart racing with anticipation and the adrenaline of daring, she stretched until her mouth met his. He groaned deep in his throat as he claimed her lips and found her nearly naked body beneath the robe.

He continued moving, taking her with him, drowning her in need and desire, not stopping until he pinned her against the nearest wall. He held her with his hips, his erection hard against the metal buttons of his jeans and the fly pressing into the soft flesh of her belly.

He cradled her face in his right hand, holding her; his left moved relentlessly, touching, titillating, building her need. Though his touch was gentle, his kiss imparted the raw desire ravaging him. He couldn't get enough of her, nor she of him. Again and again she let him test, kiss, explore, until she could stand it no more and thrust her questioning tongue into his mouth to do the same.

When he broke the kiss, they were both breathing hard. Cally wanted more of his mouth, his hands, and whatever came next. The sinuous rocking of his hips against her promised what he wanted.

Very deliberately, his fingers skimmed the sides of her neck. At her collarbone, he hooked the lapels of the robe and slid it over the top of her shoulders, down her slim arms, finally catching against the wall. Suddenly exposed, she experienced a moment of panic. The fleeting vulnerability passed when he lifted her chin and gifted her with a slow, deep kiss that enflamed her soul.

Yes, she would walk through fire for Requiem Maguire, which was exactly what it felt like she was doing. She had no idea it could be so hot or so sweet. But that was typical of him. From the beginning she had seen through his harsh, abrupt demeanor. Regardless of what he said, he treated her with deference and a gentleness that made her feel special beyond belief even when he thought her crazy. If this was insanity, she welcomed it.

"You missed me," he whispered, devouring her flesh with his gaze.

The exquisite torture of his fingertips gliding from the tops of her shoulders, across her upper chest, then lingering at the swell of her breasts offered in lace cups wrung the truth from her. "More than I wanted to believe possible."

She inhaled sharply when his thumbs grazed her turgid nipples straining against the lacy bra.

"Good," he murmured, "we're getting married in Reno tomorrow."

The words registered slowly through the need he built layer upon heated layer with each caress, each touch, and each sensation that became more compelling than the one before. Wherever he had gone, whatever had happened, Req wasn't optimistic if he wanted to marry her tomorrow. "You don't have to marry me—"

"Maybe not." His hands closed over her breasts. The press of his hips grew insistent. "But *you* need to marry me." His head tilted, and he slanted his mouth over hers.

Any protest she might have considered incinerated in the heat of his slow, thorough kiss. Cally's arms twined around his neck, her fingers wound into his thick, shiny hair. She wouldn't have let go even if the house was on fire.

She cried out when he broke the kiss.

"Christ, you don't want to do this," he said in a raspy voice. "I don't want to—dammit. You're messing with my mind, Cally."

Stunned by the sense of loss, struggling to regain her breath, she couldn't tell him that she did want to make love with him. Almost as much as she wanted to go home.

Home. Responsibility. Propriety.

A reiteration of her life-long litany, coupled with the rejection of a man at war with himself, sobered her.

Req picked up the robe off the floor and arranged it over her shoulders. He backed away, holding his hands up and away from both their bodies. "Go to bed, Cally."

She retreated. Cool air washed over her body. How easily she had succumbed to the magic of his touch. The frustration of unanswered need and her confusion about his abrupt change dulled her embarrassment.

When she took a final look over her shoulder, he had one hand braced against the wall and was staring at the floor. It took her last shred of fortitude to keep from going to him.

If it was this difficult to walk away from him now, how hard would it be to leave him forever if they made love?

Cally clutched the lapels of her robe and ran to her room.

When Req said they would fly in and out of Reno, Cally thought he was using a figure of speech she failed to comprehend. From the time Req settled her into a soft leatherlike seat in what he called "first class" until they landed in Reno, Cally experienced the true meaning of the phrase "stark terror."

Never mind the dictator with her decreed they were getting married.

Never mind he'd made her wash her hair with stuff that turned it burgundy-brown.

Never mind he'd insisted she answer to the name Mary Johnson, then made her sign that name to documents.

Never mind she was dressed to blend into the gray seat that was the same color as her face during the flight.

And never mind that Req had changed his appearance so drastically she'd never find him if the hoards of people in the airport separated them.

Woman was not meant to fly. At least, women from 1890 weren't meant to.

By the time Req helped her off the airplane, Cally began to understand why people in this time consumed the wide variety of medications advertised in every medium.

An hour after leaving the airport, Cally stood in front of a boutique with Req. She couldn't get used to him in a suit that made him appear close to 250 pounds. As flummoxed as her thinking was, she nearly laughed aloud each time she looked at his blond head of hair, mustache, and goatee. She squinted whenever she looked into his eyes. The thought of putting thin sheets of material over his eyes to turn them brown held a macabre fascination. "Contact lenses," he'd called them. However, his efforts to disguise the both of them worked. She wouldn't have recognized either one of them.

"Why are we here?" she asked in a voice that betrayed an inner unsteadiness.

"I brought you here to pick out a wedding dress. You ought to have that, at least."

"A wedding dress," she whispered. This wasn't how it was supposed to be. She was going to be married in grand fashion with pomp, ceremony, and tradition. Her father was going to walk . . . The sudden sense of loss weakened her already shaky knees. She sagged against Req.

He caught her in an embrace before her rubbery legs failed completely. "Is marrying me worse than flying?"

Gazing up into his camouflaged eyes that hid every scrap of emotion, Cally shook her head in denial. "I thought my father would walk . . ." she started, but couldn't finish the private thought.

"Yeah, I know how it is," he exhaled. "Take your time." The tender way he cradled her head against his padded chest made her want to cry. The wealth of understanding imparted by his stingy use of words when emotion ran high made her want to hold onto him forever. The reason for the marriage made her want to grab his hand and run. Where, she didn't know. So she stood in the middle of the sidewalk and held him as people walked by.

"Better?" he asked when she straightened.

Cally nodded. "Is it possible to get married in something other than a traditional wedding dress?"

"The clothes don't matter. What you've got on is fine. I just thought, well, you'd want the dress." He seemed suddenly uncomfortable. "How about it? You pick one out. We'll get you outfitted from skin out. Okay?"

"I can't let you buy my trousseau." A horn blared on the street behind her and the sounds of the city intruded on their very private conversation.

"Why not? Money is one of the two things most women think men are good for." He placed a kiss on her forehead, then opened the embrace, but took her hand in his.

"What's the second?" She glanced at his mouth in time to see a familiar, quirky smile tug at the right corner.

"Sex. And I'm very good at that."

Cally pressed her lips shut. She'd just bet he was.

"We've got four hours before we get on the plane. Let's do business," he said. All hints of tenderness fled.

Moments later, the proprietress was showing them various dresses. Cally watched Req. When his eye lingered a fraction longer on a seductive blue satin gown, she chose it.

When she emerged from the dressing room to look in the three-angle mirror, she didn't have to ask Req's opinion. In an unguarded moment, it showed in his stance, his face, and in his gaze that devoured each curve of the snug satin dress.

"If you want that one, you can have it."

She turned toward the mirror, amazed at how revealing the modest scoop of the neck and long sleeves were. The way it made her feel when she saw the reflection of Req's appreciating appraisal made itself known when the satin caressed her aroused nipples.

"Yes," Req whispered, meeting her gaze with a knowing lift of his left eyebrow. "We're definitely buying that number."

Cally shook her head. She could never wear the dress in public.

"Yes," he said with a finality that made argument futile. "Now, how about picking out something a little more conservative for the wedding," Req said, effectively ending anymore arguments. He glanced across the store to the proprietress gathering gowns for their approval. "I don't want people remembering us, and you're unforgettable in that dress."

Cally nodded. "Help me, then."

Req plucked a sedate, light-brown suit from a rack.

"Fine." She took it and hurried to the dressing room. The blue satin gown revealed far too much of her.

"If the suit fits, wear it."

The next stop was a jewelry store where they argued over wedding rings.

An hour later at the Washoe County Courthouse Req juggled clerks and documents bearing their real names. Cally asked no questions and answered only when asked a direct question. She was glad they had rehearsed the answers early that morning on the long drive to the San Francisco airport.

Twenty minutes after leaving the courthouse, they stood in front of a justice of the peace. A rare case of nerves turned Cally's hands to ice.

After three engagements, she was marrying a man she hardly knew. It wasn't the enormous wedding she'd envisioned since her childhood. Neither the setting nor the ceremony compared with her friend Maudel's lavish celebration. Fortunately, neither did the groom.

She hadn't examined Req's motives for insisting on the marriage too closely. Doing so meant delving into her own reasons, something she wasn't ready to do beyond acknowledging the marriage as the most supreme, outlandishly selfish thing she had ever done. She simply wanted to marry Req and for once she didn't let all of her self-imposed rules stand in the way.

If he thought they should be married, she saw no reason for argument. Time would annul the marriage when she found her way home. After all, how could she be married to someone who hadn't been born? And how could Req be married to someone who had been dead for decades? Meanwhile, she'd revel in the excitement of being Requiem Maguire's wife.

The whole situation seemed so logical when she kept her inevitable return to 1890 in mind. Unfortunately, logic had nothing to do with what her heart felt. Had he asked her to marry him in her own time, she would have said yes—because she loved him, because he made her pulse race when he walked into the room, and because she saw sterling aspects of his character emerging with greater clarity every day.

They found the justice of the peace on the third floor of a stone building half a block from the courthouse. The small office with worn furniture and plastic flowers was a far cry from the altar she had anticipated. She had no family or friends in attendance, only strangers. And Req.

With her father gone, Req was all that mattered.

She married him because she loved him.

He married her because he thought he was going to die and she couldn't take care of herself without his assets.

When they left the justice of the peace, Cally was ready for the terror of flying. It would take her mind off her husband.

"I'll get your papers from Mrs. Murphy in the morning," Req said as he drove out of the parking garage of the San Francisco Airport. "We're in rush-hour traffic. It'll take a few more hours to get home."

After the airplane ride, the car was a haven. She wondered why this was called "rush hour" when nobody's car, including their own, seemed to be moving. The only thing rushing was her mind as it flitted from one ominous thought to another as though each was a hot coal.

She hadn't expected to walk through fire so soon after their marriage. But contemplating the reasons why he wanted the wedding in the first place felt like being burned by fire. She grabbed onto the subject he offered and tried not to think about him dying.

"I'm anxious to see what Mrs. Murphy has for us. I went over and over the documents we copied and my notes," she forced a smile at him, "and your notes. I feel like I'm looking through the fog and the image keeps shifting. The answer is there. Somewhere. I'm going to find it." There had to be answers—somewhere.

"What good will it do you?"

Incredulous, she looked at him. "Knowing who killed my father, and why, will help me get justice for him. And myself." She straightened and stared at the car ahead of them. "I lost my mother to consumption when I was fourteen. It was difficult to accept, but I saw her decline and had no choice. My father, however, was taken from me abruptly and violently. I refuse to accept my father's murder without seeking justice. He deserves better. So do I. Anything else is unacceptable."

"Do I understand you right? You think you're going to go back to 1890 and hunt down your father's killer?"

She ignored the doubt in his voice and lifted her chin. "Yes."

"Do you know how that sounds?"

"It's certainly no more stupid than you marrying a woman you think suffers from delusions, is it?"

"Touché."

"We'll both do what we have to do, Req." She looked out the window without seeing the cars beside them. Falling in love wasn't in her plans any more than falling through a time hole was. Both happened and she couldn't change either of them. But she could stay the course of her responsibility to her father, and herself. Whatever responsibility she had concerning her marriage with Req had yet to be defined.

"What if you can't return?"

"You believe me?" Dear God in heaven, a miracle in her lifetime!

"For argument's sake, let's say I do—for the moment."

"You cannot have it both ways, Req. You either believe me or you admit to marrying a woman you think is demented. Which is it?"

"I wish it were that simple. One minute, I believe you, Cally. The explanation you give is the only one that fits, even though it's theoretically impossible. The next minute, I can't accept the universe is so screwed up that even time has . . . what? Defects? Flaws?" The struggle behind his rare candor increased with his admission.

"You don't trust yourself."

"About this? No. So let's get back to my question: What if you can't return? I'm no scientist, but it's hardly plausible, is it?"

Cally hesitated, mulling his skepticism over in her mind. "To put it in the vernacular of the times, failure is not an option. This is something I must do. There are people counting on me. They're looking for me. I will not give the men on the beach the satisfaction of thinking I've joined my father. I want them to have a fair trial, and then I want to watch their executions.

"I swore on my father's grave I wouldn't rest until I got justice for him, Req. I have to do this." *I have to find a way home, but I'll leave you my heart.* "I think you know exactly why I will succeed, why anything else is unacceptable."

He changed lanes for the third time, then sped up as the traffic momentarily lightened. "How are you going to return, Cally? It's not like hopping on a plane."

"No, it isn't," she agreed, her determination building. Nothing in her wildest imagination had been quite like that. "The answer is at the beach, at the rocks. I'll find it. I have to. I'm not asking you to help me, Req. Just don't stand in my way."

When he didn't respond, she changed the subject and felt grateful when Req went along.

They rode in silence for an hour after clearing the worst of the traffic. The question that had nagged her begged an answer until she asked, "You know I have to leave you, don't you?"

"I may leave you first."

"It's not the same. I have to go home. I have a duty. Responsibilities. Sometimes you have to follow the choices you've made to the end, regardless of the cost along the way."

"You're talking to Mr. Responsibility, middle name of Duty Calls, last name, Sucker. We'll both do what we have to. If for some reason things don't work out favorably for either of us . . ." His voice trailed off as he accelerated around a long truck.

Don't tell me you're going to die. Don't step in the middle of the danger surrounding you. Don't make me a widow when I've just become a bride. She took a deep breath, then exhaled slowly. She was in no position to make demands. "Then what?" she asked in a neutral voice.

"There are some things we need to go over, things you'll have to do if that happens. I'll have some papers for you to sign in the next couple of days too."

"Will you answer me this time? Will you please tell me where you went this past weekend? What happened?"

"Don't ask, Cally. Things aren't always what they seem. Drop it."

"Drop it? As in a ton of bricks? As in you want to know my plans, but won't tell me yours?"

"It's not the same thing."

"Our perceptions of this whole, bizarre, impossible situation are totally different. You think I'm headed for disappointment and I think you're shopping for headstones. I can take your opinion or leave it, but you're not going to tell me what's happening, are you?"

His silence was confirmation. He continued looking straight ahead and keeping pace with the traffic.

She wanted to shake him, do something to break his stubborn silence. In the end, she settled for wheedling the truth out of him one admission at a time. "Did whatever happen have anything to do with us getting married? Or had you decided on that before you confronted those men in Monterey?"

"Our marriage is a precaution."

"For what?" she asked softly.

"If something happens to me, you'll be a wealthy widow. Whether you're living a fantasy or you really came through time, you aren't equipped to function in society, Cally." He glanced at her in the glow of oncoming headlights. "If you find your time gate or whatever it is that's supposed to take you back, it won't matter, will it?"

"You're not allowed to die, Req. You do not have my permission to put yourself in danger," she commanded. Every cell in her body quivered in fear of losing him. Death was so painful for those left behind, so irrevocable.

"Your permission? Goddamn, you already sound like a nagging wife," he said in a deep voice far too calm for the intense way his eyes prowled the road.

"I might be old to be a blushing bride, but I'm too young to be a widow."

"A rich widow," he reminded her.

"Any kind of widow," she snapped back, her stomach churning with emotion. She didn't want to imagine Requiem Maguire in a casket and as cold to the touch as her father.

"Then why the hell did you marry me?"

"Because . . ." *I'm in love with you.* ". . . you're the most intriguing human being to walk the earth. You roar like a bear, but you have the heart of a lamb. You're generous. Attentive. Considerate. And most important, you need me."

A genuine laugh shook Req's shoulders. "Right," he managed.

She had spoken the truth and he didn't believe her. If she had planned to stay with him, they would have to work on that. In the end, it was probably best he didn't know the extent of her feelings.

"The only way I need you, Cally, has a price tag on it I'm not ready to pay."

"What?" A dunk in a vat of ice water couldn't have startled her more.

"I'm not talking about money, Cally. Money's easy. You, you're something else completely."

When the words penetrated her stunned mind, she realized she'd have to wait for a real wedding night. Requiem Maguire feared being in love more than he feared death.

• • •

Req worked at the computer into the small hours of the morning. Paul had taught him the fine points of cloak-and-dagger hacking. With the right equipment he could access the sensitive information he desired without risking detection.

He needed answers from somewhere, and he sure as hell wasn't finding any within himself. Bringing Caladonia Hornsby into his life was a mistake of the best and worst kind. She was the epitome of innocence lost too easily; she was also an enigma he could neither unravel nor accept at face value.

That he actually believed her at times scared the hell out of him. The trouble was, she knew things about the time period she claimed as hers that no one could have known. He could have dismissed the details she spouted like yesterday's news if not for the repeated confirmations he kept stumbling over. When she told him to look in the newspaper archives for something on a specific date, it was exactly as she'd said it would be.

Then there was William Potter's unintentional endorsement of her authenticity.

"Where did you come from, Caladonia Hornsby?" Req shook his head—she was now Cally Maguire. His wife in the eyes of the law. A formal responsibility. The notion should have terrified him. Instead, he found himself thinking in terms of heart and hearth, kids and chaos, and long nights of lovemaking and crying babies.

He was loosing it. Badly.

He reminded himself that he could take care of her only as long as he didn't lose focus. Neither one of them had a shot at surviving if he failed to keep a clear head.

Sunday, Daryl Rydell had assured him they had no confirmation of the cartel putting out a contract on his life. Req believed Rydell may be unaware of a contract, but he also knew there had to be one on him. No one turned on Gutierrez without paying the supreme price. The lucky ones got off easy with a bullet in the brain.

Req didn't believe in luck.

By now Gutierrez knew he was a narc and wanted to cut out his liver personally. Two years undercover assured Req that the cancer of Gutierrez's organization pervaded state and federal law enforcement. Dropping out of sight and staying hidden would last only so long. Already, the odds were shifting against him.

Req read the computer screen a second time, then began the process of extricating himself from the network he'd wound through to avoid discovery. He had the information he needed but wasn't what he wanted. Not by a long shot. The water had never been muddier.

According to the report on Sal Terragno's private computer, Daryl Rydell was on Gutierrez's payroll. Shaken, Req reread the report. Each word became a hot poker of betrayal. He didn't want to believe what he read, but couldn't afford to ignore it.

Req reminded himself that he was dealing with his boss, Sal Terragno, a man with a private agenda who always put his political and personal interests above his people. It was just as probable Terragno had expected him to search his files and put the report in to sow seeds of distrust.

However, if Rydell was on the take, Req could bend over and kiss his ass good-bye. The chances of surviving Gutierrez's arrest and trial went from slim to none.

He took the cellular phone Rydell had given him after the Bakersfield meeting from its charger. The encryption ability made his calls impossible to track or trace.

He stared at the number pad, selected an encoded number to activate the phone, then pressed the Send button. The hum of a dial tone leaked out of the earpiece.

Once he made the call, there was no going back.

"As though there is now," he murmured.

He punched in Rydell's number.

The phone rang six times.

"Rydell," said a thick voice on the other end.

It didn't sound like Rydell. Or maybe it did and he was too tired to recognize it. He turned the chair toward the wall and put his heels on the edge of the expansive cabinets.

Req gave the name of the file on Terragno's computer and hung up.

He checked his watch. If Rydell didn't respond in thirty minutes, he'd wake Cally and they would get the hell out of Dodge. She wouldn't want to leave without the papers from Mrs. Murphy, but choices were quickly becoming as scarce as hen's teeth.

He stared at the wood grain in the cabinets without seeing it, and mentally sifted his options. Staying here together, or taking off and leaving Cally here alone weren't viable alternatives if Rydell was on the take. Rydell knew too damn much about Victor Escobar and Req's involvement in the disappearance of the dealer who knowingly had sold Malika the bad heroin that killed her.

"Req?"

The sound of Cally's voice startled him. He swung around, his feet dropping to the floor as he juggled the phone to keep from dropping it.

Req looked hard at her. A halo of sleep-tousled tresses had escaped the long braid confining the bulk of her now burgundy-tinged hair. A few more washings and she'd be blond again. She crossed her forearms beneath her breasts. Immediately he wondered what, if anything, she wore under the terry-cloth robe. The rush of heat that had become familiar since Cally entered his life surged through him. Neither of them moved to close the distance.

He hadn't meant to end up on a limb hanging over a shark tank with the chain saws warming up. And he damn sure hadn't meant for anyone to be with him.

But there she was and here he was.

The phone in his hand rang.

He diverted his concentration to the phone. "Maguire."

"Do you believe it?" Rydell asked. The slow, bass tone carried an anger Req recognized.

"Should I?"

"That's like asking a man if he still beats his wife. Any answer makes him guilty," Rydell seethed. "It's a plant. I accessed it too easily for it to be anything else."

"I'll be there Thursday and I want some answers." He would know which way the wind blew when Terragno and Rydell were in the same room again. On the other hand, by then it might be too damn late.

Rydell paused. "Something is off-kilter here, Maguire. This isn't the usual politics and backstabbing."

"Call Terragno on it, then. I don't like meeting with Hill even with a wire and surveillance. If you're with me, be in the van and cover my ass. I'm starting to feel frostbite."

"I'll be there. Hang tight. Meanwhile, think about getting laid. It'll take the edge off."

Req snorted. That was all he did these days—think about it, but not do it. "Yeah." He returned the telephone to its berth.

"Go to bed, Cally."

"It's late. You come, too."

"I'd like nothing more than to come with you," he muttered

under his breath. His present mood disavowed anything gentle in the way he'd take her. "Go to bed."

Without another word, she turned and padded down the hall to her room.

He pushed to his feet and went to the gun safe obscured behind armoire doors. Time to start getting ready for Thursday.

Cally pulled the covers around her and stared at the dark ceiling. The man she married wanted her with an undeniable hunger she saw in his eyes and in the way his body tensed when she entered the room. Heaven knew she wanted him as badly. So why were they spending their wedding night in different rooms?

She tugged at the blankets as she turned onto her side.

It wasn't a matter of who would leave first. The question was *when*? Followed closely by *how*?

The uncertainties were beyond her control and that rankled her almost as much as sleeping alone on her wedding night. She could do something to change those circumstances. But should she?

Until she knew for sure, Req could chart their direction. Of course, when she made her mind up she would have to take charge. It was her nature.

Chapter 10

"I DON'T BELIEVE this. She must have misunderstood." Cally studied the faded writing on the brittle, yellowed pages of Penelope Cunningham's century-old journal. Peeking into the private thoughts of her best friend's mother had made her uncomfortable before. Now the revelations had turned from discomfort to agitation.

After breakfast, Req had gone into town and returned several hours later with the papers Mrs. Murphy had promised and several original journals and ledgers from William Potter. Cally had delved into the bonanza with both hands and barely noticed when Req left again.

The day had passed in what seemed the blink of an eye and it was after sunset before Req joined her in the library. With the exception of the center of the couch nearest the window, every surface in the room was covered in papers.

"Find something?" Req set aside the papers he had started sifting through.

"I don't know." The entry was too bizarre to be true and too blatant to ignore.

"Let me see."

"I'm at a loss to explain this, if it's true. I'm sure my father had no notion . . ." She indicated the disturbing entry in Penelope's private chronicle. "If William hadn't lent us this diary, I suspect that I never would have known what was going on." She sincerely hoped the entry was a mistake. "My father would have been furious. He would have dissolved Golden Sun Shipping rather than be associated with such a heinous crime."

Until discovering the entry, she had believed the *Ocean Princess* sank in the Straits of Juan de Fuca en route to Seattle in the winter of 1888. The Straits were notorious for sudden storms. The treacherous section of the sea lanes where the *Ocean Princess* went down had claimed numerous ships over the years.

"Why would Penelope think the ship was scuttled?" she mused aloud. The vile thought tightened her stomach.

"How the hell should I know? But you're right. That's exactly how it reads," Req agreed. He pulled on a pair of latex gloves, picked up the artifact, then looked at her. "You mind?"

"By all means." She had pored over the reproduced writings and original almanacs all day. "I need to rest my eyes for a few moments."

"Fine," he murmured, turning the page. "It's your turn to fix dinner. Anything but a potpie."

Preoccupied by the ramifications of the *Ocean Princess* entry, Cally made sandwiches, opened a couple of soft drinks, and poured potato chips into a bowl. When she had the meal on the table, she returned to the library and poked her head inside.

"I'm ready. Can you come and eat?"

Req looked up. The tension of a hunger that had nothing to do with his stomach narrowed his eyes for a moment. He set the journal aside and stripped off the gloves. "Yeah. Easily."

Content that he would follow, Cally walked past the dining room with an eye for a new place to spread her pages. Because Req preferred the convenience of the kitchen, they weren't likely to use the big table for eating.

"How far did you get in Penelope's accounts?" At the kitchen sink, Req washed off the talcum powder residue from his hands.

"I read as far as the reference to the *Ocean Princess*." She settled at the table and recalled Req's investigation tactics. "You said to look for the money and follow it. I don't see how it fits in." Nothing would fit as neatly as the black Harley-Davidson tee shirt molded over his chest and torso.

"Was it insured?"

"Yes. So was some of the cargo." She bit into her sandwich, set it down, and reached for the pencil and paper on the far end of the table. She paused while assessing the unusual flavor of the sandwich. Perhaps she'd left something out.

"Other than collecting the insurance, where's the gain in sinking a ship?" Req examined the contents of his sandwich before taking a bite. "What the hell is this?"

"Peanut butter, canned tuna, and mayonnaise." The way he

wrinkled his nose at it, it may as well have been a potpie. "Did I use too much lettuce?"

"It's a little heavy on the peanut butter for a tuna sandwich." He folded each side of the sandwich over on itself and left the mayonnaise- and peanut butter-coated lettuce out.

"Getting back to what we were talking about, the insurance is the very reason I think it's possible Penelope misinterpreted a conversation she overheard. We lost a sizable amount of money when the *Ocean Princess* sank. As I recall, she was carrying an expensive cargo from the Far East to a client in Seattle: silk, spices, ivory, a collection of rare chests, and some rare wood." She took another bite, then started listing what she could remember from the ship's manifest on the tablet.

"Was anything salvaged?"

Cally shook her head no. "The storms on the northwest coast are legendary for their severity. When a ship goes down, the crew's only thought is saving their lives, which is as it should be. As I recall, three survived and made their way to Port Townsend."

"I think I missed something. Was the cargo insured for its full value?"

Again she shook her head no. "Cargo is seldom insured for its full value. That's far too expensive. In fact, there are times when we do not insure the cargo at all. The decisions are made well in advance of a ship's departure. The amount of insurance is dependent upon the client using our ships. Occasionally, as was the case this time, we act as importers for specific clients."

"Sounds risky." Req pushed the bowl of chips at her.

"It can be. It can also be very lucrative."

"I take it Golden Sun Shipping reaped a healthy annual profit."

Cally dabbed at the corners of her mouth with the paper napkin. "Quite so."

"While you collect all your papers and the things William lent us, think about this—"

"Collect them?" Cally's soda rested in her hand, halfway between her mouth and the table. "Why? I just got them organized."

"I need to take you somewhere safe for a little while."

"What's wrong with here?"

"It's compromised by the people I work for. I'll be gone three days. Maybe four. Meanwhile, I want you safe and out of their reach. The fewer people who connect you to me, the better off you'll be."

Genuine alarm spread through her. "What are you saying, Req?" She set the soda down. "Are you telling me you might not be coming back?"

"I didn't say that, did I?"

"You say more by what you don't say. I've learned to weigh your actions, not your words."

Req shrugged. "I'm planning on picking you up in four days max. But shit happens."

"So your clothing has stated." As usual, whenever she started probing too deep, the steel curtain of stoicism he hid behind fell into place. He wasn't going to explain, just dictate. Oh, he would let her pose all her objections and argue in defiance. In the end, she would acquiesce, but not before prodding him for answers. "You think something bad is going to happen, don't you?"

"I've stayed alive by remembering I'm not invincible. I don't want you dragged into this." He rose and went to the far end of the kitchen. The large brown envelope he slid from beneath his jacket seemed ominous. "You need to sign a few papers. I'll drop them in the mail on our way out in the morning. There are some other papers in here you need to keep handy." He paused as he resumed his seat at the table. "Anything happens to me, you go to the address on the business card in here and ask for Carl Sontag. He'll take care of everything. You can trust him."

"When you said I would be a wealthy widow . . ." The words shriveled in her throat, the possibility of losing him too devastating to contemplate.

"Don't start inventorying the community property assets yet. Any number of things can happen." He pushed aside the remnants of their dinner and opened the envelope. "Including me achieving one of my greatest ambitions—living long enough to collect my share of Social Security—if there's any left."

She caught the gist of his inference. "I don't want your things. Or your money, Req. What I want is for you to live a very, very long and happy life."

"Sure you do, but humor me." He arranged three forms on the table in front of her. "Put your John Hancock next to the check marks. Consider it insurance."

She couldn't. Wouldn't. How could she consent to receiving even a dime from a man who didn't believe she'd married him for any other reason than to become a wealthy widow?

"Look, it's nothing personal—"

"But it is! I didn't marry you for protection. I don't want you to die. Why is it so hard for you to believe the things I say to you, Req? Why can't you believe me?" The man was infuriating in his stubbornness.

"Suppose I was the one who stumbled backwards in time and you offered some guidance. Some help," Req cajoled. "Don't you think ignoring it would be . . . unwise?"

She stared at him. If he had approached her in 1890 spouting nonsense and profanity, she would have taken one long look at the clothing that fit him like a second skin and turned away, though she would have savored the form of a well-built man. She might never have gotten to his hair curling on his shoulder. Certainly not to his diamond earring. And if by some miracle of curiosity or tolerance she had gone that far, one look at the tattooed pattern circling his upper left arm would have been the end of it.

The truth turned the peanut butter-and-tuna sandwich she'd eaten into a rock in the middle of her stomach.

Cally pushed away from the table and headed straight for the front door. She punched in the security code, then went outside. The chilly night air felt warm in comparison to the cold inside her. She wrapped her arms around herself and rubbed the gooseflesh as she walked around the side of the house with no destination in mind. The motion was enough to provide the illusion of distance.

"What the hell is wrong, Cally?"

Her heart skipped a beat when she looked up. The darkness embraced Req as one of its favorite creatures. If not for the fingers of light poking out of the library windows, he would be just another night shadow.

The urge to run flickered then fled. As Req had succinctly pointed out earlier, Cally had nowhere to go and no way to get there. A knot tightened in her throat, and she felt the prickle of barely suppressed tears.

"What's the matter?" Req asked again, this time in a softer tone.

Shame kept her from meeting his eyes.

"Tell me." He stood close enough for her to catch the scent of his clothing and feel the lure of his heat, but he didn't touch her.

"There are some things I'd rather not know about myself,"

she confessed. One of those things was the sensual way he affected her even through her guilt.

"Like what?"

"Like . . ." That same shame forced her into a confession. "I would have walked away from you if you had shown up in my time. I wouldn't have taken the time to get to know you. What kind of a man you are. How generous and kind you are." Giving voice to her narrow-minded shortcomings cast her in a harsh light. "It's a shock to realize how shallow I am."

Belly-shaking laughter caught the breeze rustling the last of the season's fuchsia blooms in the darkness.

Distraught, she followed the flagstone walk into the darker part of the grounds. She barely took half a dozen steps when he caught her shoulders and spun her around until she faced him. Instinctively she reached for him. The thud of his heart beneath the muscles of his chest pulsed through her palm. Her fingers tried to burrow into the warm iron of his flesh.

"You'd take one look and figure I'm trouble. You wouldn't want to know me, let alone help me. Is that it?"

It sounded even worse coming from him. She stared at the ground, but couldn't bring herself to withdraw her hand from the heat of his chest. The same chest she wanted to feel against her naked breasts. "I had considered myself more open-minded."

"And you're disappointed?"

"Yes," she managed through the weight of self-censure. Disappointed with herself. Disappointed they hadn't made love. Disappointed he had discovered how shallow she was so quickly. "It is quite devastating to realize I wouldn't have considered helping you, especially in light of all you have done for me."

Req gathered her in a loose embrace. "I'd call walking away from me smart. I'm bad news, Cally." He tightened the embrace, as though not wanting to let her go.

Emotion balled in her throat. Nothing he could say would dull the hard edge of disgust eating at her. Simultaneously, nothing but making love with him would appease the river of desire running wider and wilder each day.

"How the hell can you be so naïve and so savvy at the same time?" He kissed her hair, his breath soft and hot against her head. The acceleration of his heartbeat promised he was as affected by the press of their bodies as she. "Would you have been as afraid of me in 1890 as you were when I dragged you out of the ocean?"

"It's shameful." She nestled against his chest, grateful she wasn't looking into his face, and wished he was naked. In his arms with the darkness wrapped around them, she felt safe and in peril at the same time. In a flash of bravado, she kissed his chest. He responded by tightening the embrace.

"No it isn't. It's instinct. It's right. I'm not someone you should want to know."

"But you are, Req." He was her husband. The man she'd walk through fire for; the man she loved, the man she wanted to lose herself with in naked passion.

His heart beat a little faster against her cheek as his head rocked on top of hers in denial. "You've seen the civilized side of me. Part of who I once was, or wanted to be. Not who I've become over the past few years—what I *really* am. I'm discovering there's no going back. You can't erase the parts of your life you hate. There are no do-overs. All things considered"— he kissed the top of her head, then released her—"you would be right to walk away."

Every fiber in her cried out that she couldn't, wouldn't walk away. She wanted him.

But she would leave him. She would go home. The tear in her soul that began as a sore, frayed spot grew painfully wider.

Reluctantly, she let him remove her arms from around his warm, solid body. The cool night air chilled her with a reminder of the real distance between them.

"I hope you are from the past and can find your way home. It's the best thing that could happen to you where I'm concerned. And the safest." He turned away, all semblance of softness gone from his shadow-chiseled face. "Let's get your stuff packed into a box. You can take it with you in the morning."

"Where am I going?" The knowledge that it wasn't with him made it a moot point.

"My sister's place—the Starkeys. I trust her and Robert."

She stared into the darkness where he had disappeared. He had never spoken of his family before. What else hadn't he mentioned?

"You've told me everything except when you're coming back." Cally framed his face with her hands, then let her fingers slide through his thick hair. They were alone in the near-darkness of the Starkeys' garage. The smell of grass clippings from the

lawn mower and paint from a model airplane drying on the
workbench filled the warm confines. The sprawling house in
Cameron Park at the foot of the Sierras offered a unique
anonymity.

"Maybe five days. Maybe a week." *Maybe never.* He memorized her face with his fingers and eyes. "As soon as I can," he
said, drawing closer and turning his head as his lips approached
hers. Slowly he retraced each plane and soft angle of her face
with his lips.

He loved the way she trembled with desire. He wanted them
as naked as he felt emotionally. So did Cally. "God, but you
make it hard." In all ways.

"Not me, Req," she said breathlessly, arching her head to
give him access to her throat. "You."

She tasted of sweet seduction. His body howled for him to
take her. Hard. Fast. Now. "I know." He traced her jaw and the
little spot just below her ear that made her moan and press
closer to him—as though that was possible without them being
naked and actually making love. "When I get back . . ."

The glide of her fingers through his hair drew him closer.
Each sinuous movement she made against his eager body
promised her passion and a part of her heart that scared the hell
out of him. God knew he wasn't ready for that much emotion.
It would drown him.

"Req . . ." The plea of his name on her ragged breathing
begged him for his soul.

"If I get back—"

She stiffened slightly. "When, Req, when."

"When," he agreed, sliding his mouth over her jaw toward
her chin. He claimed her mouth in a voracious kiss and let the
rhythm of his aching, hungry body finish the promise.

"I have to go," he whispered after ending the kiss.

She clung for a moment when he eased the embrace. The
sudden flood of tears flowing down her cheeks twisted his
heart. "I'll be back, Cally."

"Promise?"

He shook his head. "Only that I'll do my damnedest to do
what I'm best at—survive."

"That's all I can ask for, isn't it?"

He nodded, then released her. This time she retreated. "Let
me out, then close it after me."

Cally nodded, not even trying to stem the flow of tears.

He opened the car door, then hesitated. She looked so devastated. She looked as though her lover was going off on a suicide mission. They weren't lovers, but the last part might prove prophetic if he wasn't very, very careful.

"Cally . . ."

She sniffed, then retreated a step and pushed the garage-door button. Amid the whir of the overhead motor, the door raised to let light banish the darkness.

Req got into his rented car and started the engine, his gaze locked on Cally's.

Req kept an eye on the rearview mirror as he drove away from the Starkey home and Cally. She didn't understand why he couldn't make love to her. He'd be lost. Letting himself feel again came with an enormous backlash from over two years of not allowing himself to feel at all. It seemed that once the invisible dam began lowering, the flood of stored emotions had no end.

A pity the survivor in him didn't differentiate between self-preservation and duty. The only way he could slip into the old role was to have as little to live for or lose as possible. If he made love to her, he doubted that he could walk away. Doubt alone was enough to get him killed.

Cally would never understand.

Heavyhearted, he headed north. Twenty-four hours later, he entered Canada at a quiet border crossing.

If things went to hell with Terragno, Rydell, and number-crunching Louis Hill, Cally was safe. As always, what he'd told his sister and her husband had been nothing short of the truth. They did not press him for what he left out, nor did he reveal anything they would have to regard as a secret.

Ignorance was bliss in this case.

Judith had quit asking questions about his personal life shortly after Malika died of an overdose. Req supposed he had Robert to thank for his sister's restraint.

As he drove to meet his first connection before reentering the United States, Req started shutting down the fragile, newly awakened emotions he had both sought and shunned after emerging from his undercover life.

The only way to survive whatever lay ahead was as the hard-assed, emotionally calloused Requiem Maguire who never gave a second thought about pulling the trigger on someone else when threatened.

• • •

Not knowing what Req faced when he reached his unknown destination kept Cally from saying the wrong thing to Judith and Robert Starkey. It didn't stop her from worrying, nor did it keep her from waking in the middle of the night with teary eyes and a heavy heart.

If the Starkeys worried, they hid it well behind warm friendship and open hospitality. Cally liked them immediately.

She wondered how they could accept her, a total stranger, into their home. In her estimation, being Req's wife meant nothing. As party to a marriage in name only, she felt like a fraud. Robert and Judith were under the assumption that Req had married her for love. Nothing could be further from the truth.

After dinner the third evening, ten-year-old Bobby joined Cally in the living room as she thumbed through an atlas.

"Are you looking for where Uncle Req is?" He regarded her with clear, Maguire-green eyes.

"No," she answered, patting the couch next to her. "Just looking at the western states. Where we are. Places to go." How terribly far away Monterey was.

"I used to look at the maps a lot before we moved here, except I used the computer, not a book." He peered down at the State of California. "You can't really zoom in on a book map."

She wasn't sure what it meant to "zoom in," but she'd take his word for it. "Where did you live before?"

Bobby took charge of the atlas and flipped the pages with purpose. "Right there." He pointed to a spot just below San Francisco Bay. "In San Jose, until I was seven."

Gauging the distance between Monterey and San Jose incited a strange prickling at the nape of Cally's neck. Req had mentioned San Jose in connection with Malika's death. "Did you like living there?"

"Yes, but I like it here, too. It's just different. For one thing, I can ride my bike to school and the ballpark here. And my Dad's home lots more and I like that. He's coaching my Little League team in the spring." The grin he shot Cally conveyed the pride of having his father's attention.

"I see. What does being a coach for Little League entail?" While she had no idea what the activity was, she understood the specialness a child experienced when a parent bestowed the gift of his precious time. After her mother's death, Cally's father had kept her close to the point of being ridiculed by his friends. She had loved the attention and absorbed the details of her surroundings like a sponge. Consequently, she had become an accomplished businesswoman. If her father had lived, heaven only knew what marvelous ventures they might have embarked on together.

Bobby gave an in-depth explanation of the responsibilities of a Little League coach and touted his accomplishments of the past baseball season. At the sight of his father approaching the living room, Bobby sighed, then slid the atlas onto Cally's lap. "I have to do a report on how the old sailing ships navigated the ocean. Dad said I can't use the computer this time. Just books."

"Books are gold mines for the mind," Robert said from the doorway.

"That they are," Cally agreed softly. "Do you need this one?" She closed the atlas and offered it to Bobby.

"Maybe. It's got oceans in it."

"All of them," she said, smiling. "The sailing ships depended on the tides, which are governed by the moon. You might look for *The Old Farmer's Almanac* if you're interested in the cycles of the moon in relation to the tides. Tradesmen have relied on it since 1792. If you like, tomorrow we can walk to the library. If they have a sextant, I'll show you how sailors used it with an ephemeris to navigate the open sea."

"Great idea," Robert agreed. "We have a copy of the current *Old Farmer's Almanac* in the family room."

"Farmers knew about tides two hundred years ago?" Bobby's eyes widened. "They wrote it all then?"

Cally laughed, identifying strongly with Bobby's misunderstanding of the authors of the book. She had been making misjudgments about words, people, and events since Req found her.

"I don't know who wrote it originally. What I do know is the basics have remained essentially the same for over two hundred years," Robert said. "The original authors could have calculated the moon and tide cycles for today, had they wanted to." He ruffled Bobby's dark hair. "Without a computer or a calculator."

"I'll bet they woulda had to do multiplication and long division," Bobby said thoughtfully.

"Count on it." Robert rounded the easy chair on Cally's right. "And count on showing me an outline."

"You mean tonight?"

"Sure. The sooner you write it, the sooner you can play your computer game. Bedtime is still nine o'clock."

Cally withdrew from the intimate domestic banter. Of late, she had discovered an introverted aspect of her personality she would never have suspected existed. Regardless of how much she saw on television, how much she gleaned from the newspaper, or how many conversations she and Req had had, the chasm of over a century was too great to breach in so short a time. Less than a month ago, she had been home. In her home, not Req's.

"You seem distressed," Robert said softly as Bobby left the room. "Is there anything we can do to help?"

She gave a quick shake of her head. "I'm afraid I'm feeling somewhat like a fish out of water. You and Judith have been very gracious. I'm just not accustomed to . . ." Her voice withered as she examined her hands. She cleared her throat and tried again. "I find it easier to extend a helping hand than take one."

"What you mean is that it galls the hell out of you to be dumped on strangers, even if they are your family by marriage?"

Startled, Cally shot a glance at Robert. "I don't know if I would put it that way—"

"I would." Robert rose and went to the wet bar. "Drink?"

"Yes, thank you." Although she was not much of a drinker, fortification seemed like a good idea. "Whatever you're having will be fine."

"I'll have the usual." Judith breezed into the room and settled on the opposite side of the couch. A diminutive, feminine version of Req, her sharp green eyes missed nothing. The first hint of gray kissed her dark hair at the temples.

Robert laughed. "The usual? Club soda?"

Judith shrugged her left shoulder and gave Cally an apologetic look. "Let's be sophisticated tonight. Put some Chivas in with the soda. Go heavy on the ice."

Cally waited until she'd taken a stiff swallow of the potent drink Robert had given her. "Ask me what you want to know, Judith, before you burst and I crack from tension."

"Restraint isn't one of Judith's virtues." Robert smiled forgivingly at his wife.

Judith shifted on the couch, tucking her left foot under her. "Forgive me, Cally. It's just that I've grown accustomed to being left out of my baby brother's life. He's kept us at a distance for a long time. I know it's best that way, but that doesn't mean I like it."

"I know," Robert said softly. "Req would never have suggested we leave the Bay Area if he didn't have our interests at heart. He couldn't stop what Malika put into motion, just warn us to stay clear of the fallout. I have a great deal of respect for your brother, Judith. I also think he did us the favor of a life-time by prodding us to move here."

Cally took in the heartfelt emotion Robert didn't try to hide. The silent looks between Judith and Robert said as much as words. It struck Cally that they had a deeper way of communi-cating—like that of her parents. She wanted that in her mar-riage. Her *real* marriage.

Suddenly the irony of her situation seemed absurd. "I'm afraid you'd be amazed at how much I don't know about your brother."

"No, I wouldn't. I doubt he's said much about his job."

"I know next to nothing about what he does. He tells me when he's going somewhere and when he'll be back. I have no right to ask for an explanation."

"Excuse me?" Judith straightened, her finely arched eye-brows rising. Even Robert sat up a bit straighter in his chair. "No right? You're his wife."

She wished she knew what she had said to raise Judith's hackles. "I mean, it's not as though I've earned his confidence or his complete trust."

"He married you," Robert said into his drink glass. "Seems trust is a prerequisite."

"Because he thinks I need to be married to him. I went along because . . ." The reasons would sound cold, callous, and do nothing to assuage the worry she saw in Judith's face. She set-tled for another truth. ". . . because I think he's the most allur-ing man I've ever met."

She took a hard swallow of her drink. The effects of Scotch and embarrassment burned up her neck to her face.

"Alluring?" Judith repeated. "Are we talking about my brother? The long-haired, Harley rider with the tattoos and ear-ring? Now if we were discussing the Requiem Maguire we knew and loved four years ago, I'd agree without hesitation."

Cally feared she had stumbled across another word-usage problem. Req, not alluring?

"Easy, Judith. Cally has only known Req as he is now. He may be emotionally disjointed—we anticipated that—but he's more levelheaded than I expected him to be at this point. It takes a strong personality with convictions of steel to do what he's done. He went into the DEA straight out of college. For seven of those ten years, he led a normal life—until things went downhill with Malika Escobar. After that, everything changed—not just the hair, the tattoos, and the apparent lifestyle—but everything else too. He changed. The other stuff is just camouflage."

"Req doesn't do much without thinking it through." Cally frowned, silently adding, *except pull lost women out of the surf, then take them home and care for them.*

"I can't argue with that," Judith murmured. "At any rate, welcome to the family, Cally. Req must love you a great deal. I didn't think he'd ever risk loving anyone like this again. Frankly, it knocked our socks off when he told us he'd married. He swore he wouldn't as long as he was . . . doing this kind of work."

Cally looked into Judith's tear-glazed eyes and remained silent. She didn't have the heart to tell Judith the truth. Req didn't love her at all. The only reason he'd married her was to make her a wealthy widow. The only reason she'd married him was because she'd have given her last penny to have found someone like him in her own time.

Chapter 11

DARYL RYDELL CLOSED his briefcase. A man who appeared formal whether he wore a black DEA tee shirt and jeans or an Armani suit, Rydell always fit in.

"I can't tell you it isn't a setup, Maguire." He put his briefcase on the floor and glanced at the motel room door. His brisk movement stirred the scent of floral disinfectant lingering in the air.

"If we get Hill on the stand as a friendly witness, we can nail Gutierrez's coffin shut." Rydell finger-combed his short, light-brown hair. "I sure as hell didn't pick the time or place. Hill worked it out with Terragno. I heard the tapes of the phone calls. It really was Hill's idea. He wanted the rendezvous point out of the country. Just not too far out."

Four days of argument hadn't changed anyone's mind.

Four days of cat and mouse with men Req should trust but didn't.

Four days of wondering what Cally was doing, how she was coping with his sister's family, added a dangerous distraction.

Req dropped his feet from the edge of the table and stood. He had a bad feeling about the meeting with Louis Hill. Worse, he didn't know if he could trust it because he had a bad feeling about everything these days. "Let's get it over with. You watch my back, Rydell. Don't let Terragno play cowboy while my ass is hanging out."

"You have my word. He wants to turn Hill so bad his teeth ache. If he could've done it without you, he would've."

A hollow laugh escaped with a cloud of smoke from the cigarette clamped between Req's teeth. "Yeah. I'll bet. But going fishing with your only barracuda in order to catch a shark isn't my idea of brilliant tactics." *Especially since I'm the shark bait.*

"I hear you." Rydell parted the window drapes slightly, then scanned the parking lot before he opened the door. "Just make sure I hear you and Hill when I'm in the surveillance van."

"You don't think I'd risk my ass for this if you weren't going to cover for me, do you?" Req punched his fist into the sleeve of his black leather jacket. "Let's get this over with."

The bite of an autumn storm laced the erratic wind buffeting the scenic British Columbia town. A few miles southeast, the Peace Arch straddled the U.S.-Canadian border.

Splashed against the steep granite hillsides like an architectural tidal wave, street upon street of well-kept houses rose behind the businesses facing the moody Pacific Ocean. Lush trees and a profusion of countless flowers and shrubs softened the sturdiness of the shops and homes. The seaside community imparted the kinship of a loner marching to a drummer no one else heard.

It was a lousy meeting site. The steep hillsides anchored with tall trees, big-windowed houses, and layers of shrubbery rose like giant stair steps. The terrain offered a million places for someone to hide.

Terragno had no jurisdiction in Canada, which suited Req fine. The border town was also the only neutral ground Terragno and Hill could agree on for the meeting.

It was time.

Req adjusted the wire and equipment taped to his body, flipped off the safety of the weapon in his shoulder holster, then opened the car door. Gutierrez's money launderer wouldn't wait around.

Req strolled the elevated esplanade perched over the tiered seawall. On the lower level, a set of train tracks followed the shoreline. Across the water, a small Washington community hugged the end of a land spit that served as a lookout guarding the mouth of Drayton Harbor.

Parked on the narrow, shop-lined street behind Req, a white delivery van sat in front of an outdoor restaurant. Inside the van, three men monitored surveillance equipment fed by the microphone Req carried.

Waiting for Louis Hill, Req thought about this meeting. He considered it the equivalent of lighting a match to see how much combustible fuel was in the gas tank. Although it could blow up in his face, part of him had to know why Hill was willing to risk so damn much to talk to him. The skeptic in him prepared for an explosion. One thing he didn't question was his reluctance to confront anyone or anything from his underground life until he entered the courtroom to testify. That couldn't happen soon enough.

When he stripped away the excuses and rationalizations, he was a cop. As such, he'd meet with Hill regardless of the danger. The opportunity of turning Gutierrez's money-laundering man into a key witness was too damn good to miss.

When Louis Hill finally showed up, Req noted how quickly worry had aged him. Character lines that had been faint tear tracks down the hollows of his tanned cheeks two months ago were now deeply plowed furrows.

Besides the telltale stress riding Louis's face like a botched acne treatment, his custom-tailored clothing hung on his tall, lanky frame. The change went beyond weight loss. Louis, the man who could out-stare Satan, now seldom let his gaze rest in one place for long. His vigilance was characteristic of a man in need of eyes in the back of his head; a man who wasn't sure another breath would follow the one he'd just exhaled.

Every conversation he'd had with Louis had begun the same way it did now. This time it was Req's turn. He offered Louis a cigarette, then lit them both and inhaled deeply, taking his time, stretching the moment when body language shouted warnings in the silence. From behind mirrored sunglasses, he watched the street, the cars, the pedestrians, and the coffee sippers chatting at picnic tables and benches on the greenbelt. The landscaped hillsides hosted what felt like a thousand eyes watching from shadows, trees, and windows and made Req's skin crawl. He hadn't felt this exposed since he and Jeannie McCann had gotten caught having sex in the high school chemistry lab.

"You screwed me, Maguire. And yourself."

Req leaned his back against the guardrails protecting the pedestrians on the elevated walkway from the railroad tracks below. He pretended to examine his cigarette. In winning the lucrative job as Gutierrez's laundryman, Louis Hill had screwed himself. If Louis was lucky, he'd meet his end as swiftly as his predecessor had when he'd lost a run-in with an eighteen-wheeler on I-10. "Is that what this is about? Who screwed whom?"

"How long you think the feds'll keep you safe?"

Req exhaled smoke into the wind. "Long enough to testify."

"Not a snowball's chance in hell of that. There's a contract on you."

"Tell me something I don't know, Louis, like why the hell it was so important to meet with me."

"Unplug your wire first. This is between you and me."

Req shrugged. "Not about you airing Gutierrez's laundry list?"

"Unplug it, or I walk." Hill continued staring across the water. He took another deep drag from his cigarette before flicking it onto the railroad tracks. "You want to hear what I have to say, Maguire?"

He glanced past an elderly couple arguing about her snoring. Hell, he could feel the tension collecting inside the van. He'd done it by the book and worn the damn wire knowing Hill wouldn't say anything that went on record.

Terragno had insisted on the microphone and fancy surveillance rig, so in the end Req obliged. Now, he'd play the situation as it unfolded. Let Hill call the shots. For now.

"What the hell. I've gone out on a limb by meeting with you." Eyeing a slow-moving Mercedes with Alberta plates, he asked, "Friends of yours in the gold Mercedes?"

He unfastened the microphone feeding the surveillance van.

The Mercedes was Rydell's problem now. If Req was wrong, he and Louis Hill wouldn't leave the walkway.

Hill glanced over his shoulder at the car. Fear flickered in his eyes; his actions appeared nonchalant. "Like you, I have no friends. Only enemies. Difference is, I know it." He reached inside his jacket for another cigarette. "I came alone, as promised."

Req dropped the microphone into Hill's open palm. "I suspect everyone."

"I thought you were smarter than to turn on Gutierrez and think you'd survive—even with the feds baby-sitting."

"Yeah, well, damn few people are as smart or as dumb as others think. Let's cut to the chase. Say what you want to say, Hill."

Hill stared at the horizon for a moment. "I'm here because I owe you one for the Aruba fiasco."

"You don't owe me shit. And I don't owe you, either."

"If I'd known you were going to set me up the way you have, then walk, I'd have taken the bullet in Aruba instead of you. Right now, I wished it had killed you, Maguire." He spat over the railing. The stream of spit arced down to the railroad tracks. "I'm holding the bag and waiting for things to explode."

Req snorted. "The laundryman is holding the bag. Life is filled with irony, isn't it?" He had little doubt Hill would like to give him a couple of lead tokens of sentiment.

"You disappointed me, Maguire. Frankly, I haven't figured out whether you're smart enough to have set me up to take the fall for you running out with half the records. Or was it dumb luck?"

"Dumb luck." And good planning. A smart man would have found a way to save Paul Sandavol.

"If I can't convince Gutierrez I had nothing to do with you getting those files, he'll kill me and my family." Hill spoke so softly the breeze broke up his words. "Time's running out."

"You must be talking fast and smooth. You're still breathing. If he doubts you, he'll take you out. Eventually. Once he's cajoled or tortured you for every secret you ever knew." Req studied the slow, winding traffic, watching for repeats. "The way I see it, you have three ways to go. Let Gutierrez kill you and your family. Or go into the Witness Protection Program and testify."

"And look over my shoulder for the rest of my life? Sweat bullets every time my wife or kid is late coming home—"

"At least you'll be breathing," Req growled. "So will they."

"What's the third option?" Hill asked after a moment.

"Light out on your own. Tell Gutierrez what he wants to know, then tell 'em all to go to hell and light out. Take your family to a movie one night and don't go back for anything. Not even the BMW you leave in the parking lot. Disappear. You've got your numbered Swiss accounts. That money won't do you any good if you're dead, will it?" He watched Hill from the corner of his eye. The guy was thinking about it. He didn't have the balls to do it. Too bad for his family.

"Why haven't you taken the invisible road if it's such a damn good idea?"

"No need. There's just me."

"And your wife," Hill whispered.

Every nerve in Req's body stilled. If Hill knew, Gutierrez knew. If Gutierrez knew—shit!

Req stared through the two middle-aged race walkers passing on the sidewalk.

"You hear me, Maguire?"

"I heard you."

"Killing you would get me back into Gutierrez's good graces." Hill spat on the ground. "He wants you dead, Maguire."

"Tell me something I don't know."

"He wants you to suffer. He'll get your wife—if he doesn't have her already. Then he'll come for you."

"He'll try," Req agreed. Damn, he needed to get the hell out of here and back to Cally.

"You think the feds'll keep her alive? Think she'll like Witness Protection? Having no friends? Never seeing her family again? Teaching your kids to be afraid of everyone? Sounds like fuckin' utopia, doesn't it?"

His gut tightened with the realization of how severely he had endangered Cally by marrying her. He wanted to run for his car and head south. Until he saw her, touched her, he wouldn't sleep, wouldn't be rid of the molten fear snipping at his veins.

"You seem to think I'm like you, Louis. I'm not. Never was. Paul Sandavol and I were partners." He couldn't save Paul from Gutierrez. He could live with that. Not easily, but he could do it. Cally was an innocent in all of this. Just another casualty of the drug wars. "Your boss better check his information. I'm not the marrying kind."

Hill drew a sharp breath and turned. "I know you're not like me. You're a damn fed."

"I'm whatever it takes." Req turned until he looked directly at Hill. "From the beginning I've had only one purpose, bringing Gutierrez down. After he killed Sandavol, I made damn sure I'd be able to kick him all the way to hell and back. I did what I had to do, and I've never cared who got in the way."

"You'll never make it to the courtroom, Maguire."

"I've got enough pieces for the Legal Eagles to build a case even if he gets me before the trial." He turned away. "I may be an S.O.B., but I'm thorough. He's going down. So are those around him. You better make your move damn quick."

"I've got time. They haven't arrested him yet." Hill spat over the railing again.

Req checked his watch and calculated the three-hour time difference from the East Coast. "The shit has already hit the fan. They arrested Gutierrez about forty minutes ago. And except for you, his chiefs are in custody by now, too. So, how's it going to look? They're arrested while you're taking in the sights of the Canadian resort town during the off-season? Think they'll finger you, Louis?"

Hill paled and fumbled for another cigarette. "You're bluffing."

"I'm way past the bluffing stage."

"That bastard Terragno set me up for this, didn't he?"

Req remained silent. He knew too well how it felt to be caught in one of Terragno's squeezes. The trouble was, somebody usually died.

The day wasn't over yet.

A gaggle of laughing teenage girls on rollerblades bustled past them on the walkway.

"Shit." The cigarette shook between Hill's thin, colorless lips. Even cupping his hand around the lighter flame couldn't keep it from jumping with a sudden case of nerves. He turned his back on the ocean and faced the street to shield his cigarette from the wind.

"Look at it this way. You're still breathing." A movement at the surveillance van caught Req's attention. The driver's door opened. He saw Terragno lean out.

"Sonuvabitch." Hill dropped his cigarette and lighter. Blue eyes round with shock stared at a neat, round hole in his chest, then lifted toward the hillside layered with trees, homes, and a thousand hiding places for telescopic eyes trained on them.

Req grabbed for Hill out of reflex. Suddenly he was balancing almost two hundred pounds of collapsing weight. Before he could shout for help, an explosion rocked the street.

Pieces of the surveillance van flew in all directions.

Hill's left hand gripped Req's wrist in a death grip. "Gutierrez," he rasped.

"Yeah." Req pulled out his weapon and visually scoured their surroundings.

"Envelope. Inside pocket."

Pandemonium swarmed, hiding them from the sniper on the hillside. Eye-stinging smoke mingled with the screams of innocent victims. The gaggle of teenagers half a block down screeched in panic.

Watching the hillside through the chaos seizing the streets, Req reached inside Hill's coat and found the envelope. Blood-stained white parchment protected a computer disk. He slipped it into his pocket.

"Where's your family?" Req hissed.

"Safe . . ." Hill's contorted features began to relax as though the pain had stopped. "Leaks."

Hell, nothing and no one was safe. "Where's your family?"

Surprise opened Louis Hill's eyes so wide Req thought they'd pop out of their sockets. A long exhale collapsed his chest. The black pupils bloomed wide in Hill's lifeless, blue eyes.

Confusion gripped the narrow street. The stench of burning rubber swirled in the black smoke.

Req swore under his breath and closed Hill's sightless eyes. He rose and started for the smoldering van. People jostled him and each other on the sidewalk. With every heartbeat, he felt more like a target. Maybe he hadn't been the primary target— this time. Damned if he knew why, unless Gutierrez had something very special in store for him. *Cally.*

The intense heat shimmering from the blazing van thinned the crowd. The bitter stench of the thick, black smoke permeated his senses with the finality of death.

The arguments with Terragno were over. What remained of his body continued to burn beside the van.

And Rydell . . . Shit! Rydell.

A painful need to get back to Cally made him want to run. Disciplined, he turned away from the van. His car was on a side street a block away.

Cally. He holstered his weapon and started running.

Before he'd taken a dozen steps, what felt like a freight train slammed into the center of his chest and sent him flying backward. His last thoughts were of his wife.

Cally and Bobby spent the afternoon in the history section of the library. What the two of them had learned about the moon, tides, and navigation with a sextant and ephemeris opened new doors for both of them.

Lost in a realm of silent speculation, Cally jotted down times, tides, and figures while Bobby wrote his report.

It was possible she had found the answer she needed for returning home—well, as possible as anything like being washed through time could be.

The only way to know for sure was to try it. She had nothing to lose—except Req. Her heart plunged each time she reminded herself that he was of this time and place. He wouldn't give that up. Even if he was so inclined, duty kept him here. She had discovered a fiercely loyal aspect of his personality. Had their marriage been real, she would have treasured such a priceless trait in a husband.

"Have you two bookworms just about finished?" Judith

smiled across the library table strewn with open books, notes, and notebook paper. "Or should I go grocery shopping and come back in say," she glanced at her watch, "forty-five minutes?"

Cally looked at Bobby's report. "We're almost done."

"Wow, Mom, you can't believe how much she knows about the tides and the stars and navigating the sea." Bobby's face brightened with excitement. "And she knows things about shipwrecks that aren't even in the books."

Judith started to say something, then paused and looked around. "Looks like I'll be grocery shopping alone. Pick you up out front?"

"We'll be ready, Mom." Bobby grinned, then got back to his report.

Cally finished the time and tide matrix she had spent most of the afternoon making. Anything that felt so right had to hold a grain of truth. Even impossible truth.

Not once did she doubt her hypothesis. Doubt was a mind-killer. Long ago she had recognized it as an enemy that traveled with a companion named Fear. Her resolute determination allowed no quarter for either.

For Cally, it was a simple matter of getting home—where she belonged, where people depended on her. Once there, she would deal with explaining her absence and unmasking the men responsible for killing her father and Freddy the Thief.

Preoccupied with what lay ahead, she barely spoke on the way home. Bobby's glowing appraisal of her navigational talents filled the void.

Still contemplating how the time portal might work with the new information she had gleaned from the library, she cleared the dinner dishes.

Five days and no word from Req. He had better hurry back. She had a schedule that nothing short of death would stop her from keeping. The idea of leaving without seeing him again wielded a double-edged sword.

Not saying good-bye or thanking him for his hospitality was akin to sneaking out of a hotel room in the middle of the night. Cally always paid her debts. On the other hand, the man was incredibly enticing. Holding a decent thought in his presence was becoming increasingly difficult. Keeping her composure and adhering to a decorum this society had abandoned was becoming more of a challenge in itself.

"I'll do it the right way," she murmured to herself as she closed the dishwasher.

"Sweet God in heaven." The horror in Judith's voice brought Cally around. Judith stood beside the counter, her gaze glued to the small television set on the counter. Trembling fingers pressed against her lips and chin.

"What is it?" Concern brought Cally closer. When Judith didn't answer, she watched the screen. Fiery carnage littered a narrow street beside a walkway along the ocean. Thick, black smoke billowed from a ruined mass that may have been a vehicle.

". . . of the mayhem that broke loose on this small coastal town in British Columbia earlier today. This afternoon, a source close to the investigation claims allies of alleged drug czar Gustavo Gutierrez are responsible for the deaths of the four U.S. federal agents and two civilians. Gutierrez was arrested in Miami, Florida . . ."

The name rattled through Cally's brain. She knew the name *Gutierrez.* In the final days before leaving her with Judith, Req had hammered a set of dictatorial instructions into her brain.

"It isn't Req," Cally whispered. Whether this was denial or natural optimism, she neither knew nor cared.

"I pray you're right," Judith said, her voice tight as tears beaded on her lower eyelids. "Don't mention this to Bobby for now. Robert and I will deal with it when we're sure."

"I don't understand."

"Bobby has no idea what Req does. He thinks his uncle works at a wastewater purification plant." Judith sniffed and let the hint of a smile leak through her worry. "It didn't seem the kind of job a boy would feel compelled to brag to his friends about."

"You mean a sewage director?" Cally asked.

A tremulous twitch caught the corner of Judith's mouth. She pulled Cally into a sisterly hug. "I can see why he fell for you. You have a bright, unusual way of assessing things."

Cally returned the affection, but watched the small screen over Judith's shoulder.

"The following video was shot by a tourist . . ."

The words faded into the buzzing growing louder and louder in Cally's head. The camera panned a man lying spread-eagle on the ground. His black leather jacket gaped to reveal a black tee shirt with the message "Bite Me" in blood red across the chest.

Cally held Judith tighter, preventing her from seeing the horror of her brother lying in a Canadian street.

•   •   •

In the small hours of the morning, Cally was still trembling. Staring at the dark ceiling of the Starkeys' guest room, she saw Req lying on a Canadian sidewalk. Motionless. Defenseless.

Her brain refused the obvious conclusion.

Req wasn't dead. He couldn't be. He was too cautious.

But what if he *was* dead?

She groaned and flopped onto her stomach. The painful thought sent tears flowing onto the pillow.

It was one thing to leave him alive and in his own element when she returned to 1890. It was quite another to know he would never draw another breath.

Life just wasn't that unfair. Was it?

Of course it was.

The only logical path was discovering the fate of Requiem Maguire. Her husband.

The tears flowed faster as she realized he had anticipated the possibility—no, probability—of violence. Again, she considered the enormity of his measures to ensure that she was provided for, protected. Pampered.

Curling onto her side, she rejected his money and his property. She didn't want them.

She wanted him alive, surly as a dockhand, and looking at her as if he'd just returned from a year-long whaling stint.

When she found him again, she would yield to the desire she had restrained out of propriety. Here and now, she was a married woman.

Or a widow.

No. Not a widow. It wasn't Req sprawled on the sidewalk. Please, God . . .

Sniffing, she straightened her legs. Worrying, crying, railing against the injustice of the universe wasn't going to change anything. She had to keep a level head. Be practical.

She forced the direction of her thoughts to the present.

A prickling at the nape of her neck destroyed the semblance of calm she'd mustered. Sensing something was terribly wrong, she lay motionless amid the tangled sheets. Barely breathing, she listened with keen awareness.

The noise in the far corner was small, but the terror that shot through her felt as big as California.

Someone was in her room.

Before she could scream, a hand clamped over her mouth.

Chapter 12

CALLY'S HEART BEAT in her throat hard enough to choke her. The stealth of her attacker had caught her off guard.

The realization of being snared so easily robbed the starch from her backbone.

She went limp in feigned submission, and the man relaxed his grip slightly.

Cally slammed her right elbow into his abdomen with all her might. Her attacker let go and doubled over. She tried to bolt from the bed.

"Damn it, Cally."

She twisted, not yet free of the bedclothes. "Req?"

She fumbled for the light on the nightstand, then caught his bowed head in her hands. Delirious over his presence, not quite believing he was really here, she turned his face to the lamp.

Shadows accentuated the stark hollows of his face. Gazing into his dark, glittering eyes, relief swamped her senses. "Oh, God. It *is* you. You're alright. Thank God." Her fingers flexed against his warm flesh in reassurance. The prickly stubble of his whiskers against her palm had never felt so good. The horrendous weight that had settled on her heart melted immediately.

"Quiet. You'll wake the whole house. And let go of my head." He straightened slowly, then rolled onto his back.

She crouched beside him and a sweet, pervasive joy sang in every nerve in her being. "I knew you couldn't be dead. I refused to believe—"

Req's fingertips trembled against her mouth. "Shut the hell up, Cally," he said in a raspy voice.

She drew a quick breath to launch into the multitude of questions rushing through her brain. Before she got the first one out, he pulled her down and rolled on top of her. His weight pinned her amid the bedclothes and his mouth replaced his fingers on her lips. The effective weapon of his tongue silenced her.

She held him. The heat of desire blossomed between them. The sudden tightening of his arms around her sent a thousand pinpricks of need along the contact points of their bodies.

As unexpectedly as the kiss started, then ensnared her in a dazzling array of sensory bliss, he broke it. She gasped in dismay. The sudden harshness of his embrace fed the waves of relief that he was alive. Having him in her arms, breathing into her hair as though he'd run a race, felt so good, so reassuring. Only this kind of physical reassurance softened the image of him lying as still as death on a chaotic Canadian street. She slipped her hand inside his jacket.

"On the television, you looked . . . dead. You—"

"Shh. I'm okay," he crooned into her hair.

Her fingers stumbled over the constriction of a bandage wrapping his ribs and chest under his thin tee shirt. "No, you're not."

"I will be if you don't argue with me. We have to leave, without waking Bobby and the sooner, the better."

"Judith and Robert—"

"I've already spoken with them." The slow movement of his open hand along the side of her breast, into the dip of her waist, and over her hips softened his voice. "She's making coffee for the road. Get dressed."

She preferred to remain where she was with him stroking little fires into flames on her skin. Being touched, touching him, became a balm of reassurance. He was alive and well. She'd never seen a more welcome sight in her life.

"Thank God you're here," she whispered, then kissed his jaw below his earring. "I thought I would have to go find you."

He laid a trail of leisurely, thorough kisses along her neck to her collarbone. "Only an airhead would ignore my instructions to stay put." His arms tightened around her with a possessive ferocity. "Much as I hate to let you go, you need to get dressed." He released her and rolled onto his back, then carefully sat on the edge of the bed.

Reluctant to let him go, yet resigned that she must, she untangled the bedclothes twisted around her legs. She'd rather be undressing him. She eyed the way he absently rubbed his chest and knew he was hurting. "Perhaps I should meet you in the kitchen."

Req went to the closet and pulled out the gym bag they had packed her few belongings in when they'd left Monterey. "I'll pack for you."

Sensing his urgency to be on their way, Cally kept her back to Req and gathered her clothes. With a glance over her shoulder, she ducked into the adjoining bathroom. Elated Req was here, she dressed quickly in denims, a pink jersey, and a maroon sweatshirt.

Moments after making her good-byes to Judith and Robert, she sat in the car as Req drove along the quiet suburban lanes. The dark houses lurked beyond manicured lawns and shaded trees that stood like giants ready to defend the inhabitants. They soon gave way to quiet shopping strips, then a ribbon of road that never slept, I–80.

The tense silence rolling off Req and thickening with each mile tempered the elation of her relief. Req was a long way from being all right.

"How badly are you injured?" The question tumbled into the darkness with a life of its own. *Please tell me it isn't serious.*

Req stared ahead without answering.

Cally couldn't pry her gaze from him. Experience had taught her that he would talk when he was ready and not a moment sooner. That wasn't good enough this time. Obviously he wasn't as glad to see her as she was to see him. The only reason he had kissed her was to silence the excitement that bubbled through her when she realized he had returned. Never mind that he had frightened her half to death by creeping into her room.

"Get some rest. We have a long drive ahead of us."

"Is that your way of telling me what happened to you should be of no concern to me?"

"What happened, happened. Period. I'll take care of things."

Cally drew a long breath then let it out slowly. The minute-by-minute battle pitting her desire for comprehension against the restraint of decorum continued unabated. "Being in this car with you dispels any doubts I might have entertained about your ability to survive. That wasn't my question." She started to reach for him, then dropped her hand into her lap. "How badly are you hurt, Req? Were you shot? Are you in need of medical assistance? Do your bandages require regular changing? Tell me. Please."

"I'm sore. The elastic bandage minimizes the aches."

"How did you get hurt?"

"Someone fired a couple of shots. One hit me."

"My God. You *were* shot." She wanted to shout at him to stop the car and lie down. The man had no regard for his own well-being.

"I wore a vest under my shirt."

Exasperation screamed in her head. "What difference does it make what you were wearing?"

"The difference between sitting here and laying on a slab in a Vancouver morgue. It was a Kevlar vest."

Cally rubbed her temples. Calvin Klein she knew. Kevlar she didn't. And what difference could it make?

"The vest stops most bullets," Req explained. "The momentum of the impact is dispersed, but the hit still carries a helluva punch." The hard look he gave her sent a ripple of gooseflesh over her arms. "My heart stopped for a few seconds."

"Oh, my God," Cally breathed. He had looked dead on the television.

"When I came to, a guy was leaning over me doing CPR." He glanced at her. "He was compressing my chest to start my heart."

"Thank God you're alright."

"We'll stay that way as long as we disappear without a trace. I had planned on leaving you with my sister—"

"And wisely changed your mind," she finished.

"As far as the rest of the world is concerned, I'm an orphan. I never wanted Judith or her family in jeopardy. Their cover is intact. But we have other problems. Gutierrez knows we got married. He's looking for you."

"Me? Why?"

"He probably figures if I married you, they can get to me through you."

"They'd be wrong," she murmured, finally looking away. She was a responsibility he'd taken on and provided for much the same way he might take in a stray animal. He didn't love her. He didn't even want her enough to have a real wedding night.

Req crushed his cigarette in the ashtray. "That's part of the problem."

"At least it has a solution." She'd solve both their problems. She hadn't planned on revealing the fruits of her research until he had slept for a while. She had wanted him clearheaded when she told him how she intended to go home.

"Yeah. Dig a hole, crawl in, and pull it in after you until the firestorm passes."

"I must be in Monterey in three days."

"We're not going anywhere near Monterey for at least six months, maybe longer."

"Speak for yourself. Even if I have to ride a bicycle, I'll be there." Her mind said she didn't need him; her aching heart pleaded that she did. Her mind espoused the wisdom of parting in the morning; her heart never wanted to let go. Sitting within touching distance, she wanted to stroke him, to reassure herself that he was here and breathing. God, she still wanted to kiss and touch him, to feel his warm, hard body against her.

"I'll make sure Potter gets his treasures back."

"I'm sure you will. Mr. Potter has nothing to do with my reasons for needing to be at the beach where you found me."

"What's so damn important there in three days? You got a bus to catch?"

She reached over and touched his arm. "You could put it that way. In three days, all the conditions will be right for me to leave this time. I'm going home, Req. I must."

Req leaned his left elbow on the windowsill and rubbed his temple with his fingertips. He felt like he'd lived a century since the last time that he and Cally had had one of these conversations with the topic mired in quicksand. He wasn't up to it. Hell, the way his chest hurt, he wasn't up to much beyond taking his next breath.

"How about we explore that bit of sensationalism after we're clear of Sacramento." He no longer knew what to believe in respect to Caladonia Hornsby. Cally Maguire, he corrected mentally. Some days, accepting that she came from another time was the only plausible explanation.

Right now, the only truth he knew was the pain in his chest. It seemed to worsen when she spoke of leaving him.

"It matters little to me when or even if we discuss it, Req. If you will not help me get to Monterey, I ask that you not try to stop me. I fear such an action would create ill feeling between us."

"Yeah. Sure. Sure." She didn't have a clue as to how much danger they were in or just how bad it could get if Gutierrez's men caught up with them. Just as well.

She didn't need to know how bad it could get. *Ill feeling* was the least of his concerns.

Christ, he felt like an olive in a press and oil was selling for a hundred bucks a bottle.

Heading south on I-5, he turned on the radio and scanned the news stations for any mention of yesterday's deaths in the Canadian border town.

When fatigue turned his eyelids to lead, he pulled into a truck stop and found a secluded space between two eighteen-wheelers. "Let's catch a few winks, Cally. I'm beat. Pull the lever on the side of your seat. It'll will go all the way back so you can sleep."

Cally put her seat into a full recline as Req had instructed, folded her arms beneath her breasts, then closed her eyes. "Good night."

He'd hurt her, but didn't know when or how. He was too tired to soothe her ruffled feelings. Instead, he touched her cheek with the back of his fingers. "Good night."

He crossed his arms over his aching chest and let himself sink into a light sleep.

"Req?" she said after several minutes.

"What?" He opened a weary eye and looked at her shadowy image.

"Thank you for not dying." She turned her face away from him.

"My pleasure." He wouldn't dare leave Cally Maguire a widow before they made love. Which they would do soon.

Just before sleep crashed on him, he wondered how she planned to hop a train through time. Worse, how was she going to handle the disappointment when it didn't go anywhere?

But tonight was one of those times he believed in time travel. At the moment, it sounded like a helluva good escape fantasy. Just him and Cally . . .

They approached Stockton at sunrise. Cally resumed pouring over Mr. Potter's borrowed treasures. She had memorized Penelope's journal, then scrutinized each word, seeking a nuance that might have escaped previous readings.

The lonely old man's artifacts were more precious than he would ever suspect. For her quest, their content proved invaluable. The fresh insight the journals, papers, and ledgers shed on the people Cally knew was priceless.

An hour after returning to the freeway, an accident kept them parked with their fellow travelers for nearly two hours. The delay with a nearly empty coffee cup did nothing to improve Req's mood.

Req hadn't said more than a few words beyond asking whether Cally wanted coffee or needed to visit an upcoming rest stop. He confined his activity to driving and changing radio stations. She hoped that whatever grated on his nerves would wear itself out soon, then he would say what was on his mind. His unapproachable mood was a mixed blessing she wasn't sure she was thankful for. Sometime between the time he'd kissed her in the small hours of the morning and now, she'd come to a resolution.

Shortly after noon they reached the coast. Req stopped at a restaurant claiming to be someone's mother's kitchen. By then, Cally had finished reviewing her notes on Mr. Potter's collection.

"Let's eat." Req parked the car.

She waited for him to open the door for her, then took his hand and got out. Fatigue that reached far beyond physical showed in the depths of his green eyes.

"I'm sorry," she murmured.

"What the hell for?" He flipped the car door shut, then activated the automated locks and alarm. A quick gesture indicated the entrance to the restaurant.

"I don't know how to drive."

"Even if you did, I don't think I could stand you speeding down the freeway at twenty miles an hour."

It still seemed an excessive speed. The seventy miles an hour he drove had an ethereal unreality from which she had learned to disassociate her thoughts.

"We're not going another mile until you convince me," Req said after ordering breakfast.

"Convince you? Of what?" She felt like she had walked in on someone else's conversation.

"Monterey. Why it's so damn important for you to be there in a few days."

Across the smooth table, the horror that had ensnared him on the Canadian street haunted his gaze. "So I can go home."

He said nothing while the waitress delivered steaming mugs of coffee; just continued looking at her. The maelstrom of conflict raging inside of him showed in the dark circles beneath his eyes. He looked like he had lived through one war only to face another. Fiery red traces lingered in the bloodshot white of his eyes. The only comforting sensation at the table was the aroma of fresh coffee.

"Cally, four men died the other day. Three more people, innocent bystanders, not players in our meeting, are in the hospital with serious injuries. A dozen more will be nursing wounds for weeks. The men who did this will soon discover I'm not dead. One of the first places they'll look is Monterey."

"Why would they look for you there? I thought—"

"There was a leak. There had to be. Only a handful of people knew I was meeting with Hill. It would be foolish to think the agents Terragno had hunting me didn't file a report mentioning us in Monterey. It would be on the record. That means computerized. And that means a good hacker on the inside can find it." He cradled his coffee mug in both hands. "He *will* find it. Understand?"

Dishes clattered to Cally's left as though emphasizing her ignorance of the vast reaches of technology. The laughter of a young man in cutoff denims at the counter seemed too cheerful for their circumstances. Cally reached across the table and caught Req's left hand in both of hers. "Then you shouldn't go there. Ever. I'll go alone. It isn't that much further, is it? You can tell me how to—"

"You'll go to Monterey alone when hell freezes over." His hard scowl denied the possibility of negotiation.

"Considering the amount of frost already present, it shouldn't take me more than a day to get there," she answered evenly. "I have responsibilities. Duties. People who depend on me. I owe it to them to go home. What kind of a person would I be if I walked away from them, left their livelihoods in peril, their families in jeopardy, if I did not at least attempt to fulfill my obligations?"

"Damn it, Cally."

"I'm not asking you to go with me, Req, though from what I understand of the circumstances we're in, it might be a good idea. You won't have any of the conveniences or the technology you rely on, but you would have your life. No one would be trying to kill you there." *You'd be safe. With me. You might even learn to love me.*

The laugh that escaped Req held little mirth. "And who would make sure Gutierrez was put away for good? Who would make him pay for Malika? Sandavol? Rydell? Or Terragno and the rest of them?" He squeezed her hands, then withdrew his. "I know all about duty and being on the side of right. I also know the reality and power of the other side, Cally. Don't confuse hiding until the time is right with running away. I don't run."

The waitress's friendly smile accompanied the steaming plates of food she arranged on the table.

Their silent truce became a stretched rubber band ready to snap during the meal. The food settled like rocks in Cally's stomach. She had counted on Req understanding why she had to return, had even expected he would be glad to help her. Once she went through the time portal—she was sure it was there, it had to be—his life would revert to the way it was before she'd interrupted his solitude.

She stole glimpses of the man who had married her because he thought she needed his protection. Here and now, he was her husband. In a few days, God willing, he would be part of a memory she would share with no one. That memory would be both a balm and an open wound for the rest of her life. Once she left, she'd never see him again. That realization crashed through her emotions with the force of a typhoon ripping through a sand castle. The winds of its devastation scoured her soul, then eased, leaving the crushing ache of loss in its wake.

Briefly she met Req's questioning gaze, then looked down at her half-filled plate. They were still together—for now. Through their separate misery, the incessant pressure she had come to recognize as relentless, unfulfilled desire killed her appetite.

"Perhaps if I explain what I've hypothesized, you might be convinced of how imperative it is that I be at the beach where you found me in a few days." She arranged her utensils on the edge of the plate. Not trusting herself to refrain from touching Req, she folded her hands in her lap. Sorrow that he would soon be forever out of her reach stabbed her heart.

"Feel free to give it a try."

"Will you listen with an open mind?" *Will you come with me where these awful people can't reach you?*

He pushed his plate away and reached for his coffee. "Do I look like a man with a closed mind?"

Closed as tight as a full barrel of whale oil, she decided. "I believe there is a flaw in nature." *It's there. It has to be. How else would I have gotten here? Find it with me.*

His only reaction was a long blink.

"The flaw is well hidden and may or may not be permanent." She wished she had the notes she'd left in the car. Perhaps he would grasp what she wanted him to understand if she couched it in mathematical logic. "There is an old adage about time and tides. Throughout history healers found their decoctions more effective and death a kinder master during ebb tides or flood tides." Perhaps it affected an aching heart. She would know soon enough.

"That's the same hype as there being more babies born during a full moon."

"There are," she assured him. "Ask any midwife."

"I'm not seeing the connection between birthrates and time jumping."

"It has to do with syzygy." A flicker of the excitement she had experienced when piecing together the circumstances of a trip through time momentarily dimmed her growing sense of isolation.

"With what?"

"Syzygy is a time when the sun and the moon line up on the same side of the earth. It occurs twice a month. Once during a new moon, the other during a full moon. The effect on the tide is noticeable even during unsettled weather." It was remarkably similar to the effect Req had on her; and like the tide, it was forever.

"Go on." He folded his arms on the edge of the table with apparent interest.

"Syzygy intensifies the tidal shifts. So when a low spring tide occurs during syzygy, the tide is lower. At high tide—"

"The tide is higher. Got it. But it isn't spring, Cally. It's damn near winter."

Patience, she admonished. His moods were like those of the tides. Could there be anything more powerful, glorious, or devastatingly beautiful than the storm of his passion? The deep ache in her lower abdomen promised to embrace such long-awaited turbulence. "Spring tide has nothing to do with the seasons. It's from a German word meaning to 'leap up,' I believe. In the case of a very low tide, think of it as leaping away." Each word she spoke etched the painful finality of leaving him deeper into her raw soul.

"I did some calculations and discovered the precise tide cycle for when I . . . left home and came here. Low spring tide during syzygy, Req." The discovery still excited her, but the ramifications became clearer with each facet of her explanation. "Whatever anomaly exists in the pool is accessible then. If it goes one way, it must go the other."

"What makes you think the door goes both ways?"

"Why, the laws of nature." *And your nature keeps you here, on the edge of death, upholding your laws and duty.*

His jaw tightened. He stared at her until she grew uncomfortable and began to squirm under his intense gaze.

"Exactly which laws of nature cover this particular phenomenon?"

"You've only to look around you, Req. The tide goes out. The tide comes in. If you throw a rock straight up into the air it comes down in the same place. The earth turns every day, and turns around the sun so the seasons arrive at the same time every—"

"You know just enough science to be dangerous." He pushed out of the booth, dug into his pocket, and came out with payment and a healthy tip for the meal. "Show me hard data—calculations."

"You believe me?" Barely able to accept that she had won him over so easily, she slid out of the booth. Her breath caught in her throat when she met his eyes and saw the skepticism melt into something she didn't recognize.

"How long before all this is supposed to happen?"

"Not quite three days." *Then I'll never look into your dangerous green eyes, never touch—*

"Okay."

"Okay, what?" she asked, jolted from the litany of loss running through her mind.

"Okay, we'll go home. No matter what happens, four days from now neither one of us is going to be in Monterey. Got it?"

She did, and hardly knew what to say. He didn't believe her, at least not that she had found a way back, but he was going to help her. Again. No wonder she loved him.

Chapter 13

ARLY-EVENING FOG thickened the night air. Req keyed the gates guarding the estate driveway. After garaging the car, he checked the grounds, then double-checked the security. Returning to the estate was dangerous. With a little luck he had another day before Gutierrez's henchmen realized they hadn't killed him in Canada. Besides, he needed to gather his resources and do some planning before he and Cally disappeared.

And they had to keep Cally's appointment with time and the tide. She seemed so damned convinced that he didn't have the heart to dash her hopes with logic or flat-out refuse to give her a shot at her latest dream.

Something about Caladonia Hornsby Maguire wouldn't let him say no. He'd said no to money, authority, and serious intimidation in the forms of Gutierrez, Terragno, and most recently, the Justice Department, the latter whose protection he didn't want. The last refusal had turned ugly, loud, and ended with him leaving the computer disk from Louis Hill on the table when he'd walked out. He'd return when the trial started. Until then, they could find some other plumber to fix their leaks. Not him. He had his hands full with Cally and her wild time-hopping schemes.

Following a dream was dangerous. Too often, dreams became nightmares. Still, that didn't stop the need to follow.

Optimistic as she was in her search to find a tunnel in time, she never seemed to consider the negative aspects. At least he'd be with her when her collision course with disappointment slammed into her at ninety miles an hour.

Once satisfied the estate was secure, he avoided Cally the rest of the evening. It was becoming damn near impossible to be around her without touching her, kissing her, needing to make love with her so damn badly that he had to keep his hands in his pockets.

After showering, he pulled on a pair of jeans and an undershirt, then ate a sandwich in front of the computer while keying in and evaluating her hand-written computations. Her accuracy was mind-boggling.

Shortly before midnight, he saw the logic of her hypothesis and pushed away from the computer. "Not just logical—friggin' brilliant," he whispered. From her account of how she arrived at her conclusions, science had played an important, but secondary role in the basic thought process.

Staring at the computer screen, Req laughed out loud. If a more optimistic woman with unbending convictions ever trod the earth, he hadn't met her. Nor did he want to.

The computer gave Cally's plan to return to her own time a high probability rating—even though it was based in maybes, supposes, and what ifs, not on hard science.

Req had his own set of maybes, supposes, and what ifs.

Maybe he ought to forget everything beyond the moment and make love with her. Seduction wasn't out of the question; considering the way she looked at him at times, it shouldn't be too difficult. Indulging in erotic speculation forced him to straighten his body to relieve the growing tightness of his jeans.

Suppose they did make love. Suppose he explored all the places he ached to touch and taste. He'd want more. Worse, he supposed it would change him, make him more protective of her. Make him feel more than he already was, and that was already painfully dangerous.

What if they actually found a basis for the marriage they had entered into for altruistic reasons? One that had nothing to do with money or protection?

Love.

He didn't know what it was anymore, but he was certain that Cally did. What if he fell in love with her? And what if she left him when her plan to return to 1890 crumbled into disillusionment?

Falling in love . . . Stupid idea, he concluded, then flipped off the computer. Most days, he doubted that he'd ever been capable of loving anyone.

"The probability of that happening is a gnat's hair better than her going back to 1890," he whispered. Caladonia Maguire wasn't going anywhere, except away from Monterey in four days. With him.

Massaging his sternum where a black-and-blue bruise flowered beneath his chest hair, he got up. When he looked across the room, Cally stood in the doorway like a vision of erotic innocence.

"Something wrong?" he asked, noting that she no longer clutched the lapels of the terry-cloth robe at her throat. The loosely knotted belt let the front gap to a point. The robe shadowed, but did not completely hide, the pale valley between her breasts.

Req's mouth went dry. God, how he wanted to bury himself in her in every way possible, starting with kissing her mouth until neither one of them could breathe.

"Nothing you can't make right." The sudden color rushing to her cheeks and the tilt of her head revealed her nervous bravado.

He crossed the room and stopped in front of her. The sharp vee at the front of her robe invited his gaze to delve inside.

He indulged.

She wasn't wearing a bra. The quick rise and fall of her breath made him aware of her femininity on a plane that ran from the elemental to the ethereal. His erection became painfully hard as he wondered if she wore anything at all beneath the robe. A casual tug of the loose half-hitched belt would show him.

"What do you want me to make right, Cally?" Multiple shampooings had washed the dye from her hair. The hall light reflected in errant blond strands clustered around her shoulders. He shoved his fingers into his front pockets to keep from touching her.

"Us."

"Us?" he asked, wary, not wanting to interpret the situation incorrectly.

"Make love with me, Requiem Maguire. The way a husband and wife do." She reached for the belt around her narrow waist. "I'm not asking you to love me forever, just make love with me for tonight." A subtle tug released the tie on her robe. A shrug of her shoulders sent it to the floor. Her chin lifted a notch and she made no move to cover her nudity.

His fingers curled in his pockets. She was beautiful beyond his dreams. The ache to touch her threatened to turn his skin inside out. But the dark times of the last two years refused to let him believe things were as forthright as they seemed. "Why? What's in it for you?"

"You," she said so softly he almost missed it. "Memories."

The honest desire in her eyes and her blush of indignation

when he questioned her motives underscored the truth he sensed. There was no greater aphrodisiac than having the woman he ached to make love with tell him she wanted him. He didn't care what kind of price he paid later. He was going to have her. The only remaining question was whether he could go slow enough to keep it from being over too soon.

In a single motion, he swept her up and carried her down the hall. She tightened her hold around his neck, drawing close enough to nip the tender skin behind his earlobe. The sensation of her mouth on his flesh hurried him into the bedroom.

"Memories, huh?" His voice sounded thick and distant, coming from somewhere deep in his chest.

"To last forever." The vibration of her lips on his skin sent the implications straight to his heart.

"I'll give you more than memories, Cally Maguire."

With a knee braced on the bed, he lowered her into the center, coaxing her to let go when he retreated. When she did, he instinctively wanted to reach for her. But he wanted to see the entire prize she offered. He turned on the lights recessed in the headboard looming behind her.

"God, you're beautiful."

Cally smiled shyly, somewhat embarrassed at his frank perusal of her naked body. Her need to touch him, however, quickly banished any lingering bashfulness. She twisted onto her knees and wound her fingers into his tee shirt, then tugged the hem from his jeans and slid the thin fabric up his back. "I want to see you naked."

"You got it." He eased her aside, then sat on the edge of the bed. His boots hit the floor in quick succession. One-handed he pulled the tee shirt over his head.

High on his right shoulder blade, an image of Pegasus rearing on his hind legs looked at Cally, his wings spread to take flight.

Req stood, facing her. Muscle and sinew sculpted his body. It took a moment to realize he'd removed the wrapping from his chest. An ugly black-and-blue bruise the size of her palm stained the skin beneath the ebony chest hair glistening over his heart.

She tentatively reached for the bruise, but didn't touch him. "Will it be all right?"

"Yes. It will be even better when I make love with you." A practiced tug freed the metal buttons on his jeans.

Cally's heart thundered against her ribs. He was an incredi-

ble masterpiece of flesh and muscle. Powerful. Breathtaking.
Enticing. Hers.

All the dabbling on the fringes of intimacy with three fiancés
had led her to this. The mysteries between a man and a woman
had never been intriguing enough to explore.

Until tonight.

Nothing had prepared her for the overwhelming emotions
swamping her senses and the desire charging her body.

In that instant, everything she wanted in life stood before her.
The realization she was the reason for the fine tremors of anticipation rippling up his arms both humbled and thrilled her. Primal need seethed in his predatory green eyes. It sharpened his
uncompromising features and revealed a single-minded sense of
purpose coiled in the muscle and sinew advancing toward her.

"I don't know if you're my salvation or my ruination, Cally.
Either way, you're mine now. God help us both."

Req allowed her no time to collect her tumultuous thoughts.
He slid across the bed, claiming her mouth, her senses, and her
body. The sheer animal strength evident in his tight abdomen
intrigued her as much as the texture of his skin against hers.

Then nothing mattered beyond exploring him and reveling in
the sweet torment he created with his mouth on hers. His kiss
melted her from the inside, teasing, probing the corners of her
mouth, coaxing her lips apart, and then taking everything she
offered and demanding more. Shocked by the unfathomable
depth of the need he created in her, she gave him everything.
And became desperate for more of him.

She cried out when his mouth slid away from hers.

He loomed over her, his eyes wild, his hair framing his chiseled face. "So sweet, Cally. Let me taste more of you."

Dazed by the voracious hunger dilating his pupils, she barely
made a sound.

His long, powerful fingers caught one breast as his mouth
claimed the other. His teeth scraped against her nipple, sending
a sharp, clear jolt of pleasure through her.

She gave herself over to the sea of sensation nearly drowning her. This was the man she loved; the one she would hold in
her heart regardless of time or distance. She hadn't wanted to
love him, but what she wanted and what was, were two different things.

Her senses nearly exploded when he cradled the blond curls
between her thighs. A new world of sensation burst on her as he

teased, tormented, and promised to please with the stroke of a finger.

Her breath went ragged. The response of her body begged for more, and he delivered with an ardor that nearly incinerated them both.

In a distant part of her dissolving reason, she heard a small voice laugh and cry simultaneously. This was what she wanted, the intimacy, the totality of joining in all ways. This was the memory she would carry with her into the past. She savored every nuance of the invisible talisman Req created, then fashioned with each touch, each kiss. If there were words to describe the pleasure he gave her, she did not know them, nor could she have uttered them.

"Don't leave," she cried out when he retreated. The night air stung with a chill that left her bereft.

"Not on your life," he murmured as he took something from a drawer in the nightstand.

Not wanting to miss anything during their lovemaking, she knelt behind him. Her fingertips barely touched the winged Pegasus tattooed across his shoulder blade in blues, reds, greens, and black. It was only when she looked closer that she saw tethers lashing the creature to the ground. Sadly, it reminded her of Req—ready to soar, but unable to break the restrictions that would allow him to do so.

"Condom," he said, glancing over his shoulder at her. "Safe sex. Remember?"

No, she didn't remember, but she'd take his word. Leaning over his shoulder with her body pressed against his back, she watched him unroll the thin protection over his erect penis.

Now that she had a good look at what she had wanted inside her with every fiber of her being a few minutes ago, she couldn't wait to feel how they fit together.

Req returned them both to the center of the bed and settled between her thighs.

Braced on his elbows, he smoothed errant strands of hair from her face. She watched his dilated green eyes study her face. Her own excitement grew with every heartbeat. She laid her hand across his cheek and felt the muscle working around his hidden dimple twitch against her palm. She would love him for all time.

Hard and hungry, he devoured her with a kiss that banished the last iota of rational thought. Just when she thought he'd

scorched her soul, he broke the kiss. The infernos of need engulfing every fiber of her flared.

With his body, his hands, and his mouth, he touched her
everywhere. The most poignant was the way something in him
reached inside her and cried out that he loved her. Over the thunder of her heart, she heard the whisper of her name on his lips.

A subtle shift of his hips brought him to the entrance of her sex.
Chest heaving, she met his intent gaze. Her heart, her very soul
belonged to him that moment. She offered her entire being openly,
willingly, eager to know the sweet mystery of lovemaking.

"I want to watch your face when you take me inside," he
whispered.

Had she been able to speak, she wouldn't have known what
to say. Instead, she tucked her arms under his, then embraced
his ribs.

The slow, sinuous motion of Req's hips teased her thighs farther apart.

"Wrap your legs around my waist." His voice was thick with
a sensual urgency.

Looking him in the eyes, she lifted her right, then her left leg.
Open, exposed, vulnerable, her breath caught in her throat as a
myriad of emotions and sensations rolled through her. Trust and
love banished the cloud of foreboding that lingered on the
fringe of her awareness.

Req entered her with a hard, swift stroke.

Cally gasped, then winced, forgetting everything but the sudden stab of pain that accompanied his invasion.

Req swore, but remained motionless buried inside her. "Why
the hell didn't you tell me?" he hissed as though in torment.

"Tell you what?" The pain receded to a sting.

"I knew you weren't experienced, but I thought . . ." His
voice trailed and he shook his head. "I didn't think. Christ, I'm
sorry, Cally."

She looked away. The beautiful chaos of anticipation and the
joining that now made them one became a throb.

"Hey," he said softly, then cradled her face with his hands.
"Look at me."

Reluctantly, she complied. The tenderness that replaced his
wildness of moments ago melted her embarrassment.

"Why didn't you say something?"

"I didn't think I should. I just assumed you'd know what to do."
He stared down as though she had slapped him.

"It just seemed . . ." She drew a deep breath, then exhaled, her arms tightening to keep him close. At last, he was part of her. She had never been so close to knowing the full beauty of love. "I know things are different here, but I didn't think I was the only twenty-four-year-old virgin in California."

A virgin. The realization added to the fire in his brain. "Yeah, well, you were, but not anymore." Hell, he didn't know what else to say. If he didn't move soon, the way she was wiggling and squirming would set him off. "Put your legs down."

"Kiss me first." Her arms flowed around his neck and drew him down.

What had started as gentle lovemaking required all his strained control to keep from turning into wild rutting. Holding still, allowing her time to adjust tested him to the limit. Perspiration tingled on his skin. The cool air of desertion cut across his waist when she lowered her legs.

"Req," she said against his mouth. "Need . . ."

Need. His body screamed with it. So did his malnourished soul. Realizing the magnitude of what she gave him by making love awed him, but did nothing to diminish the drive to claim her in the most elemental, primitive way possible.

She clutched at him, her fingers digging into his shoulders, her legs up around his waist again, flexing, lifting, urging him deeper with each thrust.

When he felt her spiraling toward a climax, he drew back to watch. Her expressions became a kaleidoscope of adoration, awe, and something he might have recognized as love had he not dwelled in an emotionally insulated hell for so long.

Surprise lit her wide eyes and filled her voice when she called his name as she climaxed, and he followed her over the brink. For a few moments, time ceased. The echo of his name on her lips would stay with him for the rest of his life. He buried his face in the sweet scent of her hair and kissed her neck, gathering her in his arms, holding her against his heart, cherishing her, mourning her, but most of all savoring the genuine emotion silently tearing at his heart. The slow retreat of her legs from around his waist and her soft, throaty laugh conveyed her contentment.

He grabbed the comforter, damp with the labors of their passion and fragrant with their desire, rolled onto his back, and took her with him. He grinned at her as she laughed, all the while wrapping her in a cocoon of comforter and him.

"Can I ask you a question?"

His grin broadened. "*Now* you're asking if you can ask?"

She gingerly brushed clusters of hair from his face. "Have you any idea why you were named after . . ." The smile faded into confusion.

"A death ritual?" he finished.

"Yes."

"Yeah." He watched curiosity burn in her eyes and felt the shift in her body as her patience shortened. "My father was a cop. He was killed in the line of duty shortly before I was born. It devastated my mother and caused me to be born early. I was the surprise during the requiem mass for my father. Actually, I was born twenty feet from his casket.

"The incident made the local papers. It read, 'Police Officer's Requiem Brings New Life.' Mom thought it appropriate and named me Requiem." He caught her finger making lazy circles in his chest hair and kissed it. "It's also responsible for me learning how to fight at an early age."

"Requiem," she whispered. "It sounds almost holy."

"There's nothing holy about me."

"I've never felt closer to heaven than where you just took me."

Req pondered what twist of fate gave him a woman with a naïve passion that had stolen his callused heart, an unbridled optimism that lit the dark corners of his soul, and a fickle intellect he didn't quite know whether to believe or not.

The soft whisper of her breathing stirred the hair on his chest. She fit so well into the crook of his arm. Her head rested on his shoulder, just above his heart. The placement was perfect for stroking her long, silken hair.

While he made love with Cally during the early hours of the new day, his old companions—fear, death, and betrayal—had sulked in the darkness that nurtured them. The freedom Cally gave his soul with her body and the shiny jewel of her laughter was the most precious gift imaginable. In the afterglow, he vacillated between amazement and the need for reassurance by making love to her repeatedly until he grew tired of her in a century or two.

But they didn't have a century or even a week. Hell, there was no telling how she would react when her plan to return to 1890 washed away with the incoming tide.

It had taken him damn near a month to believe what had been in front of him all the time. Caladonia Maguire needed to go home to 1890. It was strange how clear things became after making love with her.

He kissed the top of her head, then looked toward the window. A wisdom born of experience warned that he had to get Cally somewhere safe, then not see her again. But he was beginning to think he wasn't a wise man. Rather, he was a selfish one. He wanted Cally with him, where he could keep her safe.

Other than himself, he could think of no one he'd trust with her preposterous secret. When he examined their situation in that light, there was no point in searching out a haven for her. The best place for her was with him.

The premonition that they were rushing headlong into disaster almost made him wish he'd never allowed himself to feel again. Almost. Had such a wish been made and granted, he would never have known Cally. Nothing was worth missing out on the sweet passion evident in the naked heaven molded against him.

With the exception of the way their bodies fit, little else in life approached perfection. He intended to revel in that perfection by taking her to the Cypress By The Sea Resort. He would put the car in storage where no one would see it. Room service would ensure she didn't leave their room until checkout time except for the excursion down the beach to the rocky spine. Until she met with the reality that she couldn't go home through a swinging door of time at the tide pool, he'd make love with her at every opportunity. When the time came, he'd find a way to soften the blow for her.

Cally alternately savored and begrudged her time alone in the elegant resort hotel suite. They seldom left the room during the day. Occasionally, Req ventured out alone. Following his suggestion, she soaked in the warmth of the whirlpool tub. She had never dreamed such opulence existed.

Eyes closed, she relaxed in the delicious warmth. Her mind continued whirling faster than the water massaging muscles she hadn't known she had the day before.

Recalling the wondrous delights she and Req had explored, she let the tingling of the water reverberate through her. The sweet, erotic sensations were now memories that would have to last the rest of her life. Hopefully they would create more each hour they spent together. She wanted as many as she could greedily pack into their remaining time together.

The optimist in her refused to dwell on the emptiness ahead. She was going home in a day and a half. The only way to remain focused on her goal was to ignore the nagging voices crying in the dark corners of her mind. There were consequences for everything, she reminded herself when the voices gained too much strength, even things that happened beyond her control. The consequence of stumbling into Req's world had been falling in love with him. And from the beginning, she had known she would have to leave.

True, she had hoped to fall in love someday. But not here. Not with Req, a man she couldn't call hers for more than a few days.

But she had a day and a half left. If she made every hour count, it would be enough. It had to be.

"Daydreaming?"

Startled, she sat up. Habits of a lifetime sent her grappling for a towel to draw over her breasts. Water sloshed in all directions. "You frightened me."

"That towel won't save you from what I have in mind, Cally." Water soaked into his jeans when he sat on the edge of the tub and removed his shoes.

Her gaze settled on the holstered gun he wore under his left arm. The weapon remained within his reach even when they made love.

"We should be safe for the next couple of days." He removed the harness and set the gun on an elevated ledge above the tub. "Gutierrez's henchmen wouldn't think to look for us here. Their mentality is geared to an urban hiding place."

"What of Gutierrez? Will he remain in jail?" She slid onto her knees and ran her slick, wet hands beneath his shirt.

"That was the plan. It'll work if Pierce gets the right judge." He pulled the shirt over his head with his left hand and unfastened his jeans with his right.

"Who is Pierce?" Watching his taut body shift and flex as he undressed was a potent aphrodisiac. "Someone you work with?"

"He's the man I'm counting on to put Gutierrez and his kingpins away. Pierce is a prosecutor. Now that Rydell is gone, he's damn near the only person I can even come close to trusting."

Cally made room for him to join her in the tub. "I'm turning into a prune," she murmured looking at her fingertips.

Req took her hand and kissed it. "If so, I've got a new favorite food." The hunger that lived in the shadows of his eyes flared.

Head bowed, she hid the smile of anticipation for what she was sure would follow. The slight tug of his hand drew her body against his. He kissed her forehead, then wrapped an arm around her shoulders and pulled her across his chest. The water bubbled and sputtered along the sides of the tub.

Cally basked in the sense of intimacy that reached the most private corners of her heart. The rhythm of his breathing pressed his ribs into hers.

"Cally . . ."

The way his voice trailed made her look up at him. A faint furrow rode his brow and hinted of worry. "Is something wrong?" She hoped not. She dearly wanted to add making love with him in this warm, bubbly cocoon of steamy water to her mental scrapbook.

"Your plan for returning home might not work."

"Shh. Pessimistic thinking is not allowed while we're naked and in such opportunistic circumstances." Her fingers closed around his erection. The sudden flex of hard flesh against her palm quickened her pulse.

"Time isn't a swinging door." He caught her wrist.

She slid a glance at him, but continued caressing her underwater prize. "I found nothing in my research to support that assertion."

"Okay, so nobody wrote it down or made a movie out of it but think about it. Logically it just doesn't make sense for a swinging door to exist between your time and mine."

"I've thought about how time might stretch, bend, break, twist, or turn from the moment I realized what happened to me." She released him, then straddled his thighs. The ugly bruise discoloring his chest shimmered below a fat line of bubbles dancing across the obstacle course of his chest hair.

"Believing something will happen because you need it to won't make it so, Cally. Wanting, needing, even believing that you can return home this way won't let you manipulate nature. Unlike the laws of man, those are immutable."

She smiled at the worry in his eyes. His attempts to express his concerns and defuse the disappointment he expected her to meet were as subtle as a bull moose at a ballet.

Her smile broadened with the realization that she had indeed devoured the elephant of change she had faced when he pulled her from the sea. One bite at a time, she had consumed it. Now it was part of her, albeit not a particularly comfortable one.

"Kiss me, while you still have the opportunity." She lowered her mouth.

"Stay."

Everything stopped. Her breathing. Her forward motion. Her heart. Only the mechanically induced bubbles continued to spew from underwater jets. The aroma of fresh flowers penetrated the steam rising from the water. Her gaze locked with Req's.

"Stay," he repeated. "I'll keep you safe, Cally."

She sat back and let her hands rest on the side of the tub. "You are a tempting man, Requiem Maguire." Her heart cried out for her to stay, to remain in his arms, his life, his time.

"Not just any man. Your husband. I won't run out on you, Cally. Choose to stay. Please."

A vise clamped down on her heart. "Is that what you think I'm doing? Choosing? Running out?" If only there really was a choice involved.

"No."

"I can't stay. I have a business to run. A partnership to uphold. People who depend on me." She brushed back a clump of wet hair that fell across her left eye. With all her heart, she wished she could stay with him until they were old and did little more than rock together on the porch at sunset. But they would see different sunsets. "I have to find out who murdered my father. Those are duties, responsibilities I cannot walk away from regardless of the personal cost. It is a matter of honor, not of choice. If anyone should understand why I must go, it's you. You uphold your responsibilities even when people let you down. When you almost get killed."

The shadows in his eyes told her more than any words he might say. "Oh, Req. You don't want me to stay—you just don't want me to try to go back. You think I'm wrong, that all I'll find in the pool is disappointment, don't you?" Chaotic emotions tightened her throat. She wanted to hold him against her heart forever. Simultaneously, she wanted to run from the potency of his pessimism.

"Disappointment can be an ugly demon, Cally."

"Will you be disappointed if I am right and leave you as I've told you I will?"

In the silence that followed, the depth of his disbelief crystallized. Yet, at great risk and considerable expense, he was doing everything possible for her to test it.

"What worries you more, Req? That I'll go? Or that I'll stay?"

"Damned if I know," he hissed. In a flurry of motion, he sat up straight, caught her in an embrace, and seized her mouth in a kiss.

Tears spilled down Cally's moisture-beaded cheeks. There would never be another love for her.

Chapter 14

THE DIM BEACONS of streetlights weakened before reaching the beach. Billows of predawn fog ebbed and flowed lazily in the still morning. Ribbons of kelp left stranded by the high tide emitted the tangy odor of decay. The surf broke against the rock stacks in the riptide.

Cally and Req walked the beach hand in hand. In part, he had chosen the resort because of its proximity to the ocean. Even so, it was a long walk to the rocky spine where he'd found her a month earlier. In the foggy darkness, no one would see them. And should they come upon someone in the dark, Cally's 1890s garb would draw attention away from their faces. Cally had insisted they bring it with them, arguing that returning in clothes from the 1990s would raise too many questions that she couldn't answer. Funny how the dress, once so familiar, now felt cumbersome.

There had been so many changes since Req rescued her from the cold sea. The greatest was the warmth in her heart for the man at her side, the man she married and would always love. The man she'd be leaving behind in such a short time.

She couldn't think about life without him. Doing so created such anguish that she could barely breath.

"What will you do after I return home?" Now that the time of parting was at hand, she focused on the million questions besieging her. The answers provided the basis for future memories and fantasies.

Both of them ignored the boulder of disbelief he carried in a gym bag stuffed with dry clothing he'd brought for Cally. He had done nothing to conceal his expectation for her failure to return to 1890 by climbing into a tide pool. "Change my appearance, then find a place to lay low and live high."

"Do the two not contradict one another?"

"Not if you have enough money and contacts that stay greedy." A gentle squeeze of his hand tried to provide a reassurance she would never feel. Once she left, there would be no way of knowing his fate.

"I assume you have both."

"Yeah. The contacts I built up over the years. The money is from Victor. I believe he'd consider it well spent if it kept me going long enough to testify against Gutierrez."

"What will you do after that?"

"I thought maybe I'd try a desk job. If I didn't like it, I'd do something else."

She couldn't imagine him confined by a desk and the restrictions of an office. "Such as?"

"Hell, I don't know. When you're undercover, you don't make long-range plans. Guess it becomes a habit. But it doesn't matter because once I testify, I'm quitting this job." He gave her hand a playful squeeze. "What do you think about exploring the country from the back of the Harley? We'll go see Yosemite. Yellowstone. Zion."

"I think you'll see those places without me," she said softly. With each step toward the craggy spine bending into the sea, her feet grew heavier, her pace a fraction slower. There was so much she still wanted to say, but what would be the point? Telling him she loved him would only make their parting more difficult.

They reached the rocks. The languid shushing of the sleepy waves over the fog-saturated sand should have calmed her pounding heart. Instead, each lap of water on the beach became a time marker of precious seconds with Requiem Maguire that she would never experience again. Suddenly, they were moving too fast.

Req dropped the gym bag and checked his watch. "We timed it well. Ten minutes until the tide changes."

It didn't seem a sufficient margin to her. Unlike Req, who lived on the swordtip of seconds, she preferred the shield of padded minutes. Arriving this close to the time of tide change made her feel late for her appointment with destiny. "Let's get down to the water."

"Cally." He took her hand, but didn't move.

"You've gone this far with me and I thank you from the bottom of my heart. It would be unfair of me to ask you to go another step. I didn't know what I was facing when you helped me to shore a month ago. Now ..." her voice cracked, ". . . now I know I never could have muddled through on my own." It was a difficult admission. The warbling of her voice betrayed the tears welling up from what felt like the center of the earth.

Req swore under his breath, then released her hand.

In that instant, the sense of isolation that crashed on her in the darkness became a portent of the loneliness ahead. Whether it was more strength or weakness she needed to turn her back on her obligations, it didn't matter. She didn't have enough of whatever it took. She knew only one course: forward on the path of duty.

She turned away, unable to speak. After several steps, she realized he was following. When he placed his hand on her shoulder the connection shot through her like lightning.

"Look, Cally—"

She flung herself into his arms. Unerringly, she found his mouth and kissed him until neither one of them could draw a steady breath. In desperation for this final embrace, she cherished the unyielding firmness of his body, the coffee and chocolate taste of his mouth, the enticing warmth of his breath on her cool cheek, and the spicy scent of his damp hair. The symphony of indelible sensual memories built to a crescendo against the relentless backbeat of the ocean waves lapping up the seconds ticking away.

Teary-eyed, Cally tore away from Req and ran the final distance to the break in the upthrust. Lifting her skirts, she threaded her way out to the series of pools, using her feet as guides on the slippery rock. The foggy darkness hid the tears streaming down her face. The combination made seeing where she was going impossible.

"You're going to break your neck." Req caught her arm just as she started to slip.

"I-I'm f-fine."

"Like hell you are. If you step the wrong way . . ."

As if speaking a prophecy destined it for fulfillment, Cally fell into the water. Reaching out to break her fall, Req tumbled in after her. Grappling one another, handfuls of seaweed, slimy growths, and struggling for footing, she sputtered until Req hauled her up by the shoulders.

". . . you'll fall," he finished.

"I've found the bottom," she said, pushing hair from her face, her teeth already chattering from the cold.

"Yeah, I wish," Req breathed. "The tide ought to start changing any minute."

Cally searched for the niche where she had hidden before. Time and weather had eroded the stone, but there was enough left of the caprock for her to get a bearing. With her skirts gathered and tucked between her legs, she hunkered into the recess. The gentle waves caressed her shoulders.

"Are you going to watch me go?"

"Hell, I'm looking right at you." Standing in the water up to his ribs, he was a specter breaking the line of waves rushing toward her.

Despite her tears, she couldn't help a weak smile. He really didn't want to be here, didn't want her here, but he was going to stay to the end. A wave slapped at her throat and splashed onto her face. Her feeble smile faded. The rock at her back felt softer.

"When you think of me, do so with tenderness, Req. I love you and it pains me deeply to leave."

"Yeah." He shifted, bracing against the incoming waves.

"Stay safe," she whispered, lifting her chin to keep the sea out of her mouth.

What would he do when she disappeared into the tunnel that would take her home? How would he cope with the miscalculation of disbelief when proved wrong?

The incoming tide pressed her further into the recess, which seemed to yield more with each wave.

"Req?"

"Ready to go?" He reached to help her up.

"I am going. But—" Another wave slapped her in the face and washed her words away.

"Let's get into some dry clothes and go back to the room."

She pushed his hand away. "I love you, Req. I always will." The water rose over her face. The back of the niche became spongy. She caught a full breath in the trough of the next wave.

Req grabbed her wrist.

The rock dissolved behind her. Reflexively, she turned her hand and closed her fingers around Req's wrist.

The back of the niche dissolved. The riptide of time drew them both into the vortex.

They were drowning.

In a friggin' wading pool, no less.

Req kept a tight hold on Cally's wrist. He kicked, flailed, and groped for the sides. The powerful currents tore at him, threatening to rip Cally from his grasp.

He held onto her and let the water carry them to the surface. His lungs shrieked for a breath. In a heartbeat, he realized they were no longer in the shallow tide pool.

He surfaced, dragging Cally up with him. Air shrieked into his lungs with the force of a thousand needles propelled through a wind tunnel. Heedless, he kept them afloat and worked with the waves to find the shore.

By the time they dragged themselves above the waterline on the beach, every muscle in Req's body screamed as loudly as his lungs. He splayed his fingers across Cally's breast.

Her heartbeat rose and fell.

He relaxed a notch.

When their steam-engine gasps eased to heavy panting, Req found the energy to flex his fingers. All he thought about was breathing, his and hers.

Cally rolled onto her stomach and against him.

A few minutes later they pushed into sitting positions, each leaning on the other.

"Thank heavens I didn't wear a corset," Cally panted.

"Or petticoats," he added. How she thought she'd survive in the water with that damn heavy dress was beyond reason. "You gotta get rid of that dress."

"I'm afraid you're right. It's ruined." Straight-shouldered, she looked around. "We did it, Req." She reached over and grabbed his arm with fingers trembling with cold. "We did it!"

"What we did is avoid drowning," he growled.

"Look around. We're here. We made it. I was right!"

Req did look around. They were on the beach, in the fog, and it was starting to rain. The woman chose the oddest time for a happy fit. "Yeah, I can tell by the texture of the sand. This is 1890 all right."

"We're safe, so cheer up." She shook his arm, then let go.

"Safe my foot. Let's get going. It's cold out here."

"I see our success has improved your disposition."

"I'm always in a bad mood when I come close to drowning with you. Call it PMS."

"PMS?"

"Pissed-off Man Syndrome." He'd had it for years and was beginning to think it incurable. "Let's go. It's cold and it's starting to rain."

"Worried about getting wet?" With great effort, Cally pushed to her feet. She gathered up yards of her skirt and twisted. Water splattered onto the sand. "We don't have far to go."

Sometimes her outlook baffled him. The hotel was two miles down the beach. In the rain, when they were already cold and wet. He heaved to his feet, suddenly feeling much too light. He reached inside his jacket. His holster was empty. Swearing, he trudged toward the rocks where he'd dropped the gym bag with dry clothes. On the way, he collected his hair behind the nape of his neck and wrung out the excess water.

"What is it, Req? Are you hurt?"

"I lost my damn piece."

"Your piece of what?" Cally rubbed her upper arms for warmth.

"My gun." Dark as it was, he'd never find it in the pool, nor was he likely to locate the bag before they both suffered from exposure. The temperature had dropped an easy twenty degrees in the last few minutes. Being soaked worsened the plummeting chill. "Damn, I liked that gun." He kicked at the sand. "Help me find our dry clothes."

"Forget the bag, Req. It isn't there." Her fingers caught his. "Let's go home and get warm." On tiptoes, she planted a kiss on his jaw.

"What was that for?"

"Helping me to shore. Again. And my way of welcoming you to 1890."

His heart skipped a beat. Christ, he'd been wrong all along. She was delusional. "Look, Cally, wishing—"

"Remember that. Now take a good look around and tell me what you see."

"Drizzle. Fog."

"You are the most infuriating, obstinate, closed-minded—"

"Quiet," he ordered. Something *was* different. Something he couldn't put his finger on. Something not quite right in the air. He listened through the drizzle falling on the rocks, the rhythmic whisper of the surf, and heard . . . nothing. The *nothing* reached into his bones and warned that the *something* was very, very wrong. Still, it eluded him.

"It's the silence," Cally whispered. "In your Monterey there is noise you are so accustomed to that you don't even know it's there. Here, that noise doesn't exist." Her fingers brushed his ear. "Strangely, it's like hearing something. Am I making myself clear?"

"No." If he accepted her assertion, this situation became far worse than anything he'd ever faced. In a place where everything was wet, his mouth turned dry. Unfortunately, Cally had made herself clear. He just didn't want to acknowledge it. His instincts battled back and refused him the luxury of denial. "Holy Mother of God. You were right, weren't you?"

"Yes. Let's go home. Irene may be up and have a pot of coffee on the stove."

Req remained motionless in the rain. Experience coupled with the training that had kept him alive during the dark times wouldn't allow denial. Everything had changed. Except him. And Cally. The enormity of change would knock him over if he took a step.

Christ, he could barely cope with it, and he hadn't even left the beach. Try as he might, he couldn't imagine the area over the dunes as, what? Primitive? Pristine? Or simply void of civilization as he knew it. How had Cally survived the change? It must have seemed like she'd gone to another planet. And he'd helped, how? By labeling her an addict, then as a candidate for the psychiatric ward.

Conversely, he was already feeling deprived without knowing the extent of the changes he faced in 1890.

"What the hell am I doing here?"

"You're paying an unexpected visit to my home."

"Not for one friggin' minute did I want to . . . to . . ." He couldn't say it.

"Come home with me?" she finished with an aching softness that reached through his confusion and twisted his heart. "I know. But then, why did you grab my hand when I waved good-bye?"

"Is that what you were doing? Shit. The water was getting higher with each wave. You looked like you were going to sit there until you drowned. I thought you'd come to your senses and wanted a hand up."

"Regardless, you're here. It's cold. Let's go home."

Home. For a man who hadn't felt at home in years, the concept was laughable. He didn't need his training as an investigator to confirm her assertion. It was cold. Damn cold. He heard her teeth chattering and felt the shivers of exposure ripple along his own skin.

He started to remove his jacket.

"Keep it," she said, slipping her icy hand into his. "Please, Req, come with me. We'll confront the changes together."

His legs refused to move at first. This spot was his last connection with his life. "I have to go back, Cally."

"Not tonight. The pool is underwater." She kept tugging on him.

The step he took in her direction smacked of defeat. He hadn't believed her. Hadn't believed it possible. If he had given her assertions a crumb of belief, he wouldn't have reached for her, wouldn't have risked leaving his world behind.

Would he?

He hadn't thought of Cally leaving him because she chose to although she had spoken of it repeatedly. From the start, she had been up front with him. In return, he'd acted like a blind-folded jackass. It was time to take the blinders off. She really had left him. If not for the accident that sent him tumbling after her, she'd be gone forever. The realization chilled the core of his soul.

"How did you do it?" he asked as they slogged over the top of the last dune. The silence and the absence of streetlights probing the fog served as constant reminders of a difference he had yet to comprehend.

"Do what?"

"Accept the differences."

She squeezed his hand. "A wonderful man named Requiem Maguire helped me."

"That's not what I mean." Peering into the darkness where the road should be, he knew he hadn't helped her the way he should have. He hadn't believed her.

Cally sighed and hugged herself in the rain. "Have you ever eaten an elephant, Req?"

"No. Why?"

"You do it one bite at a time. Eventually, you consume the entire beast. Some of it has a foul taste. Some makes you laugh. Some of it staggers you with wonder. And a lot of it gives you mental indigestion. But all of it gives you insight and facilitates acceptance of what you cannot change. It can be done, Req."

Just what he needed—a twelve-step program for pachyderm consumption. "Lead on, Mrs. Maguire."

"Perhaps we should make some plans," she said slowly.

"Like what?" Suddenly irritated beyond reason, he couldn't help pushing her. Clearly, the use of her married name was something she hadn't planned on her own turf.

"Like finding out how long I've been gone, then explaining your presence and my absence."

"This is starting out to be a really bad day."

Irene Kenny brandished a broom in one hand and clutched her ample bosom with the other. Snow-white braids coiled behind her ears laid flat against her head. The shiny part down the middle of her crown reflected the fastidiousness evident in her perfectly starched and ironed gingham dress and apron. Squinting into the darkness over wire-rimmed half-glasses, she challenged the intruders attempting entrance to the Hornsby domain. "Come another step, and I'll knock ya senseless."

Cally's heart leaped. Her housekeeper's temper and protectiveness were a formidable combination. "It's me, Irene. Caladonia."

"Don't try any tricks with me. And don't you take another step closer." She raised the broom a little higher.

"Put your broom away, Irene. Mr. Maguire and I are cold and wet." She led Req into the fringe of the muted light cast by the lantern hanging on the back porch.

"Miss Caladonia?" Wonder set off a fine tremor in the housekeeper's voice. Her hand muffled a gasp of surprise, then fell to the broom handle. "Is that really you, Caladonia Hornsby?" she demanded with unexpected ferocity.

"Yes, Irene." They fully entered the half-circle of light at the bottom of the porch steps. "This is Mr. Maguire, my friend and my rescuer." She glanced up at Req who looked like a creature from one of the late-night horror films she'd watched. Dressed completely in black, as was his habit, his presence became more foreboding than ever when she looked at his face. Clumps of hair were plastered against his clenched jaw and snarled tendrils clung like seaweed to the shoulders of his leather jacket. The diamond in his left earlobe sparkled when he turned his head. Req had the eyes of a predator, wounded and dangerous. Determining the color of his dark eyes in the faint light was impossible. However, if the sharpness of his gaze had substance, he would have cut Irene and the back of the Hornsby house to ribbons.

"Praise Jesus, Miss Caladonia, you're home. Where have you been? What's happened to you?" Irene dropped the broom and bounded down the three steps above the stone walkway on which Cally and Req approached. "Dear God in heaven, thank you for bringing her home. Sweet Jesus, we sing your praises."

Cally released Req's hand just in time to keep him from being knocked aside. Irene's beefy arms engulfed her with love, worry, and warmth. The wash of tears flooding down the elder woman's cheeks mingled with the moisture saturating Cally's dress and warmed her more than the body heat.

"How long was she gone, Mrs. Kenny?" Req asked with a composed authority contrary to his wild emotional state.

"Four terribly long weeks. This entire doing has become a nightmare."

"Yeah, I can relate. Is half the town up in arms over her absence?" Req pressed.

Cally lifted her head. Even when shaken to the marrow of his bones, Req held control and exerted authority.

"Mr. Cunningham told everyone you were ill," Irene sobbed, "too ill to leave the house. Oh, Miss Caladonia, we've been so worried. Just beside ourselves not knowing what happened to you. Where you were."

She hugged Irene. The housekeeper worried about few things, but when she did, all her energy went into it. Cally realized how much she had missed her, and how diligently she had cast aside thoughts of those close to her because she could not cope with their probable grief as well as her own plight. "I've missed you, Irene. I'm back now, and it is so good to be home. Let's get inside and start sorting this out. I can't believe that only you and the household knows I was gone."

"Mr. Cunningham and Mr. Morton know. Can't say I know what Mr. Barry thinks," Irene said, bristling with indignation. "Mr. Morton feared you dead, Miss Caladonia, but I kept on praying." Irene sniffed, her shoulders heaving with the depth of her emotion.

"I'm here now. I'll tell you about it after we warm up and get into dry clothing," she promised, giving Irene a final squeeze because she hated letting her go. Irene had symbolized home and safety for as long as Cally could remember.

"Oh yes, of course. It is cold out here, especially for you being soaked to the bone and all. Fresh coffee is on the stove. Bread and breakfast buns are in the oven, just waiting for your hungry mouth." Irene wiped the tears from her cheeks with the hem of her apron. "Why did you not send word? Brendan and I have been at odds with worry."

Cally looked into the kitchen. "Where is Brendan?"

"Laying a fire in the boiler for hot water."

Cally caught Req's hand. Informalities and permissive

touches were inappropriate here. She would have to remember that and ignore the spontaneous impulses to touch him. But right now, she couldn't let him go. He was so distant, so isolated even though he was standing right beside her. The ice emanating from him went far beyond the chill of the cold, wet night. It came from his soul.

Cally shivered with fear. He was with her, but never more far away.

Chapter 15

"YOU MASQUERADED AS a criminal among unscrupulous men who actually were criminals. Surely, this plan is less complex, and the risk much smaller." The set of his jaw sent her spinning away from him, exasperated. Now that they were both bathed and warm, she had to address the rest of their survival concerns—starting with Req's sour disposition. "You can be so stubborn."

"Not stubborn, Cally. Practical." He picked up the starched white shirt she had lain across the bed in the guest room she had consigned him. "How does Brendan move in all this starch?"

"Very well. You're changing the subject."

"I'll do my damnedest to blend in, starting with this body brace. I'll even forgo the earring and get a haircut."

One concession at a time, she thought. "Alright." Although his willingness for a haircut went beyond her expectations, his reluctance to embrace her entire plan vexed her. She started for the door, then stopped with her hand on the knob.

A look over her shoulder let her gaze slowly climb from the tips of his bare toes, up the damp, black jeans he insisted on wearing after his bath. The denim clung to his thighs as tightly as did her legs when they made love. Her gaze rose higher, lingering at the enticing bulge of his sex, and then upward to his narrow waist. She gave into the smile of appreciation rising from the heated desire she worked to keep down to a simmer.

Following the thin ebony hairline rising from his waistband and over his navel until it flared, she studied the jaundiced rainbow bruising his chest. Her fingers tingled, eager to glide through the silken strands and soothe his bruises. She licked her lips, wishing she could kiss away the colors of violence. A sense of happiness glowed in every part of her being for the fates that had conspired for him to accompany her home.

A subtle movement drew her gaze to his. The liquid emeralds she looked into were molten with desire.

"These clothes were all Brendan could find that might fit you. Do you need assistance dressing?" Huskiness reserved for their bouts of lovemaking weighted her voice.

"Miss Caladonia!" Irene's strident call shot up the stairs and down the hall. "You bring Mr. Maguire and come eat something now. The fire is taking the morning chill out of the air. Even so, I won't have your breakfast getting cold."

The intrusion of the outside world took the edge off the seductive heat shimmering between them. Their stares locked in icy stubbornness rippling with an undercurrent of desire.

The air in Cally's throat took on substance and thickened until she could barely breathe. She turned away and twisted the knob.

"Cally?"

The warning vibrating in the space between them kept her from turning around.

"Next time you undress me—be ready to get naked."

God, she was ready! "This is going to be difficult for me, too, Req." She slipped out of his bedroom and closed the door. All her plans for catching her father's killer had been pushed into the back of her mind when Req tumbled through the time door with her. Within minutes of realizing he had accompanied her, she had run through an emotional gamut that still lingered.

Selfishly, she was glad he was here where she could see him. Talk with him. Touch him. But his presence disallowed her carefully constructed defense of keeping the two time periods separated emotionally. She had not anticipated loving him in the flesh in her own home.

Of course, he would leave. It was as inevitable as her returning home. Meanwhile, if she acknowledged their marriage, how would she explain the ceremony in Reno? The dates on their marriage certificate—even if she had it, crossed the time barrier.

She *couldn't* explain it.

Even an expert liar, which she was anything but, would have trouble juggling the stories necessary to make the truth believable.

Still, for all the complications, she was ecstatic. He was here, even if they couldn't live as man and wife. When she had tried to explain why their arrangement had to change, Req had protested, then became sullen. For a wild moment, she thought his reasons for wanting to continue the marriage may have extended beyond the physical.

Spinning the ring on her left ring finger with her thumb, she started for the stairs.

"Miss Cala—"

"Coming, Irene," she called. "Mr. Maguire will be down shortly." Irene's fawning had reverted to the comfortable routine of their old ways once she was satisfied Cally was safe and healthy.

Cally started down the stairs. Her clothes, particularly the undergarments, seemed to belong to someone else. Belatedly she decided the scanty items Req had selected for her to wear were more comfortable. She drew a slow, deep breath that tested the will of her corset, then released it along with her thoughts of making love with Req.

As long as he avoided the face in the mirror, Req didn't recognize himself. The trousers were a size too large. The shirt fit snugly across his shoulders. The sleeves on the jacket were a bit short. He regarded the false shirt collar and sissy bow tie in his hand with all the disdain he might give a hairy spider.

In an era without chewable antacids, how did a man eat the elephant of change—even one bite at a time?

Cally had done it with little or no help.

He sat on the edge of the four-poster bed and put on Brendan's shoes. They were uncomfortably small. A cherry-wood dresser sat beneath a sculptured mirror. Rich wainscoting ringed the room below pale rose-colored watered silk wallpaper. He fingered the elegant floral comforter spread on the bed like a pristine snowfield, then stood and squared his shoulders.

He was a pro. He'd been an undercover agent for over two years. If he could do that, he could do this with one hand tied behind his back.

He'd adapt. Fit in. Bide his time. Then go home and do what needed doing. He couldn't think beyond that goal.

"Syzygy my ass," he muttered. How had she put it all together? He still didn't understand it, but knew he should. A man had a higher survival potential if he understood what was going on around him. Christ, no wonder he had such a lousy track record with women. If he lived to a thousand, he'd never understand Cally. Regardless, there was no room for denial, only a deep-seated admiration for her nimble mind. He doubted he'd have figured out the riptide of time that carried them between centuries.

He left the beeswax- and lamp oil-scented bedroom convinced that the good old days could benefit from the technology of synthetic blends when it came to comfortable clothes. The right size would help, too.

The aroma of freshly baked bread and bacon made his mouth water. He followed the alluring smells into the dining room where he found Cally pouring coffee. The sight of steaming food made his stomach roll over and beg.

"Once you compare the fruits of Irene's culinary skills with mine, you'll understand why I stay out of the kitchen." Cally set a full cup of coffee on the table and gestured for him to sit.

Req eyed her place at the head of the table and scowled. "You're really going to deny we're married?"

"I'm not denying it, just . . ."

"Just what?"

"Keeping things simple by not acknowledging it."

"Yeah, that sounds real simple." While he hadn't expected undying love and devotion from their unexpected marriage, he hadn't anticipated denial either. It stung in a way that defied reason.

"I don't see that I have a choice." Exasperated, she started uncovering dishes and serving them. "How would I prove we were married, Req? Even if I had it in my hand, our marriage license doesn't look real, and I was there. The date is so far removed from today, who would believe it a mistake? It certainly wouldn't stand up to scrutiny. In fact, you might argue that we wouldn't be married for—"

"Whatever you want, Cally." She'd have it her way anyway. What did he care? She was safe. She was back where she belonged. When the next tidal syzygy occurred in a month or so, he'd be home too. He hoped. Until then, he had little choice but to play it her way.

She let the cover fall over the serving dish with a reverberating clang. "What do you mean, 'whatever I want'? I didn't plan on bringing you back, even though I'll admit I wanted you to come."

"Explain that one." He tried not to read anything into her admission.

"I wanted you to want to come."

He stared into her coffee-colored eyes. Drug lords, addicts, ambitious bosses, road rage, grieving families: those were things he understood. Caladonia Hornsby did not come close to that realm. "You wanted me to come so you could deny making love with me when I got here?"

Though she didn't move, color rose up her neck and into her cheeks. "I never said we wouldn't make love. I said we couldn't live openly as man and wife. We'll have to be discreet."

"Right. That's why we aren't sleeping in the same room." He stabbed at a piece of ham, fleetingly wondering if it was from a rear flank of the animal. He could identify with the butt.

"I hope you brought a good supply of condoms with you." Cally's question concerning birth control turned her cheeks pink, and Req hoped it was with desire. However, when her gaze challenged him, he knew better. She started cutting her food with the same deliberate precision with which she delivered her logic.

"I didn't bring any." Hell, he'd thought they would be packing for Alaska by now, between bouts of lovemaking in their hotel suite. A side trip to 1890 had never crossed his mind.

"Then we have a problem. I don't plan on raising a child alone, Req."

"Hell, we had a box full of them in the room. Remember? I thought you'd end up cold and wet, then we'd go back to the room and I'd warm you up in the bathtub."

"Your faith in me nearly makes me swoon."

"Give me a break." Nothing like rubbing a little salt in the wounds.

She stabbed a piece of potato. "Thank you for the invitation. I accept. Let's start with your jaw. You might be able to get your foot out of your mouth then."

"It doesn't matter whether I believed you'd actually do anything more than get wet and catch a cold. Me coming along was never part of your plan." And he couldn't imagine the torment he would have experienced if she had disappeared in the tide pool while he stood by and watched. Relief that he hadn't lost her surged through his heart.

"No. You would have preferred staying there where people were looking to kill you. They blew up that van—with people inside—in the middle of a peaceful street. They shot you, Req." Her fork dropped on the fine china plate with a clatter that hung in the silence.

Damn, she did feel something for him when they weren't in bed. Maybe she did actually love him as she had professed in the tide pool. He hadn't wanted to believe it. The admission irritated him to no end. Being loved incurred a new set of obligations, ones he didn't know how to deal with, ones he didn't want. "They didn't kill me."

"They'll try again when you go back and they find you," she murmured.

"They aren't likely to find me here." He broke a biscuit in half, slathered it with butter and jam, and then took a bite. He gave half of it to Cally as a peace offering. "Irene makes apricot jam better than anything I've ever tasted."

Cally accepted the biscuit. The man's moods swung like a well-oiled door. She seized the moment. "We have a number of things to discuss."

"Starting with where I'm sleeping," he said, then lifted a questioning eyebrow. "I'm your husband, Cally. Let me be what I am."

"My plans don't include a husband."

"You had three fiancés before you married me—"

"Our marriage doesn't count."

Shards of silence cut the air with razor-sharp ice.

"It did count," she amended. "But we both thought it was temporary."

"No, *we* didn't."

"Yes, *we* did. I planned on doing just what I did—discovering a way home, then going. You . . . you thought . . ." Her voice trailed, her expression darkening as though her thoughts were painful and too private to share.

"Finish it." He wanted the truth. All of it.

"No."

"Well, hell, Cally. How can I argue with you if you aren't going to tell me what I think so I know what to say?"

Cally twisted the napkin in her lap the way a butcher would wring a chicken's neck—or how she'd wring Req's. "I think you think you know what's best for me, when the truth of it is, you don't even know me, Requiem Maguire. Being my husband, making love . . ." The color drained from her face.

"Go on. Making love . . ." He waggled his fingers, infuriating her down to her toes and taking a perverse satisfaction in doing so.

". . . does not endow you with a divine revelation of who I am. If it did, you would apologize immediately and do as I suggested."

"Apologize?" He had the audacity to pinch his eyebrows together and squint in a hurt yet amused expression. It was all she could do to keep from screaming.

"For acting like an ass!"

"I wasn't aware my true nature was showing. However, if you think I was thinking—"

"Req!" she seethed.

The slow lifting of the corners of his mouth grew into a smile that eased the furrows from his brow. The smile grew into a grin as he leaned back in his chair.

Cally watched, amazed, as his typical world-weary expression melted into one of a mischievous, fun-loving imp with a grin that brightened the room. The deep dimple in his left cheek begged for her touch. The transformation further tightened the Gordian knot of her emotions.

"Damn." Req shook his head slightly. "You're a dangerous woman, Cally Maguire."

"Me?" The only thing dangerous about her was her feelings for him. At the moment, she wasn't sure whether to kiss him or bean him with the chafing dish cover.

"Yeah, you."

"I fail to understand why you would make such an outlandish assertion." Failure to understand many things about the man she loved was becoming a chronic condition.

"You make me unreasonable."

"I make you unreasonable," she repeated slowly, not comprehending the meaning any more in her own voice than she had when he'd spoken the words. At least they agreed he was being unreasonable—never mind the cause.

"I've spent the last few years trying like hell not to care about anything or anyone." The grin began a steady retreat. "I swore that would change when I dropped my cover. I was working on it very gradually. Then I met you. A goddamn bulldozer when it comes to change."

Cally gave her napkin another twist. "I don't know what to say, Req; whether I should be flattered or insulted."

"Neither do I." He pushed away from the table. "Meanwhile, how about giving me some money and pointing me in the direction of a clothing store so I can buy clothes that fit?"

"Money?" she repeated absently.

"Yeah. My bank account is a little out of reach at the moment." He stood. "This is the part of our nonexistent marriage where you give and I take. Unless you don't mind me wearing my own clothes?"

"Oh. Yes, we'll go into town." Finished with her half-eaten breakfast, she stood. "Just as soon we agree on an explanation that will withstand public scrutiny. Unlike you, Req, I am normally surrounded by people, all of whom will want to know where I went, why, how, and who you are. Understand?"

"Perfectly, which is why I can't pass myself off as a doctor as you suggested." The puckish gleam in his eyes and the reemergence of his grin sent a chill up her spine. "Unless I pre-empt Sigmund Freud and claim to be a psychoanalyst."

"Who? And what is a psychoanalyst?"

"Someone who spends years learning how to teach others the common sense of living and dealing with life's problems."

She glared at him. The brief truce was over. "Since no one has heard of psychoanalysts—"

"A shrink, Cally. Therapist. Counseling. Or in this time, an asylum doctor. That's what I'll agree to and that is as far as I'll go in this scheme of yours. No way am I going to let you tell people I'm a doctor. Christ, I don't know a thing about medicine."

Compromise was what he wanted. Again, he was offering half a loaf when she wanted it all. The man defied logic. He defied manipulation, a small voice warned Cally. "All right," she snapped before he changed his mind. "I suppose the need for a shrinking doctor is as good a reason as a real doctor would have for staying in the house with me." She looked hard at him, all pretense gone. "Oh Req, it's just that I want it both ways. I want you here for as long as you will stay. But when you do leave, I don't want my reputation compromised to the point of affecting my business. What is it you say . . . work with me on this? I know it will change as we go along, but we can deal with those changes as they happen."

Traces of a smile tugged the corners of her mouth. Requiem Maguire, undercover agent and all-around tough guy, had barely glimpsed the elephant he'd be dining on while in 1890.

Req got a close look at another kind of change before either he or Cally was ready. The doors of the dining room opened without warning. The houseman, Brendan Caulder, stood aside while Consuelo and Manuel Rodrigues rushed inside. Both spoke at once in excited, emotional voices and rushed to Cally. Consuelo continuously crossed herself and thanked God in Spanish for answering her prayers.

The pair, in their mid-thirties, had worked for the Hornsby

family for over a decade. Their joy at having Cally safely home overflowed; Consuelo, Cally's maid and assistant housekeeper, couldn't stop hugging her while Consuelo's husband, Manuel, the gardener and caretaker, hovered beside his wife. His wary glances at Req let him know that he regarded him as an eyesore in need of pruning from the Hornsby property.

Req chose that moment to extract himself from the group and corner Irene in the kitchen. He pulled a tall stool near the stove.

"Are you needing something special, Mr. Maguire?" Irene regarded him from the far side of the worktable. A swipe of flour marked her right cheek. Wary blue eyes scrutinized the length of his hair and the one-carat diamond sparkling in his ear.

Req grinned, aware of his formidable appearance and unwilling to apologize for it. "Nope. You fix a fine meal, Mrs. Kenny. My mouth is already watering at the sight of that piecrust you're rolling out."

"You're sure it's a pie I'm making."

"I'm sure I'm hoping it is." Hands braced on his thighs, Req closed his eyes and inhaled deeply, his spine straightening as his head lifted. "Smells like my favorite."

"Are you daft? You don't even know what kind of pie this will be."

"Homemade. Golden crust. My favorite."

"You must be an easy man to please, if that be the case."

"Oh, I assure you, the simplest things please me. How about you, Mrs. Kenny? Are you difficult to please?"

Her bosom shook as she laughed softly. "Heavens, no. I just like order and keeping things as they should be." The mirth faded from her round features. "I thank you from the bottom of my heart for bringing Miss Caladonia home. She never did say how she got lost or where she went."

"She may never be able to say exactly what happened," Req said slowly, wheedling his way into the role he reluctantly agreed to play. "Sometimes, that's for the best."

"For who?" Irene demanded. The thunk of the rolling pin on the dough seconded her demand. "I don't see no good coming from that, but I won't be questioning the way the Lord's answered my prayers for her safe return."

"What happened while she was gone?" Req probed lightly, careful to keep Irene Kenny's loyalty to Caladonia unchallenged.

Irene regarded him with a shrewd look that promised she was debating how much to tell him.

"I realize I'm a stranger, a curious one, asking questions you're not sure about, Mrs. Kenny. Trusting strangers isn't an easy thing to do, especially when someone we love is involved." He gave her his best apologetic smile and met her wary gaze.

"Don't you go getting any ideas about falling in love with Miss Caladonia. She knows her own mind on that score. She'll let you know if you can fall in love with her. Meanwhile, I'd feel better knowing just how you came across her and why it took you a month to bring her back."

"I assure you, Mrs. Kenny, we got here as soon as possible." He hooked the heels of his too-small shoes in the stool rungs and braced his elbows on his thighs. "I couldn't bring Cally home until we knew where home was and how to get here."

"Are you saying that girl forgot where she lived?" The rolling pin hung over the flattened pie dough. "I don't believe it. She's lived here most of her life. That ain't something a body is likely to forget."

Req shrugged. "Unfortunately, it happens, Mrs. Kenny."

"How'd you come across her?"

"When I'm near the ocean, I like to watch the sun rise. That particular morning, I happened to be at the right place and the right time for Miss Hornsby. I saw her in the water and helped her to shore." Req opened his hands as though he was opening a truth spoken from the heart. "It took some time to get things straightened out and return here. Believe me, there were no delays. She was anxious to get home." It was as close to the truth as he dared. He liked it that way.

"Oh, Lordy," Irene murmured, flattening the piecrust to the thickness of a crepe. "What if she forgets where she lives again?"

"That's hardly likely," Req assured her. "Traumatic amnesia is usually an isolated occurrence. Now that Miss Hornsby has recovered her memory, she isn't likely to forget again." Req kept his expression unchanged as he launched into the first of many lies necessary for his cover. "My best guess is that she was watching the tide come in a little too closely. A wave snatched her from the rocks and carried her out to the riptide. She nearly drowned."

Irene rolled the dough until it was paper-thin. "You saved

her, brought her home, and now you figure you have the right to ask questions. Is that it?"

Req couldn't contain the smile twitching at his mouth. Irene Kenny reminded him of a bulldog who wasn't going to give up any part of her bone without a knock-down, dragged-out fight. He liked her. "I don't figure you owe me anything. I'm concerned about Miss Hornsby and would like an idea of what she's going to face after a month-long absence."

"Well, I'm supposing it will depend on Thomas Barry," Irene conceded.

Req tried not to appear too pleased the conversation was finally going where he wanted it. "Mr. Barry?"

"If he continues pressing his suit for marriage, all will be fine. But if he takes one look at you, then Miss Caladonia, and thinks what I think . . ." Her voice faded into an uncomfortable silence.

"Just what is it you think, Mrs. Kenny?" Christ, his being here did complicate the hell out of both their plans. He hadn't realized how inconvenient he'd be for Cally to explain away until now. In his time, none of that mattered. However, 1890 was an entirely different story.

"I think, with the way you two look at one another, you just may know each other a little too well. You strike me as the kind of man who gets what he wants, Mr. Maguire." Irene's blue eyes spoke the rest of her assessment. "Under any other circumstances than saving her, taking care of her, and bringing her home, I'd have turned a shotgun on you by now."

"Save the shotgun for whoever killed her father," Req said softly, his gaze never wavering from the threat in Irene's eyes.

"I've got a barrel for him, too."

"Do you know who?"

Irene shook her head. "If I did, there'd be some justice for one of the kindest, most honest men Monterey has ever had the privilege to know."

"Tell me, Mrs. Kenny, what happened while she was gone? I'll warn you up front, I'm not leaving until I'm sure she is secure here." And he had about a month, until the next tidal alignment of the earth and moon, to make that happen.

Irene gathered up the piecrust dough in the same fashion a kid would take his marbles and go home. She wadded it between her powerful hands with a vehemence that forced the dough between her fingers like cream-colored fans. "Nobody in town knows Miss Caladonia was gone. Leastwise, nobody except Brendan, Mr. Cunningham, Mr. Barry, and Mr. Morton."

"How is that?"

Caladonia's soft question intruded on the private conversation.

Irene glanced from Cally to Req then back again. "Mr. Cunningham was wringing his hands about how it would look if you disappeared. He didn't want folks thinking he and Mr. Barry were trying to thin out the partnership."

Cally stood prim and proper; her hands loosely stacked at her waist. "And what did they tell people?"

"They said you were ailing. Not even Consuelo and Manuel knew you were not in the house. Mr. Cunningham told everyone I was the only person you'd see. Keeping people away from the house was no small task, Miss Caladonia. Mr. Cunningham managed it, though."

Req just bet he had. It appeared that Chauncy Cunningham was up to his eyebrows in mendacity and murder.

"Were there any events in town after I left . . . any unsavory occurrences?" Cally asked, making her way to Req's side.

Irene mashed the piecrust dough onto a new bed of flour. "Some sailor washed up on the beach just south of here. He had a bullet hole in his head."

"Did he have a name?" Req asked, his arm slipping around Cally's waist when she stood beside him.

"If he did, nobody knew it or recognized him right off, but the bullet hole was unmistakable." Irene held the rolling pin up. "Take your hands off her."

He reluctantly released Cally. In response, she rested her hand on his shoulder as though just as reluctant to break the contact between them. Req met Irene's knowing eyes with a sense of amazement, then pressed forward. "How does Thomas Barry fit in?"

Irene hesitated for a moment. "Mr. Barry has been beside himself with worry. He's set to marry you, Miss Caladonia, the minute you return, so he can take care of you proper."

Cally walked to the window and drew the curtain aside. "I won't be marrying Mr. Barry."

For a second, Req thought she might admit to being his wife.

"I don't love him," Cally said flatly. "I'll never love him."

"You're in love with this charming pirate here, aren't you?" Irene demanded.

"He's not a pirate."

"I'm a psychologist." Req's gaze fixed on the slight easing of Cally's rigid shoulders. What was one more lie to him?

"What's that?"

"A nuthouse doctor." Suddenly, the title felt apropos. The whole damn world had gone crazy and it was his turn to be king. As long as he was stuck playing this insane charade, he was going to use it to his advantage and get some answers. He may not have volunteered for this assignment, but he wasn't leaving until he was sure Cally was safe.

Regardless of how he'd gotten here, he owed her that much before he left.

Chapter 16

THE SMELL OF the ocean, pine trees, and horses hung in the early-afternoon air. The wagon took a hard bounce as it turned onto the main road to town. Req needed clothing. The only way to ensure that his new attire fit was to do it the old-fashioned way—go into town and try it on first.

Manuel Rodrigues provided the ride. Req had looked forward to questioning the gardener/handyman during the trek. But the opportunity faded when Manuel stared straight ahead, ignoring anything Req said to him. Bouncing on the seat of the supply wagon, the ride seemed long although it was only a short distance from the Hornsby home. To make matters worse, Cally had remained behind. Until they learned more about what took place during her absence, it seemed prudent to continue the ruse of her illness. Req had his own plans for investigating Cally's close brush with death.

After Manuel dropped him off, Req quickly concluded that shopping for clothing in 1890 was a challenge. For the past three years, he'd lived in jeans and tee shirts. He didn't know the first thing about country suits or cut-away waistcoats. The only certainty he clung to was that he wouldn't wear a plaid suit as seemed to be the style, judging by some of the men he had seen on the way into town. Fortunately, it didn't come to that. With the help of a patient clerk, he managed to put together several fashionable outfits that fit the times.

The town barber—with a handlebar mustache and a haircut that was a walking advertisement for his competition—made Req nervous as hell with the straightedge he put against Req's throat. By the time he left the barbershop, Req felt lucky he wasn't leaving a trail of blood to go with the mountain of hair on the floor.

Studying the pedestrians going about their daily business, he slowly walked the streets of Monterey. The elephant of change trumpeted everywhere he looked. Just as Cally had promised, the geography and geology of their respective eras were similar, but that was about it.

He relied on his training to help him adjust to his new world; listening, watching, absorbing, easing into the chameleon skin of the setting. An hour after arriving in town, Req's manners blended perfectly. Next, he sought ways to fill in the gaps. He began by picking up a copy of *The Wave*. On a bench in front of a dry goods store, he found part of a discarded San Francisco newspaper. He tucked the papers under his arm and went to the train depot where he studied the schedule. Any long trips he and Cally made were not going to be in a wagon.

Standing in the depot watching the railroad workers reminded him of the Westerns he had grown up watching on television.

With an hour to spare before he was to meet Manuel at the wagon, Req entered a café where most of the patrons were women and young couples. He supposed every era had its own versions of hot spots for the in-crowd. Interested in gossip, he deliberately chose a spot amid several tables populated by chatty women. With a cup of coffee and his newspapers, he settled in to learn about the good citizens of Monterey.

When he rose an hour later, he smiled, wondering what the women might have said had they known his true identity as Caladonia Hornsby's husband, former undercover drug agent and novice time traveler. It didn't take long for the societal differences of eleven decades to surface. After ten minutes of listening to the patrons around him, he had to admit that Cally had chosen the right course of action by insisting on hiding their marriage. He should have trusted her to know best. But then, he wasn't used to trusting anyone.

Cally was no shrinking violet. Hell, the longer he was in 1890 Monterey, the deeper became his respect for her mental toughness. She had not only coped with the vast cultural differences time had created when he'd hauled her out of the sea, but she had endured the cutting edge of his disbelief and the barbs of his skepticism.

Mentally he winced. She might be a fortunate woman, but she wasn't a lucky one. A lucky woman wouldn't have ended up with an emotional cripple like him as a rescuer. Now, the circumstances were reversed. He was damn lucky she was compassionate and caring.

With a sigh, he set out on the two-block walk to the wagon.

On the way home, he asked Manuel questions in Spanish—and got no more answers than when he'd asked in English.

Cally sighed, wrapped her shawl around her shoulders, and followed Req down the front steps into the damp night. The glow of the house lights illuminated the fog rolling in from the ocean while in the distance, the warning horn wailed out its message to seafarers in Monterey Bay. They walked slowly. The emotional distance between them was greater than the careful physical separation.

Since his return from town shortly before supper, Cally had been staring at him. Initially she wasn't sure whether to laugh or cry. Requiem Maguire didn't look out of place in the fashions of 1890. He should have: his physique was too sculptured for a store-bought suit. His shoulders were too wide for his coat, his hips too narrow for both his coat and trousers. The man needed a tailor. Badly. But in true Requiem Maguire fashion, he had improvised with the available fare, then exerted his individuality. Other than his shirts and possibly his undergarments, all his clothing was black—even his waistcoats.

Quietly, she lamented the loss of his long hair. How she had enjoyed running her hands through his dark, thick mane during the quiet moments after they made love, that special time when everything glowed and nothing intruded. Inhaling a long breath of cool night air into her lungs, Cally tried not to think about intimacy with Req.

"You were right." A faint glow from the parlor windows lit the side of his face. He peered straight ahead with an intensity that made her suspect he was searching for someone hiding in the darkness.

"About what?"

"Doing things your way. This is your turf. You know best how things will work."

The night cloaked any insight she might have gained from his expression. "Is this your way of apologizing?"

"I guess you could call it that."

"Hmmm. I believe I will. I've never heard you apologize before."

"Yeah, well, write it on your calendar. It doesn't happen very often." Though he tried to make it sound light, the truth wouldn't knuckle under easily.

"In that case, I'll most certainly do as you suggest. While I'm at it, perhaps you would narrow the apology down to a subject." Feeling him tense, she bit back a smile and quickly added, "You needn't be specific, but it would help."

They followed the contour of the rambling Victorian-style house around to the side. A stepping-stone walkway led into the garden, then branched out in several directions. Without hesitation, Cally selected a path that led to a stone bench in the heart of the gardens.

"I, uh, was being selfish about sleeping with you." He braced one foot on the bench when she sat down. "The marriage thing . . ."

Sensing there was more, she waited, curious about his strange mood.

"I don't have a claim on you. Not here, that's for sure."

"Do you want a claim on me, Req?" Had any double-edged sword ever had such sharp edges? Regardless of the edge it cut with, it produced pain. Regret.

"I want to sleep in the same room with you."

"Why?" she pressed, emotion thickening in her throat. Though she couldn't see more than his solid silhouette against the dim light leaking into the garden, she felt the heat of his desire. She doubted he would have revealed so much of himself in the daylight. Still, she wished for enough light to search his face for a hint of what was going on inside him.

"Why the hell do you think? So we can make love." Irritation clipped his words. "At least that'd take the edge off."

"Take the edge off what?" she asked guardedly.

"Being here. Being out of place."

She watched him slide his foot from the edge of the stone bench and step away. His restlessness was contagious. It was also irritating. "Are you telling me that you want to sleep with me because sleeping in strange places makes you edgy?"

The air around them instantly warmed with the fire of their mutual annoyance with each other and their circumstances. "Don't start picking at my words, Cally. This isn't easy for me. I know I acted like a Neanderthal when I found you on the beach. Hell, I still do. And I like sleeping with you—and not because sleeping in strange places makes me edgy."

Her body quaked with desire when he faced her. In the faint light from the house, she saw more of his soul than in the bright light of day. Consigned to the solitude of the guest room, he'd awaken from his nightmares alone. That realization was almost enough for her to relent.

"I'm changing, Cally. I hate it, but I can't stop it." The admission tore at her.

"Will my risking discovery of our intimate relationship stop it, Req?" If so, she'd open the bedroom door wide. Anything was worth easing the torment that lived in the depths of his eyes.

"No. I'm a selfish bastard. You're right to protect yourself and your future here. You caught me at a weak moment when I found you in the water. A month earlier, I would have left you on the beach, walked away, and never given you a second thought." The angst in his voice betrayed a darker turmoil she had glimpsed more frequently in recent days. "I wouldn't have cared about your future," he concluded.

"In that case, it sounds like I arrived at the best possible time," she said softly. "I wouldn't have cared for detox or any of the places I may have ended up if you hadn't taken me home with you." *And let me fall in love so you could break my heart,* she concluded.

"I'm no benevolent do-gooder, Cally, and you damn well know it. I'm trying to do my job and survive the best way possible, just like the next guy. Coming here wasn't in my plans, but that won't stop me from doing what I do best. We need to catch your bad guys and put them away."

"I realize that." She hesitated, suspecting that a refusal of his help would add to his turmoil. "Meanwhile, I'll do everything I can to help you adjust to the here and now. Tell me what you need."

The despair evident in his hollow laugh made the fine hair on the nape of her neck rise. Unexpectedly, he caught her face in his hands, hesitated, then kissed her forehead. "Damned if I know, Cally. Go inside. I'll be in later."

"Req—"

"Leave it be. I need to think."

As much as she wanted to hold him, kiss him, and ease the tumult rolling off of him like breakers on the beach at high tide, she refrained. Req was a solitary man struggling hard to rejoin a society he had abandoned in the name of vengeance, all the while wearing the mantle of justice. He would never forgive her if he thought she considered him weak even for a moment.

Cally rose, her hands clasped tightly against her skirts. Why did his pain hurt her so much? "Will you accompany me to the shipping offices in the morning?"

"Yes. Now go to bed." He straightened and shoved his hands in his pockets. "Good night."

Awash with empathy for his sense of displacement, a dozen platitudes clamored in her head. But that's all they were—platitudes. She turned away. There was no substitution for him finding his own way of devouring the change.

She felt him watching her retreat, felt the way he stripped off her clothing one layer at a time, and knew the fiery excitement of his gaze on her skin. The heat of anticipation flowed from her in the cool night. How easy it would be to get lost in the quick passion that ignited between them with a careless look. How foolish. How marvelous.

She hesitated. "Good night, Req," she whispered without turning. He was beyond her reach in so many ways.

Adrenaline rushed through Cally when she entered the offices of Golden Sun Shipping the next morning. She had taken care to dress in her best business attire. The blue wool with ecru bands as borders on the skirt and sleeves fit the occasion perfectly. Wide point de Gênes lace formed the cuffs, sleeves, and cravat of the tailored gown.

A day of isolation was the limit of her tolerance away from the center of activity. She needed resolution. The daring of her plan barely got a thought amid the myriad emotions brought on by being back in the bosom of the life she loved. Her father had built this business with Chauncy Cunningham. The greatest tribute Cally could pay him was to nurture it and do her best to guide policy in the direction he advocated.

At the Golden Sun offices, Cally waded through everyone's good wishes and prayers for her recovery from the mysterious illness. She suspected Req held her upper arm as much to ground him as to issue a warning to any whom attempted to approach her. However, his formidable presence did expedite their progress to the office with her father's name still painted on the door.

"You'd gain a helluva lot more credibility if you put your name on the door," Req muttered, studying the mahogany walls replete with paintings of Golden Sun vessels skimming the waves. Her gaze lingered on the painting of the Golden Sun flagship *Venture*. The oil held the hallowed position on the wall behind a massive teak desk polished to a high gloss.

The remark caught her off guard. "Thank you for your opinion."

Req prowled the office. "My opinion about your business doesn't mean jack." He paused beside the window and studied the wharf on the other side of the curtains. "We've got about a month to clean up this mess. Let's round up the players."

"You've done enough for me, Req. It isn't necessary—"

"You're not stupid. Don't make noise like you are. I'm here. I'm not going anywhere until I'm sure there isn't some soulless bastard waiting for you in the shadows after I'm gone."

"You're going to be my hero as well as my rescuer?"

Before Req could answer, the door opened. Thomas Barry, the third partner in the shipping firm, hurried in. Cally barely had time for a breath before he wrapped her in an intimate embrace.

"My God, Caladonia, I've been so worried," he breathed into the mess he was making of her hair. "What happened? Are you well?"

She knew Thomas had tender feelings for her, but not the depths responsible for such a blatant breach of propriety. Stunned, she pushed away from him.

In the blink of an eye, Req was at her side. One-handed, he caught Thomas by the shoulder and eased him away.

"What?" Perplexed, an angry Thomas turned on his attacker. "Who the devil are you?"

An instant rivalry potent enough to ignite the air around them sprang up between the two men. "Gentlemen," Cally started, carefully inserting her shoulder between them, "please allow me to introduce you."

Before she got any farther, the door banged open. Cally's dearest friend, Maudel Morton, rushed at her, then stopped short. "Thank God you've recovered, Caladonia. Father said the doctors weren't sure how you would fare." Tears filled Maudel's big brown eyes. Thick, dark lashes caught the overflow and spiked her cheeks. "When Irene refused to let me see you this past month, and you didn't answer my letters, I feared the worst." She reached out. Trembling fingers clutched Cally's arm.

The abject misery Cally's absence had inflicted on those she cared for, those who had become her family, tore a new chasm of hurt in her heart. "Oh, Maudel, everything is going to be fine. I'm here, and I'm healthy."

One moment, she and Maudel were hugging and making plans for an evening together. The next, Maudel was rigid and staring at a spot behind Cally.

"Ma'am," Req said softly. How did he make a single word sound like he was tipping his hat? He wasn't even wearing one.

"Oh, my. I apologize for intruding," Maudel said.

"Not at all." Cally caught Maudel's arm and drew her closer to Req. "Allow me to introduce—"

"Where were you? Why the hell didn't you send word?" Chauncy Cunningham boomed, then slammed the office door, saw his daughter, and abruptly added, "From your home?"

A man with a generous share of height and girth, his presence seemed to take up half the office. A thick mane of gray hair subdued from years of taming parted to the left. Heavy gray-brown eyebrows arched over eyes the same golden-brown as his daughter's. Yet, unlike Maudel's, Chauncy Cunningham's older, wiser, eyes held secrets. "We've been worried sick over you, Caladonia. Who is your companion?" His jowls continued vibrating when the rest of him stopped short and stared across the office.

"May I present—"

"Requiem Maguire." The easy grace of his manners instantly put everyone in the room at ease.

"—Requiem Maguire," Cally finished, stunned by the sudden complete change in him. "He's my—"

"I'm overseeing Miss Hornsby's care. She's been through a difficult time." Req shook Chauncy's hand, then reached for Thomas's. "Because we have no clear scientific explanation for the reason that necessitated Miss Hornsby's absence, I think it best for you to keep a safe distance."

"Are you saying she had something contagious?" Maudel brushed the lingering tears from her cheeks. "My goodness." She took several steps back, ran into her father, then stopped. She dropped her hand to her abdomen. "I had no idea."

"I'm not contagious," Cally insisted, hating the distress that etched Maudel's waifish features. What was Req up to?

"Under normal circumstances, I'd agree, Miss Hornsby," Req said, coming to her side. "The problem lies not with you catching a malady, Miss—"

"Mrs." Maudel corrected. "Mrs. Cameron Morton."

"Mrs. Morton," Req acknowledged. "The danger lies in Miss Hornsby catching something as simple as a cold from those around her."

"The hell you say," said Chauncy, his brown eyes squinting, never wavering from Req.

"Miss Hornsby has endured severe trauma this past month,

Mr. Cunningham. It was only her tenacity to regain her old life that enabled her return to you now."

Cally didn't have to fake any trauma. Req was traumatizing her with each word he spoke. She knew he had to be convincing when he went undercover, but she hadn't expected him to take charge so well, masterfully weaving a bridge over the missing month with strands of the truth. It gave her pause to consider how many ways there were to tell the truth—all of them conjecture.

"I see," Chauncy said. "I wonder if you would mind stepping into my office, Mr. Maguire."

"That's Dr. Maguire," Req said with a friendly smile.

"We could use another doctor," Chauncy said, reaching for the door.

"I don't practice general medicine," Req said. "I'm specialized."

A sigh of relief tempered Cally's growing trepidation for what Req would say or do next. When she saw the abject sympathy with which Maudel and Thomas regarded her, she knew it was her end of this charade she had to concern herself with. Req was doing fine.

"Perhaps you should sit and rest," Thomas suggested. "Maudel and I have only your best health in mind."

"Oh, yes, Caladonia. Please. I could not bear it if you were to become ill again."

She was the antithesis of a frail invalid. Having Req so close without making love last night had filled her with excess energy. Even so, she settled in the chair Thomas pulled from behind the enormous desk she had inherited from her father.

"Tell me what I've missed," she prodded.

"I believe Maudel is quite capable of that. Suffice to say I am delighted you're well. We have much to discuss, Caladonia, but that will keep for a more auspicious time."

"Yes," she agreed, "there are several things in need of discussion." *Right after I talk with dear* Dr. *Maguire.*

"I'll send word. Perhaps in a day or two?" he asked from the door, obviously eager to join in the conversation between Chauncy Cunningham and Req.

"That would be fine, Thomas."

Oblivious to the silent agendas growing around her, Maudel settled on the sofa. A smile lit her face with the full intensity of a lighthouse beacon. "Oh, I am so glad I stopped by to see Father today. I can tell you our marvelous news." She leaned forward and clasped Cally's hands. "There will be one more in our family this spring."

A boy, Cally thought, squeezing Maudel's fingers in shared excitement and trying to banish the foreknowledge. "This is great news. Exciting news."

The comfort of old friends catching up slipped beneath the worry of what was going on in the adjacent office. Req would handle himself well.

Maudel spoke about the social happenings during Cally's absence with increasing animation. Watching, listening, Cally wondered how long it had been since her friend's effervescent personality had danced in the daylight as it did now. Why hadn't she noticed before that something was amiss in Maudel's life? Was it the pregnancy? Or something else?

Shortly, Req returned to the office, indicating it was time to leave.

Maudel's radiance dimmed when she realized their hiatus from daily pressures and responsibility was at an end. Although Cally invited her back to the house, she declined.

Req led Cally out of the Golden Sun Shipping offices. The crisp morning air carried the raw odors and sounds of a fishing trawler unloading her catch.

She bit her tongue until they were safely out of earshot from the Golden Sun offices. "Why are we leaving so soon?"

"Trust me, it's time to go."

"What did you three discuss in Chauncy's office?"

"I asked a few questions. They asked plenty more." He caught her elbow and guided her across the street. "Mostly I explained your medical condition. I did learn that Cunningham thinks you're going to be content to put in an occasional appearance, look at some paperwork, and turn the actual operation over to him and Barry."

It dismayed her, but didn't surprise her. "I might have started convincing him how wrong he is if you hadn't whisked me out of there. I really need to catch up on the business, Req."

"I think you've created enough of a stir for one day. Cunningham and Barry were full of questions, and the best way to put them off was to tell them I had to bring you home to get some rest."

"Sooner or later, we're going to have to answer their questions. Tomorrow, I'm going to see what my partners have done with the time I've been gone. We had several interesting opportunities in the way of new clients before I left. I want to know what happened."

"I suspect Cunningham is going to want you to keep your distance, as you've done since your father's death."

"Those days are over. I'm a full partner and I don't intend to sit quietly in the corner."

Chauncy Cunningham was certainly in for a surprise. Cally's jaunt into the late twentieth century had showed her the great strides women could make if they asserted themselves. One-third of Golden Sun was hers. She intended to assume one-third of the workload in running it, just as she expected to bank one-third of the profits or pay the same share of the debt. "And Thomas?"

"He's harder to read. Offhand, I'd say he has big plans." Warning narrowed his eyes when he met her gaze. "Plans that include marrying you and taking over the company. We already know he's going to sell out in a couple of years. The question is, why? If you marry him—"

"I'm not marrying Thomas Barry." The notion of settling for Thomas after Req was laughable. Just walking beside Req put all her senses on alert, always waiting for the delicious moment of an improper touch, an intimate glance, or a soul-searing kiss. She wanted it all. "After watching you in my father's office, I must say you certainly know how to do your job very well."

"I can be subtle." With the grace of a dancer, he moved to the street-side of Cally as they turned toward the rougher part of the waterfront.

"Not with me," she murmured.

"No. You're separate from everything else."

She decided to let it rest. Later, she would press him for the meaning of his words. "Our next stop is Helmut Schmit. He's dealt with the all the Golden Sun captains and their crews." She drew a long breath. "Getting them to work with the dockhands for a common purpose is not an easy task. After my brief stint in your time, I think Helmut's extracurricular activities might be considered the beginning of unionism. Golden Sun pays him to assist in procuring the best price for provisioning our ships before they go to sea."

"You haven't spoken about him much. Did he have anything to gain from your father's death?"

"Nothing. He had a lot to lose. Helmut never wanted to be anything other than a sea captain. A whaler, specifically. An angry whale changed his life. A couple of years later, my father helped him find a new avenue of making a livelihood for his family. Helmut loved my father. He encouraged Helmut's organizing activities with the sailors. I would trust him with my life and have on the docks."

"Tell me you don't come here alone."

Cally ignored him. "We're here." She stopped in front of a weathered green door in a single-story battered building sandwiched between two larger, equally dilapidated buildings.

"Cally? Do you come down here alone?"

Again she ignored him.

"This conversation isn't over."

"It certainly isn't," she agreed, then opened the door. A bell jangled nearly as loud as the hinges squeaked.

Fresh air fanned the dank atmosphere inside the long, narrow interior. Dust devils scurried along the scarred, wooden floor and danced in the rays of sunlight filtered by windows in dire need of washing. The office was empty. Even the battered desk Helmut had kept as orderly as a ship captain's quarters was gone. The only evidence of life was the trails of rat droppings along the baseboards.

"Helmut," Cally whispered, her fingertips hovering over her lips. "Oh, my God, what's happened?" She swayed, barely aware of Req holding her up.

The only thing that would have convinced Helmut to abandon this office was death.

Chapter 17

No ONE ANSWERED the door at the Schmit home. When Cally cupped her hands and peeked inside the windows, she saw the house was as empty as the waterfront office. Flummoxed, she knocked on the front door of a neighbor's home.

Round-faced Ardith Murray dabbed at the corners of her sad brown eyes with the hem of her apron while explaining that Helmut Schmit had died, killed on the waterfront in San Francisco. Cally leaned against Req, hardly able to believe what she heard. If she started crying for Helmut, she might disintegrate into a weepy puddle. "Where did his wife go?" Cally asked the Schmit's neighbor.

"The shock of Helmut's death was more than Katya could bear alone. Now she is gone too. Gone to San Francisco to live with her daughter and son-in-law," the woman said. "Their absence is a great loss to my husband and me. We've known them since we came to Monterey nine years ago."

"When did Mr. Schmit die?" Req asked. The comforting arm he slid around Cally's waist kept her from swaying.

"Four weeks ago this coming Friday, though we didn't know it until Katya returned for her things. It's so hard to believe we'll not see him again." Ardith Murray sniffed, then gathered her composure. "My husband is overseeing the sale of her house. We'll get what we can. Katya would hate being a financial burden to her daughter."

"Do you know why Helmut went to San Francisco, Mrs. Murray?"

Cally listened in disbelief as Mrs. Murray explained that Helmut and Katya had left for San Francisco unexpectedly.

When Katya returned, she said that Helmut had left their daughter's house to take care of some business and never returned. The police had found his mangled body a week later, a bullet through the side of the head.

By the time Req led her away from the Murray home, Cally was sure Helmut's death wasn't a case of him being in the wrong place at the wrong time. "They murdered him," she murmured, pointing toward an alley shortcut to the livery where their buggy waited.

"Who are *they* and why did they murder him?" Req asked calmly.

"*They* are the same ones that killed my father and Freddy the Thief. The ones who wanted to kill me."

"Did you have a divine revelation? Or is this emotion talking, Cally?"

Her shoulders sagged in realization that all she had was emotion. "It makes sense," she countered. Her intuition screamed that all three murders were connected. The question was, how?

Req eyed a trio of sailors watching them. When they turned away, he asked, "How popular were Helmut's union efforts with the ship owners and captains?"

Cally looked up at Req. Suddenly, things weren't as clear as a moment ago. "Do you think someone would kill him for that?"

Req shook his head. "Let's just say unionization of the labor force, particularly on the docks, came with a high price. In its infancy, murder was common. Sometimes it was thinly disguised as an accident or a random mugging. Regardless, a bullet in the brain is a universal message."

"Well," she started, slowing her pace, "Helmut and I were supposed to meet with Chauncy and Thomas about standardizing wages. When I got caught in the time pool, I assumed Helmut would have attended the meeting on his own. But since he left for San Francisco so quickly I'll have to ask Thomas."

Her mind spun between grief and outrage. "What would have lured him up to the San Francisco docks? What could they have said to him?" Cally continued.

Req guided her around the corner. "We don't know the same men who killed Freddy the Thief also killed Helmut. But for now we'll assume your gut instincts are right and all three murders are connected. The way they're interwoven around you and your father is too convenient for coincidence. We need to find the links between your father, Helmut Schmidt, and Freddy the Thief."

"Hansen," she said abruptly. She had been struggling all day trying to remember the exact words spoken on the beach. "He said his name was Freddy Hansen."

"Good girl. A name gives us a place to start looking for answers. Someone on the docks or in the bars must have known him. Even a man like Freddy leaves a hole when he dies."

Cally let him guide her down the sidewalk. It sounded like Req was developing a plan to help find her father's killer and she was eager to do her part. "I'll make inquiries among the men on the wharf and those who frequented Helmut's office." Something she couldn't quite identify wiggled in her brain.

"Leave Freddy Hansen to me," Req said. "Men like him are cut out of the same cloth no matter what year it is. I know the weave well. You stay clear. There's no telling what kind of snakes will crawl out from under the floorboards once I start asking about him."

"I'm not going to sit at home and watch the minute hand on the clock make circles every night while you're out solving my problems." That was unthinkable. Unacceptable.

"Good. You can work another angle that I can't. Go sit at your friend's home." He nodded at a passing couple who bid them a good afternoon. "Seems to me one of the major players was absent this morning."

"Major players?" At times, she still had trouble interpreting twentieth-century idioms.

"Where was Cameron Morton?"

"I don't know," she answered thoughtfully. "Now that you mention it, it seems strange for Maudel to be at the company without Cameron accompanying her." Because she had never cared for Maudel's husband, she had not noticed his absence.

"If you can't wrangle an invitation with the Mortons for to-morrow evening, then invite Thomas Barry, the Cunninghams, and Cameron and Maudel for dinner. I'll stay in the back-ground. Be careful how you probe Cameron for information. We need to find out what he knows about the *Ocean Princess,* and how deeply he's involved. With three possible leads and not a lot of time, we need to find the weak link and go after him without tipping our hand. Thomas Barry could be involved all the way up to his starched collar."

"Or he could have only the noblest motives and be innocent of any subterfuge."

"There's nothing innocent about your business partner. Considering the way he manhandled you today, he's already got two strikes against him in my book."

"Two strikes? And they are . . . ?"

"He's ambitious."

"You disapprove of ambition?" She certainly hoped not.

"When it burns in a man's belly to the point where there's nothing he won't do to achieve his goals, yes. Thomas Barry has smoke rising around his shirt collar."

"He is ambitious, and he does have an uncanny business sense," Cally agreed, remembering the reasons her father cited for taking Thomas Barry on as a partner—besides the size of his bank account. "But I never sensed anything sinister about him."

"I'm not saying there is. He might have the strength of character to resist shortcuts, or he might not. I didn't spend enough time around him today to size him up, but I suspect that the man has as many layers as an onion. How well do you know him, Cally? Well enough to trust him with your life?"

She thought hard about Thomas, and then sifted through what she knew. "When I put my mind to it, it is amazing how little I actually know about him. My father trusted him. I trusted my father. But I can't tell you much about Mr. Barry."

She mulled over the disturbing revelation until the livery was in sight. "What was the second strike against him?"

"He damn well better keep his hands off you. He undresses you when he looks at you."

Cally lowered her head to hide a satisfied smile. "So do you, Req." And she felt it in the center of her being each time.

"I am your husband. I have the license to do so. It's valid as long as we're together. When I leave, as far as you're concerned, I haven't been born."

"And for you, I'm dead. Is that it?" Realizing how little she meant to him dropped a fifty-pound anvil onto her heart. Memories of making love, tender touches, and sudden bursts of laughter during lighthearted moments played out on top of the anvil of heartache.

"Looks like it," he snapped. "Don't see what the hell I can do to change it right now. Do you?"

"Either way, death parts us and nullifies—"

"Just keep a distance from him, Cally. Like it or not, you're married to me. If he tries anything when I am—"

"What's the matter with you, Req? What warped your perspective?"

"My perspective hasn't changed."

Cally let out a yelp when he picked her up and put her in the buggy, then climbed in after her.

"Be a liberated woman. Drive us home."

"Be a macho man. Take the reins while I admire your horsemanship and watch the scenery," she said, confident he knew as much about horses as she knew about motorcycles.

He released the brake on the top surrey. The horse sensed movement and danced in the traces. "Too bad we don't have seat belts." He reached for the reins.

Exasperated, Cally snatched them away. "You don't know how to drive."

Req sat back and folded his arms over his chest. "So teach me. It can't be any more complex than steering the Harley through rush-hour traffic on the freeway. No helmet requirement either. How hard can it be?"

"Suppose I teach you how to ride a horse instead."

He shrugged. "I did that once. For that, I'd *want* a helmet."

She snapped the reins and sent the horse on his way. "And you think that was enough to learn all there is to know about riding a horse?"

"Unless you know how to put one in reverse, it's enough. I'm not entering the Kentucky Derby, just going back and forth from town."

He'd been here for less than two days and no longer needed her. She didn't know whether to feel humbled, awed, or just plain irritated. She settled for the latter. It was less threatening.

Req decided to go into town after supper and poke his nose around the dockside taverns. He wished for his Harley, but in its absence opted to walk instead of climbing onto the back of a horse.

Cally was waiting for him when he returned after midnight. It didn't surprise him that she had waited up. Hell, she haunted his dreams and invaded his thoughts the instant he let his guard down. The long golden braid draped over her shoulder begged to have his fingers unwind it. The sturdy robe hiding her nightgown reminded him of the terry-cloth armor she had clutched to her throat in his kitchen. She wasn't holding the pale-blue robe closed. A cotton tie did that for her.

"What did you find out?" She closed and locked the front door.

"It's late. You ought to be in bed." *My bed.*

"I was so worried, I couldn't possibly sleep until you returned. There are so many unfamiliar things for you to cope with. . . ." Her voice trailed off and she licked her lips as though salivating for the kiss he ached to give her.

"I coped. I'm back. Go to bed, Cally. We'll talk about it in the morning." He dug a finger behind the starched collar chafing his neck. Damn, being so close to her, wanting her twenty-four hours a day was going to toast him into a cinder before the next tidal cycle.

Arms crossed under her breasts, she glared at him.

He could ignore her or grab her and haul her up the stairs to the closest bed. At the stairs, he slowed, tempted to give into his base needs. "In the morning, we're going hunting."

"For what?"

"The contents of the office Helmut Schmit ran."

"That has been bothering me all night too," she said from two steps behind him. "Learning he was dead was such a shock at the time, I didn't stop to wonder what happened to the office. Once we got home I realized the papers and records were gone. So was the furniture, such as it was. Helmut went to San Francisco a couple of days after I left. Who cleaned out the office?"

"That's the $64,000 question." At the top of the stairs, he stuffed the starched false collar and tie he'd removed into his coat pocket. "Round two of the question-and-answer period will resume in the morning."

"Req . . ."

The soft plea in her voice cut through him. He gripped the doorknob and turned, but didn't open it. "I'm tired, Cally, but not too tired to get off on that earthy growl you make when you come." He opened the door. "I'm going to bed now. Don't come in here unless you plan on getting naked with me."

"Req, it doesn't have to—"

He closed the door and stood in the darkness, aching, wondering why he wanted her so damn badly. Not just wanted—*needed.* Over the years, he'd wanted many women, but this was the first time he needed a specific one. Not even Malika had gotten to him in such a primal manner.

He chalked it up to the reemergence of his long-suppressed emotions. The trouble was, they all seemed to have been reborn with birth defects.

He listened for her in the hall as he undressed. When he got into bed, he called out, "Good night, Miss Hornsby."

Without acknowledging him, she walked away.

Req stared at the ceiling. It was going to be a long month. The prospects of what came after were too bleak to contemplate. For now, he'd concentrate on finding the killer stalking circles around Cally. Eventually, whoever it was would move in for the kill unless Req unmasked him first.

Other than the supreme sacrifice of not seducing her, it was the least he could do for her.

Pressing business matters at the Golden Sun Shipping offices consumed Cally's days. An astounding number of contracts required her signature. In true, thorough Hornsby style, she would not sign any document until she had read and understood the content of each. It was going to take days for her to deal with the most critical ones.

Resigned to their slow progress at exploring who at the shipping company knew what about the murders, Req seized the opportunity to roam the docks. By noon he began to grasp the reverence and respect in which the men who went to sea had regarded Peter Hornsby. Some lamented the death of Helmut Schmit as the demise of their last advocate with the large shipping companies who were repressing their earnings.

Wage structures and labor relations were the last things Req wanted to concern himself with. He entered a rough-looking tavern, ordered a beer, and sat at a table with his back to the wall. The ingrained habit of making sure of his surroundings isolated him from the rest of the clientele.

He listened and waited. The word was spreading that someone was asking about Freddy Hansen. Eventually someone would ask him *why*. That was the man he wanted to meet.

The ebb and flow of dockside business filtered through the dank, smoky air of the tavern. Req listened to the brags, boasts, and laments of the sailors.

The conditions of hard drinking and even harder working men would change over the next century, but the basic composition of character evolved little. How easy it was to distinguish the men who came in for a social respite from those whose lives revolved around the tavern.

"Mind if I join you?" The young man across the table from Req had old eyes although Req guessed him to be in his mid-twenties. The tension in his shoulders had reached into his face and carved worry lines around his eyes and mouth.

"Depends." Req took the first sip of his beer that had turned warm and flat. The strong flavor tickled the back of his tongue. He reminded himself that the uniformity of alcohol content was still something in the distant future.

"On what?" The visitor stepped over the bench on the far side of the table.

"Whether or not you're a good conversationalist."

"If I heard right, we have something to talk about. You can find out for the price of a beer."

Req studied the sailor. He was cleaner than the regular patrons. Tall and rangy. In his own time Req would have thought him a runner. Light-brown hair overdue for an appointment with the barber's scissors framed the sharp features that were chiseled into a long, narrow unshaven face. The pea coat he carried like a prized possession looked new. Req watched the stranger's movements. He was far too conscious of the occasional bellow and raised voices from the sailors at the bar to be one of them.

"Who are you?"

"The name's Lemuel." He signaled to the tavern keeper.

"Requiem Maguire." He nodded, not ready to extend his hand until he finished sizing up his visitor. "Is Lemuel your first or last name?"

"Last name's Hansen. Freddy was my brother. I understand you've been asking about him."

"Yeah." So Freddy the Thief had a brother who cared enough to ask questions. What was he interested in? Freddy, or Freddy's business at Cally's house?

"What do you want with him?"

Req waited until the tavern keeper served Lemuel a beer, then paid for it. "I had a few questions I wanted him to answer."

"What about?"

Req studied the way the younger man's hands gripped the stein. They were the hands of a hobbyist, perhaps an office worker; not the hard, callused hands of a man who did manual labor. The dress and cultivated mannerisms may have convinced others that Lemuel and his brother shared a trade, but not Req. Beneath the veneer, Req saw something more promising than a man who was his brother's keeper. A fire burned in Hansen's belly.

"I'm interested in the men he worked for." Req cast an experienced eye over the patrons. None showed the slightest bit of interest in either him or Lemuel.

"That's common knowledge. He'd just come off the *Pacific Bounty.*"

"I checked at the registry. That ship sailed without him six weeks ago." Req pushed his beer away and approached from another direction. "It isn't common knowledge Freddy had a brother. How do I know you're related?"

Lemuel's dark-brown eyes glittered as though he enjoyed the challenge. "Who would claim Freddy Hansen as a brother and look for his killers if he wasn't?"

Req grinned. He liked Lemuel. "You have an excellent point. Who would? Unless it was his killer looking to see how well his tracks are covered."

Lemuel lifted his stein. "Touché. Now it's up to you to decide which one I am."

His brother, Req decided. "Do you know who he was doing his night business for?"

Lemuel shook his head. "Why are you interested?"

Req shrugged. "A number of things have happened that are too convenient to be coincidence. Freddy's death is one."

"Are you referring to the death of Helmut Schmit?" Lemuel took a long drink on his beer, then wiped his mouth with the back of his hand.

"Among others."

Lemuel perked up. "Such as?"

"Who was he working for?" Req had given him enough. Now he wanted answers.

"I don't know. From what I've pieced together, someone influential and wealthy. Freddy thought he was going to make a handsome sum of money for one night's work." Lemuel pushed the half-empty stein away. "My brother was never one for lifting a hand when he could lift a wallet." He crossed his arms on the table and leaned closer. "What is your involvement with Caladonia Hornsby?"

"Miss Hornsby has asked for my help. Why?"

"From what I've gathered, Freddy was very interested in her shortly before he was killed. Suddenly he's dead and Miss Hornsby becomes so ill she can't answer a simple note of inquiry. Next, Helmut Schmit is murdered in San Francisco. Mr. Schmit worked with Miss Hornsby on organizing the fishermen, as I understand it. All things considered, I think she is in the thick of things."

Req studied the man. Whoever he was, he had a good mind. A curious mind. Perhaps he was just what he said, a man seeking answers to his brother's death. However, Req's inability to trust anyone made him delve deeper in search of ulterior motives.

"What do you know about Miss Hornsby?" Req asked in his most persuasive tell-me-everything-you-know voice.

"Not nearly as much as I need to make up my mind about her involvement. You were right earlier when you said it's all too convenient."

"I won't waste our time trying to convince you of her innocence. You'll reach that conclusion soon enough."

"You know her well?"

"Well enough to know she didn't kill anyone. She has her own demons and it's very possible the same men who killed, or arranged the killing, of your brother, are also responsible for Schmit and her father."

"Her father?" Lemuel straightened. "I didn't realize her father had been killed." He stroked his chin thoughtfully. "That does shine a different light on it."

"Where are you from, Hansen, and what's your line of work? It sure as hell isn't a seaman."

"I'm a stockbroker from San Francisco," he answered, obviously distracted by the new piece of information that changed his suspicions. A fresh alertness sharpened his gaze. "You think all three murders are connected?"

Req said nothing.

"I suppose anything is possible," Lemuel mused. "Helmut Schmit paid me a call on the day he was killed. Unfortunately, I wasn't home. I thought very little about it because I didn't know him. When I read about his death in the newspaper, I couldn't help wondering why he'd come to see me.

"Ten days ago I received a letter informing me my brother had died. Answers concerning the circumstances are practically nonexistent."

"You're determined to find out what happened to him," Req said, weighing the man's sincerity in on the high side.

"Freddy was many things, Mr. Maguire. One of them was

my brother. A man doesn't turn his back on his brother's murder and forget about it because it's inconvenient to seek answers."

"It could also be dangerous."

"I'm aware of that." His unwavering gaze met Req's and did not shy away. "Particularly since the authorities have no intention of pursuing the matter."

"You've spoken with them?" At least Lemuel Hansen had started with a plan.

"Yes. For a while I thought Detective Goodman might pursue the matter. However, I was mistaken. Going to the authorities is a futile endeavor."

Req nodded. He hadn't intended to reveal his interest in the three murders to the police. According to Cally and the newspaper accounts, Detective Goodman had shown interest in her father's murder, then dropped the matter. The odds of the authorities raising an eyebrow over Freddy Hansen were lousy even for a seasoned gambler. "Have you learned anything of use?"

A hollow laugh accompanied Lemuel's reach for his beer. "Besides things I would have preferred to remain ignorant of concerning my brother? Very little." He took a drink, then settled the stein before him. "One thing puzzles me."

Req offered a slight nod of encouragement. Lemuel Hansen was well on his way to unburdening his troubled mind, so there was no point in interrupting. Besides, the façade Lemuel had carefully constructed to help him fit in with the dockside dwellers already had slipped away. The man was an amateur.

"In the past week I've wondered a hundred times why Freddy came to Monterey." Lemuel shrugged in resignation. "Perhaps he signed onto a ship for work and he had no choice. Still, it puzzles me."

And interested Req. "Had he been avoiding Monterey? Why?"

"Yes, and I have no idea why. Whatever it was, I suspect it has something to do with the reason he was killed."

All Req was sure of was that Freddy's payment had been decided well in advance. His killers had sought to get one final job from him and limit their sphere of players. What did Freddy know? "Unless the 'reason' he avoided Monterey contacted him and asked him to come. Have you thought of that?"

Lemuel sat so still that he hardly seemed to breathe. "No," he answered after a long pause. "I had not and I have no idea how I would find out. It seems my brother kept his own confidences—regardless of the amount of drink he had consumed.

"Freddy had few possessions. I went through them, of course. While doing so, I discovered an empty envelope with Helmut Schmit's name on the front. The only person in Monterey I could have connected Freddy with is dead too."

"Are you going back to San Francisco?" Req asked casually.

"Eventually." Lemuel dropped his hands to his thighs and sat up straight. "Is there anything you can tell me to further my quest for justice for my brother's death, Mr. Maguire?"

"I'm afraid not." Req leaned over his forearms. "Poking around down here is damn dangerous for you, Mr. Hansen. You're a fish out of water."

"I can't walk away until I've done all I can to find my brother's killer," Lemuel stated in a tone that denied argument.

"Then take it from the other side. San Francisco is your turf. You know the city, probably have contacts there. Find out who is responsible for Helmut Schmit's death, and odds are you've got your brother's killer too."

"Do you think the answers are there? In San Francisco?"

Req studied the man's earnest expression and decided to level with him. "Not the ones you're looking for, but there might be some loose threads floating around. That's what we want to tug until they unravel. We're not after the shooters, Mr. Hansen. We want the people who hired them."

"I want both," Lemuel insisted.

"Fine. Just don't muddy the water and lose sight of the big picture. Whoever hired the men who killed Helmut Schmit can hire more to come after you if you get careless and step on their toes."

"Who are you, Maguire?"

Req stood. "A pale rider passing through." Yeah, like Clint Eastwood, only he doubted that 1890 Monterey would get a red paint job. "When you go back to the city, send word to me at Miss Hornsby's home. I'll let you know as soon as I find something. You do the same?"

He hesitated for so long, Req thought he'd lost him. "All right," he said finally. Lemuel picked up his coat and withdrew a card from one of the pockets. "You can reach me here."

Req tucked the card away. "Watch your back, Lemuel." Casting a surreptitious eye on the patrons and cataloguing them along the way, he left the tavern. Finding an unlikely ally wasn't bad for a day's work.

Chapter 18

CALLY KEPT AN eye on the entrance to the ship's galley where she and Captain Norm Wakefield sorted through Helmut's records. At this late hour, Req would show up any moment and want to take her home. The subtle motion of the waves on the ship's hull soothed her frustration at not finding anything that might provide a clue as to why Helmut was killed.

His records and furnishings had proven easy to trace. What Katya Schmit hadn't taken to San Francisco, Captain Wakefield had moved onboard *The Dawning*. Wakefield was one of the few men who understood that Peter Hornsby had patterned the fledgling union's structure after the American Federation of Labor. Although barely four years old, the Ohio-based organization was the most promising union yet. The loss of the files would have dealt a significant blow to Helmut's organizing efforts.

During the past week, Cally had devoted her late afternoons and evenings poring over the disarray of Helmut's files. Somewhere, something tied Helmut, Freddy Hansen, and her father together. All she had to do was find it. Fortunately, Captain Wakefield had proven a wise choice as Helmut's first mate in the office. Now, Wakefield oversaw agreements between ship owners and the buyers for the seamen's catches.

The aroma of food nudged Cally from deep concentration. Captain Wakefield touched her elbow, then nodded toward the stairs leading up to the deck.

"Maguire's takeout," Req announced as he entered the galley and held up a large wicker basket. "Food to die for."

"Aye, if it's as good as it smells, it might be worth it." The captain stuck a piece of paper into the account ledger then closed it.

"Where did you get this? It looks delicious." Cally slid down the bench to the side of the galley table where Req began laying out the food he'd brought. Between trying to catch up at Golden Sun Shipping and reconstructing the records of the independent federation of fishermen her father had worked so hard to bring together, she hadn't had time to think about food yet today.

"It doesn't matter. It's here now and you need to eat." He folded the quilted towels as he removed them from the dishes he had taken from the basket.

Cally's stomach growled in anticipation. A sudden image of Req laughing and talking with a winsome tavern maid displaying an open invitation with her plunging neckline hung in Cally's mind. She took the dinnerware Captain Wakefield brought from the heart of the galley. "Req? Are you not eating?"

"I ate at the tavern." Indulgence softened his features in the kind glow of the lanterns blazing over the table. "It's nearly ten o'clock. Eat, then I'm taking you home. Your work here will keep."

Cally tried to dismiss the images of Req at the tavern. Jealousy was a new emotion for her, one she didn't like. "I need to do a little more tonight. Tomorrow morning, I must be at Golden Sun as early as possible. Then—"

"You're help is appreciated. And I know what we're looking for in these here papers," Captain Wakefield assured her. "Come back when ya can, Miss Caladonia. I'd never forgive meself if ya took ill again on account of helping me put things to rights."

"I'm fine," she assured the captain.

"And to make sure you stay that way, you're taking tomorrow off," Req said.

"Impossible." She cut into the flaky crust of a meat pie and inhaled the steamy herbal aroma. "We're almost done."

"Tomorrow is Sunday, Cally. Even the shipping offices are closed," Req reminded her.

"I have a key." How easy it was to lose track of the days when so many things clamored for her attention. The only positive aspect to juggling the countless balls she had spinning in the air was that they left her little time to dwell on Req. The long hours made exhaustion her sleeping companion. But Req visited her dreams in agonizing, erotic splendor.

"He makes a good point. A day's leave from these papers would not harm either of us, Miss Caladonia." Captain Wakefield offered her a piece of bread with butter melting on it.

Cally accepted the bread, her mind churning. "You certainly should have some time away from all of this. I can make a great deal of headway on this tomorrow. We have a good idea of what's missing. Next week, I'll take the Del Monte Express up to San Francisco, visit Katya, and bring back the remaining files. I'll send word and let her know my intentions."

"If you come tomorrow I'll be obliged to help, Miss Caladonia. Neither these papers nor Missus Katya are going anywhere. Besides, organizing the men into a labor federation isn't your responsibility. 'Tis ours, though we truly appreciate the help you've given." He scraped the last of the potatoes onto his plate. "Heed Mr. Maguire's advice before he makes it an order."

"An order?" She didn't take orders from Requiem Maguire.

"Is he not yer doctor?" A bushy gray eyebrow rose over Captain Wakefield's left eye.

Doctor, husband, it made little difference. Men gave orders. Women did what was necessary. However in this instance, she had no choice but to accede to Req's dictates. He had something in mind; she was sure of it.

"Suppose I compromise?" Looking at her plate and really seeing it reminded her of how thoughtful Req had been to bring her favorite meal, which she had virtually inhaled.

"What do you have in mind?" Req asked.

"Suppose I take that last bunch of loose papers? I'll go through them at my leisure tomorrow."

"Before you keep your date with Irene to review the household affairs? Or maybe you'll do it after the dinner you're giving for Maudel and her husband?"

His unruffled patience mixed with logic irritated her. "Over breakfast." She rose and gathered dishes until Captain Wakefield put his hand on hers.

"Take the papers then." Req fetched her coat, then held it for her. "Call it a night. It's time to put Bessie in the barn."

"You wouldn't know a gelding from a mare. And his name isn't Bessie." She shoved her left arm into her coat.

"I always thought it more important to know a Harley from a Honda," he murmured, pulling her coat into place. The back of his knuckles grazed the nape of her neck ever so slowly. The touch provided a reminder to every cell in her body of just how sweet it was to experience his full attention. "All things considered, this Harley man would even settle for a Japanese bike over a horse any day."

"I'm sure you would." Needing to ease the tense flame of desire that flared hotter and brighter each time he touched her, she bid Captain Wakefield good night and collected the sheaves of paper.

"You work too hard." Req took her arm to escort her across the ship's deck. The fog was thin tonight, the air remarkably warm for autumn.

"I've always worked hard," Cally said, glancing around the deserted dock. The rhythm of the waves served a reminder that the sea never slept. "I'll probably work even harder when you leave." The words nearly stuck in her throat. Knowing his departure was inevitable didn't change the torrent of sorrow that gripped her whenever the topic arose.

"Christ, you'll work yourself to death."

"Not to death. Just into oblivion," she seethed. Why did he have to be so tough on her? "You're leaving, so don't perspire over the little stuff."

He lifted her into the buggy, grinning. "You mean, don't sweat the small stuff?"

"I'll massacre the language any way I please, thank you very much." She started to reach for the reins, but he caught them first. "You're driving?"

"Yes."

Now she did want to reach for a seat belt. "It's night."

"I noticed." He released the brake and clicked at the horse. "So did the horse, and I'm willing to bet old Bessie here knows his way to the garage."

"The carriage house," she corrected absently, amazed how well he handled the reins on the first turn.

"In the morning, I'd like you to draw the layout of the Cunningham house."

Everything stilled inside Cally. "Why?"

"While your guests gather for your dinner party, I'm going to do some private investigating."

"You're going to break into their house?" Her chest tightened and she could barely breathe. "Sweet heaven above, Req, you cannot do that."

He tugged on the reins. The horse turned onto the road leading home. "It's the best possible time. They'll be at your home.

Most of their staff will be gone. Hell, it's not like they have a sophisticated alarm system, cameras, or lasers." He shifted toward her. "Do the Cunninghams have a dog?"

"A dog?" How could he even think of doing this?

"Yeah, a dog."

"No. Why are you going to break into their house, Req?"

"We've hit a dead end. I need a clue as to where to look next. My mother used to keep a diary. She'd stick important things in it. I got to thinking about Penelope's journal and wondered if maybe she did the same. We've spent a week looking everywhere for a hint of what Penelope wrote about, but we haven't found anything. Unless we look in the corners and crannies, we aren't going to get any closer. Besides, if her diary is any indicator, she seems fragile. I'd prefer not having to interrogate her."

Cally's mouth became a desert in the moist, cool night. The ramifications of confronting demure Penelope with the nefarious accusation of knowing who scuttled the *Ocean Princess*—if indeed she was scuttled—were beyond belief.

"What if you get caught?" She voiced her worst fear.

"I'll take precautions to make sure I don't." He muttered something under his breath.

"What did you say?"

"Nothing."

"You said something. Tell me."

"Ah, your favorite words. Tell me. Then when I tell you, you go all weak-kneed on me. Murder isn't for the fainthearted, Cally. These men aren't going to knock on your door and reveal themselves until your name is on the top of their hit parade. By then it'll be too late.

"Tomorrow, I'll enter the Cunningham house as soon as they leave. I'll be back by the time Irene serves dinner."

"You make it sound like a trip to the office."

"For me, it is."

"Are you telling me this now so I'll think about it all night?"

Req remained silent for a moment. When he answered in a husky voice, gooseflesh rippled over Cally's skin. "If it means you'll think about me, I'll wish I had thought of it sooner."

"I dream about you, Req." She turned her head to the darkness. "You're all I dream about."

"But that's all you do. Think. Remember. Dream."

"You're leaving in less than three weeks. I have enough heartaches as it is."

"What's that supposed to mean?"

"It means I don't want you to leave me. Did you think I was lying when I declared my love for you, Req? Did you think I spoke my heart just because I thought I was leaving you forever? That revealing my deepest, most private emotions was without trepidation?"

He turned his head toward her, but she could not read his features in the night. The intensity of his gaze carried enough heat to burn color into her cheeks.

"You love me," he said after a long pause.

"Yes," she whispered. "I will always love you, Req."

"And that explains why you won't make love with me."

"I didn't say I wouldn't."

"I sleep alone every night. It's your call, Cally."

"Do you love me, Req?" It wasn't a prudent question, but she didn't care.

Again, he took so long to answer she wasn't sure he would. "I'm not sure I know how to love anymore. I want you with a force that brings me to my knees when I think about making love with you. I'd lay down my life to keep any harm from you. There's damn near nothing I wouldn't do for you."

"Except stay and raise a family with me." The perpetual pain of knowing she'd lose him forever forced the words out. Having a family with him was what she wanted more than anything. It was the most natural evolution of her love for him that grew stronger with each passing day. His rejection now couldn't hurt more than his departure later.

"I can't." He cast a guarded look her way. "You know how it is, Cally . . . people who rely on me, business to take care of . . ."

Hearing the same explanation she had given a few weeks earlier stung. She hadn't realized it sounded so cold. So calloused. "Duty," she whispered. "I know." And that was the crux of it; she did know. "I won't raise a child alone."

"I don't blame you. I've been here long enough to see which way the wind blows on that score. Mr. Responsibility won't let that happen." He tugged the reins and the horse ambled toward the carriage house. "I can't stay, Cally, and you can't leave. Hell, I wouldn't take you with me if you were willing. Neither of us knows what waits when I go back, but it damn sure won't be a walk in the park."

"There's something I need to tell you." She had dreaded mentioning it and hadn't intended to say anything until it was necessary. However, now seemed a good time to prepare him for the worst.

"Then tell me." The horse stopped beside the carriage house.

"We don't know for sure you can go back, Req."

He shifted on the seat. "What do you mean?"

"The passageway seemed smaller this last time. I have no idea if it just seemed that way because two of us went through at the same time or because it's shrinking."

"Shrinking," he repeated.

Suddenly, speaking the truth seemed a poor decision, but it was too late. "It's not like either one of us has any control over it, Req. We won't know until . . ." Stunned by his lack of reaction, all she could do was watch him climb down from the buggy. When he beckoned her to slide across the seat so he could help her down, she pushed the sheaf of papers in front of her. "You don't believe me."

"I believe you, Cally." The smell of dew forming on the pines mingled with the scent of fresh hay stacked in the carriage house. The harness traces jangled when the horse snuffled and tossed his head. Req caught her at the waist and lifted her from the buggy. For the split second he held her in the air he had total control of her destiny. A giddy sensation lingered when he set her down. But he did not let go. He gathered her into a tight embrace that revealed all the hard places on his body.

"I believe everything you tell me."

In the darkness, she couldn't read his eyes. She had expected him to be angry, show his frustration, anything but the *nothing* she faced. Not even his body betrayed an inner turmoil.

Perhaps he did not understand. "You could be stuck here."

"I've been stuck in worse places." He kissed her forehead. "What you mean is, you could be stuck with me. If I can't return, you'll have some hard choices facing you, Cally."

"What sort of choices?"

"Whether or not you could handle having a full-time husband on your hands. I wouldn't settle for separate rooms and secrets. I'm an all-or-nothing kind of guy in that area."

Her heart leaped. What she wouldn't give for him to stay. But not that way. "I win by default? Second, last, and only choice?" she asked.

"First, best, and preferred—make no mistake about it. Circumstance doesn't always allow choices."

Her heart in her throat, she held him and stood on tiptoes to get closer to his tantalizing mouth. "We can at least choose to kiss one another."

Req settled a chaste kiss on her expectant lips, then drew back. "Kissing you is a pleasure in itself. It's like fine chocolate—I won't want to stop with a sample."

"Chocolate?" The comparison made her laugh.

"I'm greedy. I want all of it."

Drawn by the seductive timbre of his voice, her body pressed against him. The mix of playfulness and barely harnessed sexual excitement thrilled her. In that instant, she wished she was naked with him and life had no demands, no consequences, no responsibilities.

The back of his hand caressed her cheek. "If I hold you much longer, I'm going to kiss you, Cally."

Yes, please, her body begged as she stretched toward his mouth.

"If I kiss you once, I'll want to kiss you again."

Her fingers dug into the hard planes of his muscular back, urging him, imploring him. The evidence of his desire prodded her lower belly and silently decried the separation created by their clothing.

"And again, until I've kissed all the sweet spots that make you beg for more."

The hard, round muscle of his left buttock felt like molten steel under her hand. The inner pulsing his words incited reverberated between them, prying open the doors of abandon.

"I won't want to stop until you're hot, and sweaty, and wild beneath me. Until I'm inside you."

"Then kiss me," she repeated, breathless. Her fingers flexed with a rhythm that left no doubt how badly she wanted him. "I don't care about next month or next year. Just now. You. Us."

"Not smart, Cally."

Smart had nothing to do with the desire welling up, robbing her of her breath. Even the night around them seemed to brighten with the glow of passion burning between them.

"Señorita Caladonia," came a voice from what seemed the other side of the world. "Excuse me, Señorita Caladonia. Shall I take care of the horse for you?"

The tension rippling through Req shifted, as did her own. Sanity was an awful thing.

"Señora Kenny tell me see to the horse. She say, do it now." Manuel hung the lantern from a post beside the walkway, then opened the doors of the carriage house.

Req released her, leaving her bereft.

"I'll take care of him," Req said. "Good night, Miss Hornsby."

"Req," she started.

"Let it go, Cally." He scooped the papers from the buggy seat and handed them to her. "Get some sleep."

"Fine chocolate doesn't sleep," she murmured, then turned toward the house where Irene waited for her on the back porch.

"Neither do late-night chocolate addicts," she heard him say as he led the horse away.

Irene touched her arm as she turned to walk into the house. "That man's going to break your heart, Miss Caladonia. Meanwhile, you be careful a broken heart is all he leaves you with."

It was going to be a long night.

The hum of dinner guests conversing in the early evening filled the parlor.

Cally glanced at the clock beside the fireplace. Ten minutes to seven.

Where was Req? What had gone wrong?

Biting the inside of her lip, she knew they should have done it differently.

She should have gone with him. She knew every room in the Cunningham mansion. She should have been his guide. At the very least, she could have been his lookout and sounded a warning if he was in danger of discovery.

"There is something I must know," Chauncy said sotto voce.

Warning bells went off in Cally's head. A quick glance around the parlor confirmed they were out of earshot from the other guests, and Req was still not back from his dangerous endeavor. "Yes?"

"Is this man, this Requiem Maguire, holding something over you, Caladonia?"

"Of course not," she answered, surprised he would suggest such a thing.

"Then what made you run and hide for a month?"

"Goodness, what would possibly make you consider either possibility? Both are preposterous." It stunned her that a man who had known her since birth didn't understand her better. Caladonia Hornsby had never run from a problem. It wasn't in her character.

"What else can I think? I've been patient this past week and I've kept your secret. I thought it best to allow you time to get your bearings. Now I want answers, Caladonia. Where were you during the past month? Why did you leave without letting anyone know?" Chauncy demanded his answers with the sternness of a disciplinarian requiring an explanation before he pronounced punishment.

"Perhaps what you really want to know is why I came back. Is that it?" He wasn't the only one in search of answers. Where was Req? Why wasn't he back?

"Both. Something unsettling is going on and I don't like it. I could not bear for anything to happen to you. The loss of your father has been difficult for all of us. Your unexpected hiatus was a tremendous shock none of us wanted to accept."

Much as she abhorred considering Chauncy's involvement in the murders and the scuttling of the *Golden Princess,* the speculative evidence was stacking up against him. Most bothersome was the lie and secrecy in which he shrouded her disappearance. He had no way of knowing when, or if, she would return. "Is that why you kept my absence a secret and told everyone I was deathly ill?"

"It seemed the wisest course."

"Oh? How so?" *To give you time to restructure the partnership agreement,* she suspected. *Then have me declared dead?* A noise drew her attention toward the foyer. Her heart sank when Brendan closed the front door then crossed the foyer alone.

"We expected a ransom note. Every day without word from you or about you worried us more. We thought the kidnappers would feel braver if there was no public acknowledgement of your abduction." Chauncy pinched the bridge of his nose. At that moment, his fifty-two years showed clearly in the creases of his face. "We would have paid whatever they asked to get you back."

"When you say *we,* who do you mean?" She had grown up at Chauncy's knees. How could she believe this man would ever wish her or her father harm? Yet considering what she and Req had pieced together, how could she not?

"Why Thomas, of course. We discussed the proper course of action at length."

"Who else knew I was gone?" She tried to phrase her questions the way Req would. With mounting anxiety, she glanced at the ormolu clock on the mantle. Req was nineteen minutes late.

"Irene, Brendan, Thomas, Cameron, and I. We considered the possibility of whoever abducted you—"

"Why did you assume I'd been abducted, Chauncy?"

The fatherly arm he settled around her shoulder rested lightly. "You would never put us through so much worry without good reason. Or so we thought. When you returned as unexpectedly as you left—with Mr. Maguire, I started questioning our judgment. I thought I knew you, Caladonia. As your business partner and your friend, I'm entitled to an explanation. Tell me what happened. Silence is unacceptable."

Cally schooled her reaction as she studied Chauncy. He glanced across the room at Penelope who was even quieter than usual.

"Where did you find Dr. Maguire?" he asked when she remained silent.

"He found me," she said with the convincing openness only honesty afforded. *And showed me the glory of loving him.* "As you know, I've had trouble sleeping since my father's death. I went for a walk along the beach. The changing tide caught me and swept me into the water. I didn't know where I was and would have drowned if not for Mr. Maguire. He rescued me. Protected me. Fed me. Clothed me. And sheltered me." *Married me. Made love to me.*

"Then I suppose we owe him an enormous debt of gratitude," Chauncy mused, his thick eyebrows puckered over the bridge of his nose.

She decided to let him arrive at his own conclusions and redirected the conversation. Req was twenty-two minutes late. "I was looking through some papers at the office and I noticed you and Thomas changed insurers during my absence. Why?"

"I suspected we were paying too much. Cameron worked with some of Thomas's contacts in San Francisco and got us a better rate for our ships." He hefted his glass of bourbon, but hesitated and set it down again. "Are you going to question every decision Thomas and I make?" he asked with fatherly disapproval.

"I wasn't questioning the wisdom of this one, merely inquiring about the benefit of doing so. Had I been asked—"

"You weren't here to ask, Caladonia."

"—I would have questioned the reason we were paying more with the old company," she continued as though he had not interrupted. "Not being here does not make me less a partner with a share of the profits and the losses, so I'm asking now." Just as Req would expect—if he weren't twenty-four minutes late. *Please, dear God, keep him safe.*

Chauncy squeezed her shoulder, then reached for his glass of bourbon, all the while looking around to make sure they were not overheard. "Several months after the *Ocean Princess* sank, the cost of our cargo insurance increased. As you may recall, we anticipated the higher premium because of the size of our claim. While we haven't lost a ship or any cargo since, they continued charging us as though we were a risky company. It was suggested that we could do better."

He set his drink on a doily. "Cameron found a reputable company willing to insure our ships and our most valuable cargo. Thomas helped negotiate an excellent rate. His efforts will save a great deal of money over time."

"Thomas is very savvy," she agreed, her curiosity peaked. "I thought we delegated the cargo insurance procurement to Cameron when I . . ." she paused, still finding any allusion to her father's death difficult, ". . . became a full partner."

"We did. It was his suggestion that I look at the cost and evaluate the benefits of another carrier. Thomas wanted involvement."

She watched Cameron across the room. Like Penelope, he was a quiet individual. Had he not been married to Maudel, Cally would have ignored him and completely dismissed his secretive ways. But no one could keep a secret for long around Maudel. That was, no one except Cally. Right now, she wished Req's whereabouts weren't secret from her.

"Ah, there you are!" Thomas crossed the room and took her hand. "I cannot tell you how good it is to have you home, dear Caladonia. It warms my heart to see you. Your smile lights up the room. There you stand, creating sunshine, and you speak as if nothing had happened. Naturally, I'll want to hear every detail and clear up all the nagging questions so we can put this incident behind us and get on with it."

"Get on with what?" she asked, then managed a smile at his infectious delight. It was difficult to reconcile the ebullient man gracing her parlor with the shrewd dealmaker and ruthless negotiator she knew at Golden Sun. Regardless of which personality he donned, he was always impeccably dressed in a tailored suit and his blond hair meticulously groomed. Such habits provided a spotless backdrop for the charm that came naturally when his blue eyes fixed on a target.

"Why, the delectable treat of the dinner Irene has fixed for us, of course." Nearly as tall as Req, golden-haired Thomas carried his height like a trophy. "Irene asked that I inform you she'd like to serve now. May I?" He extended his arm to escort her to the table.

Cally glanced at the clock, then at the guests scattered through the parlor. Req was twenty-seven minutes late. A fine bead of perspiration collected between her breasts. What if someone had caught him in the Cunningham home?

She could not delay the meal without calling attention to his absence. "Then let's not keep her waiting." She took Thomas's arm and announced dinner, then wondered how she would explain the empty place setting.

The seating arrangement put her in close proximity to Thomas and Chauncy, leaving Maudel and Penelope to the absent Req. For now, she wasn't particularly concerned about Cameron who seldom participated in dinner conversation. He preferred peering at his food through his half-glasses and listening to everyone else's version of the world. Cameron was the personification of the twentieth-century nerd; Cally did not underestimate his sharp mind. She would have to pick the right venue carefully before she began probing his knowledge of the *Ocean Princess*. She smelled a rat, and couldn't help wondering if the real reason behind the change of insurance companies was still hidden.

Shortly before her father's death she had made the same discoveries that Chauncy had mentioned, and decided that the benefits of staying with their insurance carrier outweighed the slightly higher premium. The projected savings were not sufficient to warrant the time Chauncy and Thomas had spent to pursue the change.

Tomorrow she would examine all the figures again. The motives behind the gruesome events that had started with her father's death increasingly pointed at the sunken ship. Perhaps the changing of insurance carriers played into whatever plan her enemies concocted. It would be easy for her to make a quick evaluation because she had taken care of the insurance until she'd assumed her father's office. After that those duties had fallen to Cameron. Tomorrow, she decided as she settled on the chair Thomas held for her.

When she looked down the table, instead of an empty place, she saw Req settling into his chair. She was so glad he'd returned unharmed, she nearly bolted the length of the table to touch him. Her heart skipped a beat when he returned her frown with a cocky smile. Her million questions would have to wait. Once the introductions concluded, Irene and Brendan served dinner. Cally concentrated on Chauncy and Thomas. The dinner evolved into an informal business meeting.

By the end of the main course, an apologetic Chauncy had admitted to contacting her attorneys in search of a will. Because she did not have one, he had broached rewriting the partnership agreement without her. Thomas had refused. Toward the end of the meal, Cally had found answers, but she had more questions too.

Laughter and an occasional exclamation distracted Cally throughout dinner. Req had already begun cultivating a serious conversation with Penelope and her daughter. The man exuded charm with the same ease with which most men breathed.

"I don't believe I've seen Penelope enjoy herself like this for months." Thomas's gaze darted over the apple pie Irene had placed before him. At the far end of the table, Req gave Maudel one of his rare, dimple-deepening smiles.

Cally thought Thomas's voice carried a hint of jealousy for the easy manner in which Req won over the ladies. She noticed Chauncy's slow smile as he unabashedly enjoyed the animation in Penelope's demeanor.

"Any man who can make my wife laugh these days can't be all bad," Chauncy muttered, then cut into his pie. "I have been concerned for her health lately." He cast an accusing eye at Cally. "Her insomnia was particularly bad this past month."

"The arrival of a grandchild should brighten her outlook," Cally offered, recalling the dated entries in Penelope's journal. The onset of Penelope's malaise coincided with the entry date where she wrote about the *Ocean Princess*. Cally suspected Penelope knew far more than she had written and that nothing would cure her insomnia until the entire matter came to light in all its ugliness. Soon, she thought, very soon—if Req had his way.

Chapter 19

"CALADONIA, WOULD YOU do me the honor of accompanying me to dinner at the Del Monte Hotel on Tuesday," Thomas Barry said as he collected his overcoat from Brendan.

"Tuesday?" The invitation caught her off guard, though she knew it shouldn't have. She and Thomas had been frequent dinner companions at the Del Monte before her sojourn into the future.

"Sorry, Barry, not possible. Miss Hornsby will be in San Francisco on Tuesday." The smoothness of Req's delivery denied the tension festering between the two men. "I have a colleague I'd like her to speak with. We shouldn't be gone more than a few days." He offered his hand and a patient smile.

"You'll be away from the office again? Why didn't you mention this earlier?" Thomas asked Cally.

"I was preoccupied," she answered. *And I didn't know about it.* "I will return as quickly as possible."

"Perhaps I should accompany you." He lingered at the door.

Cally rested her fingers on his forearm. "Thank you for your concern, Thomas, but I will be fine. Dr. Maguire will escort me. You have my word that we won't linger."

"As in the past, I'll make sure she is perfectly safe, Barry. At the present, my only interest in Caladonia is in helping her bring things to a close," Req said in a tone so convincing that it took the edge off Thomas's blatant skepticism.

"If this is what you want, Caladonia, so be it. However, when you return, I'd like to clear up a few things with you, Dr. Maguire."

"At your convenience," Req agreed with amiability that

made Cally grit her teeth. "Meanwhile, rest assured, I'll watch over your business partner."

After Brendan closed the door on the last guest and retreated into the kitchen, Cally glared at Req. "Would you join me in the library for a few moments?"

Irritated, she didn't wait for a response. An unexpected hurt nettled at her tender heart. She'd nearly given herself apoplexy from worrying about him. What a fool she was. He considered her little more than a self-imposed assignment. One more responsibility he had to protect.

It was best that she knew his feelings regarding her. Oh, yes, he wanted her in bed. He thought about her, perhaps as much as she thought about him. He would protect her.

Of course he would. Everything about him was honed to handling the dangerous side of life. Acknowledging feelings that went well beyond the physical impulses or the sphere of his expertise left him vulnerable. Requiem Maguire would never allow himself to be at risk emotionally.

She loved him. While it was too late to slow her descent into inevitable heartbreak, she could retain a modicum of dignity. It would be cold comfort in the years ahead.

She closed the library door, then lit the lamps to banish the cold in her heart and the evening shadows that never seemed to end. "I think you owe me an explanation."

Req took the match from her hand and blew it out. "What's bothering you?"

"The list of what *isn't* bothering me is far shorter." Before she drew a breath, he spun her around and claimed her mouth in a rapacious kiss that robbed her senses.

Not until she mustered the fortitude to push him away did she realize he wasn't holding her, just kissing her in a way that excited her down to the soles of her feet.

She retreated a step, then turned away sadly. "Answers, Req, not diversions into dead ends."

"I wouldn't call kissing you a dead end."

"Trust me, at the moment it is. Save your chocolate craving for another time."

"What's got your panties in a wad, Cally? My cutting it close for dinner? Or was it springing the trip to San Francisco on you in front of your fair-haired future fiancé?" He stalked the shadows of the library as he put distance between them.

The venom of his jealousy brought her up short. The optimist in her taunted with the possibility that Req might have deeper feelings for her than he showed. "Why are we going to San Francisco, Req? Did you find something in Penelope's journal?" Although necessary, she loathed the invasion of privacy they had inflicted on Penelope.

"She had a piece of paper tucked between the pages referring to the *Ocean Princess*." He leaned against a beam in the wall of bookcases running from floor to ceiling. "It had a name on it. That's all."

The excitement coursing through her swept away the irritation she'd felt a moment ago. "Whose name?"

"Helmut Schmit."

"Helmut?" The news rocked her. She swayed and caught the back of a chair. "But she didn't know him."

"Are you sure about that?" Skepticism tinged his voice.

"I'm surprised you didn't ask her over dinner." She lifted her hand in a peace gesture. "I apologize for that remark. I forget what a chameleon you are, Req. Again, you took me by surprise. Why is it you can charm the stays out of Penelope's and Maudel's corsets and just irritate me to no end?"

His head bowed with a faint smile. "You know me better than they do. They're both lonely and looking for someone to fill the gaps. You, Cally, don't look for anyone to do anything for you. If you're lonely, you do something about it. You make a choice.

"Yeah, I charmed them. It was pathetically easy. They're nice ladies. Intelligent. Likeable. And eager as hell for a man's attention. Even mine."

"I understand." She wanted his attention too. She wanted his love for the rest of her life as much as she wanted his lovemaking.

"Do you?" His left eyebrow rose.

"Yes." Cally ambled along the bookcases. "Even Thomas and Chauncy remarked how nice it was to see Penelope enjoy herself. Thank you for giving her that."

"Don't thank me. I didn't do anything for you or anyone else." The bristly quills of his defensiveness reminded her how he detested being caught doing something nice.

"In that case, I withdraw any appreciation for giving two people very close to me a pleasant, entertaining evening."

"We're speaking about a woman whose house I entered and whose privacy I invaded in a manner she'd find reprehensible. All during dinner I kept wondering how she knew Helmut."

"She doesn't," Cally thought aloud. "I'm sure of it. Penelope doesn't concern herself with events at the wharf or at the shipping company. She was raised in Boston. Here in Monterey, the Del Monte Hotel is as close as she can find to her idea of society. The docks? Never. She knows nothing about wages, working conditions, or organizing the fishermen or dock workers."

Req crossed his arms over his chest. "I have to agree with you about her going to the docks. She's charming, one of the most socially adept women I've encountered—present company excluded."

"There's no need to pamper my feelings, Req." She stood by the window and looked out at the night. "I don't bruise easily."

"Yes, you do, when something matters deeply. I've bruised you and I'm not sure how or when. Lay it on the table, Cally. I'm not good at walking on egg shells, and I don't read minds."

"I resent you making plans without consulting me." She examined her reflection at the window. This was not who she was, nor who she wanted to be. "But that's only part of it. The rest is too absurd to even discuss."

"Not if it upsets you, it isn't."

Feeling foolish and emotionally overexposed, she faced him squarely. "When had you planned for us to leave?"

"Tomorrow."

"Why so soon?"

"We have no time to waste, Cally." He crossed the room to the door.

"Why are you doing this?"

"You're my wife. Regardless of the reasons we married, I made some promises to you. Some I can keep. Some I can't. But I damn sure won't leave until I know you're safe here. Right now, you're not. It's that simple."

"For you." Would that she could segregate and categorize which promises to keep and which to ignore.

"I'll meet as many obligations as I can, starting with the most important ones. Neither of us planned on a marriage like ours. You think you love me, but that'll fade. A month or so from now you'll realize how poorly I fit in here. Then you'll be glad I'm gone." He closed the library door behind him when he left.

A tear slipped from the corner of Cally's eye. "I'll never be glad. Never."

The heat in Cally's cheeks denied the cool San Francisco weather as she and Req walked toward the Palace Hotel dining room. She glared at him. "Why didn't you tell me Freddy Hansen had a brother before today?" She had to hand it to him, he had a way of getting information from thin air. The trouble was, he kept it there too, just out of sight.

"From what I've been able to gather, Lemuel is nothing like his brother. For starters, he's well educated, has a steady job, and a sense of familial loyalty strong enough to send him looking for his brother's killer." In truth, Lemuel was a civilian poking his nose into people's business and places that could get him killed. Req wondered if it was a mistake to have arranged a meeting between Lemuel and Cally. Their thirst for justice was frustrated enough to drown them both if they weren't guided properly.

"I take it meeting with a stockbroker wouldn't be out of the ordinary for you," Req murmured as he perused the enormous Palace Hotel dining room. It was impossible to count the number of tables in the minijungles of palm fronds serving as privacy screens.

"No. Let's check with the maître d' for Mr. Hansen." With the elegant poise of a queen, Cally assumed control of the situation. Req noted that she came forward as a manner of course. Never pushy or overbearing, she used a gentle hand to guide a situation. Because he trusted her, he had taken a backseat and let her orchestrate the arrangements of their stay. The woman was an asset any way he looked at her and God knew he'd never grow tired of doing that.

The myriad of potent emotions she evoked tore him up inside. Sometimes when he looked at her, he knew his inability to sort out those emotions was taking a nasty toll on her too. He hated hurting her more than he loathed the talons of chaos digging and twisting his heart.

The maître d' led them to Lemuel Hansen's table. As they sat, Req noted that Lemuel wore the trappings of prosperity with comfortable grace. He had traded his pea coat for a fine, smartly tailored suit and a shirt so white it glowed. His short, light-brown hair and clean-shaven face were in character with the person Req had sensed beneath the waterfront disguise.

"Have you learned anything about Helmut Schmit's death?" Req asked Lemuel when they finished the sumptuous meal.

"Nothing that will help us. I even contacted some acquaintances who are highly placed in law enforcement. If there was any information, they would know it. What I did learn is that we aren't the only ones asking questions."

"Who else is interested in Schmit's death?" Req asked softly.

"Detective Bertram Goodman."

"But he hasn't found my father's killer—"

"Nor my brother's, Miss Hornsby. I do not believe the good detective has extended much effort on Freddy's behalf," Lemuel said.

Req doubted that the detective had as much information as he and Cally. In that light, making a connection between the three murders was nearly impossible. He kept his speculation about Detective Goodman's possible motives to himself.

"Did your contacts mention any witnesses in Helmut's death?" Cally set her fork down. "Surely someone must have seen something."

"If so, Miss Hornsby, they have no interest in speaking with the police or to me. I've met a dead end and disappointed all of us." Genuine sorrow sharpened Lemuel's fine features.

"Not necessarily." Req considered the political intricacies of interdepartmental cooperation as he knew them. Though there were far fewer rules here, there were also fewer ways of uncovering criminals. "When you spoke to the police, did they indicate whether they had assigned a man to the case?"

"Yes." Lemuel reached inside his coat and withdrew a piece of paper. "Here is his name and the hours you can find him at the station. I also wrote down the policemen known on the wharf where Helmut was attacked."

Req memorized the information, then handed the paper back to Lemuel. "Did you find any of your brother's associates while you were on the docks?"

"I'm afraid Freddy inspired neither loyalty nor kind feelings among those who knew him best. However, those same people assured me he was reliable once he gave his word, which he seldom did. The things I discovered about my brother were most unflattering, Mr. Maguire. In retrospect, I marvel that we were related at all."

"That doesn't give me much to work with." Req checked the time. "Have you learned anything else?"

"Yes. Your speculation about Freddy being called to Monterey may have been correct. When Freddy was here, he had a room over a tavern. The proprietor told me Freddy received a letter. He remembered the occasion because he didn't think any of Freddy's cohorts would write to him let alone on fine parchment."

"Did he see the contents of the letter?"

"No, but the following week Freddy signed on as a mate on *Pacific Bounty.* Until receiving the letter, Freddy was a stevedore and had had his fill of the sea." Lemuel gave Cally an apologetic smile. "And no, Mr. Maguire, the letter was not among his belongings. The tavern keeper stored the few possessions my brother left behind. I retrieved them after being notified of his death."

"Other than the letter, was there anything that might indicate why he changed his mind and went to sea again?" Req asked, mulling over the information.

"No," Lemuel said. "My brother's legacy consisted of worn clothing. The duty he performed on the *Pacific Bounty* apparently did not line his pockets."

"What about his residence in Monterey?" Cally focused her warm brown eyes on Lemuel with an intensity that set Req's neck hair on end. He had no right to be jealous. Too bad his splintered emotions didn't heed his more rational intellect.

"Nothing," Req said. "He lived in a rooming house on the wharf. The landlady confiscated his possessions when he didn't show up to pay the next week's rent. Whatever possessions he had were long gone by the time either Lemuel or I got there."

"We're back at the beginning." Lemuel nodded at the waiter who looked for permission to clear the dishes.

"Not necessarily," Req said after the waiter departed. "Miss Hornsby has a list of names she needs to look for in the Maritime Registry. If you can go with her, it'll free me to check out a few things."

"I'm perfectly capable of checking the registry myself," Cally snapped, then flashed a dazzling smile at Lemuel. "But I'm sure the task will go must faster with both of us looking."

The prospect of spending the day with Cally made Lemuel beam. Req gave him a warning look that promised a broken neck if he got out of line with Cally. Lemuel acknowledged the unspoken command with a nod. Some things were universal, regardless of the era.

"Where will you be?" Cally asked, her smile melting into the irritation that never left her eyes.

"Doing a little freelance investigation. May as well make the most of the time until we can arrange for Katya Schmit to see us." The social proprieties of civilians were cumbersome at best. It would be a helluva lot easier to bang on a door and flash a badge instead of setting up appointments.

Given the opportunity, he'd rather pass the time making love with Cally.

• • •

Washing off the stench of the wharf taverns was Req's only thought when he returned to his hotel room later that night. He longed for a shower, then fantasized about the big bathtub he and Cally had shared at the resort only hours before he swam into 1890. The trouble with remembering that was the physical ache for her that never went away. Not even his cold-water bath stifled the involuntary physical response to the memory of making love with her.

No sooner had he gotten into bed and pulled the blankets over his naked body than he heard a soft tapping on his door.

Cally.

He should have known she'd wait up. If he opened the door connecting their rooms she would demand to know everything he'd learned. He wanted to tell her to go away, but the thinness of the walls cautioned silence.

He reached across to the night table and turned out the lamp, then got out of bed and answered the door.

With a whoosh of her long nightgown and wrapper, she entered the room. "Why did you turn out the light? Everyone is asleep."

"Not everyone," Req assured her. As a point of fact, part of him was wide awake and aching to share the fire burning in him. "I'll debrief you in the morning."

She closed the door and faced him in the darkness. "Why do you do this to me?"

"Do what?" He was the one standing buck naked with a killer erection. She remained oblivious to the potent effect that just the memory of making love with her had on him.

"You go off on a tangent." She fumbled around in the dark. "You wait until we're in the company of strangers or people I don't dare refute you in front of before you spring your plans."

Knowing she was right reminded him of how out of touch he was with sharing his thoughts. "So I'm not a talk-show guest when it comes to telling you my plans. Ask me again in the morning and I'll tell you whatever you want to know."

"Unless I know you're planning something, how am I to know what to ask?" She struck a match, then did a double take in his direction. "Oh, my." Her eyes grew with excitement.

Req didn't think he could get much harder until her gaze made a slow assessment of his naked body. In that moment, he would have sold his soul for her to come to him.

She blew out the match.

"The smartest thing you can do right now is leave, Cally." It would be so damn easy to seduce her right now. But how would she look at him in the morning? It mattered. A lot. Too damn much to act on base need.

Her fingers closed over the doorknob, as she groped for the key in the darkness. The sound of the key turning in the lock spoke her defiance.

Her silent invitation charged Req into motion. He fisted the yards of her nightgown and wrapper, then lifted the material over her head. He skimmed the curves of her naked body with eager hands, all the while drawing the fragrance of wild flowers and excited woman deep into his lungs. Nothing smelled sweeter. It reached into his soul and evoked painfully tender emotions that felt dangerously like love. Like a starving man, his hands clung to her delectable curves; his mouth tasted, then devoured hers in a ravenous search for satiation.

She returned his kiss with a ferocity that grazed her teeth over his. The pressure of her soft, sweet body against his dissolved any threat of her departure and allowed him to relish every moment she was naked with him. The great, wild hunger roaring through his veins demanded fulfillment.

The kiss broke when he scooped her up and carried her to the bed a scant dozen steps away in the dark. He laid her down, then settled on top of her.

The sense of power shifted. Although he was physically stronger, the impact of her unquestioning submission tempered the near-violent intensity of his need to claim her.

"I've been foolish. No more, I promise. For as long as you're here, Req, we won't spend another night apart," she breathed, then drew his head down so she could kiss his neck and run her fingers through the chest hair along the top of his pectorals.

"Just as long as you know what you're doing, Cally, I don't care what changed your mind." His erection prodded for the heaven at the juncture of her thighs. He held back, savoring her hands hungrily testing his body, pushing, pulling, gliding over his flesh like hot satin.

He cupped her warm breasts. Simultaneously, he slid his mouth down to join his hands, not trusting himself to refrain from entering her. His mouth watered for a taste of the flavors that spun the sugar of his nightly fantasies.

Tonight, she had walked into his arms ready and heated by the promise of an end to the anguish imposed by abstinence. If it killed him, he wouldn't rush anything. Not her. Not the moment.

A soft protest escaped her when he relinquished her breast. The reflexive arching of her back thrust her breasts at him. She tugged on him, trying to lure him within her reach.

"Req," she panted, her fingertips plowing furrows across his shoulder blades and biceps. A thin coat of perspiration kept her hands fluid on his heated skin.

"Shh. The walls have ears," he whispered, his voice cracking from the strain. The need for quiet added a forbidden aspect to the excitement steaming just below the eruption point.

She wrapped her legs around him, locking her ankles above his buttocks, then tipped her hips in a way that pressed her intimately against his torso. Her unexpected invitation was more of a demand and damn near drove him over the edge.

"Cally . . ."

This was what he craved, what released the emotions he had locked away for safekeeping. But there was no keeping anything safe from Cally. She laid his essence bare. When he made love with her, his emotions ran amok. He needed her, fed on her sweetness, her passion. Her love. Each time she touched him she claimed a little more, sank a little deeper into his heart, and wedged the coffin of old emotions open wider until the light shone inside and revealed his secrets.

She was breathing heavily, her breasts pressing against his chest, enticing him to touch her. His tongue danced with hers for a moment. When he could wait no longer, he entered the heaven she offered.

The strength of Cally's orgasm nearly carried him along. Straining to hold onto his control, he barely breathed. Tremors of denial wracked his body, clamoring for the release pulsing in his testicles.

He had memorized her face. In the darkness, he still saw the way her eyes widened in surprise and the dreamy quality that lingered in the afterglow of her orgasm.

Through sheer determination, he outlasted the firestorm. The perfume of their lovemaking intoxicated him with desire. He let her float alone for a few, brief minutes in their niche of paradise as he wrestled back the power she wielded over him.

In a fusion of pain and pleasure, he withdrew, giving them time to recoup. He loved driving her wild, and then feeling the intensity of her pleasure as it welded their souls together.

When he entered her again, the tiny spasms lingering from her climax caressed his sensitive flesh. He abandoned all restraint. No other woman had made him feel so damn . . . sacred.

That was it. Sacred. Each time they made love, something in him changed subtly, but irrevocably.

As bold and brazen as she was naïve and eager, she demanded all he had to give and responded in kind until they came in an explosive climax suffocated by the kiss they shared.

Req turned them onto their sides. He held her, kissed her softly, and stroked her hair and skin for a long time before he spoke. "We didn't use a condom."

"We didn't have one," she said against his chest.

"We should have used some protection."

"It's too late to think about it now." She kissed his chest, then snuggled against him. "I knew the risks when I came to your room tonight. As you said earlier, it was my choice." Her splayed finger slid along his belly. "A wise and satisfying one too, I might add. Too bad it took me so long to risk loving you regardless of the consequences."

"The hell you say." He rose on one elbow but could barely make her out in the dark. "We're going with morning-after protection."

"Huh? And what might that be?"

"We're getting married again." Hell, it was the least he could do. The way his luck was going, she'd get pregnant tonight. It would be hard enough for her to raise a child alone, but one regarded as a bastard, in this era, would be even harder. That would not happen to his kid. Not if he could help it.

Cally sighed. "Are you going to protect me by marrying me every month?"

"If that's what it takes." At least she hadn't balked at the notion.

"All right."

"We don't have to tell anyone, if that's what you want."

She yawned. "Tomorrow," she managed while snuggling against him.

Req drew the blankets over them.

"I love you too, Req." She tucked the edge of the blanket over her shoulder.

Chapter 20

CALLY REMAINED SILENT when Req detailed the marriage ceremony he had planned. In a sense, marrying him two times in as many months was amusing. He'd never asked her to marry him, never ordered, commanded, or cajoled her to do so. Instead, he used the irrefutable logic of marriage for her protection. He was protecting her and it was the equivalent of showing her that he loved her. She could hardly object because she intended to make love with him at every opportunity. Doing so dramatically increased her chances of becoming pregnant. At least her child would have his father's name, if not his father. From afar, he would continue to protect her, shielding and taking responsibility for the consequences of her loving him.

Standing on the front steps of city hall, Cally felt an undeniable sense of purpose in Req.

This time, she would marry him because she sincerely wanted to be his wife.

This time, she knew she loved him.

Shortly after breakfast, they met Lemuel Hansen in the hotel lobby. Surprised by the news of the marriage plans, Lemuel was a witness during the civil marriage of Caladonia Hornsby and Requiem Maguire. The impartiality of the brief, perfunctory ceremony was similar to their first exchange of vows in Reno.

This time, they looked into each other's eyes and spoke their responses with a conviction from the heart.

After finishing the paperwork formalities, they left the courthouse as man and wife. Again.

"I'll meet you at the hotel this evening," Req told Cally.

"Wait." Lemuel caught Req's arm. "You're not going to

abandon her in front of the courthouse. My God, man! You just married her."

Cally met Req's gaze. That was exactly what it must have looked like, but not what it was. "He's not abandoning me, Mr. Hansen. He's simply doing what he needs to do today, just as you and I will."

Riveting green eyes caught Lemuel in a gaze that spoke volumes to anyone who knew how to read them. To Cally, the wellspring of Req's jumbled emotions flowed swiftly. He seemed more at odds with himself today than ever. A ripple of gooseflesh rode up her spine as she pondered why. Maybe, just maybe, he was beginning to realize he loved her.

"Take good care of my wife, Lemuel. I don't want anything upsetting her."

A churlish frown revealed Lemuel's disapproval, though he afforded a curt nod of agreement.

Cally touched Req's arm. The decision she had made last night heightened a growing sense of freedom she ached to explore with Req. They had so little time before duty sent them down separate paths. She would be a complete fool if she didn't make the most of their time together. "Be careful, Req."

"Always." He started to turn away, then reversed himself. To her astonishment, he cupped the back of her neck and drew her into a quick, hard kiss. "I'll try to make it back early. It's our wedding night."

Ignoring the stare his actions drew, Cally laughed again. She pressed his hand to her cheek, then released him. "I'm not likely to forget." She watched him walk away. The tenderness of their early morning lovemaking left a smile in the corners of her mouth that resisted fading.

Lemuel moved to her side. "When I met Requiem Maguire in Monterey, I thought him a cold man, one void of emotion, possibly even incapable of it. That isn't the way of it, is it?"

Cally shook her head. It wasn't that Req didn't feel anything; rather, he felt too much. The only way he kept it from overwhelming him was to keep it tightly controlled. "Requiem Maguire does what needs doing regardless of the cost to himself," she answered. "He has a rare depth of honor and a sense of duty that makes the rest of us appear to be slackers in comparison."

Lemuel took her elbow and guided her toward the curb. "Those are admirable qualities. Even so, I suspect you married a very dangerous man, Mrs. Maguire."

"You have no idea," she murmured, catching a final glimpse of Req as he turned the corner. Her fingers closed tightly around the handles of her valise containing the names of the ill-fated crew of the *Ocean Princess*.

"Dangerous men are necessary in dangerous situations. Our chances of finding Mr. Schmit's killers may be better than I first hoped," Lemuel said thoughtfully.

"Let's do our part and get to the Maritime Registry. Somewhere there's a connection between my father, your brother, and Helmut. Maybe fortune will smile on us there." The sooner they brought the killer to justice, the more time she'd have with Req.

Cally and Lemuel had no luck at the Maritime Registry. If any of the crew from the *Ocean Princess* had survived, they hadn't signed on through the registries in Monterey or San Francisco.

Req's quest fared marginally better. In the seedy taverns of the wharf, he found only a small number of men willing to talk about Schmit's death. A few confidentially speculated that Schmit was asking for trouble by trying to organize the sailors and dockworkers. None admitted knowing more than the rumors. The general feeling was that someone from out of town had killed Helmut Schmit, but no one had any idea who it was—at least no one was willing to speculate.

The last and best hope for information lay in the items Katya Schmit took from Helmut's office. Cally anticipated their appointment with a mixture of hope and dread. What could she say to Katya? There were no words to ease the widow's aching heart. Murder was a particularly harsh way to lose someone you loved. For Cally, it had engendered a rage that sought a focal point. She had directed her energy toward finding her father's killer and she refused to think beyond that goal.

Hand in hand, Cally and Req climbed the steps of the front porch to the Behrens's home. The Victorian architecture was typical of the nicer homes in the neighborhood.

A younger, thinner version of Katya Schmit answered the door. Gertrude Behrens's anger over the loss of her father was almost palpable. The thinly veiled hostility in her blue eyes sought a place to strike.

Katya stood on the far side of the foyer and watched them enter. "Miss Caladonia, you're welcome, as is your companion." The resignation in Katya's voice sent a ripple of sympathy through Cally.

The stress of losing Helmut had obviously taken the widow's appetite and changed her appearance. Her blue Sunday dress no longer accentuated the contours of her *zaftig* form. Rather, it hung on her with the same voluminous depth as the sorrowful pallor that enveloped her.

Cally offered what consolation she could. It had little effect. For Helmut's widow, it was too late; too much of her had died with her husband. For his daughter, it was too soon; her anger stood in the way of her grief.

"My husband carried down the boxes my mother brought from Father's office. Please," Gertrude implored, "my mother has answered enough questions from strangers. Just take the boxes and go. I fervently hope whatever you're looking for is in them and it helps you reveal why my father was killed and by whom."

"I assure you, Mrs. Behrens, we are doing our best," Cally promised. She followed the direction of Gertrude's worried gaze.

At the parlor window, Katya stared down at the street leading toward the wharf, her shoulders rigid. The movement of the sheer lace curtain caught Cally's eye.

Katya Schmit was slowly picking apart the lace. The curtain was in tatters, the holes framed by a hint of pink from Katya's cracked and bleeding fingertips.

Before Cally recovered from the abysmal realization of how deeply Helmut's death had affected Katya, Req approached the woman. He stood behind her and gazed out the window. The bass timbre of his voice remained just low enough for Cally to catch an errant word now and then, but soft enough to keep his conversation private.

"Perhaps you should take Mr. Maguire and go now," Gertrude suggested.

"Give him a moment with her," Cally said, transfixed by the pair at the window across the room. The thickness of unshed tears constricted her throat. She reached out and gripped the doorjamb.

"Are you ill?" Gertrude asked softly.

Cally shook her head; her gaze fixed on Req.

Req was a hard, unrelenting man who posed a lethal danger to anyone who threatened those close to his heart. But seeing him with Katya left no doubt that he was also a sensitive, deep-feeling man. The way his big hand rested around Katya's shoulder as though she were a Dresden doll revealed his perception of her emotions.

Though Cally couldn't hear his words, she knew how gentle he could be with a wounded soul. The way he looked at Katya and made her the center of his universe touched Cally with a reminder of why she loved him. Requiem Maguire might be a formidable giant, but his heart was full of tenderness and caring.

Even as the outpouring of her love rendered her speechless, her heart grew heavy with the reminder of how brief their time together was. As Cally watched him speak softly to Katya, who was now visibly relaxed, Cally wondered who would console him. Who would guide him to peace when he returned to finish the business that could very well kill him?

The urge to run screaming at the injustice of the world, of life and death, of duty and love became so strong she had to turn away. He had to return to his world, and she couldn't be there to comfort him when he needed it most. In truth, both of them would be alone after the dark hour of their final parting.

While she had him within reach, she would love and comfort him; her love would span the century between their worlds.

Tears blurred the images of Req and Katya Schmit.

"Oh, sweet God in heaven," Gertrude whispered in a shaky voice. "Mother is crying. At last."

Cally turned away as her own tears slipped down her cheeks. Silently, she cried for all the losses people suffered for the sake of love. There seemed so many.

Late that afternoon they sat on the floor of their suite at the Palace Hotel. Taking care to categorize the contents of the three boxes Katya had given them required a great deal of time. Maps, folded charts, a broken compass, a variety of newspapers; and pages of repairs, lists, and communications in need of interpretation cluttered the hotel-room floor.

"Req," Cally whispered, barely able to believe her eyes.

"Did you find something?"

"Merciful heavens, look at this." She reached into the bottom of the wooden box and brushed aside several loose papers.

Req slid away from the box he was sorting and joined her. "Do you recognize that?"

"This was my father's." She extracted the blue leather pouch, then pushed the box away so they could examine their find.

"Look, those are his initials." Her fingertip ran around the letters tooled into the leather. "This may be what Freddy Hansen was supposed to find in our library the night he was killed."

"Open it and let's see what someone wanted badly enough to kill for."

Cally untied the leather thong holding the bulging pouch closed. She had barely begun smoothing out the trifolded papers when recognition struck.

"It's the manifest from the *Ocean Princess*. Look. Some of the cargo is checked. It looks like the most valuable items."

"What's this, Cally?" Req picked up a second set of papers. The ship's name was unfamiliar. She doubted she had even seen it docked in Monterey.

"They really did it," she said. "They scuttled the *Princess*."

"After they transferred some of the cargo to this ship." Req flipped the papers over. "The *Carpathian Queen*. Golden Sun Shipping collected the insurance money, and sold the cargo they diverted. And they got away with it until something made your father suspicious."

"The mysterious 'they,'" Cally agreed.

"Yeah, they. All we have is speculation. These papers don't prove murder. Who had the most to gain? Who would come out ahead?"

"Chauncy." An invisible rock settled in her stomach. "And it makes sense that Penelope would have overheard one of his conversations."

"He's not acting alone. And we know he wasn't on the beach the night Freddy Hansen was killed. You would have recognized his voice."

"Yes, I would have. I keep thinking there was something familiar about one of the voices, but I still can't place it." She collected the last papers from the box. "It definitely was not Chauncy Cunningham."

"Thomas Barry?" Req asked.

"No. I would have recognized his voice too. Still, everything sounded distorted. Maybe because I was afraid. Maybe it was the fog. Maybe it was them and the danger they were facing."

"What about handwriting? Would you recognize Chauncy's?"

"Yes." She studied the papers he offered. "That's his writing," Cally paused as something else caught her eye. "Oh, God, Req." Heavy-hearted, she fished out one of the papers from the cluster in his hand. "In a strange way, I suppose it makes sense."

"What?"

"This is Cameron Morton's distinctive scrawl. See the curlicue on the capital letters? Whatever will Maudel do? Not only her father, but her husband—the father of her child—is involved in the most heinous crime possible on the high seas. Men died when the *Ocean Princess* went down." Nausea churned in her stomach. Revealing the truth was going to devastate her best friend.

"She and the kid are better off without Morton," Req said. "Let's get this sorted and see what we've got. Keep a sharp eye on the handwriting, Cally. Look for Thomas Barry's."

"You don't like him, do you?"

Req shrugged. "It isn't a matter of liking him or not. If he's in on this, he's the most dangerous. He's glib, smooth, smart, and as you've said, he's ruthless when it comes to business. If the man has no conscience, he'd kill anyone who got in his way and smile when he walked away."

Cally shivered. "I don't think Thomas . . ." Her voice faded with the unfinished thought.

"But you don't know for certain."

"No," she agreed. She realized somewhat belatedly that she couldn't trust anyone except for Req. After all, two months ago she wouldn't have suspected Chauncy of jeopardizing everything he and her father had built either.

"Our next step is to define the players. We have two: Chauncy and Cameron. We need to know about Barry. If he's not one of them, we need him on our side."

"How do we find out?"

"Unless we get lucky and find something among these papers, it may take a while. We must move very carefully, Cally. We don't want to tip our hand."

With the exception of Irene, Brendan, and the Rodrigues, Cally and Req told no one about their marriage when they returned to Monterey. The housekeeper accepted the news with disgruntled satisfaction.

By keeping a status quo, they kept new elements out of the social interactions. This was paramount importance where Thomas Barry was concerned.

Req's black sweater lay across the bed they shared in the master bedroom of the Hornsby home. The exquisitely carved headboard and dressers invited the eye to linger on the richness of the design that flowed in harmony with the wood grain. Cally sat at her dressing table putting the final touches on her hair. She and Req had agreed that she would try to glean information from Barry at the Hiltons' party while Req used the opportunity to search his home.

"Be careful with Barry," Req cautioned her as she leaned toward the mirror and smoothed down a stubborn curl. "I hate you doing this." He'd rather spend the night here undoing each one of the curls she had painstakingly put into her long, blond tresses.

"Thomas is a gentleman, Req. He won't make a scene in public."

"Gentleman, my ass. Don't be alone with him."

"There will be a crush of people at the Hiltons' tonight. Most of them were on the train with us yesterday." Cally straightened, took a deep breath, and angled sideways. Satisfied she looked her best in an off-the-shoulder burgundy gown with a velvet bodice and peek-a-boo pleated skirt, she confronted Req's scowl. "I'll be fine. It is you who needs to take care."

He ran a fingertip along the neckline scooped low enough to display her cleavage and the swell of her breasts. "If he touches you, I'll break every bone in his body. If he hurts you, I'll kill him."

Cally's heart leaped into her throat. She pressed her fingers to his mouth to keep him from expounding on that last thought. Her husband was a man of many dimensions and he cherished her. Of that, Cally was certain.

"We will both behave with proper care and be safe," she said. The heavy, black sweater she smoothed over his chest was far more befitting him than any suit. However, she preferred him wearing nothing except her. "When we finish the night's business, we'll share our triumphs and disappointments. But we'll do that after I make love with you, Req. After I touch you with my hands, my mouth, my body." *And my heart.*

"Damn, but you're a beautiful woman." His fingers closed around her bare shoulders. "And a dangerous man-eater to boot." The kiss he settled on her was so sensuously gentle and deep she wanted to tear off their clothes, but couldn't move for want of experiencing each electric charge it sparked throughout her body. "If I were a jealous husband, I'd never let you carry out this part of the plan alone."

"You are a jealous husband." A smile she couldn't suppress escaped.

"Maybe. But I'm also a trusting one. Go on, Cinderella. The hand-picked prince of Golden Sun awaits you downstairs." He stepped back leaving her suddenly chilled in the warm bedroom.

She reached for her black velvet cape, but he beat her to it. He settled the fine wrap around her, then caressed her shoulders as though he envied the fabric.

He opened the bedroom door and made a formal bow as she passed through. No sooner was she in the hall than the door closed behind her.

"I love you," she whispered to the silence.

She drew a deep, cleansing breath and headed for the stairs. As she descended to join Thomas Barry, the man who hoped to wed her, she thought of her husband. If Req could use the evening to further their investigation without a qualm, so could she.

Rain added a sinister dimension to Thomas Barry's home. Req jimmied the lock on the French doors opening into the sunroom from the flagstone patio leading from the garden. Breaking and entering was pathetically easy without sophisticated alarms and electronic monitoring devices.

The staff moved freely through Thomas Barry's household. Sometimes they came within a few feet of him as he moved just as freely though Barry's private papers.

When the house became quiet and dark, Req slipped into Barry's bedroom. He checked every drawer, nook, cranny, and hiding place imaginable. The search produced a great deal of information about Thomas Barry, but nothing that remotely tied him into the bad business with the *Ocean Princess*. The correspondence and mementos Req scanned indicated a strong moral streak and a genuine fondness for Peter Hornsby. Such evidence might have swayed Req before he went undercover and watched Gutierrez order the deaths of men he liked, including his own brother-in-law.

Conflicting and unreliable, Req's burgeoning emotions wouldn't differentiate between Gutierrez and Barry.

Cally was involved. He couldn't afford discrimination; it increased the chance of error.

As he slipped back into the rainy night, he wondered how Cally had fared on her so-called date.

The notion of his wife *dating* Thomas Barry for any reason stuck painfully in his gut. Ever since his emotions had started to creep out from under the rock where he'd buried them years ago, he was finding it harder and harder to keep the personal and professional separate. This was particularly true when it came to Cally.

If he hurried, he could search Cameron and Maudel Morton's house before they returned from the party.

Somewhere, someone had the answers he needed. All he had to do was find them.

"Something has bothered me the last several days, Thomas."

They threaded a path through the throng of partygoers in the Hiltons' parlor and down the hall toward the solarium where they found privacy among the exotic plants. Cally leaned closer to Thomas's tall, lean frame. She had learned a great deal about him tonight. The surface elegance swathed in propriety disguised a barbaric ferocity with which Thomas protected what was his. If not for Req, she might never have discovered the true nature lurking below the polished surface of her golden-haired escort.

Cally settled in the middle of a bench and spread her skirts.

A knowing, half-hearted smile curled Thomas's mouth. "Your proclivity for single-mindedness has always fascinated me."

"I don't know what you mean." Had she inadvertently revealed herself? She hadn't thought so. But Thomas seemed different tonight, more intense and attentive than usual. Gone was the cloak of casualness and the repartee that kept a conversation going without making it personal. That was the difference. Tonight he was taking a more intimate approach.

"I'm wondering if you will give the same kind of undivided attention to the man you marry."

Suddenly at a loss, Cally looked away. Heat colored her neck. Only Req knew the real answer. "Did you bring me in here to make me uncomfortable, Thomas?"

"My apologies if you are. You're a very intelligent woman, Caladonia. Surely by now you've realized I want to court you with marriage in mind." He settled on a bench across from her.

"No," she said, wanting the conversation to take any direction other than this one.

"No, you don't want me to court you, or no, you didn't realize that was my intention?"

Cally gathered her wits. "We're business partners. I'm content to keep that arrangement."

"You may change your mind in time."

Cally shook her head. "I admire your keen sense of business. I respect and value your friendship. But I do not love you the way a man considering marriage should be loved, Thomas."

"It's Maguire, isn't it?"

She met Thomas's imploring gaze and took a chance on the truth. "Yes. I love him in ways I never thought possible."

A crooked smile lifted the side of his mouth as he shook his head in open disbelief. "Where did he come from, Cally? How did he get into your life?"

"It doesn't matter. He's here now."

"And asking questions about your father's death." Thomas became very serious and spoke in a voice so soft only the closest plants could overhear.

"On my behalf," she agreed, her palms growing damp. She gathered her determination and refused to let him control the conversation. "Though there are a few questions you might answer for me, if you would be so kind."

Thomas regarded her for a long moment before the tension eased from his features. "So it's to be business all the way."

"Thank you, Thomas." She smiled, assuming victory.

Thomas laughed, then settled back on the bench across from her. The earthy smell of loam and mulch mingled with the sweet scent of exotic plumeria. "Ask away. Partner."

She stood, quickly gauging their proximity to other guests in the solarium. She had good reason for her nervousness. If Thomas was the man behind the three murders and the scuttling of the *Ocean Princess,* Cally was setting herself up as the next target, if she wasn't already. "Thomas, what if I told you that some of the items on the manifest of the *Ocean Princess* were offered for sale in San Francisco?"

He stared at her without blinking. "I'd say there had to be a mistake."

"And if there wasn't?" Her heart hammered in her breast. If she was wrong about Thomas's involvement, revealing so much might force him to ensure that she didn't see another sunrise.

He regarded her for a long, tense moment during which she had second, third, and fourth thoughts about the wisdom of her revelations. An impenetrable mask slipped smoothly over his features and hid any glimmer of his reaction. At the far end of the solarium a woman laughed and a man swore. The tempo of a waltz overpowered the fading sounds of conversation and laughter.

"Then I'd say we have a severe problem. Is that what you and Maguire were doing in San Francisco? Searching for pieces of the *Ocean Princess*'s cargo?"

"Among other things, we went to visit Helmut Schmit's widow and pay our respects." And for Req to weave the magic only another lost soul could weave in order to show Katya the path leading toward the mending of her tormented soul.

"And?"

"We aren't finished going through his papers, nor have we begun looking for any of the items on the ship's manifest." She straightened when he relaxed, then added, "Yet."

"Yet? Do you really expect to find items from the *Ocean Princess's* on the open market?" Incredulity laced his voice but his expression did not change.

"Yes."

"My God, Caladonia. Do you realize what you're saying? You're implying—"

"Yes, Thomas. Unfortunately, I know exactly what this means. I wish it was otherwise, and I am not sharing this confidence lightly. Don't insult us both by trying to take it so."

He drew a long, deep breath, his shoulders squaring, his gaze never leaving hers. "How did you arrive at this reprehensible conclusion?"

"I'd rather not say right now." She hoped she hadn't tipped her hand too far.

"Did your father tell you this?"

"No, but I think that's why he was killed. I suppose when you've been responsible for cheating Golden Sun Shipping and sinking a ship with all hands, another death or two or three means little."

Thomas paled visibly in the soft light of the greenhouse lamps. "I had no idea you were such a hard woman, Caladonia."

"Not hard. Honest." It was self-preservation, pure and simple. Embracing the broad scope of what she perceived a monstrous series of tragedies was too overwhelming. Like the elephant of change, she consumed it in small pieces and ignored the rest.

"Clearly, you believe this. Knowing you, you must have a

solid basis. I'll help you resolve this. Meanwhile, don't mention this conversation to anyone." He rose and extended a hand.

She took his hand and rose, absently smoothing her skirts in the process. She hadn't believed he had any part in the nefarious actions. His last request gave birth to doubt.

"Shall we join the party?"

"Certainly." Cally gave him a dazzling smile and accompanied Thomas into the fray.

Chapter 21

THE RAIN SLACKENED. Through the fine mist draping the night, Req made out the lights of the Hornsby home. The detour through the Morton house had made him much later than he had originally planned.

The sound of voices and a carriage warned that Cally had beaten him home by several minutes. To avoid discovery, he left the road. A shorter, more direct route through the soggy trees brought him to the house just in time to see Barry try to kiss Cally.

Req stopped in his tracks. His blood alternately froze and sizzled in his veins. His hands curled into fists itching for a landing spot on Thomas Barry's face. With what felt like superhuman willpower, he remained in the shadows. An orchestra of drips played from the house and trees. The flat tune muffled the conversation on the porch, making their words indistinguishable.

His fists tightened when Cally put a gloved hand at the center of Barry's chest, then said something and gave Barry an apologetic smile. Barry shrugged a shoulder and said something that erased the smile from her lips.

Get used to Barry going after her. The bastard wants her. Bad, he warned himself. Cally's life wasn't going on pause for over a century once he returned to what awaited him. Life would go on. She'd do what was necessary. So would he. Just as they were now.

He closed the distance to the porch steps Barry was descending while watching the front door close behind Cally.

"Looks like you're pushing damn hard where you aren't wanted." Req itched to hit the fair-haired prince of Golden Sun who showed only faint surprise at Req's sudden appearance from the shadows.

The jangle of harnesses and the creak of the carriage bespoke the driver's anxiousness to be underway. "You're reaching too high on the social ladder. Let her go, Maguire. She's too good for you." Barry faced him squarely.

"But not for you, eh, Barry?"

"I can offer her a future. Security. Decorum at the level of society she's known most of her life." The light from the house glittered menacingly in Barry's eyes. "I don't know where you came from, Maguire, but if you care for Caladonia, do her a favor and go back."

"You mean do *you* a favor," Req growled, aching to hit Barry for telling the truth. Hell, even if he were foolish enough to contemplate staying, he couldn't make much of a living. Certainly not one to rival the lifestyle she enjoyed now. He damn sure wasn't going to live off her, which was another reason why he had to leave.

Cally looked around, glad Brendan had the good sense to retire for the night as she'd suggested before leaving. She hung her cape on the hall tree and stripped off her gloves on the way to the library. Anxious to talk with Req, she draped her gloves over the newel post. There was so much to tell him.

Until his parting comment in the Hiltons' solarium, she had never seriously considered Thomas's involvement in the nasty business of the *Ocean Princess*. Now she questioned her previous judgment. Why else would he want their conversation kept quiet?

Her heartbeat quickened at the sound of Req's footsteps in the library. Closing her fingers around the ornate doorknob, she wondered what, if anything, he had discovered in Thomas's home.

Not seeing Req as she stepped inside the library, she called out his name.

Certain she had heard him just a moment earlier, she shut the door and started forward, then halted in her tracks. The papers she and Req had meticulously categorized and chronicled lay scattered across the floor on the other side of the room.

Only the lamp on the far table and the one on the desk lit the room. A sense of foreboding slowed Cally's step. A chilly breeze set the hairs on the back of her neck on end.

Instantly, her gaze shot to the open window through which

Freddy the Thief had gained entry nearly two months earlier. Why, oh why, hadn't she remembered to have Brendan fix it?

She backed up a step, wanting to run, yet uncertain where Req was. What if he lay hurt on the other side of the room? What if the intruder had come and gone? What if . . .

An arm snaked around her waist with the force of a bullwhip, and a sweaty hand clamped over her mouth.

"Make a sound, and it'll be your last," a voice hissed against her ear.

She instinctively squirmed, trying to escape the reach of her captor, struggling for freedom.

"Hold still, Miss Hornsby, or you'll discover how fast my knife can slice through your corset. Overall, I have little to lose. You, on the other hand, have your life in the balance." The miasma of wine and spices rolled from his mouth with the warning. He stood half a head taller than she. His whipcord frame seemed all buttons and bones. Fear tainted the pungent odor of perspiration that Cally vaguely realized was his.

The voice seemed familiar, but in her state of near-panic she couldn't recall from where. Eyes searching frantically for a weapon, Cally forced her body into stillness.

Where was Req? Had the intruder killed him? Had Thomas's household help discovered him?

With no weapon in reach, Cally quickly decided on deception to obtain her freedom. She went completely limp.

Instantly, her captor struggled to hold her dishrag body without falling over.

Cally smiled slightly as her head lolled from side to side while he struggled. Any minute he'd have to put her down. Then she'd have a chance.

"Cally isn't a piece of meat being auctioned to the highest bidder," Req said, itching for a good fight. He wouldn't start it, but he'd damn sure participate until one of them couldn't get up. Judging by Barry's size, he'd make it a contest, but he was no match for Req's street tactics.

Barry descended the final step and took a stand in front of Req. "At least we agree on something, Maguire."

"She makes her own choices, Barry. And it isn't you, so give her the respect of knowing her own mind and leave her alone." *Before I rearrange your face,* he added. Adrenaline high, he was ready, silently begging Barry to take a swing.

"Miss Hornsby is a fine lady who has had more trouble than

she deserves. You managed to find her at a particularly vulnerable time. You've wheedled your way into her affections. When she comes to her senses, she'll see you for the Neanderthal you are, Maguire."

"The point is, she *didn't* choose you, Barry. Don't make a nuisance of yourself. The lady works with you. She's your business partner. Nothing more. Accept her decision." What was wrong with him? He'd never goaded anyone into a fight before. Trouble usually found him all by itself.

"You're a flash in the pan, Maguire. You won't last a day longer than her last fiancé did. Caladonia is independent, but she needs the strong guidance of a man who genuinely cares for her, someone of her class and position in society. Me.

"I'm a patient man, Maguire. After you're nothing but a bad memory fading from Caladonia's nightmares, I'll still be at her side."

"Some bad memories take a long time to fade. Others never do." Req's finger's splayed wide then tightened into a fist in search of a place to land.

"You may be content to live off Caladonia's fortune, but she'll soon come to her senses and cut off financial access."

"You're a real asshole," Req murmured, then stepped forward.

"Buck up, Miss Hornsby."

She knew that tenor voice. Oh God, he was the man on the beach, the one who shot Freddy Hansen. The realization made her head swim and the false swoon nearly became real.

He was losing his grip on her waist along with his balance. The imperative to capitalize on whatever opportunity she could create intensified. She had to be ready, for there would be only one chance.

Unfortunately, there was only one direction open—straight ahead and into the library. If she could elude him for a few seconds, she might be able to rouse the household.

Without warning, her captor released her. Eyes closed, she crashed to her knees, then swayed as the pain of landing on the hardwood floor shot up her thighs and into her hips.

He slammed a fist against her right shoulder. With nothing to keep her steadied, she toppled. She lay on her side, her cheek pressed to the floor. Desperate, she thought of every ploy and defensive ruse she'd ever known. Only one came to mind.

"Damn shrinking violet," her captor muttered.

Cally watched his feet through her eyelashes, careful to keep her eyes closed long enough to fool him into believing she was in a faint. Barely breathing, her heart racing, she was determined to outwit him.

Finally, mercifully, he turned and opened the library door just far enough to see out.

Heart thundering her fearful bravado, Cally rolled, scrambling to her feet amid the yards of skirts and petticoats. She reached the desk and began throwing things. Her only thought was to drive him out of the room she occupied.

Scream, she ordered her throat. Panicked, her desperation made her breath come too rapidly to form more than a whimper. Staring at him, she knew she'd never forget his face. Bushy gray muttonchops. The sharp contrast of his black hair. His thick eyebrows that met over the bridge of his crooked nose. And his eyes—close together, black, like a ferret.

Frantic to turn him back, she picked up the closest object, an ink bottle, and hurled it at him.

The intruder slammed the door with his foot, his arms raised to protect his face from the barrage she unleashed. His swearing grew louder and more vile each time an object struck him.

Cally gathered up the pens and hurled them like darts. They struck against the door, the walls, the intruder, then clattered to the floor.

She threw the pen holder, the other two ink bottles, a wooden tray, and a polished geode, all of which connected with a satisfying thud and evoked an infuriated oath from the target. Angry now, Cally kept throwing things until the desk was bare.

He blocked most of the objects with his forearms and batted away the smaller objects. Despite the blood seeping from his hands where the pen points found their mark, he kept advancing.

In a desperate measure, she threw the lamp and sent oil flying across the carpet.

"Damn lying bitch! You'll get no mercy from me now."

A glance at the window, which seemed half a mile away, denied escape. She opened the center drawer and found more ammunition. If she could draw him around the desk, then dash for the door . . .

He rounded the desk and lunged for her, his fingers missing her by inches. The close call shot a bolt of fresh fear through her.

She screamed, kicked the chair into his shins, and threw the paperweight she'd plucked from the drawer. It connected solidly above his left eye and opened a gash that bled immediately.

She ran for the door.

He caught her halfway there, then spun her around.

Panicked, reaching for anything that might save her life, she used her elbow as a club and caught him squarely in the left muttonchop. Her arm instantly went numb. No one on those action shows on television had mentioned that it hurt when bone slammed into bone.

He yelled and reached for his face with one hand.

She bolted, but he hauled her back by the hair. Her screams vented pain and frustration.

She tried elbowing his ribs and succeeded only in throwing them both off balance. They tumbled against a wingback chair, which toppled backwards and slammed into the desk. Locked in battle, they crashed to the floor.

"Killing you will be a pleasure," he seethed through clenched teeth as he struggled to subdue her.

Wild-eyed with angry terror, sure she was going to wind up as dead as Freddy Hansen, Cally tried to knee the attacker in the groin. A growl of fearful frustration escaped through her gritted teeth. The yards of skirt and petticoat softened the blow to the point of doing nothing more than alerting him of her intent.

In retaliation, he swung his leg over her body and straddled her ribs. The full force of his weight squished the air from her lungs. He was bigger and stronger, and he was going to kill her.

His anger growing in proportion to her continued struggles, he backhanded her.

Req brushed past Thomas Barry and started up the porch stairs. What the hell was he doing playing an adolescent game that didn't amount to a hill of beans?

"Go home, Barry. When she wants you, she'll let you know. Until then, leave her alone." He fished the house key from his trouser pocket and stuck it into the lock.

"Do you derive enjoyment from enticing vulnerable women?" Barry asked from the bottom step.

"Let it be before we both do something neither of us will be proud of in the cold light of morning." He turned the key and pushed open the door.

Cally's muffled screams cut through the silent house with the impact of a sonic boom on Req's ears. He ran across the foyer and down the hall.

The doors banged against the wall as Req assaulted the library. He saw the writhing, clawing tangle of arms, legs, and skirts near the desk and his blood turned to lava. A man had her pinned and was trying to get control of her.

A primal yell of outrage tore from his lungs. Red fury filmed over his vision. All he saw was a man attacking Cally. Everything in him focused on the single purpose of rescuing her.

He caught the attacker by the scruff of the neck with one hand and lifted him off Cally as she continued to scream. At last, his fist had a worthy target. Req slammed the man against the desk, then vented the heat of his anger by unleashing the power of his right fist.

The impact spun the attacker off the edge of the desk and onto a lamp table. The delicate piece shattered under the man's weight.

Req followed with the intensity of a grizzly bear. He'd never wanted to kill anyone with his bare hands as much as he did now. Req grabbed the man and roughly hoisted him off the floor. Eye-bulging fear accompanied the man's twisting search for freedom. Req rewarded his efforts by burying his left fist in the man's abdomen.

The attacker doubled over, then sank to his knees when Req released him.

"Get up," Req demanded, frustrated that he had been denied the opportunity to fully vent his rage. He felt he'd never quell the emotional storm crackling in every nerve.

The attacker sagged to the floor at Req's feet and curled into a ball.

"What? You only beat on women? Get your ass up or I'll kick you to death where you are."

The man moaned and started to rise.

Req helped him up by the hair and hit him a third time in the ribs. "Can't take it when someone your own size hits back?" Req's fist found the man's nose. "This one's for Cally." He released the man's hair and delivered another blow to his left jaw. Arms spread, the man careened against a nearby chair, then staggered as his legs gave out. He collapsed into a battered heap on the floor and promptly passed out.

"Goddamn coward! Get up! I'm not done with you." Wild with anger, seething with the need for retribution, Req started toward the man lying only a few feet out of his lethal reach.

Before he reached the crumbled heap on the floor, Cally's face filled his gaze. She lifted her hands and held his jaw, forcing him to look at her, forcing him to abandon the soul-cleansing catharsis of beating the man to a pulp.

"Jeezus, Cally." It hurt deep in his gut to see the red hand imprint on her face. A droplet of blood leaked from the corner of her mouth. Tears streamed down her cheeks. He wiped his bloody, sweaty hand on his pants, then used a gentle thumb to caress her cheek. "Jeezus, Cally," he repeated, letting the pain of his angst emerge.

He gathered her in a desperate embrace and held her, stroking her disheveled hair, unable to speak, knowing if he tried, the ball of emotion expanding in his chest would burst.

The awful truth reached out of the maelstrom of emotion. He tried slaying it, but it refused to die. He tried forcing the ghostly specter down deeper into the depths of his awareness where it belonged.

The truth was dangerous; he could not afford to love his wife. To do so would destroy them both when he left.

His head lowered further against her as though part of him bowed in defeat. Inwardly, he shook as hard as she trembled. His rapid breathing drew her scent into the very heart of him.

"He's one of the men from the beach. He's the one who killed Freddy Hansen," she said when her breathing returned to normal and he eased the deathlike grip of their embrace.

Req stroked the soft skin along the side of her neck and leaned back to look at her. Wild, blond curls hung down to her shoulders. Tears streamed over the angry, red handprint on her cheek. In the liquid brown depth of her eyes, fear from the discovery of her vulnerability lingered.

He should have seen accusation, censure, and disdain reflected in those eyes as the result of his failure to protect her. The fact that he saw none of those emotions, only love and the lasting remnants of fear created a thickness in his throat that kept him from speaking.

He'd almost lost her. He loved her, and he'd damn near lost her. Both realizations rocked the roots of his soul. It filled him with more rage than he thought existed in the entire universe. He yearned to tear the attacker apart with his bare hands, yet craved isolation with Cally. He needed to see every inch of her, ensure she was all right, then worship her with apologies and tender kisses to help heal the inner bruises.

"You do have your uses, Maguire." Thomas Barry kicked

aside the remnants of the small table. He had picked up a lamp from the hallway and sat it on the edge of the desk. He lit it, letting the light illuminate the utter chaos of the library. "Who the hell is this?"

The intrusion of an outsider's voice broke the spell. Req had forgotten about Barry. Req reluctantly released Cally and turned away.

"A killer." Cally answered the question in a voice that sounded miles away. The tremor in her proclamation reflected the terror lingering from nearly becoming his next victim.

Thomas crossed the room, curled a finger under Cally's chin, and turned her face toward the light. "Your mouth is bleeding. Shall I send for a doctor, Caladonia?"

"Unless you want to join the asshole on the floor, take your hands off my wife. Don't touch her again, Barry."

Shaken by the venom in Req's voice, Thomas turned away from Cally. He recoiled, his eyes wide in surprise.

Req kept an eye on Thomas while he unwound a gilt cord from the drapery. The violent turmoil raging inside him was still dangerously close to the surface.

"Your wife?" Thomas asked Req, but looked at her. "Caladonia? Is this true?"

"Yes," Cally answered, wishing she could shield Req from the derision evident in Thomas's scowl. "Requiem is my husband."

"You married Maguire, and told no one? This is priceless Caladonia." He prodded the cretin on the floor with the toe of his highly polished shoe. "And who is this one? A relative of his paying a social call?"

"I realize you're surprised, Thomas, but I won't tolerate you insulting Requiem in his own home." She rested her hand on Req's shoulder as he tied up the intruder.

"Quit badgering my wife and make yourself useful, Barry. Bring that chair around." Req pulled the semiconscious attacker upright, a dangerous gleam in his eyes. "We're going to have a little discussion with Cally's visitor."

Barry set the heavy chair down with a loud thunk. "I'll send my driver for the authorities."

"Not yet." Req positioned the chair, then grabbed the man by his clothing and lifted him up.

The attacker came alive with a howl. Fully alert, he rubbed at his chest with his bound hands. "You're pulling out my chest hair."

Req unceremoniously dropped him into the chair.

Cally watched without sympathy. The spot on her scalp where he'd hauled her up short by the hair still throbbed.

"Who is he?" Thomas pulled the lamp closer to the edge of the desk for a better look at the intruder. The increased brightness washed over the man in the chair clearly illuminating the captive's features.

Thomas didn't show any concern the man might identify him as a coconspirator. Cally watched both men closely, her trembling fingertips absently moving over Req's shoulder.

"You don't know him?" Req asked evenly.

"Now that I have a better look at him, he does appear familiar." Thomas gathered up his great coat hems and dropped onto his haunches to study the intruder from another angle. "What's your name?"

The prisoner stared at Thomas as though he wasn't there and held his silence.

"I think I recognize you." Thomas braced his right elbow against his knee; his chin perched on the apex of his thumb and curled forefinger. "You were in the office yesterday."

Cally's heart dropped. Any lingering hope she had held of someone close to her not being involved in the three murders evaporated.

"Seeing who?" Req demanded.

Thomas shook his head. "I didn't pay attention. Busy as we were, it's sheer happenstance I remember seeing him at all."

Req removed an oilskin pouch from inside his rain slicker, slipped it into his pocket, then took off the slicker.

"You're wet. I'll start a fire." Cally turned toward the fireplace, her intent obvious.

Req caught her hand. "Your business associate will light the fire, won't you, Barry?" He led her to the couch. "It will give me a reason to let him stay. Otherwise, you can get the hell out of here."

To Cally's surprise, Thomas rose, removed his overcoat, and got busy at the fireplace. "I'm most definitely interested in learning more about this. Do either of you have a hypothesis?" Thomas asked.

Cally exchanged knowing looks with Req who was rifling the captive's pockets. She caught his nod, then settled on the edge of the leather couch. Thomas certainly didn't act as though he had anything to hide. Quite the contrary, he seemed as intense as when he negotiated a deal. However, Cally remained skeptical about Thomas's innocence and her own objectivity about him. After another sharp look at Req, she decided to trust his judgment in this matter. "He's Freddy Hansen's killer."

"Freddy Hansen." Thomas dusted his hands and stood in front of the growing flames. "Who is he?" His gaze roamed from the man in the chair to Req, then to Cally. "Or shall I ask, who *was* Freddy Hansen?"

Cally brushed a clump of hair out of her eyes, then settled fully into the couch. The way Req was tying up the intruder, there was a better chance of the chair becoming part of his anatomy than of his escaping. Pushing its way through the residual adrenaline, a sense of overpowering love for Req rolled through her in waves. He was her protector, her husband. Tonight, he was her savior. Her hero.

"A dead man." Req caught the man's foot and finished lashing him to the chair. "Think hard, Barry. Who was this guy with when you saw him yesterday?"

"Give me a moment and it will come to me. He was there." Thomas crossed the room and confronted the man in the chair. "Would you care to prod my memory?"

Revulsion twisted their captive's features. A small trickle of blood leaked from the left corner of his pursed lips.

Req grabbed the man's hair and pulled his head back. "I'm tired of chasing killers. I'm pissed at the whole damn world, and I'm really itching to beat the hell out of someone."

"I should say that you already have, Maguire," Barry said.

"That's just a warm-up. Crude, and nowhere near as effective as some of the methods I know," Req murmured. The fine hair at the nape of Cally's neck rose. Seeing this side of her husband unveiled a new myriad of emotions. When he had assumed the role of her protector, she had no idea of the depth of his lethal commitment.

He leaned closer. "Give me an excuse to demonstrate some of those methods—all I need is an excuse."

Cally realized that Req meant every word. "My husband hasn't irreparably harmed you. Yet. A wise man would heed the warning he's received." She met Req's inquiring gaze with a confident nod. He would do what he thought was right.

"Perhaps I should send my driver for the authorities." From behind Req's back, Barry cast an amused glance at Cally.

"No," Req snapped.

"Not yet," Cally answered at the same time. There were

things they needed to do before the man's capture became common knowledge.

"He's not going anywhere until I know who his accomplices are." Req pulled up a footstool and sat down, his elbows resting on his spiked knees, his hands loosely folded in the gap. "And he's going to tell me. The easy way or the hard way," he gave the man a pointed look, "even if it's the last thing he does."

"Why don't you have your driver wait in the kitchen until he's needed, Thomas?" Doing her best to appear at ease, Cally folded her hands in her lap. The glass of champagne she had drunk before leaving the party soured in her stomach.

She waited until Thomas reluctantly donned his coat and departed before addressing Req. "Why?"

Req caught her hand and rose, bringing her with him. He led them to the fireplace where he warmed himself, but never let the intruder or the door out of his sight. "Speak softly. I'd prefer our captive audience not hear."

Cally glared at the man tied to the chair, then nodded. "Why did you let Thomas stay?"

"He's not in on it, Cally. At least, he's not in on the *Ocean Princess* project."

Exasperated, Cally shook her head. "How do you know for certain? I'm not sure it is wise for us to divulge *everything* to him."

"What we know and what we can prove are two different things."

The man was exasperating. "What exactly are you saying Req? Do you or do you not have definitive proof that Barry is innocent of any involvement with the *Ocean Princess*?"

"I didn't find anything at his house—"

"That doesn't mean—" The gentle skim of his fingers along the length of her jaw silenced her.

"I found what we need at your friend's house, Cally. The notes in Morton's handwriting we found among Helmut Schmit's boxes were only the tip of the iceberg. He's involved all the way. Think hard. Could it have been Cameron Morton you heard on the beach?"

Her mouth went dry. The bottom of her churning stomach felt like it had dropped to her feet. "Cameron. Oh, God . . ." It very well could have been him. "What did you find?"

"Enough to hang him." Req nodded at their captive. "And Horace Dowd, which is who we have here." He offered the man's wallet that he had found earlier when rummaging through the thief's pockets. Cally refused it with the shake of her head. "For now, I need to know how comfortable you are with Barry."

Less so by the hour, she thought. His zealous profession of emotion had shaken her. But all she said was, "Why?"

"We need him to buy into helping us. He's the key." A scowl darkened Req's angry green eyes. "The mole. If you're comfortable with it, I'll do the recruiting. If he's willing, we'll lay the trap for Morton and Cunningham. Coming from his direction, they'll never see it."

She studied her husband. "That's what you did, isn't it? You acted the part of the mole who gathered information from Gutierrez, didn't you?"

Req ignored the question. "We're taking a gamble with Thomas Barry, Cally. He's smart, but he isn't a pro. If he's as clean on this as I think, we'll have to be very careful. If we slip up, Barry could end up just as dead as Freddy. Cameron has already proven they're capable of murder and deception. What Barry will need to find out is how deeply Cunningham is involved. We need a confession and the names of their accomplices."

Her husband had never seemed more distant from her than at this moment. He was about to turn one business partner against another.

Her best friend would soon learn that the man she married, the father of her unborn son, was a cold-blooded killer.

The anvil of angst over her father's death settled hard on her heart. Despite the fire, Cally felt cold. It was going to be a long night.

Chapter 22

"How did Horace Dowd become involved with Cameron?" Thomas Barry asked over Sunday brunch. Despite the late night, he had appeared at the Hornsby house promptly at ten o'clock.

Cally glanced at Req. When he didn't answer, she spoke up. "Each had a nefarious interest in the *Ocean Princess's* cargo even before the manifest was set. Both had ties to the ship's captain, Captain Sweeney. Dowd was his brother-in-law. Chance brought them together and sealed Captain Sweeney's and the rest of the crew's fate." The brunch fare of breads, eggs, ham, sweet rolls, and meat pies failed to spark her appetite. When she thought of all the innocent men who had perished, she felt decidedly queasy. She set her fork down and pushed away her plate.

The thought that there had been no survivors reminded her that there would be no survivors when Req left her. Although she would continue breathing, inside there would be only an aching black void.

"One man did survive," Req said. "Freddy Hansen."

"I believe you're mistaken. I checked the names of the crew last week. He wasn't listed," Cally said slowly. "I doubt I would have overlooked it."

"Me either. Don't forget Freddy had a brother who came looking for the reason he died. Freddy would know Lemuel would get involved if he discovered that Freddy had a role in the sinking of the *Ocean Princess*. Freddy signed on under an alias." Req pushed his plate away.

"Did Dowd tell you this?" Admiration tinged Thomas's

voice. Last night's events had forged an uneasy bond between the trio neither man wanted tested.

"Part of it. The rest was easy to piece together. What Freddy lacked in formal education he made up for in street smarts. Either he figured something was afoot, or he was involved from the start. Dowd wouldn't say much about Freddy. When Dowd had cargo transferred to the *Carpathian Queen,* Freddy made sure he went with it. He knew what kind of men he was dealing with, so he disappeared when the ship docked in Seattle. Dowd found him five months ago.

"There's an axiom that says to keep your friends close and your enemies closer. Dowd believes that. He persuaded Freddy there was a place for him in Monterey."

"As it turned out, there was," Cally said softly, recalling the terrified surprise on Freddy Hansen's face split seconds before a bullet took his life. "However, it wasn't the one he anticipated."

Req retrieved an oilskin pouch from his pocket and laid it on the table. "We're dealing with men accustomed to defining responsibilities and rewards. Men steeped in the rituals and rigors of business. Had they been hard-core criminals when they started on this caper, they'd never have written a damn thing down. They weren't. They drew up a contract. This is the proverbial smoking gun." He handed the pouch to Cally.

"How did you come up with that?" Thomas asked, his fingers drumming on the tabletop. The tilt of his head and the gleam in his eyes underscored the respect in his voice. "Or is it more prudent not to ask for details?"

"For now, leave the details to me." Req's gaze settled knowingly on Thomas. "We have a lock on Morton and Dowd."

Cally read the chilling agreement between Cameron Morton and Horace Dowd. The mechanics of their plans were vague, but the intent, right down to identifying the cargo that they transferred, was clear. Their utter disregard for the crew of the *Ocean Princess* turned the scant amount of breakfast she'd eaten into a lump. "Req, you are a nimble-fingered genius. Cameron would never have volunteered this. But we're missing something, aren't we?"

"Yes," Req answered. The hint of an understanding, sad smile tugged at the corners of his mouth.

"What's missing?" Thomas asked while eagerly examining the agreement Cally had passed over to him.

"Even with this, we still have nothing that proves either of these men killed my father."

"Unfortunately, this is just circumstantial evidence that matches a hypothesis we've formed, Cally. Tying it to your father's death for a jury is still a hard sell," Req agreed. "We're going to have to force a tip of the scales if we want to get a conviction. Delivering the sting to Morton and Cunningham is your job, Barry." Req placed his napkin on the table. "We have today to prepare. We're only going to get one shot at tripping them up and getting the proof that these men killed Cally's father. Tomorrow, it's for real. You're dealing with men in a life-and-death situation. Theirs. Cunningham's involvement is not a sure thing. But I feel it in my bones. He's in."

"Perhaps," Barry conceded. "But I cannot believe he's involved in Peter's murder." Genuine sorrow softened his expression when he focused on Cally. "I'm sorry I wasn't more helpful when you insisted your father wasn't the victim of some itinerant dockworker."

"You're helping now," she said. "That's more than I can say for Detective Goodman and the rest of the Monterey authorities. I was gone a month, and they made no progress on my father's killing."

Barry stroked his chin. "As I recall, Detective Goodman did pay a visit to Chauncy several weeks ago. I believe he was asking about you. Chauncy brushed it off as unimportant."

"If Detective Goodman wanted to speak with me, he has had ample time to do so," Cally said, then motioned Req to continue.

"Cunningham's role is yet to emerge. Meanwhile, don't let Morton's quiet mannerisms fool you," Req said. "His life is on the line here. The worst mistake you can make is to underestimate him. He's counting on that camouflage. Look straight through it and see the man.

"Dowd told me that he was supposed to meet Morton this morning. By now, he will probably be getting nervous. By tomorrow morning when he can't find Dowd, he'll start looking. That's when he's vulnerable."

"How long are you going to keep Dowd locked in the root cellar?" Thomas glanced up from the agreement he had been reading, his features drawn sharply in his pale complexion.

"Today. Tomorrow." Req shrugged. "He broke into this house, so here he'll stay until we decide otherwise. If we turn him over to the authorities too soon, we lose our edge. I want Cameron sweating. He'll make mistakes then."

"You won't make any mistakes, will you, Maguire?" Curiosity sharpened the admiration punctuating Thomas's question. "Who are you?" He rose slowly, pushing the agreement aside.

"Your best friend or your worst nightmare, Barry. For the moment, the choice is yours." The tension between the two men returned with a crackling sensation.

Thomas looked at Cally. Absently, she slipped her fingers over Req's forearm. The diamonds in her wedding ring sparkled in the light.

"You intrigue me, Maguire. I believe I'd rather count you as one of my friends. I suspect your enemies do not fare well." The winning smile that Thomas used for persuasion beamed with sincerity. "Besides, I suspect we could learn a great deal from one another."

"Friendship and the freedom to pick my brain don't go hand in hand."

"Well, I'm confident you'll explain what's necessary. I do hope you realize what a compliment you're receiving with my acknowledgement of your intellect."

"You're an arrogant snob, Barry."

"So your wife has informed me on numerous occasions. Perhaps the two of you have more in common than I initially suspected." Barry extended his hand to Req. "I have a well-deserved reputation of making good business deals. Those instincts tell me you're a man I can trust." He gave Cally a wistful smile. "Even if I do envy you."

"Fair enough." Req rose and shook Thomas's hand. "We have a lot of work to do today."

"Then we had best be about doing it." Thomas held onto Req's hand. "I never cross my friends. For anything."

"I understand." Req pumped Thomas's hand a final time. The agreement between the two men eased the tension from the air.

Cally swallowed the lump in her throat. Given time and circumstances, she had no doubt her dark, moody husband and her golden, extroverted partner would become fast friends.

Time.

It was her dearest friend and most formidable enemy.

She rose when Req held her chair. Out of habit, her hand slipped into his. Emotion twisted around her heart. This was how it should be—for the rest of their lives.

With effort, she tucked the ache away, concentrating instead on the plans that Req was outlining.

While he was speaking, explaining all the minute details, Req assumed the persona of a benevolent dictator. The satin-and-steel quality of his voice hypnotized Cally and created a sense of urgency.

She quickly studied the salient points of the plan he outlined on paper. Then she and Thomas repeated their objectives.

With the dedication of a tyrannical saint, Req rehearsed hypothetical scenarios with them and shared his expertise.

She ached at the way he showed her he loved her without ever admitting it.

The telegram arrived late Monday afternoon. The contents changed everything.

After a word with Brendan, whom Req was beginning to like, he checked on Horace Dowd.

Dowd sat up as Req entered and shot him a fierce glare.

"You can't keep me locked up down here forever," Dowd spat. "People'll come for me."

Req set a pitcher of fresh water and the tray of food on a crate. "Who, Dowd? Other than Cameron Morton, who knew you were coming here?"

"If you're going to turn me over to the authorities, do it. You can't keep me imprisoned indefinitely."

"Sure I can. You're my houseguest, albeit an uninvited one. I'm just showing you some old-fashioned hospitality." He gestured at the pallet of blankets. "You have a comfortable bed."

"You call that comfortable?"

"You will when they lock you up." Req splashed water into a glass. "Irene is an excellent cook. Enjoy this while you can. I guarantee that you'll look back on this with fond memories once you get to prison."

"Who the hell do you think you are?"

Req looked sharply at his prisoner, smiling, anticipating the attack lurking on the fringe of Dowd's desperation. "Come on, Dowd. I've been aching to hit someone all day."

Dowd cursed under his breath, then retreated to the shadows.

The attack Req expected died a cowardly death. He secured the door and turned the key over to Brendan.

Half an hour later Req walked into Thomas Barry's office at Golden Sun. Cally flowed into his arms immediately.

Without consideration of place or audience, Req drew her

close. The desire for privacy created a separate space for them in the realm of the carnal kiss neither wanted to break. There was something so right about holding her against his heart, so complete and soothing to his eroded soul, that he loathed giving it up. But he would go when the time and tide were right. God help him, he had a duty to perform and an old debt to pay. For now, however, he'd steal whatever piece of heaven he could grasp.

"Where's Cunningham?" he asked softly.

"In his office," Barry said moving from his desk to join Cally and Req.

"Morton?"

"Working in my office," Cally said, her lips dangerously close to his, tempting him to kiss her again.

"Why are you so concerned about where they are," Thomas said. "Have you discovered additional information, Maguire?"

As much as he hated to release Cally, he did so and addressed Thomas. "Actually, Lemuel Hansen has stumbled onto a trail we need to pursue."

"A trail? Whose?" Thomas asked.

"He's found pieces that match descriptions and the *Ocean Princess*'s manifest. He needs confirmation. The note said we have to move fast. Someone is interested and he's not sure whether she's the buyer or the seller." Req spoke so softly that his voice barely carried to Thomas who was standing right next to him.

"She?" Thomas echoed.

"With a little luck, Lemuel will have a name for us when we get there," Req answered.

"Therein lies the rub, folks. One of you has to go to San Francisco and identify it. It's also time to bring in the authorities. If the pieces are from the *Ocean Princess,* we'll need them involved up front. Sounds like Detective Goodman is still nosing around. Let's deal with him. The last thing we want to happen is for either of you to appear involved in a mass murder cover-up for insurance fraud."

"You are correct, of course," Barry mused. "However, we'll need to move on this quickly, before Chauncy and Cameron realize what we've discovered."

"I'm the most logical one to verify Lemuel's discovery," Cally volunteered. "I had duplicate drawings made of the items we submitted insurance claims for. Some of the Chinese pieces were well documented and we actually had photographs made so we could identify them."

"I, on the other hand, know nothing about Chinese art," Thomas said. "I doubt I could distinguish it from Japanese art. My preferences lie on the European side of the Atlantic."

"You are such a snob, Thomas," Cally retorted with an easy familiarity that sent a twinge of jealousy through Req.

"Proudly so," agreed Thomas.

"Now comes the tricky part. We'll have to make some adjustments to our plan," Req said.

"I'll continue alone with what we discussed yesterday," Thomas said. "I'm sure I'm correct in assuming that you are accompanying Caladonia to San Francisco."

"Right. That leaves the matter of Mr. Dowd. We'll have to turn him over to the police." He'd struggled with the decision on the way into town.

"And tip our hand?" Cally collected and stacked papers. "That will leave Thomas in peril. And he'll be alone."

"Not to worry, Caladonia. I've dealt with unsavory cretins before. I shall undoubtedly prevail this time."

They would all *prevail* a helluva lot easier with the instant communication and surveillance equipment Req was accustomed to having at his fingertips, Req thought. Even with the modern technology he yearned for, they were spread too thin.

"Grab your hat, Cally," Req said. "Barry, you come, too."

"Where?" Barry asked, tidying up his desk.

"We're hiring a lawyer and dumping the Dowd problem in his lap." He caught Cally's hand, then squeezed it. A mental image of the elderly William Potter poring over his ancestor's legal files almost brought a smile. "Mitchell Potter."

Cally's surprised expression gave way to a grin. She gave Req's neck a quick hug, whispering, "William will love it." Then she let go. "You are positively brilliant."

"Excuse me, but who is Mitchell Potter?" Barry asked.

"More important is what he is." Req accompanied Cally to the office door. "He's a lawyer. An honest one known for his inscrutable integrity." And his reputation can withstand the test of time, Req added silently.

"Then why haven't I heard of him?"

"You just did." Req handed Thomas his hat.

Shortly before the dinner hour, Req was in the Hornsby parlor with Mitchell Potter and Detective Bertram Goodman. Although unhappy about it, Cally and Thomas had returned to Golden Sun Shipping after their initial meeting with the attorney. At Potter's request, they would remain until both Cameron and Chauncy had left for the day.

While relating an abbreviated version of events that led to Horace Dowd occupying the root cellar, Req watched Goodman's expressionless brown eyes for a reaction. Ironically, the absence of the laws that would have prohibited Req from questioning Dowd the way he did, then holding him in the basement of the Hornsby house, left him at the Detective's mercy. Goodman didn't seem a merciful man.

"Why didn't you notify the authorities immediately?" Goodman asked. "Why did you keep Mr. Dowd here?"

"My client is the aggrieved, not the aggressor. He's given you his statement," Potter reminded Goodman. "Mr. Dowd invaded his home, destroyed his library and brutally assaulted his bride. What I find amazing is the fact that Mr. Dowd is still alive, not that my client detained him."

"That's what has me interested in you, Mr. Maguire. You show up with Miss Hornsby after she's been ill. No one saw you come to town. If fact, no one saw you in town—"

"Are you going to take Mr. Dowd into custody or not, Detective Goodman?" demanded Potter.

Req liked William Potter's great uncle. Mitchell had the sharp features of a terrier and a mind as quick as a barracuda strike. A slightly built man who barely reached Req's shoulder, Mitchell's light brown hairline was receding. His clear, bright blue eyes held no guile, only outrage when he perceived a wrong.

By contrast, Goodman was nearly six feet and had a full head of unruly brown hair he didn't bother taming with pomade. His only concession to fashion was his mustache that curved up at the ends just enough to soften his sharply chiseled features.

"Why did Mr. Dowd break in and attack Miss Hornsby?" A small tic made the ends of Goodman's mustache twitch. "Your wife," he corrected, rising from the settee.

"That's something you can ask him, once you take him into custody," Req said softly. He didn't want to tell Goodman more than necessary, nor did he want him as an adversary. "While you're at it, you might want to check into how he makes his money. Cally interrupted him in the library. Perhaps others in the area have been victims of his thievery, too." He hoped the suggestion provided the incentive necessary to hold Dowd until he and Cally returned from San Francisco.

"What did Mr. Dowd take?" Goodman asked skeptically.

Req glared at him. "He didn't have the opportunity to take anything of monetary value. Instead, he stole something more precious: my wife's peace of mind. Her personal safety within the walls of her own home. Her security. And if I had returned a few moments later, Detective Goodman, Dowd would have taken her life." The heat of outrage made him perspire. He'd come so close to losing Cally forever. "There are few things I'd kill a man for; Dowd is damn close to one of them."

"Is that why you kept him here, Mr. Maguire? To decide whether or not to kill him?"

Req stared into Goodman's brown eyes for a moment. "You think whatever you want. Then think about the situation with Dowd choking the life out of your wife, in your home."

"This conversation is over, gentlemen." Potter stepped between the two men. "Detective Goodman, please take Mr. Dowd into custody. If you need corroboration, Mrs. Maguire and Mr. Barry will give you a statement at their convenience."

Furious, Req turned away. If Goodman released Dowd, he'd hunt him down and kill him with his bare hands for hurting Cally. At least she wouldn't be looking over her shoulder for him after Req entered the time pool.

Cally and Req caught the next train to San Francisco. Their purpose was simple, their destination clear. The warehouse section of the city was a short distance from the hubbub of the main wharf. The screeching gulls echoed the organized chaos of the dockworkers unloading a ship from the Orient. The myriad of languages blended into the protests of groaning wood and squeaking ropes creating the irreplaceable sounds of dock life.

When she allowed herself to dwell on it, Cally both loved and hated relying on Req to help unravel the snarl of deceit and murder. In the worst moments, it gnawed at her with the razor teeth of dependence. Yet she would not trade any of the moments she spent with him. Nor would she turn her back on finding her father's killer.

To that end, she had packed simply and relied on the season's latest fashion trend of a surprise dress. The versatile design of black silk opened on a pale rose-colored gown and lining. Buttoning the lapels turned the dress into a walking coat.

Accompanied by Lemuel Hansen and Inspector Benjamin Curtis, the foursome approached the warehouse leading a contingent of half a dozen uniformed policemen. As soon as they had arrived in San Francisco, Req and Cally had gone to the police and enlisted their involvement. Inspector Curtis had admitted that he found their story far-fetched but agreed to help nonetheless.

Curtis was an eagle-eyed man with a gray half-halo of receding hair. The soft-spoken, wiry inspector looked Cally straight in the eye and listened more than he talked. Req had assured her the trait was a good sign.

The cry of gulls pierced the hum of noise wafting through the streets and narrow alleys separating the platoon of warehouses.

Inspector Curtis withdrew a key from his pocket. "Sam Christopher owns this warehouse, and most of the other ones on this block. He claims he has nothing to hide."

"Everything in here is his?" Lemuel asked, looking around them with a nervousness that set Cally on edge.

"No. Only the building belongs to him. This one's leased to three different companies, each of whom have space." With Req's strong arm lending assistance, Inspector Curtis opened the heavy warehouse door.

"It's dark as midnight in there," Lemuel said nervously. "Workers were stacking cargo into the back of the warehouse last time I was here. They had lanterns burning and the side doors open."

"These lanterns?" Inspector Curtis reached around the door and lifted a pair off the wall.

Lemuel reached for one. "Are there more?"

Minutes later, armed with lanterns, Cally followed Lemuel and Inspector Curtis into the depths of the warehouse. In the flickering light, the crates and bales of cargo bearing markings from all over the world formed vertical spires. The lantern light moved through deep shadows where musty, stale air protested the disturbance by releasing fine dust particles.

The corridors through the goods twisted and turned.

It took Lemuel several tries to find what he was looking for at the back of the warehouse. "I marked the corner panels so I could find them again." He pointed at a pair of crates stacked two high and set his lantern aside. Excited, he climbed onto a lower crate, then reached down for the pry-bar Req offered him. "They caught me spying through a window, you know."

"Good heavens, what did you do?" Cally asked.

"I told them I was looking for work. I had donned my seaman's attire and looked the part of a dockhand. To my surprise, they hired me to help pack and stock the crates that contained the very items I'd traced to this place."

"Good work, Hansen." Req's praise made the stockbroker stand a little taller.

The screeching protest of nail retracting from wood filled the warehouse. Req leaped up to help on the other side. Together, they pried off the upper front panels. They extracted a mountain of packing material before carefully lifting out a wrapped object slightly larger than a breadbox.

The two men maneuvered the heavy object onto the cleared surface of an adjacent crate. Cally set aside her lantern then freed the last layer of padding from the treasure.

Her eagerness quickly turned to dour certainty as she stared at the antique chest. The figures adorning every side of the chest were exquisite carved. The meticulous inlay of jewels and gold accentuated the superb workmanship.

Cally's mouth became very dry. She tried to swallow. "Inspector, do you have the drawings and photographs I gave you?"

"Right here. Is this from the *Ocean Princess*?"

"I believe so. I'd like to make a confirmation. Either way, this piece is worth a small fortune."

"There are two possibilities for why it's here," Req said. "Either someone doesn't know what they have, or it's a helluva place to hide it. You were right, Lemuel. You were also damn lucky no one recognized you."

"In truth, I've slept little since I discovered these items."

"Cally?" Req prodded.

Inspector Curtis carefully turned the piece then lifted a lantern over the top. "It matches the written description perfectly. Do the photographs match, Mrs. Maguire?"

"Yes," Cally whispered. "This proves they transferred some of the cargo and that Golden Sun *is* involved in insurance fraud."

"And you filed the claim, Mrs. Maguire?" Lemuel murmured.

Cally nodded. "I had signature authority. My name was the only one necessary. Why did they do it? Our profits were high that year."

"One thing at a time, Mrs. Maguire. Let's repack this," Inspector Curtis said, "then check the other crates you marked,

Hansen. My men will confiscate everything we identify as evidence." He stood back and assessed the tiers of crates surrounding them. "We're going to seal off the warehouse and go through the cargo piece by piece with the manifest and descriptions."

"There may be more stolen pieces hidden in here. It could take days to go through all of it," Cally mused, anxious to conclude their business in San Francisco and return home. "Did you learn the identity of the woman you saw with these crates?"

Lemuel put his weight into prying the lid from another crate before answering, "Mrs. Penelope Cunningham. I followed her to the Palace Hotel." He set the pry-bar aside and gave her an apologetic look. "I have friends there. There's no mistake."

Cally dropped the packing and staggered back. Inspector Curtis caught her arm to steady her.

"Penelope? You saw Penelope?" Surely she had heard wrong.

"Penelope?" Req echoed.

Stunned, she met his gaze and found a rare show of surprise. Of all the things they had speculated, this had never crossed their minds. "Dear God, it was there all the time. We read it. Again and again."

"And didn't read between the lines. She didn't overhear anything. Someone overheard her." Req hopped off the crate and reached for Cally.

She leaned against his arm for support. "My father."

"Bingo."

"All this time I was feeling sorry for her. So guilty for suspecting Chauncy, knowing it would tear her world apart. . . ."

"Shh. They're the guilty ones, Cally." He led her into a shadowy ell for privacy.

The circle of his arms was all that held her up. Accepting the magnitude of the conspiracy crushed something inside her. "For as long as I can remember, we were like family."

"When it's over, you and Maudel may be all that's left. She'll need you, Cally. Your strength. Your wit and wisdom. She'll need you to walk beside her and remind her to keep her head up," Req crooned into her ear.

The bleak picture he painted increased the quaking in her limbs. "Maudel," she whispered. A woman so willing to remain in the background, so fragile. "Her baby."

"There isn't much you can do to soften the blow, but you can cushion the landing with your friendship."

From nowhere, a rage so consuming she couldn't breath seized her. "Why? Why did they do this! Look at the death! The misery and devastation that so many have suffered." Her fist beat at his chest. Hot tears stung her eyes. "For what? You always have all the answers. Why, Req? Tell me!"

"You're asking the wrong person." He caught her hands and held them. "Sometimes . . . sometimes we don't get to know the answers. Sometimes we just have to accept that people often make bad choices and things are the way they are. We move on, Cally. We do what we have to do, or we get lost ourselves. Understand?"

The sorrow in his eyes warned that he wasn't talking about betrayal and murder; he was talking about them. "I can't move on without you, Req," she whispered, tears streaming down her cheeks.

"Yes, you can. You can and you will." He kissed her forehead.

For the life of her, she didn't know how.

"You and Maudel will help each other," he whispered in her ear. "That's later. Right now, we need to see this through and find out who killed your father."

Cally nodded, gathered her crumbling emotions and tucked them behind a frail net of composure. Req wiped her face with a handkerchief then curled his finger under her chin. When she was steady, he released her.

Inspector Curtis cleared his throat. When he looked back at them, he addressed Req. "Did you say Helmut Schmit's death is associated with these dealings?"

Req met Cally's gaze quickly before addressing Inspector Curtis. "Yeah. I doubt Schmit knew much. I suspect he recognized Freddy Hansen's body when it was found, then came up here looking for answers. He may have even suspected a connection between Freddy Hansen and Peter Hornsby's death. On the surface, it seems an unlikely association. But whatever Helmut Schmit knew, he took it with him to the grave."

"We'll bring his killers and those of Peter Hornsby and Freddy Hansen to justice. I'm certain of it." Conviction hardened Inspector Curtis's voice.

Cally believed him. What she had trouble believing was the bitter taste and hollow feeling that accompanied the justice she had craved. Instinctively, she reached for Req, knowing that he too would be gone soon.

Chapter 23

OVER THE NEXT several days, Inspector Curtis's men uncovered six more pieces in the warehouse. An insurance representative and Cally verified each item and noted its value against the payment of what amounted to a fraudulent claim. The long afternoon at the insurance company offices proved as tiring as searching the warehouse.

The first traces of drizzle coated the carriage windows when the driver turned onto Market Street. Minutes later, he pulled into the circular, marble-paved courtyard of the Palace Hotel. Seven stories overhead, a domed ceiling of amber glass muted the late afternoon light. The glass ceiling protected the patrons from the brunt of the weather's temper. Req helped Cally from the carriage, then paid the driver.

Cally drew her wrap tightly around her shoulders and ducked her head. The chill in the air was tepid compared to the one in her heart.

They went straight to their opulent room and locked the world outside. Req gathered Cally into a eager embrace. The slight rocking of their bodies provided an age-old comfort.

"It will take a couple more days to tie up all the loose ends here," he said. "What do you say we make the most of the time?"

"How?"

"For starters, let's order room service and eat in bed." The suggestive flick of his tongue against her earlobe revealed the nature of his greatest appetite. "We'll talk about today and plan tomorrow later—after you've rested and had something to eat."

"Each time I look at one of those pieces or read another insurance document, I think of Penelope and the reason so many

men died. I didn't believe her capable of such . . ." Her voice
faded as her arms tightened around him.

"Cold indifference to life?" he offered, tucking her head
under his chin.

"Yes," she whispered and nodded against the coarse fabric of
his coat. "She was always so kind, so willing to lend a hand and
listen to those around her. I don't understand."

"Don't jump to conclusions. We don't know whether she's an
accessory before or after the fact. Determining that isn't our job
here, Cally. We've done what we came to do; you identified the
pieces. I told Curtis we'd stay two more days while his men
search the rest of the warehouse and he runs down a couple of
leads. When they're done, we'll be on the train headed for
Monterey."

"But Req, the time for your return is close. The tide won't
wait for you. We must go whether Inspector Curtis is finished
or not," she said in a frail voice.

"If we miss it, I'll go next month." He lifted his chin quickly
to keep the crown of her head from ramming into his jaw. "I'm
in no hurry to leave you." Not now; not ever, he realized. He
couldn't look too hard at that side of himself. It was much too
dangerous.

She gazed up at him with big, brown eyes he could easily
lose himself in for a decade or five. "Yes, but I thought you
were going now, because of the trial."

"I'll testify at Gutierrez's trial. The wheels of justice don't
move very fast where I come from. Pierce, the prosecuting
attorney, is pushing hard for a quick date. Even if he gets it,
Gutierrez won't have his day in court for at least three
months. I'd rather wait here with you than be back there
alone." He didn't want to leave for any reason, but he knew
he had to. His sense of duty was part of what made him who
he was. He couldn't walk away from old wars and obligations without meeting the commitments he'd sworn to see
through.

"Eventually, I will have to leave, Cally."

"I know. Kiss me," she breathed. "I want everything you'll
give me for as long as you can stay."

Req unfastened her stylish felt hat with an ostrich plume
tucked neatly in the fold of the brim. Knowing it was her favorite, he looked around for a safe but convenient resting spot
for it.

"Toss it on the table," she said. "I'm not letting go of you."

Her gaze roamed his face with the same yearning that a child regarded a big, shiny new toy.

A perfect lob positioned the hat in the center of an end table. One by one, he removed the pins holding her long blond tresses in an artful arrangement and tucked the pins into his pocket. "When you look at me the way you are now, I wonder how the hell I got lucky enough to have you as my wife—twice."

"Luck has nothing to do with us, Requiem. It was fate that brought us together." A sorrowful thought flickered in her clear, brown eyes. "And fate has determined our future."

"I don't believe that." Drawn by the motion of the mouth he wanted against his, he lowered his head. "We'll talk philosophy later." Her lips parted, inviting him, then demanding without reservation. The conversation of desire, of love, and of the need to share that love took place in the span of a kiss that said everything.

A kiss wasn't enough. However, the rewards of patience were sweetest when savored. "I'm going to undress you," Req said in a black-velvet voice that made them both smile. "Slowly."

"Then I'll undress you . . ."

A timid knock on the door interrupted what promised to be a wonderfully wicked description of her libidinous intentions for retaliation.

"The door's locked. We can ignore the noise."

"Alright." She snuggled against him. The smile begging to be kissed off her lips was as provocative as the feeling of her breasts against his chest.

He bent to claim her lips again when the pounding on the door was repeated with fresh insistence.

"Requiem," she pleaded, rising on her tiptoes to brush her lips against his.

Releasing her without another sample of the passion simmering between them was beyond his power. He wanted to sink to the floor with her, remove her clothing piece by piece, all the while kissing her, tasting her, drinking in the love she lavished on him without hesitation.

The pounding on the door resumed, the strident cadence lasting longer.

"That isn't knocking. It's air in the pipes," Req said, willing the intruder to give up and go away.

"Caladonia." The desperate female voice on the other side of the door could only belong to one person.

"Maudel," Cally said against his mouth. Abruptly, she stiffened. "Maudel! What's she doing here?"

He groaned, then rested his forehead against hers. "We're about to find out. Stay there. I'll answer it." He released her. "Her being here is not a good sign."

"Surely you don't think Maudel is involved."

"Thinking has nothing to do with it." He crossed the room, checked that Cally was out of sight for both eyes and bullets, then opened the door.

Maudel was alone. She brushed past him in a swish of black brocade as if he wasn't there. He leaned out of the doorway and checked the hall. It was empty. If Maudel's knocking had brought the attention of other hotel guests, they hadn't been irritated enough to look. Suspicious about Maudel's unannounced visit, Req waited a moment before closing and locking the door.

"No! No. Don't embrace me, Caladonia." Maudel's hands flew up, palms out, as though someone had put a gun in her back. A black drawstring purse dangled from her wrist. "It's so awful. So terrible I can barely speak of it, but I didn't know where to go or who to turn to, or what to say." The words gushed into the quiet room with the force of a sonic boom. Maudel's shorter, heavier form seemed a cannonball ready to explode.

"How did you know we were here?" Req folded his arms across his chest and leaned against the closed door.

Maudel spun at the sound of his voice. Big brown eyes regarded him with the same fear he'd once seen in the eyes of a deer caught in the headlights of his oncoming car. "Thomas told me. I think he felt sorry for me."

"I see." What he saw was Thomas Barry's Achilles' heel: a near-hysterical pregnant woman on the precipice of tragedy. Barry had sent her to the only life raft in the terrible sea of misery drowning her and Cally received her with open arms.

"Oh, Mr. Maguire, you and Caladonia have every right to be angry with me and my family. I cannot believe what has happened. I cannot . . ." Her mouth continued moving, but no sound emerged. Instead, tears pooled in her tormented eyes, then spilled down her cheeks.

"Come. Sit." Cally took her friend by the arm and guided her to the plush blue-and-yellow-striped settee. "Req, would you get her a glass of water?"

He nodded, then went to the wet bar and poured a glass of water for her and drinks for Cally and himself.

"Drink slowly. That's it. Now, take a deep breath and tell us what's happened." Cally took the brandy snifter from Req and gave him silent thanks with her eyes.

Req settled into one of the blue brocade chairs facing the set-tee. "From the looks of you, Maudel, I'd say all hell has broken loose in Monterey. When did you get here?"

"Just a few hours ago. I took a room down the hall and I've been waiting for you to return. Oh, Caladonia, you are the only one I can turn to." The torment in her eyes was painful to see. "I didn't know where else to go." She glanced shyly at Req, then turned away. "Thomas said you had married Mr. Maguire."

"Yes," Cally said, affording Req a tender look.

"We are married," Req confirmed. The weight of the marital obligations that he took more seriously with each passing day sat on his shoulders with an ominous pressure. He had meant the vows he exchanged with Cally—both times. Circumstances and the fickle nature of time made his responsibilities to his job, the Escobars, and Paul Sandavol felt as heavy as the world the mythical Atlas toted on his shoulders.

"Tell us what's happened." Cally put down the snifter and took Maudel's hands in hers. "We know you're caught in the middle, and—"

"Oh, you don't know, Caladonia. You can't possibly know. They've run away!"

"Who? Who ran away? When?" Cally asked.

"My mother and Cameron!"

"Together?" Cally asked, horrified.

Req wasn't sure which was more of a surprise, that Cally made the connection, or that she'd asked Maudel. Regardless, the revelation added a new element to the situation.

"Yes. No. Oh, it's so sordid! They were going to leave to-gether. My mother and my husband. Oh, God! But she changed her mind and went back to Boston alone. She came by the house to say good bye late yesterday afternoon. That's when she told me about ... about her and Cameron. She simply blurted it out, then kissed me on the cheek and left. I was so stunned, I didn't think to ask questions."

The tears spilled freely down Maudel's cheeks. The front of her velvet mantle became damp with her misery. Req withdrew a handkerchief and offered it to Cally who accepted it with gratitude.

"She left me standing on the porch. She just went. She didn't even look back. I must have stood there for nearly an hour. Only later did I realize that her trunks were strapped to the carriage and they drove off toward the docks." When words failed, she accepted the handkerchief Cally offered and blew her nose.

"Where's your husband, Maudel?" Req was more interested in the men involved. There was no doubt in his mind that the tenacity and thoroughness of Inspector Curtis would reunite mother and daughter in a courtroom long before Penelope was ready.

"Gone."

"What do you mean, *gone*? Gone where?" Cally asked while removing Maudel's hat.

"He left me the day you boarded the train for San Francisco. I didn't know why. At least not then." A fresh flood of tears cascaded down her face. "Worse, I don't know why I'm glad he's gone." Maudel covered her face with her hands, bent over, and sobbed.

Req took a sip of his brandy. Every time Maudel opened her mouth she revealed one surprising turn after another. Or maybe his lack of insight concerning the fairer sex was standing in the glare of his ignorance. Until now, he had thought Maudel was madly in love with her husband.

Cally rubbed her friend's shoulders and tried soothing her. "Take your time. Cry it out, Maudel. You've been through a terrible ordeal and it may not be over for you."

"What do you mean? How can it possibly get any worse? My mother betrayed me. So did my husband. Then he deserted our unborn child. My father has locked himself in his office and he won't come out. He won't talk to me. He won't even talk to Thomas.

"Ooh, Caladonia! What about my baby? What is my child going to face when all this is over? What has my family done to my baby?"

Req rose from the chair and walked over to the window. From the sixth floor of the Palace Hotel, the city looked completely alien to him. He shivered thinking of the censure Maudel and her innocent child would face as a result of Cameron and Penelope's actions.

"This baby will be loved, Maudel," Cally promised. "I'll love him. You'll love him. What more does he need?"

"A father," Maudel lamented. "A child needs a father. How will I raise this baby alone? Cameron took every penny we had. I am absolutely and completely penniless."

"You'll do fine," Req said, watching the traffic below. "My mother raised me alone."

"Oh, Caladonia. What ever will I do?" Maudel covered her face and sobbed.

Req looked over his shoulder and caught the sympathy in Cally's gaze and the turmoil that racked Maudel's body.

Although itching to interrogate Maudel as though she was a hostile witness, he listened to Cally console her friend. The two women would need one another in the years ahead. His questions would wait. For now.

A sharp rap sounded on the door, startling all of them.

"Stay right there," Req ordered as the women began to rise from the settee, then he went to answer the door.

It was a day for surprises. Inspector Curtis stood in the hall with Detective Bertram Goodman. Req opened the door wide, wondering if the two officers were any better at sharing information or jurisdiction than Terragno had been. Both men removed their curly-brim felt hats upon entering the hotel room.

"What brings you to San Francisco, Detective Goodman?" Req asked.

"Murder, Mr. Maguire," Goodman answered softly. "And an amazing story from your house guest, Mr. Dowd."

"Really?" He would have loved being a fly on the wall during Goodman's interrogation of Dowd. "I'm sure it was fascinating. The question is, was it true?"

"In light of what Inspector Curtis tells me, quite possibly so, Mr. Maguire." Goodman's flat brown gaze sought and found Maudel on the settee and remained on her throughout the introductions. He settled on the closest of the two blue brocade chairs and addressed Maudel as though she was the only other person in the room. "Mrs. Morton, your presence makes this easier for Inspector Curtis and me. Unfortunately, the news I have will distress you."

Req caught a glimpse of genuine emotion in Goodman's face. Whatever the detective thought he knew, he believed in Maudel's innocence.

Maudel cradled her empty water glass in her gloved hands.

"Circumstances could not be more dire for me, Detective Goodman. Please, say what you have to say."

"Detective Goodman, I want it understood that Maudel has done nothing wrong," Cally interrupted. "I am assuming you and Inspector Curtis have discussed the horrendous fate of the *Ocean Princess*. Surely, you must realize Maudel is an innocent caught in the consequences."

"I believe that's the case, Mrs. Maguire, which is why it is my uncomfortable task to inform her that we've traced her husband's whereabouts," Goodman said without his gaze even flickering from Maudel.

"Wh-where is he?" Maudel didn't seem to notice when Cally removed the glass from her hand and gave it to Req.

"He left Monterey yesterday and sailed for San Francisco. We have good reason to believe he was on a ship bound for Mexico last night."

"The man has no imagination," Req muttered, then refilled Maudel's water glass.

"He didn't go first cabin, Mrs. Morton. Your husband was shanghaied," Goodman continued as though Req had not spoken. "We found his trunks boarded on a vessel bound for the Sandwich Islands. When we did not find him, Inspector Curtis called in a favor from . . . shall we say, someone who would know about these things."

Req nodded at the Inspector, impressed by the quickness of his resources. Being shanghaied seemed a fitting experience for Cameron Morton.

For the first time, Detective Goodman looked at Cally. "We've initiated contact with the authorities in Boston. They'll meet Mrs. Cunningham's ship."

"Have you ascertained the depth of Penelope's involvement? Was she involved with the sinking of the *Ocean Princess*?" Cally asked Inspector Curtis.

"Without her confession, I cannot substantiate what we've pieced together. Mr. Dowd made no mention of the *Ocean Princess*, Mrs. Maguire. However, I'll have more questions to ask him when I return to Monterey."

"But you and Inspector Curtis have put some of the pieces together, haven't you?" Req said, then met Cally's gaze. "They need to know, Detective Goodman. Please, tell them what you suspect."

Cally cast a grateful look at her husband. He always seemed to know what she needed, even if it wasn't what she wanted.

"It appears Mrs. Cunningham and Mr. Morton have been, ah, involved for a time."

Cally slipped her fingers through her friend's. A chill radiated through Maudel's gloves. The pulse point in her wrist was the only indication Maudel was still breathing.

Rage burned a path through Cally. How much misery could poor Maudel endure? She swallowed hard, then nodded at the detective. "Tell us all of it."

"According to Dowd, Mr. Morton needed money to carry out his plans to leave with his, ah, mistress." The stoic Detective Goodman shifted, clearly uncomfortable with what he revealed. "Mr. Dowd did not know the identity of the woman."

"My mother," Maudel whispered. "My mother and my husband. And what of my father?"

"I spoke with your father earlier today. He remains loyal to your mother."

"He suspected she was having an affair," Maudel said in a small, distant voice. Her brown eyes looked straight through Detective Goodman until Cally squeezed her hand. "And we both—may God forgive us, but the one time he spoke of it, we both thought it was with your father, Cally."

Stunned, Cally gaped at Maudel while the words settled in. "You thought my father and your mother were having an affair? My *father*?" Somehow, it never occurred to her that her father had even wanted sex after the death of her mother. Their devotion to one another had been all-consuming.

She looked across the room at Req who had assumed his usual position of holding up a wall with his arms folded over his chest and his ankles crossed. Beyond the sympathy in his expression, she saw a virile man with an enormous appetite for sex. Someone would take her place in his bed after he left here just as someone had undoubtedly taken her mother's place in her father's bed after her death. But that someone had not been Penelope Cunningham.

Cally reached out to Maudel and pulled her close before asking the final question. "Did Chauncy kill my father?"

Maudel tried to push away, but Cally held on.

"I've been working on your father's murder since you came to see me almost eight months ago, Mrs. Maguire," Detective Goodman said. "This has not been an easy case. First, there was nothing. Then everything happened at once. You became ill.

Freddy Hansen washed up on the beach. Helmut Schmit lit out to San Francisco where he was murdered. Your emergence from your sickbed with Mr. Maguire at your side was a very suspicious circumstance."

Cally glanced at Req, who didn't even blink, then met Detective Goodman's gaze. "Suspicious? In what way?"

"It crossed my mind that you might have wanted your father's position at Golden Sun." A hint of color brightened his jowls. "You have a reputation for intruding into the business world."

"You thought that *I'd* kill my father?" In disbelief, she held onto Maudel even tighter.

Goodman met her gaze without hesitation. "Mr. Maguire's appearance and your sudden marriage changed my thinking."

"So you thought I killed him, then blackmailed her into marrying me for her money," Req finished.

"How outrageous! I never—" Cally had never felt so indignant in her life. Req came to stand behind her. His hand on her shoulder was more calming than anything Detective Goodman might say.

"Perhaps. The longer I interrogated Mr. Dowd, the more it seemed there was something else going on here. I spoke to Mr. Cunningham before I followed Mrs. Morton up here. It seemed a good bet she was making a beeline straight for you. Then I spoke with Inspector Curtis and got a clearer picture. As it turns out, I owe you both an apology."

"Accepted," Req said from behind Cally.

"Speak for yourself." Cally hugged Maudel, looked Detective Goodman in the eye, and asked, "Did Chauncy kill my father?"

"I'm still putting things together—"

"Did he?" Cally demanded over Maudel's fresh sobs. She had to know. She had to end this slow torture. "Tell us!" Only lancing the boil of uncertainty and innuendo would ease the pain and allow them all to heal.

"Yes, Mrs. Maguire," Detective Goodman said, his shoulders relaxing in resignation. "Chauncy Cunningham confessed this morning. He's in my custody. I'm sorry for both you and Mrs. Morton here."

Cally nodded. She had her answer and her thirst for justice had never seemed further from being quenched. She held her friend and rocked them both on the settee. Tears she could not begin to stem flowed down her cheeks.

"Gentlemen, I think it's time for you to leave," Req said softly. "Please get in touch with me if you receive any further news."

Cally barely noticed when all three men went through the door. She and Maudel held one another and cried.

Maudel didn't return to her room. Instead, she spent the night in the bed Req had planned to share with Cally, while they slept on the settee. When the sun rose, Req stretched the kinks out of his limbs. The settee was not designed for sleeping. Twisting his lower back, he sat up.

The bedroom was quiet. He'd listened to Maudel's soft sobs late into the night. With each hiccup the urge to hunt Cameron Morton down and pulverize him with his fists grew stronger. But it wasn't Cameron Morton he was truly angry with; it was himself. And with circumstances.

At least Cally wasn't pregnant.

Yet.

Or was she?

It was too early to tell.

He had wrestled with the demons of conflicting duties all night. Morning had not produced a victor; just a fatigued, grumpy battlefield housed in a six-foot-two frame.

He slipped into the bathroom without waking the women, bathed, and shaved. It was going to be a bitch of a day. He could feel it in his bones.

Tomorrow would be better.

But it would also be a day closer to saying good-bye.

Chapter 24

THE FUROR FROM scandalous hearings into the sinking of the *Ocean Princess* and the murders of Peter Hornsby, Freddy Hansen, and Helmut Schmit ebbed.

Winter gripped the coast hard in a January chill. Requiem stood on the deserted beach and gazed out to sea. On the day of tidal syzygy for the last three months, he had donned his own clothing and walked to the rock formation with Cally. The last two times he had merely stared out to sea. When the tide began to change the last two times, they'd come to the water's edge, then left the beach without a word. Not once did they discuss why he hadn't gone. Each time they'd gone straight to their bedroom and made love.

"You're going this time, aren't you," Cally said from beside him.

"Yes. It's killing me to stay and killing me to go." The decision carried finality as ominous as the sentences Chauncy Cunningham and Horace Dowd had received from the court.

"I suppose this is a good time—"

"You're my wife. There's never a good time to leave you. Are you pregnant, Cally?"

"It wouldn't change what you need to do if I were."

"Yes it would. It would change everything." He gazed into her eyes and knew she wasn't going to tell him what he wanted to hear. "Answer me, Cally."

"I won't know for certain for another four days. By then, it will be too late for you to leave, and next month we'll agonize over this again. We'll keep doing so until I am with child." Tears pooled on her lower eyelids. "Ah, Req, you didn't plan on

coming with me in the first place. We've known you had to go
since you got here. Let me go with you. . . ."

"I couldn't keep you safe, Cally. At least here you're out of
foreseeable danger." The words tore from his heart and left a
gaping wound in their wake. If for one minute he thought he
could protect her through the trial, he was selfish enough to
want to bring her. But he knew he'd have trouble covering his
own ass. That kind of selfishness could only get them both
killed.

The incessant rhythm of the waves underscored the need for
patience. Seagulls perched on the nearby rocks, squawked, then
took flight. In the gently rolling tops of the kelp forest, otters
lay on their back and ate abalone under a cloudy sky.

"I'm coming back, Cally." The hope that suddenly lit her
eyes bit a chunk out of his heart. "Jeezus, woman, did you ever
doubt it?"

"You never said you wanted to." The starch melted from her
rigid stance as her arms and shoulders relaxed.

"I haven't told you I love you either." He hadn't told her
many things. He needed a lifetime with her and it still wouldn't
be long enough.

"You didn't have to. I knew. You showed me a thousand
times and in hundreds of ways, Requiem. I just didn't know if
you knew it."

Req couldn't help the ironic smile that crept onto his face. "It
took me a helluva long time to figure it out. The first couple of
months with you I didn't know what I felt, just that it was too
damn much and I couldn't turn it off anymore."

"We've both changed." She managed a smile, her head tilt-
ing. The afternoon sea breeze caught the errant tendrils of her
hair and spun them like golden filaments around her head. "I've
grown up."

He turned her and embraced her from behind. He would miss
holding her every day. They both faced the jagged spires poking out of the sand and surf. "If I'm not back in a year, it won't
be for lack of trying." Only two things would keep him from returning: death and the closure of the time portal.

He held her, silently savoring the fullness of his heart and
soul when she was in his arms. The *rightness* of having her
pressed against his heart matched the sunrise in the morning.

"I love you, Cally Maguire." He kissed the top of her ear. "I
will until my dying day."

"Don't speak of dying," she pleaded in a strong voice that

denied the tears staining her cheeks. "I could not face the rest of my life without you."

"I'll always be with you." He outlined the shape of a heart on the gentle swell of her left breast. "In your heart." He laughed softly, then crossed his arms beneath her breasts. "I'm coming back and we're going to have a passel of little Harley riders."

"Oh, Requiem, there are no such things as Harley machines in this time." She sniffed and snuggled closer to him.

"There will be, my love. There will be." He turned her in the circle of his arms. "I'm going now, Cally. Kiss me good-bye and go home."

Though she trembled like a leaf in a gale, she did not cry aloud. Tears washed her cheeks, flowed down her neck, and dripped from her jaw onto the yolk of her striped day dress.

They had made love until dawn. Afterward, he had watched while she slept on his shoulder. Perhaps they had both known then that he would leave today.

He kissed her with the ardent passion of a lover and the knowledge of a husband. They shared the kiss like a cloak that protected them against the bitter coldness of the rest of the world. Through it all, he tasted her tears.

"I love you, Requiem," she said, then released him. "I'll watch you go."

He wanted to object, but understood her need for closure. If he could not return, she would know he was in a place where she could never follow.

He kissed her forehead, then guided her toward the black, craggy rocks jutting out of the golden California sand.

When they reached the pool, he took off his jacket and draped it around her shoulders. "Cally, so help me—"

She put her fingertips on his lips. "I know," she mouthed when the words remained locked in her throat. "One of the reasons I love you so much is your loyalty and your commitment to duty, even when it's . . . difficult."

"That's two." Req slid down into the pool and found the niche where Cally had sat when she pulled him through the time warp. The water was cold and the niche smaller. The barbs and barnacles covering the rocks jabbed at him but couldn't compare to the pain he felt leaving her.

Cally slipped her arms into the jacket sleeves and hugged herself as she watched him, her eyes more eloquent than any words either of them might speak.

The first waves of the changing tide made their entrance with small crests breaking atop the swells. Req feasted his eyes on the sight of Cally who had moved to the rocks opposite him. Overhead, the gray sky came undone and a patch of blue grew over her left shoulder. Gulls cried and soared in the finger of sunlight streaming down to the sea, changing it from gray to blue.

The waves gained force, slapping his face, stinging his eyes when he refused to close them against the vision of his wife. The rock softened against his back. He pushed. It gave, but did not yield.

For a bittersweet moment, he thought circumstances had removed the chalice of decision.

Then the rock dissolved and sucked him into the vortex of the narrowing time passage. The last thing he saw was Cally blowing him a kiss.

Flashing a DEA badge with his name, a picture, and a magnetic information strip, Requiem Maguire stormed into Adam Pierce's office unannounced. A young secretary chattered protests like a magpie as she trailed after him.

"It's been three months of highstakes courtroom poker. I'm done being part of the ante, Adam," Req said. He gave the secretary a withering look that sent her out of the office. He walked over and slammed the door behind her.

"They're asking for a weeklong recess." Adam Pierce rose from behind an enormous desk needed to support the weighty stacks of folders and law books open to various sections of the criminal law codes. Pierce cultivated the Abe Lincoln look and often capitalized on his slow Southern drawl in the courtroom. Anyone who watched him prosecute a case from start to finish knew it was part of the act. Being underestimated had its rewards. "Looks like its time we called their hand, Maguire."

"As far as I'm concerned, you're running out of time. My ass has been hanging out in the breeze too long as it is. Today is Friday. Start counting. In three weeks, I'm gone and you won't get another shot. If you let Gutierrez's lawyers win another recess, you'll have to get your direct and the cross-examination in during that time frame."

"Be reasonable, Maguire."

"Hell, if I was any more reasonable or obliging, I'd be six feet under by now. This isn't open for negotiations. Three weeks, then I'm gone." *Home. To Cally.*

"I'll subpoena you and have you brought back."

"Sure you will."

"Shit!" Pierce slammed a law book shut. "You disappear again, and so help me, when they bring you in, I'll shackle your ass to this desk and nail it to the floor."

"Three weeks." Req turned on his heel.

"Wait."

Req turned the knob to let himself out of the mahogany-paneled and bookshelf-lined office.

"I just negotiated the recess down from five days to three. I'll put you on the stand Thursday morning."

"Fine. I'll be there."

"I want you in protective custody."

Req turned toward the door. "It's good to want something. It gives us something to reach for." He slipped through the doorway and hurried out of the office. Instead of taking the elevator, he dashed up the stairs two at a time and ascended three floors in less than a minute. In a side corridor, he ducked into a maintenance closet. Careful not to disturb anything, he opened the trash chute and reached inside. The rope he'd taped to the side filled his hand. He grabbed it and swung inside, then closed the chute door.

He knew exactly where to hide.

That evening, a cabby helped an elderly woman from his cab and into her wheelchair at William Potter's estate. Req paid the cabby and showed his appreciation for the man's assistance with an excellent tip.

The deep, abiding love Req had for his wife colored the way he viewed William Potter. On the one hand, he envied him for having spent over fifty years with a woman he loved with every fiber of his being. On the other hand, he pitied him for losing her. Req understood what it was like to walk around with a hollow spot the size of Alaska expanding inside him.

"I noticed you sold your house," William said when they were alone in the library. "No one knew if you would come back to Monterey. Your visit answers my question." He closed and locked the door against intrusion. "I've been watching the trial in the newspaper and on television."

"Yeah, well, I wish I were that distant from it. I take the stand on Thursday. Once I finish, I'll have a helluva time getting them off my tail." He stood and took the drink William offered. "I need your help." He sipped the drink, then smiled. "And in exchange, I'm willing to tell you a story, a true one, that'll knock your socks off."

"About your little lady?" William's eyes gleamed with excitement.

"She's my wife, William."

"Your wife?" William poured another shot of scotch into his glass. "Will wonders never cease? That little gal took you to the altar. How about that."

"Yeah, how about that," Req agreed.

"Knowing you, I'm sure you have her tucked away some place very safe. I won't ask. She's quite a woman, your wife. Funny thing about the things you two were asking me last time you were here," William said from behind the lip of his scotch glass. "Mrs. Murphy called here several weeks ago to see if I knew where you were. She found another stack of newspapers. Darn near all of them dealt with Peter Hornsby's murder and the demise of the Golden Sun Shipping Company."

The ruination of the company now belonging to Cally and Thomas seemed inevitable. There was nothing he could do to forestall it. "That's part of what I need to pick your brain about, William. But first, I'll tell you about my wife."

William grinned, his eyes alive with anticipation. He was as excited as when he and Cally had compared notes on Monterey's history.

Cally rested against the rocks and watched the sun play on the waves. Seals chided one another to move over on the rocks they used for basking. The pungent aroma of kelp drying on the sand caught the breeze. Sand flies hopped excitedly from one spot to another.

The tide changed. Each wave lapped higher and higher on the shore.

Cally didn't want to consider what Req's absence signified.

Numb with disappointment, she gathered the cloth bag stuffed with towels and clean, dry clothing.

The walk home became longer each time.

He saw her turn away and called out. The riptide had deposited him further out to sea this time. He used the incoming tide to help him as the cold ocean drained his strength.

Although she could not have heard his call above the waves and the screeching gulls, she turned back, then lifted her hand to shield her eyes.

Req swam hard. His dreams and his future waited on the shore. And every stroke brought him closer to them.

He heard Cally crying his name, urging him, giving him strength. When at last he could put his feet down, his rubbery legs could barely support him.

"Stay," he panted when she started to wade into the water. He stumbled the last twenty feet out of the water and into her waiting arms. He trembled from fatigue, then held her tightly enough to feel the swell of her abdomen. Dammit, she *had* been pregnant when he'd left. He placed his hands on her extended sides. "Cally . . ."

"Shhh. We have another four months before the first generation of Harley riders makes his debut." She ran her hands over his body, then cradled his face. "You are a man of your word, Requiem Maguire," she said in a tremulous voice. "I love you with all my heart."

"There's no going back." He couldn't look at her enough. He pulled the pins from her hair and watched it unfurl like fine, pale gold filaments floating in the breeze. "God, I dreamed of you and tried to imagine all the ways you've changed."

"What is this?" She tugged at the girdle hugging his ribs.

He ran his shaking fingers through her hair. "I sold everything and bought gemstones. They'll finance our future." He brought her hand to his mouth and kissed her finger. "Victor would have approved. William certainly did."

"Kiss me, Req. I'm aching to show you how much I've missed you."

"I love you, Mrs. Maguire."

The nectar of her kiss tasted of home, love, and a future.

TIME PASSAGES

__CRYSTAL MEMORIES	_Ginny Aiken_	0-515-12159-2
__ECHOES OF TOMORROW	_Jenny Lykins_	0-515-12079-0
__LOST YESTERDAY	_Jenny Lykins_	0-515-12013-8
__MY LADY IN TIME	_Angie Ray_	0-515-12227-0
__NICK OF TIME	_Casey Claybourne_	0-515-12189-4
__REMEMBER LOVE	_Susan Plunkett_	0-515-11980-6
__SILVER TOMORROWS	_Susan Plunkett_	0-515-12047-2
__THIS TIME TOGETHER	_Susan Leslie Liepitz_	0-515-11981-4
__WAITING FOR YESTERDAY	_Jenny Lykins_	0-515-12129-0
__HEAVEN'S TIME	_Susan Plunkett_	0-515-12287-4
__THE LAST HIGHLANDER	_Claire Cross_	0-515-12337-4
__A TIME FOR US	_Christine Holden_	0-515-12375-7

All books $5.99

Prices slightly higher in Canada

Payable in U.S. funds only. No cash/COD accepted. Postage & handling: U.S./CAN. $2.75 for one book, $1.00 for each additional, not to exceed $6.75; Int'l $5.00 for one book, $1.00 each additional. We accept Visa, Amex, MC ($10.00 min.), checks ($15.00 fee for returned checks) and money orders. Call 800-788-6262 or 201-933-9292, fax 201-896-8569; refer to ad # 680 (4/99)

Penguin Putnam Inc.
P.O. Box 12289, Dept. B
Newark, NJ 07101-5289
Please allow 4-6 weeks for delivery.

Foreign and Canadian delivery 6-8 weeks

Bill my: ☐ Visa ☐ MasterCard ☐ Amex _____ (expires)

Card# _____

Signature _____

Bill to:

Name _____

Address _____ City _____

State/ZIP _____

Daytime Phone # _____

Ship to:

Name _____

Address _____

City _____

State/ZIP _____

Book Total $ _____

Applicable Sales Tax $ _____

Postage & Handling $ _____

Total Amount Due $ _____

This offer subject to change without notice.